PRAISE FOR
Lauraine Snelling

Half Finished

"This is a beautiful story about a community of women who get together for crafting....The side issues coping with loss, grief, romance, and more made this a compelling read that I loved. These are mature women, but millennials would also enjoy because of their friendships. I highly recommend this lovely story of friendships and will read other books by this author!"

—BookReferees.org

"[A] wonderful story about the power of a community that comes together to work together and help their own."

—SheLivesToRead.com

The Second Half

"A beautifully written book about how things can change in a blink of an eye and how to deal with the unexpected changes....Snelling is a talented writer and draws from real-life experiences for her novels."

—RT Book Reviews

Someday Home

"The story is inspiring and hopeful. Snelling tells a wonderful tale of fresh starts, resilience, loss, and love in this perfect summer read."

—RT Book Reviews

Heaven Sent Rain

"Snelling's story has the potential to be a big hit.... The alternating narrators make the tale diverse and well rounded. The premise of the story is interesting and the prose is very moving."

—RT Book Reviews

Wake the Dawn

"Snelling (*One Perfect Day*) continues to draw fans with her stellar storytelling skills. This time she offers a look at smalltown medical care in a tale that blends healing, love, and a town's recovery...Snelling's description of events at the small clinic during the storm is not to be missed."

—Publishers Weekly

"Snelling's fast-paced novel has characters who seek help in the wrong places. It takes a raging storm for them to see that the help they needed was right in front of them the whole time. This is a strong, believable story."

"Lauraine Snelling's newest novel will keep you turning pages and not wanting to put the book down....*Wake the Dawn* is a guaranteed good read for any fiction lover."

Reunion

"Inspired by events in Snelling's own life, *Reunion* is a beautiful story about characters discovering themselves as the foundation of their family comes apart at the seams. Readers may recognize themselves or someone they know within the pages of this book, which belongs on everyone's keeper shelf."

"*Reunion* is a captivating tale that will hook you from the very start....Fans of Christian fiction will love this touching story."

"Snelling's previous novels (*One Perfect Day*) have been popular with readers, and this one, loosely based on her own life, will be no exception."

On Hummingbird Wings

One Perfect Day

The Florence Legacy

The Florence Legacy

A Novel

Lauraine Snelling

New York   Nashville

FaithWords
Hachette Book Group
1290 Avenue of the Americas, New York, NY 10104
faithwords.com
twitter.com/faithwords

First Edition: May 2022

FaithWords is a division of Hachette Book Group, Inc. The FaithWords name and logo are trademarks of Hachette Book Group, Inc.

The publisher is not responsible for websites (or their content) that are not owned by the publisher.

Scripture quotation on page 51 is taken from the NEW AMERICAN STANDARD BIBLE®, Copyright © 1960, 1962, 1963, 1968, 1971, 1972, 1973, 1975, 1977, 1995 by The Lockman Foundation. Used by permission.

The Hachette Speakers Bureau provides a wide range of authors for speaking events. To find out more, go to www.hachettespeakersbureau.com or call (866) 376-6591.

Library of Congress Cataloging-in-Publication Data
Names: Snelling, Lauraine, author.
Title: The Florence legacy: a novel / Lauraine Snelling.
Description: First edition. | New York: FaithWords, 2022.
Identifiers: LCCN 2021041688 | ISBN 9781478920120 (trade paperback) | ISBN 9781478920113 (ebook)
Subjects: LCGFT: Novels.
Classification: LCC PS3569.N39 F58 2022 | DDC 813/.54—dc23
LC record available at https://lccn.loc.gov/2021041688

ISBNs: 978-1-4789-2012-0 (trade paperback); 978-1-4789-2011-3 (ebook)

Printed in the United States of America

LSC-C

Printing 1, 2022

The Florence Legacy is dedicated to my round robin writing group of thirty-five years. We met at writing conferences and we've been retreating once a year plus any other times we can get together ever since. First, we communicated with our round robin letters that managed to make it around the members usually two to three times a year. Now we are online and so grateful. Such friends, such a history. So many hugs and tears and prayers, always grateful God brought us together.

Acknowledgments

First came the adventure of my trip to Italy, fulfilling a dream to see the *David* in reality. Why the dream? Who knows why dreams come. But the trip was so much more. And then came the novel, another dream come true.

One of the best parts of the dream come true was the people I met who shared their love of their homeland, such as our first guide with her love of history and the Vatican. My regret? We couldn't spend more time with her and her incredible wealth of knowledge. If only I'd had history teachers like her in school.

And Raffaella, with her farm and cooking school in Umbria. Her cookbook, *Sprinkle with Flour: Shapes of Italian Pasta: Recipes, Techniques, Tools and Memories*, is now published and you can find her online at www.cookin umbria.it. How I would love to go back again and take another class—or two.

Our flat in Florence was another gift beyond measure. Thank you to a husband and wife who open their home to visitors and make one's stay another piece of history.

The Accademia Gallery in Florence houses such an incredible collection of paintings, sculptures, and touring exhibits. What a privilege it was to go there.

Thank you to a charming young man who drives guests around Florence and dearly loves the history and architecture there and sharing it with others. His sense of humor, concern for his passengers, and pride in his family made him a delight to be with.

And thank you to my friend Eileen Grafton, who did most of the planning for this adventure of a lifetime. We have been long-term writing buddies, another of the many gifts God has given me. Her daughter and my friend, Jennifer, helped make the adventures even more delightful. And thank you to my friend Judy, who went along because she lived in Italy years ago and was so excited to return.

I am thankful, always, for my husband Wayne, who stays home and takes care of our critters and makes sure all is cared for when I'm away. These several years later, I am still in awe that our Father brought all this into being.

Thanks, always, to and for my agent, Wendy Lawton, my go-between with the wonderfully competent publishing team at FaithWords, who take my stories and turn them into published novels. Producing a novel always takes a dedicated and persistent team effort. Thanks also to my new brainstorming partner, Kiersti Giron. I am so blessed.

I am always grateful for my readers, who make it possible for me to continue doing what I so dearly love, writing books. Thank you for your encouragement and joy in reading. Amazing how many ways we can read books these days. For all of these things—I am grateful.

Prologue

B reeanna Lindstrom stared at the envelope in her hand. Probably a thank-you note since it was from Jade's husband. Tears immediately burned her throat and leaked from her eyes. How she missed Jade. All these years of friendship, ever since they met at that first writers' conference, and now she was gone. Jade, who was always eating well, exercising, doing all the right things to stay healthy, taken by a freak brain cancer, despite how hard she fought it.

Breeanna laid the envelope on the table and grabbed a tissue to mop up with. Tissue boxes all over the house, in the car, on her desk at school. She'd been through the stages of grief before, all those years ago when Roger died in that boating accident. Shouldn't the knowing of the process make it easier?

Muttering at herself, she gave in and sat in her worn-to-fit recliner to cry it out. Her golden retriever, Spencer, laid his muzzle on her knees, warm brown eyes staring up at her, feathered tail swishing.

Memories paraded through her mind. Jade gathering their writing group to pray, always being the first to reach out when anyone had a need, the first to make them all laugh. The pile of crumpled wet tissues grew on the oval antique table beside her chair.

Spencer whined. Cinders, her tuxedo cat with a black

spot between her eyes, jumped up over the arm of the chair and kneaded Bree's knees before settling in a circle of comfort.

Lord, it's just not fair. Jade should not have gone home to be with you already. We needed her more than you do. She knew better. Blaming God did no good. Count it all joy... The verse waved from the edges of her weepy mind.

Breeanna sniffed a deep breath. One hand on each of her four-footed family, she finally leaned her head against the cushioned headrest as the tears slowed, then stopped. After blowing and wiping one more time, Bree stared at the picture Jade had painted for her. The scene of mother and child spoke to her again of the love of friendship that had brought them closer than sisters. So many years, so many experiences.

She stroked her two buddies, set Cinders on the floor, and stood. Whew. Made it through another weeping bout. She knew from her inside out that the tears always ceased but still... "Come on, guys, tea for me and treats for you." She glanced at the envelope on the dining room table. She needed tea first.

After dinner that evening, she picked up the envelope and slit it open. Just as she'd thought, a thank-you note from Jonathon, Jade's husband.

Dear Breeanna,

Jade ordered me to send you this so that some of your dreams may come true. Thank you for your years of friendship not only with Jade but all of us. We wish you the best in your years ahead.

Sincerely,
Jonathon Wellington

Breeanna unfolded the paper insert. And caught her breath. A check for ten thousand dollars. She could feel her mouth drop open.

Jade knew of her deep dream to someday visit Italy, to see the *David* in person. They'd discussed it often in their writing group, and the five of them had tried to go two times but something always got in the way. Just life, they'd agreed. Jade knew Bree had always worried that she couldn't afford the trip, anyway. Now she was giving her the gift of her dream, even if they wouldn't be there together as they always planned. *Oh, Jade…*

❖   ❖   ❖

Bree finally woke up when Spencer planted both front feet on the edge of the bed, whined, and slurped her face at the same time. Sputtering, Bree sat up and glanced at the clock. *Oh, my goodness, nine thirty.* If she found a puddle on the floor, it wasn't her poor dog's fault. She crammed her feet into her fluffy slippers and pulled on her fleece bathrobe as she flew down the stairs, the dog racing ahead of her. He darted out when she opened the back door and barely made it to the bottom step before stopping to pee.

"I'm sorry, I'm so sorry," she muttered as he squatted at the edge of his potty place, did the rest of his business, scratched the dirt with his back feet, and trotted back to join her at the back door. In the meantime she had poured the kibble in his dish and fed the vociferous twining cat.

"Good boy," she crooned, handing Spencer his post-potty treat before he wolfed down his morning allotment. She punched the start button on the coffeemaker and headed back upstairs to get a shower and dress for the day. Jeans, a mock-turtle long-sleeved tee, and a V-neck sweater to ward off the cold. The damp chill of western Washington penetrated even through the bones. Another drizzly gray day. Icy clear during the night and leaking clouds during the day. Not unusual for this time of year. Four hours until the other three of the writing group would convene in her family room. What would they think of her gift from Jade? Had she given something to any of the others too? If Bree did take this trip, she didn't want to go alone. But she shouldn't be focusing on the gift…or maybe she was just distracting herself from remembering this would only be their first regular meeting since Jade died.

She sipped her third cup of coffee and let her mind wander. Jade had been the most mature writer in the group when they all met, had taken Bree and several others under her wing when they arrived, wide-eyed and overwhelmed, at their first writers' conference. Before they knew it, they had exchanged contact information and agreed to meet once a month, realizing they all lived relatively close to one another. This group of friends had been one of the greatest blessings in Bree's life. They'd helped launch her writing career and given her new purpose and drive after Roger died.

Elizabeth, more often known by Lizzie, their juvenile fiction writer, arrived first. "I got hungry for my mom's flan and went into a baking frenzy, so thought I'd share. Not that it'll compare with your famous cinnamon rolls, but it's a favorite family recipe." She handed the plastic container to Breeanna before removing her belted wool coat, then pulled off her knit hat to shake out her dark, shoulder-length hair.

"Yum." Bree peeked inside at the caramel-scented custard, her mouth watering. "Thanks, friend."

The doorbell chimed again. This time Suzie and Marybell, one who also wrote for middle readers and the other historical sagas, strolled in.

"Oh good, you started a fire for us. Thank you." Suzie held her hands out to the blaze.

"Always." Bree smiled, but her insides were tremulous. Part of her wanted to weep—it just didn't feel right without Jade here—but the other part was jumping with wanting to find out if the others had received a gift too. "Let's get our coffee and bring it in here, unless you'd rather have tea and gather around the dining room table."

They'd just settled down when Suzie said, "I have something to tell you."

By the tone of her voice, Bree knew. "You got it too, didn't you? From Jade."

Suzie stared at her. "How did you know?"

"You mean you all got it?" Marybell glanced from one to another around the nodding circle. "The gift, the check?"

"I could hardly believe it." Bree cupped her hands around her coffee and let out a breath, grateful it was out in the open. "Ten thousand?"

The friends all nodded.

Stunned silence, then Lizzie shook her head. "Jade was always so generous. But this . . ." She rolled her lips together. "I miss her so much."

"Me too." Bree swallowed back a lump. No tears today, she'd promised herself. "But you know what she'd want us to do with it." Despite the grief, a shiver of excitement ran up Bree's arms.

"The Italy trip." But Marybell shook her head, her face crumpling. "But I can't—girls, I can't go."

They all turned to their friend who was twisting the bracelet on her wrist. "What is it?"

Marybell sucked in a breath. "My mother just learned the cancer is back and I'm the only one who can take care of her, get her to appointments, all the stuff." Tears gathered and leaked over. "I—I'm so sorry. I know we've all wanted to do this for so long."

"You're not the one to be sorry." Breeanna left her chair

to put an arm around Marybell's thin shoulders. So not fair. This friend gave her all to her family, and her beautiful novels rang in many hearts. *Lord, why is there so much pain in the world?* "Of course we wish you could go with us, but mostly I'm so sorry for your mother to have to go through this again."

"Thank you." Marybell leaned her head against Breeanna's arm. "You are such a comfort."

"Well, we might as well get all the bad news over with." Suzie shook her head. "I can't go either, not now. John has been offered a far better position if we are willing to move ASAP, and I can't tell him no. He's waited too long for this opportunity. We'll need to use my gift money to help cover expenses."

"You're moving? I hope not too far away?" Bree's heart sank.

"Pretty far—Phoenix. He'll leave in two weeks and I will pack us up again and follow as soon as we find a house. Guess God is giving me my dream of living in a warmer climate." Tears shimmered in her eyes now. "But I would have so loved following our dream to Italy with you all." She swallowed. "You'll still go, won't you, Breeanna? You were always more excited about this idea than anyone, Jade knew that. Someone needs to use the gift the way she must have planned or dreamed."

"I'd like to, but it sure won't be the same without all my writing buddies. Lizzie, you'll go, won't you?"

Lizzie nibbled her lower lip. "I don't know. I mean, I've always wanted to see Venice. But I've never been out of the country before."

"Really? Not even to visit your mom's family?"

"Well, Mexico a couple of times when I was little, but we just drove down. That doesn't count."

"Sure it does." Bree nudged her friend's shoe with her

foot. "Come on, if you don't join me, I don't know if I can muster the courage to go myself. And with Elisa going off to college, you need something fun to plan for."

"But that's just it—so much is happening at home, I don't know if I should leave. And Steve and I, we're still working on our marriage; it's only been a couple of years." While Steve had been a wonderful gift in Lizzie's life, their blended family still had its challenges.

Bree got that, she did. But the excitement that had briefly fizzled in her veins was rapidly leaking away.

"Well, we'll keep talking about it." She put on her hostess smile and glanced around the circle. "At least these changes won't ruin our group. We'll just keep on keeping on, online if we have to. Some of us will just need to travel farther for our yearly retreat. Maybe one of you will have a big enough house that we could meet for our week there, like we met at Jade's."

At least the conversation had broken the awkwardness of meeting again without their fearless leader. The focus shifted to writing. Bree filled the coffee, passed the goodies, listened to the excerpts her friends read from their current manuscripts. Keep smiling, keep things together, set her personal feelings aside—that was what she'd been doing for years, what she always did.

But was this trip to Italy yet another dream she had to give up? Surely Jade would want her to find a way to make it happen.

Chapter One

What would the kids say to her news?

Breeanna pulled the pot roast out of the oven, her stomach jumpier than it had been since waiting for her first grandchild to be born, almost three years ago now. She slid a knife into the fragrant beef, then poked a fork into a chunk of potato. Perfect. Scooping the potatoes and carrots into a ceramic bowl and the meat on a platter, she covered the dishes and set them in the oven to keep warm so she could make the gravy.

The doorbell dinged. Must be James and his family—Jessica would never be this early. Hopefully her daughter and the current boyfriend-of-the-month at least wouldn't keep dinner waiting this time. She wanted everyone around her table together tonight.

Breeanna turned the gravy on low and hurried to open the door. With a squealed "Gamma," her toddler grandson Luke leapt into her arms.

"Hi, Mom." James stepped inside and kissed her cheek over his son's curly head. "Smells great in here."

"So good to see you." Breeanna hugged her pregnant daughter-in-law, Abigail. "How are you feeling?"

"Pretty good now, thanks." Abigail rubbed her gently rounding abdomen. "Looking forward to the ultrasound to-morrow, though we've decided to wait to learn the gender."

"So exciting." Breeanna set Luke down with a kiss. "If you go in the living room, sweetheart, Grandma got your toys out for you." Little sneakers pattered through the entryway.

"No Jessica yet?" James arched a brow.

"They should be here soon." Breeanna deflected the criticism always ready to spring from her son toward his sister. Yes, Jessica wasn't as responsible as he was, but she'd also been younger when their father died. Some allowance should be made—though perhaps over the years, Bree had allowed too much. James certainly thought so, hence their recent conversation and agreement that Breeanna wouldn't bail Jessica out financially anymore, no exceptions. She'd yet to be tested on that.

"Need any help in the kitchen?" Abigail pushed back her dark curls and defused the tension with her ready smile.

Breeanna squeezed her hand, grateful again for this sweet daughter-in-law. She was just what James needed. "I'm fine. Why don't you go in with Luke and sit down a few minutes. All I have to do is toss the salad and stir the gravy."

As she drizzled vinaigrette over the greens, another door-bell ring announced Jessica and Ryan. She let James get it, praying he wouldn't say anything about the time. They were only just ready to eat anyway.

"Hey, Mom." Jessica came up behind Bree and wrapped her arms around her shoulders.

"You're pinning my arms," she protested, dropping the salad tongs.

"Sorry." Her daughter released her and stepped back.

Breeanna turned, her irritation melting at the sight of her baby girl, blond hair like her own though swinging long rather than Bree's chin-length bob. Her father's brown eyes with that same sparkle for life—though too often dampened in recent years, mostly by her own bad choices. If only Jess had Roger's steady head as well. Was it the resemblance to him that made it so hard for Bree to say no to Jessica?

"Hey, Jess." She enveloped her daughter in a hug. "Thanks for coming."

"Of course." Jessica snagged a crouton. "Ryan says he's getting addicted to these Thursday-night family dinners." She smiled, but something in her face wasn't quite right.

"I trust that's all he's addicted to?" Breeanna folded her arms and stared straight at her daughter. That one bout with drugs a few years ago had been enough to set her mother sensors on high alert for the rest of her life.

Jessica rolled her eyes. "Yes, Mom. Ryan's not like that. You've seen him, talked with him, he's a really good guy." Something softened in her daughter's face, a wistful vulnerability Bree had rarely seen. Her heart squeezed. Had Jess finally found a man worth finding? But a heaviness about her daughter still tugged at Bree's intuition.

"Jess, is anything wrong?"

Luke bolted into the room, a small cyclone of energy. "Gamma, I hungry."

"We're coming, sweetie." Her own news popping back up in her mind, Breeanna handed the salad bowl to Jessica. "I'll bring the roast. Tell everyone they can sit down."

Alone in the kitchen a moment more, she hefted the platter and drew a deep breath. *Lord, please help them to be happy for me. Or rather, with me.*

After James said the blessing and Breeanna served, the first half hour of dinner passed in a pleasant rumble of light conversation and chuckles over Luke's antics. He was becoming a regular little chatterbox, more like Jessica at his age than the more serious James.

Ever the older brother, James chewed a bite of pot roast and carrots, then aimed a question at Jessica's boyfriend. "So, Ryan, remind me what you do?"

The quiet, dark-haired young man set down his water glass. "I'm in IT. Work with computers at a law firm, mostly AV stuff. Setting up video conferences, that kind of thing."

"Ah, IT. Good steady job." James leveled a glance at his sister. "What a novel idea."

She narrowed her eyes at him and turned her attention to Luke, who was artfully attempting to share his carrots with anyone remotely willing to take them.

Breeanna nudged James's foot under the table. *Be nice*, her eyes said. "Well, I certainly appreciate those of you who understand technology. It took years for me and my computer to become even lukewarm friends."

"Friends might be overstating it." Jessica angled her head, her sparkle returning. "She's always asking me what this icon is or that app is for. And I've heard her threatening dire punishments on her laptop if it refuses to cooperate. You wouldn't know she manages to write bestselling mysteries on the thing."

Ryan chuckled. "Sounds like my mom. One time her computer was acting up, and I told her I'd come over and take a look. She told me, 'Better bring a hammer. I think that's the only thing it understands.'"

Everyone laughed.

"So, if you're a computer geek"—James held a finger in the air—"do I dare hope I've found a fellow sci-fi fan?"

"*Star Wars* or *Star Trek*?" Ryan grinned. "If the latter, I'd go with *Next Generation*. Can't beat Picard."

James pulled his fist down in a victory gesture.

Bree felt the tension loosen in her chest. She was liking this young man—hallelujah, she really was. Her feelings from before were indeed valid. And on that positive note...

She folded her napkin and laid it on the table, her butterflies dancing. *Come on, Breeanna, it's only your family.* "I wanted to share something with you all tonight."

No response. James and Ryan had delved into an animated discussion of *Star Trek* reboots or something, while Abigail listened intently to Jessica's story of how she and Ryan had met while Jess was doing a stint as a coffee shop barista—the job prior to the current one at Applebee's.

"Hey, everybody." Breeanna cleared her throat. "Can I have your attention a moment?"

In his booster seat at her right, Luke shook his head and poked at the dreaded carrots. "Dey no listen, Gamma."

Out of the mouths of babes. Bree raised her voice. "I'm going to Italy."

Dead silence. Four young adults swung their heads to look at her.

Luke patted her hand. "Dey listen now."

Jessica frowned. "What do you mean?"

"Well." Breeanna folded her hands, her middle still jumping. "You remember Jade, from my writers' group? It turns out she left each of us ten thousand dollars."

"Really?" Jessica stared.

"I know, we were all blown away. Jade wanted us to finally fulfill our dream of going to Italy together. Although without her, now." Her throat tightened again.

"Mom, that's awesome." A grin split James's face. "It's about time you did something like this for yourself. You deserve it."

"Yes, that's so exciting." Abigail smiled and wiped Luke's face with his napkin. "When do you leave?"

"Well, I'm still working on that." Bree drew a breath. So far, so good. "It turns out Suzie and Marybell can't go, and Lizzie isn't sure. But I want to do this, even if I have to go alone." Her determination rose again as she spoke the words. "I was thinking about late April or early May, before the baby comes."

"Alone?" James frowned. "That doesn't sound like a good idea. You've never been to Europe before, you don't speak Italian. You at least need someone who knows the ropes."

"Or an organized tour," Ryan suggested. "Those pretty much take care of everything for you."

"That's a good thought." James nodded.

"I looked into those," Bree said. "But they keep you scheduled every single day. I want to get a feel for real life in Italy, have time to people-watch, maybe do some writing. I don't want just the typical tourist experience."

"So you're going to use all of Jade's money for this?" Something strained in Jessica's voice, and she pushed back her chair. She grabbed her empty plate, then reached for Ryan's next to her.

"I wasn't... finished." He trailed off as Jess strode toward the kitchen.

Oh, boy. Bree stood also, gathering dishes to clear the table. "I'll be right back."

Lord, help me here. She headed after her daughter. What was the matter now? Why couldn't they all just be happy for her?

Jessica stood at the sink, running hot water full-blast over the plates.

"What is it, Jess?" Breeanna set her stack of dishes on the counter and leaned her hip against it.

No response. Jessica scrubbed at a plate.

"Something's been off ever since you got here. And now you're upset that I'm going to Italy?"

Jessica turned around then, her brown eyes watery. "I'm about to lose my car."

"What?"

"The bank called, I'm super behind on my payments. If I can't catch up within the next two weeks, they're going to repossess it. Then I'll lose my waitress job, because I won't be able to drive." Jessica sniffed back a sob. "I'm behind on my rent too; my landlord hasn't said he'll kick me out yet, but I'm afraid he's going to. So when you said you'd gotten this amazing gift from Jade, I thought— I thought..."

Bree folded her arms, her stomach sinking. "You thought I would use Jade's gift to bail you out." Why was she surprised? Jess was only basing her assumptions on what Bree had done before.

"Well, just to help me a little. You know. Until I can get back on my feet. I'd pay you back—"

"Jess, you've never been on your feet. We've been in this spot so many times." Tension clamped a vise on Bree's neck.

"So you're just going to abandon me?" Jessica turned back to the sink, her voice dripping tears.

"I never said that." Bree reached to touch her daughter's shoulder, but Jess flinched away. "Sweetie, you know after last time I told you I wouldn't be able to rescue you again. We talked about this. You agreed. You've got to learn to stand on your own two feet." And James would have Bree's head if she backed down again.

Jessica flipped off the water and spun around, still gripping the sponge. "But it's not my fault; it's because of what happened with Dereck. I still have to pay off all the credit card debt I racked up bailing out that bozo. And they're demanding their money too."

"Yeah, that's what happens when you date a guy with a gambling problem and then let him talk you into rescuing him." Breeanna massaged her temples. Her gut twisted, mother guilt kicking in. Maybe she should save the money from Jade, at least part of it, in case Jess really needed it. "Does Ryan know about any of this?"

"No." Jessica lowered her head, her voice dropping small

like the long-ago little girl who'd confessed to breaking several pieces of Bree's cherished Norwegian fine china from her mother.

Bree sighed. "I like Ryan. It seems like you've finally found an actual man, not a lazy good-for-nothing. But at some point you're going to have to be honest with him."

"But what if that pushes him away?" She scuffed at a spot on the linoleum with her toe. "I can't lose him, Mom."

Lord, she really is falling in love with him. "Jess. If you care about this guy, at some point you'll need to be honest with him about who you are and the mistakes you've made. If he's the man you think he is and cares like you want him to, he'll stick around. If not, well, at least you're not trying to build a relationship on false pretenses."

Silence hung a moment, broken only by the ticking of the kitchen clock and the soft murmur of conversation from the dining room.

"So what do you think about the money?" Jessica sniffled and glanced up.

"No." Something snapped inside Breeanna. "I'm not going to give it to you, Jess. I'll talk to James, see what ideas we can come up with to help you figure things out. But my friend gave that check to me for a purpose, and I've waited a long time for a chance like this. I've worked through widowhood and raising you kids, teaching and substitute teaching and writing nights and doing whatever I had to in order to put food on the table for you and your brother. And I would never be able to afford a trip like this, not after all the times I've dipped into my pitiful savings for you. Not without Jade's generous gift. So I'm going to take it, and you're going to have to grow up a bit."

"Fine." Jessica slapped the sponge into the sink. "I won't let you know if I end up living under a bridge, all by myself again. I wouldn't want to spoil things while you're enjoying Italy." She stormed out of the kitchen and down the hall, tears falling fast.

Bree heard the bathroom door close. She leaned against the kitchen counter a moment, spent, then turned to the sink and squirted soap over the pile of dirty dishes, blinking back tears herself.

Lord, am I doing the wrong thing? Maybe I should help her. I'm her mother. Who else is she going to turn to? Please, this is so hard.

She soaked the plates, trying to compose herself enough to return to the dining room. She could hear conversation, no doubt James and Abigail trying to cover the awkwardness. Poor Ryan must have been wondering what he'd gotten himself into.

Breeanna dried her hands and drew a long breath. Putting on a smile, she reentered the dining room.

"Anyone ready for dessert?"

All heads turned. Luke raised his spoon in the air, beaming. "Me!"

Everyone chuckled, breaking the tension. Thank God for small children.

Jessica rejoined them as Breeanna served squares of chocolate sheet cake with fudge sauce, quiet but composed. Maybe only Bree's mother's eye noticed the telltale pink of her daughter's nose and eyes. Ryan glanced at her with concern, but soon they were chatting about the dessert, which had been Jess's favorite since she and James were little. One of many—Bree did love to bake.

Jessica and Ryan stood to leave soon after the last crumbs were eaten.

"Already?" James raised a brow.

"Ryan has to be at work early." Jessica didn't meet anyone's gaze.

Bree hugged her daughter at the door, feeling the tension in Jess's shoulders. "I love you, honey. Let's talk soon."

"'Night." Jessica pulled away with a forced smile, no doubt for Ryan's benefit.

"Thanks again for dinner." Ryan shook her hand, then followed Jessica's tug down the walkway.

Breeanna closed the door and stared at the little leaded-glass window in it, rubbing her arms. What else should she have said, or done?

"Help you finish the dishes?" James spoke from behind her.

She turned to see her son already rolling up his sleeves. Her mouth quirked. James was so predictable at times, only offering to help with the dishes when he wanted to have a serious talk.

Leaving Abigail on the sofa reading a picture book to Luke, they tackled the kitchen.

"So." Wearing Roger's old apron, James scrubbed the roast pan. He always did confront the toughest thing first. "What's going on with Jess?"

"She was hoping I'd use the money from Jade to help her." Breeanna stretched plastic wrap over the remaining cake in the glass baking pan.

"Again."

"Yes, again. But honey, she is in a bad spot. Trying to help that creep Dereck really set her back. I didn't know till tonight that she was so behind on her rent, and the creditors are really hounding her. She's about to lose her car, which means she'd probably lose her job." Her chest squeezed again for her little girl. "Maybe I should..."

"Mom, no. You can't." James set the scrubber down and turned to look at her, eyes intent. "You know you can't. You'd only be continuing to enable her bad decisions."

"I know." Bree swallowed back tears. "I know that's not

the way to help, but I don't know what is." She'd always worked so hard to stay out of debt, even when it meant doing without a lot of luxuries and even simple wants as a single mother raising two kids. Except for the mortgage, she didn't know the first thing about dealing with debt or how to get out of it.

James sighed and ran hot water over the pan, rinsing it. "Maybe I could pay for her to work with a credit counselor. I know a guy who works with a group, a nonprofit company. I think they help people reach agreements with creditors for a workable payment plan, in addition to counseling on finance management, budgeting, that kind of thing. I could give him a call."

"Really?" Hope sent a full breath into Bree's lungs. "That sounds good."

"But she has to be willing to work with them." James flipped the pan over with a clang. "She'll probably have to get another part-time job, too, if she's in as big a mess as it sounds like."

He didn't say *again* this time, but Breeanna knew he was thinking it.

Her heart hurt for the tension between her children. James was right, she knew that. But he and Jessica used to be so close, especially in the years after their father died. He'd been such a protective older brother. Now she guessed that was coming out in different ways, in his frustration over his sister hurting herself more than anyone.

Bree dried the dishes in silence while James finished washing, then they headed into the living room. Abigail and Luke lay cuddled on the sofa, fast asleep. Luke's curly head pillowed on the small mound that would be his little brother or sister.

James eased into an armchair with a sigh. "I better get them home soon."

"Can you wait a few minutes? I want to call Jessica, and I'd rather you were here." His presence would help her stay firm. She didn't need to say that.

James nodded and leaned his head against the back of the chair, closing his eyes.

Bree softened watching him, seeing a rare moment of her little boy in the grown engineer of a son. He worked so hard, providing well for Abigail and Luke and soon another little one. And trying to take care of her and Jess too, in his own way.

She dialed Jessica's number, her stomach tensing. *Lord, please help her be open to this.*

It rang until she thought she'd land in voicemail. But finally, Jessica picked up.

"Hi, Mom." Her voice was flat.

"Hey, sweetie." Breeanna cleared her throat. "You got home okay?"

"It's not that far. For now."

Did "for now" mean *until I'm living under a bridge?* Bree didn't pursue it. "Listen, I was wondering if you'd be willing to come over again tomorrow to meet with James and me. So we can talk all this through."

"You mean so James can yell at me?"

"No." Bree pinched the bridge of her nose. At least, she hoped it wouldn't end in another of those scenes. "But he does have some ideas that I think might help. Could you come over after dinner tomorrow? Say, around seven?" Breeanna raised her eyebrows at James, who'd opened his eyes to listen. He nodded.

Static, then Jessica sighed. "I work the day shift tomorrow so I guess I could come after I get off."

"Great." Bree released a breath. "We really do want to help you, honey. Just in a way that's for the long term." She wouldn't mention anything about the credit counselor—

it might scare Jessica off. She'd let James handle that tomorrow.

"I've got to get to bed. Bye."

The call ended. Bree reached down to stroke Spencer's head as the dog rubbed against her legs.

Okay, Lord. Now, if only Jessica would go along with this.

Chapter Two

This wasn't a good start.

Breeanna could tell as soon as she opened the door the next evening that James was stressed—his eyes, the set of his shoulders.

"Hi." He strode in past her without so much as a peck on the cheek. "Jess here?"

"No, not yet." She closed the door.

He sighed and raked a hand through his hair. "Great."

"She'll be here, honey. It's only just seven." She prayed so. "Want some coffee?"

"Decaf, if you have it." James headed into the dining room and flopped his computer bag on the table.

In the kitchen, Bree lifted the steaming pot from the coffeemaker and poured them each a cup, then rejoined her son. Cinders twined around her legs. "Tough day?"

"Just a lot going on at work. Then Abigail had her ultrasound, so dinner was late and Luke was crabby." James sat down and opened up his laptop.

"Did the ultrasound go okay? And did you talk to your friend, the creditor counsel?"

"It did, everything's fine. And it's credit counselor. He's got a full client load, but he said he'd make room for Jessica." James pulled some brochures from his bag and studied them. "Sure hope I haven't stuck my neck out for nothing."

The doorbell rang.

James looked up from his computer and his eyes bored into Bree's. "No matter what she says, Mom, you can't help her this time. Not even to be a co-signer on anything. She's got to learn to do this herself."

Bree's stomach churned. Maybe she shouldn't have coffee after all. She'd hardly managed any dinner, anticipating, fearing, the evening.

She went to the door and returned with a subdued Jessica.

Her daughter halted in the dining room doorway when she saw James with the computer, briefcase, paperwork set up. "What's all this stuff?" She gripped her purse strap, eyes wary.

"James has some ideas that might help you, honey." Breeanna kept her tone level. "Want some coffee?"

Jessica snorted. "I'm not doing this again." She spun to head back to the door.

"Jess, wait." Bree hurried after her and caught her daughter's arm in the entryway. "Not doing what again?"

"Not sitting there while James tells me what a failure I am and lays out his perfect plan for my life." Jessica yanked her elbow away. "He doesn't get me—he never has."

"You know he loves you." Surely, deep down, Jessica knew that. "And so do I—so, so much." Despite her efforts, Bree's voice wobbled a little. "I know your brother can be a bit overbearing. But he has wisdom in that stubborn head of his."

Jessica snorted again, softer this time. But she didn't move toward the door.

"Ja, he's a stubborn Norwegian." Bree added a Scandinavian lilt to her voice, trying to lighten the moment. "And so are you. You come by it naturally, I'm afraid. But Jess, I haven't dealt with this kind of thing before; I don't know how to help you out of this. I think maybe James does."

"Yes, you do. You just won't."

"Giving you that money is not going to help you." She was saying the words for herself as much as Jessica. "Not in the long term. But we're not going to abandon you either. Will you at least listen to what your brother has to say?"

Jessica let out a long, shuddering breath. Her shoulders slumped. "Fine."

Bree led the way back.

Jessica plopped into a dining chair and folded her arms. She stared at the table, one ballet flat tapping the floor as if counting the seconds till she could bolt.

Bree sat down and wrapped her hands around her coffee mug. At least the warmth was comforting. *Father, be with us here—we need you. Help my children, both of them, please.*

She thought James would dive in right away, lay out the plan or lay into Jessica or whatever he was going to do. But instead he just sat a moment, staring at his screen. Then he closed the lid and folded his hands on the laptop, with a sigh that seemed drawn up from the bottoms of his feet.

"Jess, I don't want another yelling match. We've had too many of those."

Jessica glanced up, a flicker of surprise in her dark eyes. Then back down.

"Believe it or not, I want to help you." He leaned toward his sister, staring at her bent head, hair shielding her eyes. "But if you really want to get out of this mess, you're going to have to put effort in too. Like a lot. It won't be easy, not Mom just writing you a check like before."

Bree flinched inwardly.

Jessica sat up straighter and flipped her hair back. "You act like I don't do anything. I work hard. I've worked more jobs than you."

"Yeah, and how many have you kept, with you running

late all the time?" James snapped, then paused and visibly slowed himself. "Come on, Jess. Do you want to hear my ideas or not?"

James was trying, he really was. His little sister had always tested his patience, but he'd give his life for her in a minute. Bree knew that.

"Whatever." Jessica slumped back down.

James opened his laptop. "I have a friend who works for a credit counseling company. Do you know what that is?"

She shrugged.

"They help people who are struggling with debt and managing money, like you are. A credit counselor discusses and assesses your financial situation with you, gives guidance on how to address your current problems and avoid similar ones in the future. They help you with budgeting, figuring out how to get out of debt, all kinds of things. This company even offers a debt management plan, where they'll work with your creditors to help you pay off what you owe in amounts you can afford, over a reasonable time frame."

"Really?" Jessica looked up, a flicker of interest on her face.

"But you have to be consistent."

"And how much does all this magic cost?"

"The company's a nonprofit, but there are still fees. I'd be willing to cover them for you—if you meet certain conditions."

"What are those?" The wariness slipped back.

"You'll attend all the counseling sessions. And you'll increase your hours at work, get to full-time level, at least thirty-five to forty hours a week."

"My manager won't give me more hours." Jessica clamped her arms back across her chest, shaking her head hard. "I've asked before, but they want to keep the service staff part-time because of benefits or something."

"Then you'll have to get a second job. Also, I think you

need to be accountable to Mom or me for your spending. Probably me. Maybe even hand over your credit card until you can get a handle on your money."

Jessica's face reddened. "You really see me as a stupid child, don't you?"

"Honey." Bree scooted closer to Jessica, her throat aching for her girl. She smoothed a hand over her daughter's back. "He doesn't mean that."

"Yes, he does. You both do." She closed her eyes, hugging her crossed arms to her chest.

Bree got up and strode into the kitchen, Cinders trotting beside her. *Lord, help me. Wanting to help her is tearing me apart.* But James was right that if she signed on anything, if she eased her daughter's path in any way right now, she would be defeating their purpose—to force Jessica to grow up.

"But what if I screw up?" she heard Jessica cry.

Bree dared not return to the dining room, or she might offer Jessica the whole check from Jade right now. It wouldn't cover all Jess's debts or solve all her problems, but it would help, wouldn't it? Bree took a shaky sip of water. No, she knew that wasn't the answer. She had to let James deal with this.

Silence from the other room. Bree edged toward the door to the dining room so she could see her children but they hopefully wouldn't notice her.

James was rubbing his forehead. "I've got the website here if you want to take a look. Picked up these brochures too. But the decision is yours, Jessica. I can't force you. I've gotten you a spot with my friend, I've laid out your options." He pushed the brochures toward her. "I've done all I can do. Mom certainly has done all she should do, probably more. The rest is up to you."

Bree could tell by Jess's face she was deep in thought.

The quiet around the table was broken only by Spencer's whimpering from dreaming on his worn doggy bed in the corner.

"Okay."

"Okay, what?"

Jessica sniffled. "Okay. I'll do it. But—would you go with me?"

"To meet with Dave?" James blew out a breath. "You do understand I will not bail you out. This is your opportunity to clean up your mess."

Breeanna stepped into the doorway and leaned against it.

Jessica nodded, her index finger worrying the cuticle on her thumb. A sure sign she was fighting inside to stay with this.

"Then yes, I will go with you."

Bree blew out a breath she didn't realize she'd been holding. Was there hope for her family working together after all?

❋   ❋   ❋

After the kids left, Bree carried the empty cups into the kitchen and looked at the clock. Eleven p.m. A wave of exhaustion crashed over her—physical, mental, emotional. Years ago she'd thought the baby and toddler years would be the most intense of her parenting, but sometimes adult children drained her in a way interrupted nights never had.

She saw to the animals' needs. Cinders was already curled up fast asleep on top of the sofa. After a quick shower, she climbed into bed, switching off her bedside lamp as she did so. As soon as she settled her head into the pillow, her mind leapt into action, replaying the conversation this evening. Would Jessica stick with the plan? Would the credit counseling actually work, or would she fall back into her same old habits once she finished the course? Bree rolled to her other side and plumped her pillow. Ryan seemed like a good guy; even James thought so. And since he was a good guy, did that mean he wouldn't want to be saddled with Jessica and her problems? Pain stabbed her heart at the thought. Or that he truly cared, and would stick with her and support her?

She tried praying for each member of her family and reciting her favorite psalms in her head. But sleep remained a taunting imp, dancing just out of reach.

After an hour or so of this, Breeanna sat up and slid her feet into her slippers beside the bed. This wasn't working. She might as well get some pages added on her manuscript.

She tied on her robe and padded downstairs, Spencer following at her heels, no doubt wondering what the crazy woman was doing up at this hour. She flicked on the entry light at the bottom of the stairs to gently light her path, then passed through the darkened living room to the familiar solace of her office.

Settling into her ergonomically correct desk chair, she adjusted the height a little. The chair had been a gift to herself after a particularly encouraging royalty check a few years ago, and she'd never regretted it. Switching on her Sherlock Holmes desk lamp—complete with a stack of antique-looking books for the base, and quaint detective with magnifying glass peeking over—she booted up her computer and breathed in the peace of this familiar refuge. Book-lined shelves surrounded her like old friends, with her favorite authors, research books, and her own series upon series of suspense and mysteries and now her new favorite, cozy mysteries, taking up shelves of their own. Spencer curled up at her feet, as if to say, *I'll stay with you, but I won't give up my own sleep, silly human.*

Breeanna opened her latest manuscript and stared at the blinking cursor for the next chapter. Her detective in this series was a high school English teacher, harking back to her own memories of teaching before her kids were born, and again after Roger died until her writing finally took off. Spunky Miss Effie Bartlett balanced solving crimes in her small town in the Northwest with a classroom of lively teenagers always eager to hear about her latest cases—or occasionally getting mixed up in them.

The earlier novels in the series had done well. But over the last year or so, Bree had sensed her inspiration waning. Sales had fallen with the most recent books too. Her editor had suggested she try a new series after this manuscript was turned in, but so far, she had zero ideas. Maybe that was another reason to pursue this trip. Hadn't Italy inspired countless artists?

Bree tapped her fingers on the desk. For now, she had to get this novel done. Was it time to introduce another red herring? Or let Miss Bartlett actually catch a glimpse of the real killer? Following the tickle of an idea, Bree started to type, and the words actually flowed, mingling with Spencer's snoring as the hours ticked silently by.

One and a half chapters later, she glanced at her computer's clock and gulped. Five a.m.—how had that happened? The same as it always did, of course. But her fictional worlds proved such a needed break from the real world at times.

She saved the document and shut down her computer. Bleary-eyed but satisfied with her progress, she pushed her chair back. Spencer roused with a snort and a shake, then padded beside her back down the hall and through the darkened house to the kitchen, where she let him out the back door, breathing in the cold crispness, the deep dark of the wee hours still hanging.

Back in the kitchen, she filled the animals' dishes with kibble, still not bothering to turn on the light. Cinders walked in at the sound of food and stretched, tail straight up, then settled down to eat, delicate mouthfuls in contrast with Spencer's noisy scarfing. Bree turned off the telephones, grateful for the answering message she had finally set up after too many late writing nights were followed by early-morning phone calls. It just said, "Hi, you've reached Breeanna, my story grabbed me last night and didn't let go until nearly time to get up. Will call you back when I can. Thanks." Simple and it worked.

Barely able to walk straight, she hauled herself up the stairs and fell into bed with her robe still on.

Lord, please help Jessica follow through with this plan was her last thought before being swallowed by sleep.

Chapter Three

"Hey, what're you doing for dinner tonight?"

Breeanna glanced at the computer screen before her. "I wasn't doing dinner, going to keep writing. The story is ripping along now. Finally." She tipped her head from side to side to stretch out her neck muscles.

"Well, we're doing one of those salmon that Peter caught last fall out on the grill, and I made roasted vegetables to go with it, plus a salad." A hint of static broke through her friend's voice on the phone, then cleared. "And I baked an apple pie this afternoon. Come on over."

"Paula." Bree elongated the name. "You know better than to do this to me."

"Won't be for two hours yet, you'll have racked up enough pages by then."

Salmon on the grill the way Peter did it was beyond delicious. "All right, but now my arm hurts."

"I know, from me twisting it." The two friends chuckled. Ever since they'd met at church years ago, they'd grown into a friendship that understood without explanations.

"You want me to bring anything?"

"You have vanilla ice cream in your freezer?"

"You know I do." Ice cream of several different flavors could always be found in Bree's freezer. Vanilla bean was a staple. "I'll bring it."

"Good. Eating at six." They clicked off their phones so Breeanna reread the last page she had written and picked it up again. Dryness of mouth and needing to use the bathroom brought her back to reality. Five forty-five. Now, that was perfect timing. *Thank you, Lord.* She drank from the glass she kept in the bathroom, used the facilities, applied lipstick, and headed to the kitchen to feed the animals. Good thing Paula lived only three houses north of hers.

Bundled against the cold with a royal-blue wool stocking hat and matching scarf, a down three-quarter-length coat, and gloves, she blew out a breath that steamed in front of her. January in Vancouver could be heading into the teens at night.

She mounted the steps to the gray house with blue trim, smiling at the twin arborvitae potted shrubs on either side of the door, now clothed in tiny twinkling lights. With a double knock she let herself in. Spencer's best friend Bruno the Basset bayed her arrival and met her with a tail wagging so hard it created bruises on nearby legs.

Paula came into the living room drying her hands on a towel. "That's enough, Bruno, you've announced her arrival to the whole world."

Breeanna handed over the bag with the ice cream and started divesting herself of her winter attire to hang in the closet. "Bet Peter is freezing out there." She paused in front of the blazing fireplace and let the heat warm her face. "Oh, this fire feels so good."

"I thought we'd do coffee and pie in there tonight." Strains of gentle brass reminded Bree she'd not taken time to change the playlist on her sound system from Christmas yet. Often when she dug deep into a new manuscript, lots of things didn't get done around her house. James kept suggesting she install a gas log in her fireplace since she so rarely got around to starting a wood fire.

"Can I help with anything?" she asked as she entered the country kitchen decorated with both hens and roosters. "Sure smells good."

The back door pushed open and Peter carried in a cookie sheet with the salmon in a double bed of tinfoil. "You want this on the stove or...?"

"Put it on the butcher block." Paula pulled a serving platter decorated with a rooster out of the slotted cabinet over the stove and set it beside the pan of salmon.

"Ah, Peter, what a treat."

"Eating them is never as much fun as catching them but not too far behind." He lifted the salmon out of the tinfoil nest and settled it on the platter. "Glad you could join us." He folded up the smoky-bottomed foil and tossed it in the trash. "How's the book going?" His blue eyes twinkled. "Before you were interrupted, that is."

"Going well, I'm pleased to say. And as your wife reminded me, I'd have done enough pages by dinnertime. But when the story is rocketing along like that, I do hate to stop."

Peter took a knife from the block and sliced the boneless fillet into portions. "Knowing you, you'll go back to it when you get home and..."

"And work through the night," Paula finished for him. "Bring the salmon, I've got the roasted vegetables. Bree, please bring the salad." She nodded to the wooden bowl on the counter. "I already poured the dressing on the greens."

They settled at the table, Bruno taking his place beside Peter, who had a habit of accidentally dropping bits at times, and they clasped hands for grace. "Lord, bless this food and the hands that prepared it. Thank you for giving us salmon in the river and vegetables in the garden. And forever friends." They all said, "Amen."

"Pass your plates over for the salmon." Peter scooped up

the first serving for their company. "I think I got all the bones, but being careful is always smart."

"Did you grow the parsnips too?" Breeanna asked as she dished up the roasted vegetables. Peter's garden was famous in their neighborhood since he gave away tomatoes and lettuce, and this year green beans as well. The two of them still kept busy canning and freezing and even experimenting with drying. In his spare time he shared his master gardener status and knowledge with whoever asked.

"In answer to your question, no. I bought those at the produce market."

They caught up on all the Fordsmith family news during the meal, cleared the table, and took apple pie à la mode and coffee to settle in front of the fire.

"Now it's your turn." Paula took a bite and closed her eyes in delight. So Breeanna told them the latest drama with Jessica and how James had been trying to help.

"And what do you think of the new boyfriend?" Peter asked, since he'd been the one to go to Jessica's aid when she had car or boy trouble in the middle of the night.

"His name is Ryan, and I think she finally found a real man, not another spoiled lazy boy out to get everything he can from her." Bree rolled her eyes. "I was beginning to lose hope."

"I think we all were." Peter used his spoon to get the last of the pie juice off his plate. The three of them chuckled. They'd shared their families ever since they met that Sunday at the blessing of the new church built not far from them.

And now all their children were grown and had flown the nest and started nests of their own, some still single, others married and either having grandkids or not. Breeanna was blessed that both of hers were still in Vancouver so she had the privilege of loving and playing with Luke.

"But oh"—Bree straightened in the overstuffed chair—

"I almost forgot my other news." She told them about the gift from Jade. These friends knew of the long-postponed dream to go to Italy; Paula had commiserated with Bree each time the plans proved unfeasible before.

"Of course you should go." Paula gave a decisive nod. "Why wouldn't you? It's the chance of a lifetime. I'm so excited for you."

"I know—me too, every time I think about it. But I'm just not sure. What if Jessica really does end up needing that money? And then I don't know whether I can get Lizzie to go. I'm open to going alone, but James seemed to think I was crazy for even thinking that."

"Nonsense." Peter set down his coffee. "You're a strong, independent woman, Breeanna—look at all you've accomplished on your own, raising and providing for these kids, becoming a successful author. Talk with a travel agent, they could give you some insights, tell you what's feasible and what's not."

"That's a good idea." Bree felt her shoulders relax. "I knew it would help to talk with you two. And speaking of my career, I'm really hoping the trip might help jump-start some ideas for this new series my editor wants me to come up with. So far, I've been coming up dry."

"See, yet another reason to go. And don't let me hear any more of this guilt-tripping yourself over Jessica." Paula met her gaze. "You don't need me to tell you why."

Bree chuckled wryly. "No, guess I don't."

When she caught herself yawning, she told her friends thanks for the delicious dinner and that she needed to be on her way. While she suited up, Paula fixed a packet of salmon and roasted veggies. Peter shrugged into his winter jacket.

"Peter, you don't need to walk me home."

"I know, but I'm going to anyway so don't bother arguing."

Paula made a nothing-I-can-do-about-it face and handed

her the bag. "I put a piece of pie in but we used up your ice cream."

"Thank you, now I won't have to cook tomorrow." Bree hugged her best friend, who saw her and Peter out the door. "'Night now."

"Thanks for coming." Peter blew out a cloud of iced droplets as he spoke a few minutes later. "A good evening."

"Thanks, we hadn't done that for a while. Talk tomorrow?"

"Good." He waited until she opened the door and turned with a wave.

"'Night." Breeanna closed her door and, moving to the window, watched him stride back home.

After hanging up her gear, she tucked the food bag in the refrigerator and turned off the lights; then she and her faithful furry friends climbed the stairs of the split-level house. Gazing back down the stairs, she debated: *Bed or book?* Heaving a sigh, she entered the master bedroom and checked the messages on her cell.

James. *"Hey, Mom, could you possibly watch Luke tomorrow afternoon? Abigail has a follow-up appointment and she'd like me to be there, if it works out."*

Bree sighed and rubbed her forehead. Of course she would say yes, she always did. But there went half her writing day. And this story was just starting to come together. Well, she'd just have to be productive in the morning. Despite Paula and Peter's predictions, she was just plain too tired tonight.

She donned winter flannel pj's and crawled into her bed. Spencer spread out at the foot and Cinders curled up on the other pillow. Maybe she'd wake up early to get back to the book.

Chapter Four

She hadn't heard from Jessica in several days.

Bree checked her cell phone again, then refocused her attention on Luke, playing with his train set on her braided rug in the living room.

Had Jessica talked with the credit counselor yet? Had she and James pushed her too hard? Or had Breeanna just never pushed hard enough before? So many questions.

"Look, Gamma! Caboose come off."

"Uh-oh. Can you put it back together?"

"Sure." Sticking his tongue out the corner of his mouth, Luke carefully reconnected the magnets.

Bree hid a smile and ruffled her grandson's hair. What a lifter of spirits he was.

James and Jessica had been too, when they were little. Chaotic as those years had been, how she'd loved them— years when Roger was alive and her kids were small and innocent, when a kiss or time-out or adhesive bandage fixed most crises.

Not like now.

Her phone chimed, and Breeanna dove for it like a socially deprived teenager. A new message lit up the screen.

Jessica. *Hey, Mom, do you have time to talk?*

Breeanna retrieved a wayward boxcar from underneath

the sofa for Luke and speed-dialed Jessica's number. "Hey, honey. What's up?"

"I messed up." Her daughter's voice came sniffly. "I blew up at Ryan, and he left."

Breeanna almost asked her to clarify what she meant by "left." Had they broken up? But Jessica was definitely crying now, so she only said, "I'm sorry, sweetheart."

"Could I maybe come over for a little while? I don't work till four. I close tonight."

"I'm watching Luke, but—yes, of course, honey, you can come over." Breeanna disconnected and set her phone aside, closing her eyes briefly. *Oh, Lord, not another crisis. Please show me what to do, how to make this better.*

"Gamma." Luke patted her knee. "Hungry."

"Okay, sweetie." Breeanna opened her eyes and smiled at him. "Let's go get a snack."

With Luke in his booster seat at the kitchen table, happy with crackers and cheese and cut grapes, Bree glanced out the window for Jessica's car. It had started to rain again, water dripping off the eaves onto the porch railing with a dreary plop, plop. The already gray day was darkening early, though it was only midafternoon.

"Look, Gamma." Luke held up his slice of cheddar, a hole bitten right through the middle, and grinned at her through it.

"That's funny. But eat your cheese, okay?"

"Okay." He shoved the corner in his mouth.

Jessica's little red car splashed into the driveway. Huddled under her raincoat hood, Jess darted up onto the porch.

"Didn't you bring an umbrella?" Breeanna met her at the door and motioned her toward the mudroom section of the entryway.

"I forgot." Jessica shucked her dripping coat and boots.

Bree didn't comment on that but gave her a hug. Jessica

leaned into her shoulder a moment, like when she was a thirteen-year-old having a hard day. Sadness mingled with the scent of rain in her hair.

"I need to get back to Luke. Come in the kitchen with us."

Jessica followed, silent.

"Hi, Auntie Jess!" Luke waved a cracker, grinning at his favorite aunt.

"Hey, buddy." Jessica leaned down to kiss his crumb-dusted cheek. "Having a snack?"

"Uh-huh. Finish cackers cheese, then can pease have a cimmin roll." Luke nodded wisely.

"Good to know." A corner of Jessica's mouth tipped up.

"Want tea?" Breeanna carried the kettle to the sink and filled it.

"I guess." Jessica slid into a chair next to Luke and pulled her sweater sleeves down over her hands. "Sure is chilly today."

She and Luke made quiet conversation, Jessica prompting him to finish his snack while Breeanna steeped two mugs of chai. She carried them to the table with a small plate of the cinnamon rolls she'd baked that morning, knowing Luke might be coming. Baking always gave her comfort, and the fruit of it seemed to do the same for others.

"Figure we could all use a treat." Breeanna sat down and pulled off part of a roll for her grandson.

"Tank you, Gamma." Luke fingered the sticky pastry, his grin wide as he stuck his finger in his mouth.

Jessica bit into a roll too, with a trembly sigh that seemed drawn up from her stockinged feet.

Breeanna watched her daughter, heart hurting. If only cinnamon rolls could fix things as easily now as they had when Jess was little.

"So what happened?" Bree wrapped her hands around the warmth of her mug, bracing for what was to come.

Jessica picked at her cuticle. "Ryan only worked a half day today, and it's not often we both are free at the same time on a weekday, so we met for lunch. But my phone rang near the end, and it was—the bank. About my car." She swallowed. "I figured I should take it, so I stepped away from the table. I tried to tell them I was getting this credit counselor, and I would get it all paid off, but they were really pushy. When I came back, Ryan could tell I was upset."

It had never been too hard to tell with Jess. "So then you told him?"

"I tried to, because you said I should." An edge of resentment grated her daughter's voice. "I told him it was the bank on the phone, and that I have a lot of debt I'm trying to pay off, and I was trying not to lose my car. He said he understood, he had student loans and stuff too, and he knew how easy it was to get in debt. But then he kept asking questions and pressing me for more—at least it felt like it. He probably just wanted to see how he could help—he's super detail-oriented. But I got upset and then I just blurted out what happened with Dereck. I think it came out wrong, because he said if I didn't want his help, then fine. And he just left. He probably thinks I'm a complete mess." Jessica was crying in earnest now.

Well, that wasn't too far off. But Bree held her tongue.

"Ryan's the one good thing that's happened to me lately, and now I've probably lost him." Jessica propped her elbows on the table and buried her face in her hands. "I wish I never listened to you when you said to tell him."

Luke stared at his aunt, mouth half full of his cinnamon roll, then looked to Breeanna, eyes round.

Poor little guy, he didn't need to be seeing this. Blowing out a breath, Bree wiped her grandson's face and hands and lifted him down from his booster. "Come on, sweetie, let's go in the living room."

"Auntie Jess okay?" Luke trotted beside Breeanna, holding her hand.

"Yes, she'll be okay. Want to play with your train some more?"

"All done train. Trucks?"

"Okay, but we need to put the train away first." Bree sat back on the rug with him, her stomach churning. *Lord, I don't know how to fix this. Maybe I shouldn't have suggested she tell Ryan. But now what?*

A few minutes later Jessica came in and plopped on the sofa, her tears subsided at least for now. "I'm sorry. I shouldn't have come, I didn't mean to upset him. I always mess everything up. I shouldn't have told Ryan. I shouldn't try to do anything."

"Jessica, you've got to stop saying that." Frustration built pressure in Bree's chest. "You only hurt yourself—first with bad choices, then not wanting to take responsibility for fixing them. But when you curl up into a ball of woe-is-me, that doesn't help either."

"Okay, so I'm a terrible person." Jessica threw her arms out, the drama queen of her teenage years showing. "I get it, you and James have hinted it often enough. You're probably glad Ryan is saved from me."

"I didn't say that." Bree tossed wooden train tracks into their storage tub harder than necessary. Luke tugged a small blue engine and attached string of cars around the outer braid of the rug, murmuring choo-choo noises to himself. Apparently he had forgotten that he was all done with the train.

Jessica sighed and dropped her hands back on the sofa cushions beside her. "But you're right. Here I am twenty-eight years old, and the steadiest job I've ever had is waitressing at Applebee's. Did you know Ryan has been at his same job for eight years, ever since right out of college? No wonder he couldn't wait to get away from me." Tears sprang again. "I just wish I hadn't snapped at him like I did. Or that we could have talked it over more."

Maybe they still would. Ryan didn't seem like the type to split without a word. But Bree didn't know him that well—and neither did Jessica. They'd only first met three months ago.

She needed to start dinner, so she left Jess to watch Luke while she put on water for spaghetti and took a freezer container of homemade meat sauce from the fridge to finish defrosting. She could send some back with James when he came to pick up Luke before too long. Abigail was always so appreciative of home-cooked meals since she could enjoy food again.

The doorbell rang. Must be James.

"I'll get it." She could hear Luke chattering to Jessica in the living room—probably better medicine for her daughter right now than anything Bree could say. She hurried through the entryway and opened the door.

"Ryan." She stared at the young man, his dark cropped hair and the shoulders of his jacket damp with rain. He hadn't brought an umbrella either. Maybe he and her daughter weren't different in every way after all.

"Hey." Ryan shoved his hands into his jacket pockets, tipping his head self-consciously. "Sorry to just show up like this. I was wondering if I could talk with you a few minutes."

"Come in, it's freezing out there." Bree stepped back and let Ryan in, her mind spinning. "Ryan, just so you know, Jessica—"

"That's what I want to talk to you about—Jess, I mean." Ryan glanced away, then back to meet Breeanna's eyes. The vulnerability there melted her heart. "She said some things today, and I maybe didn't react real well. But I don't want to lose her, and I'm afraid I might have made her think I don't care—I just didn't know what to do."

"Ryan." Bree touched his damp sleeve. "Jessica is here. In the living room, with her nephew."

"Oh. Wow." Ryan hesitated. "Guess I should have known that was a possibility. Can I see her?"

"Of course. Let me get Luke, give you two some privacy." Breeanna hurried ahead into the living room, hope pattering her heart. *Lord, he came after her—that's a good sign, isn't it?* "Jess, Ryan is here."

Jessica looked up, her mouth dropping open. "He is?" Fear crept into her eyes. "To see me?"

"Well, he didn't know you were here, but—anyway, here he is."

Ryan moved into the room behind her. Bree scooped up Luke and a couple of trucks and carted them into the kitchen, her grandson protesting the sudden eviction.

She strained to hear anything from the living room as she poured dry pasta into the now-boiling water, but only murmurs made it through the intervening hall.

The doorbell rang again—surely James this time. Bree met him at the door with a raised hand to be quiet.

"Jessica and Ryan are here."

James frowned. "And that means silence why?" He stepped inside and set his umbrella in the wastebasket Bree kept in the entryway for that purpose.

"Daddy!" Luke dashed in from the kitchen and threw himself at his father.

So much for quiet. "Jessica told Ryan about everything today, kind of accidentally." Breeanna kept her voice low. "He got upset and left, and Jessica was falling apart. But now I hope they're talking it out."

"And she came crying to you, as usual." His jaw set, James picked Luke up. "I hope you didn't go back on any of the things we talked about."

"Of course not." Stung, Bree stepped back.

"Well, I've got to get home." James set Luke down with a pat. "Get your shoes, buddy."

Bree sighed, pressing past the tension. James meant well, as usual—he was just tired. And Jessica could push anyone to breaking. She should know. "Let me send some spaghetti and meat sauce with you. It should be ready to package up."

Boxing the food in the kitchen, Breeanna could hear James greet Jessica and Ryan in the living room. His voice was one to carry.

Please, Lord, let him not say anything to set Jessica off right now. She snapped on plastic lids over steaming food. *I've had all the drama I can handle for one day.*

James and Luke left without further incident, and Ryan followed shortly after. Bree desperately wanted to ask what they'd talked about, how it had gone, but she bit her tongue and waved him off with a smile. Jessica shut the door behind him and turned to get her own raincoat.

"I've got to get to work." She drew a deep breath, her voice subdued but not teary. A good sign? "Thanks for letting me come over, Mom."

"Of course." Bree wrapped her in a hug. "How did it go?" She couldn't help herself.

Jessica pulled back and shrugged. "Okay, I guess. I told him more of the background, about Dereck and stuff. And about the program James wants me to do, not that I fully understand it myself yet. But he—well, he says he wants to stick with me, Mom." A tentative smile touched the corners of her face. "Not sure I believe him yet, but that's what he says."

"That's good, honey." A full breath of air filled Breeanna's lungs for the first time that afternoon. "That's really good."

Jessica left, hurrying through the rain to her car.

Bree rubbed her elbows—the temperature was still

dropping—then headed to the kitchen for her one-person spaghetti dinner. She fed Spencer and Cinders, then ate in the kitchen as she usually did. The ticking of the clock, the patter of the rain, and her pets' contented munching helped fill the silence. Still, she noticed it more than usual.

She washed her dishes, too few to run the dishwasher, thinking of something her friend Denise had said once shortly after she was widowed: that she never noticed how quiet a house could get till she knew her husband wouldn't be coming home. Denise—it had been too long since she talked to her, and with her living down in Eugene, they rarely got to meet in person. She really should give her a call.

With the dishes put away, Bree headed into the living room and dialed Denise's number.

"Hey, stranger." Denise's peppy voice made Bree smile.

"Hey yourself. How've you been, friend of mine?"

They chatted about their families and their current writing projects—Denise did write but was even more a photographer, her work gracing gorgeous gift books and devotionals. Bree talked as little as possible about Jessica and instead listened to Denise rattle on about her daughter, Rachel, who had a master's in illustrating children's books.

"Right now she's looking for inspiration for a new picture book. Her drawings are fantastic—she just blows me away."

"I'd love to see some of her work." Bree swallowed back a pang of jealousy. What would it be like to have a daughter pursuing a career with her God-given gifts rather than struggling to survive? "Speaking of looking for inspiration, I'm hoping to find some in Italy."

"Italy? Now, there's a story I've got to hear. You never go anywhere. What happened?"

So Bree told her, the idea feeling a bit more real each time she shared it.

"Ah, *Italia*." Denise sighed. "There's nothing like it. I've been wanting to go back myself, take Rachel this time. I'd love to share all the places I remember with my daughter. Though going alone can be wonderful too."

An idea pricked, but Bree hesitated. Would she really want to travel with Denise? She loved her dearly, but she could be a bit bossy, even pushy. Still, wouldn't it be infinitely better not to be by herself, however brave a front she might show James? "Actually, I've been trying to figure out a way to not go alone. Lizzie is still undecided, but regardless—would you by any chance want to join us?"

"Would I? Are you kidding?"

Half an hour of listening to Denise breathlessly plan their trip later, Bree hung up the phone and gazed at Cinders, placidly kneading and purring on her lap. Listening to all the details her friend had talked about, it finally felt like more than a dream.

"I'm going to Italy," she whispered, a thrill running down her arms.

It was really happening.

Chapter Five

The stubborn ringing of the landline by her bed dragged Breeanna up from deep sleep.

Fumbling, she punched on her bedside lamp, grabbing for the phone, squinting through the sudden brightness at the clock as she did so. After midnight—never good.

"Hello?"

"Bree, it's Peter." Paula's voice came out almost unrecognizable, tight with panic. "He's in the ambulance, they took him—I'm on my way to the hospital. Can you come?"

"Of course." Not needing more details, Breeanna hung up and hopped out of bed. She pulled on jeans, a warm sweater, and extra socks, praying all the while, then snagged her purse, tucking her pocket Bible inside. She hurried downstairs, let Spencer out and in, made sure the animals had food, then snatched her coat and hat and headed for the door. At the last minute she wheeled back to the kitchen for a bottle of water and an energy bar—who knew how long she'd be gone.

Darkened highway faded past her on both sides, her headlights gleaming the ice spots on the road ahead. *Please, Lord, please. You know what's going on. Help Peter. Help Paula. Be with us, please.* She pushed back memories of rushing to the hospital after a frantic call all those years ago, only to be told it was too late.

White-faced, Paula met her in the emergency room waiting area. She leaned into Breeanna's embrace, her shoulders shivering, and not just from the bitter temperatures outside.

"What happened?" Bree led her friend to one of the vinyl-padded chairs. "How is he?"

"I don't—I don't know." Paula twisted a damp tissue between her fingers. "I was in bed, Peter had gotten up to go to the bathroom. I heard him come back out, heading toward the bed, and then...he just grunted and went down...collapsed." A shudder racked her entire body. "I flicked on the light and called him—Bree, he was turning gray." Paula lost her battle with the tears. "Right before my eyes. I c-called nine-one-one, tried to straighten him out to do CPR, kept telling him to hang on and how much I love him. Th-they came and started doing CPR, then loaded him in the ambulance." She blew her nose on the worn tissue and tried to draw a breath. "I-I don't know—they haven't told me anything. Th-thank you for coming, I'm so sorry to pull you out of bed."

"Don't you dare be sorry." Breeanna rubbed Paula's back, small, soothing circles. "I wouldn't want to be anywhere else." Paula had been there for her at the hospital when Roger...

She sat with her friend, reminding her to contact her children, texting her own prayer circle in case anyone was awake.

It seemed an eternity, but was probably only half an hour or so, before a young doctor in scrubs emerged and called Paula's name.

"Mrs. Fordsmith? Would you come back with me, please?"

She clenched Bree's hand. "Can my friend come too?"

He hesitated, then nodded.

Bree helped her up, and they followed the doctor through the sterile, swinging door.

He led them into a small corner with two chairs, not enough to call a waiting room, but more private than out in the public one, and gestured for them to sit.

"Just tell me." Paula stayed standing, clamping her hands on her elbows. "How is he?"

The young doctor blew out a breath and shook his head. "I'm so sorry, ma'am. Your husband was gone before he reached the hospital. We did everything we could...but we feel he died instantly, probably before he hit the floor."

The man's well-meant words faded into noise, something about needing to do an autopsy to be sure of cause of death. Breeanna caught her sobbing friend in her arms before she collapsed to the floor.

❁   ❁   ❁

Another funeral, for another friend. Peter was her friend too. Bree stared into her closet mirror, trying to decide if she looked suitable in her black sheath dress and tailored gray jacket, only her silver cross for jewelry. Not that it mattered much. What mattered was being there for Paula.

Why does there have to be so much grief in this world, Lord?

She was almost out the door when her cell rang. Jessica. Bree answered while transferring her keys, wallet, and extra tissues from her everyday purse to the small black leather one for more formal occasions.

"Hey, honey. What's up?" What had she done with her lipstick?

"Hi, Mom. Just wanted to let you know I'm not able to make it to the funeral. I have a job interview."

"Oh, Jess." Bree straightened, dropping the purse on the table in the entry. "Can't you schedule it for another time? The Fordsmiths have been our friends so long, all your life, really."

"I can't help it." Irritation edged Jessica's voice. "You wanted me to get another job, right? That was specifically one of James's conditions. And this is when they could see me."

"Fine." Breeanna pushed back her hair with a sigh. She didn't have time for an argument, but disappointment sank hard in her middle. Hopefully Paula wouldn't be too hurt. "Where is the interview?" She'd clearly missed some things in Jessica's life the last few days.

"The new natural grocery store downtown."

"I see." Probably wouldn't pay much, but at least it was something. If only Jess could find a job that would actually put her gifts to use. She was good with children, and at art—Breeanna had always thought she'd make a wonderful art teacher, or even a kindergarten teacher. But in college, she'd been interested in graphic design. Until she quit. "Well, I'll try to explain."

"Give Paula my love." Jessica's voice softened. "Erin and Ashley too. I really am sorry. Peter was a good guy."

"He was. Well, I've got to go." Bree hung up, noting the time on her phone. Great, now she was running late.

Pressing down frustration, she pulled on boots, wound a scarf, and buttoned her good wool coat, then hurried out to the garage.

❖   ❖   ❖

Pierre-René Dubois didn't do funerals well.

Dressed in the immaculate black suit he saved for occasions like these, he waited outside a side entrance near the front of the sanctuary, along with the rest of the immediate family. Paula, his late wife's sister, was talking with the visitation pastor right by the door. Her daughters, Erin and Ashley, and their husbands and the children gathered near, along with Peter's siblings.

Perhaps Pierre should have merely sat with the congregation, being only a by-marriage brother-in-law, and a widowed one at that. But Paula had asked him to stay with the family. And that was his priority today, being a supportive presence. Never mind what memories might try to press their way in.

Paula stepped up to him, her face pale but composed with that strength he knew the Lord gave on such occasions. "It's almost time. Would you escort me in, Pierre?"

He opened his mouth to object—wouldn't she rather have one of her children? But he shut it, realizing they had their families. Paula, now, had no one.

"Of course." He held out his arm for her to slip hers through. At the minister's nod, he squeezed his sister-in-law's hand atop his coat sleeve and led her toward the door.

Inside the church, the rustle of the congregation and sonorous tones of the organ filled his senses. He again stamped down thoughts of Lynn's funeral ten years ago and focused on following the minister to the front pews reserved for family. Safely depositing Paula in the aisle seat, Pierre stepped back to let her children file in, then sat down at the other end. Someone, one of Peter's cousins, he thought, squeezed his shoulder from the pew behind. Pierre-René turned with a quiet greeting, then back to gaze at the abundant flower arrangements. His brother-in-law had been well loved. No casket, as Peter had opted for cremation.

The minister mounted the podium. "We are gathered today to remember and honor the life of Peter Edwin

Fordsmith, husband to Paula and father to Erin and Ashley, and to celebrate his entrance into the joy of eternal life with his Savior, even as we grieve our loss on earth..."

Pierre-René closed his eyes to let the comfort and truth of the words seep into his soul. Soon he would be called on to do the Scripture reading, as Peter had requested in his funeral directions—not that he'd any idea they would be needed so soon. The tension in his muscles relaxed with the beauty of the voluntary, a medley of "O, the Deep, Deep Love of Jesus" and "I'll Fly Away." He prayed the music would soak comfort into Paula's heart too.

Taking a deep breath, Pierre moved to the pulpit as the music faded. "I've been asked to share with you one of Peter's favorite passages of Scripture, from the book of Isaiah, chapter thirty-five." A slight disturbance in the back caught his eye as an attractive blond woman slipped in late, then sat in one of the back pews next to a young family. At least she was quiet about her entrance. Pierre refocused on the Bible before him.

"...And the redeemed of the LORD will return and come to Zion with joyful shouting, and everlasting joy will be on their heads. They will obtain gladness and joy, and sorrow and sighing will flee away." Grateful his voice had remained steady, he closed the Bible and with a dip of his head returned to sit with the family.

The rest of the service passed in a blur, but Pierre-René got the sense Peter had been honored well. At last he stood in the receiving line near Paula, shaking unfamiliar hands, giving appreciative nods and thanks.

The blond woman who had come in late hugged Paula with the tight embrace of a lifelong friend.

"I'm so sorry, I wanted to get here before the service, and here I was late. Something came up so Jessica couldn't make it, she sends her love, then there was this accident on the bridge—but never mind all that." She stepped back and met Paula's eyes. "How are you doing?"

"Surviving." Paula breathed in deep, her smile teary. "You know?"

"I do." The woman squeezed her hand. "Can I do anything?"

"Rescue me if anyone tries to talk my ear off?"

"You've got it." Another couple approached, and the woman stepped away to let Paula greet them.

"Who was that?" Pierre-René asked.

"Oh, I'm sorry, I should have introduced you. Longtime friend, Breeanna Lindstrom. Wait." Paula tapped his arm. "She's the friend I tried to set you up with, back a few years ago. Remember?"

He did, now. And she had refused. Not that he had blamed her; he himself hated blind dates. But if he'd known how attractive Paula's mystery friend was at the time, he might have tried a bit harder to make it happen.

Stop it, Dubois, you're at a family funeral here.

Paula turned to greet other friends Pierre didn't know, and he glanced around the reception hall. He really didn't belong in the receiving line; few people knew him. He should get Paula a plate of food. By the look of things, it would be a while before she'd get a chance to eat.

With a word to his sister-in-law, he stepped away and headed for one of the lines at the refreshment tables, where the church hospitality committee had laid out platters of sandwiches, fruit and veggie trays, crackers and cheese. The standard funeral fare.

He picked up a paper plate and napkin and started with a pinwheel sandwich and croissant, then reached for the fruit tongs to add some pineapple and cut fruit. His fingers collided with those of a woman reaching from the other side.

"Sorry." She pulled her hand back.

"No, please." He gestured for her to go ahead. "My apologies. I wasn't paying attention."

She looked up at him, and to his chagrin, Pierre felt heat creeping up his neck.

It was Breeanna Lindstrom.

*   *   *

The dark-haired man who had done the Scripture reading, whose rich, cultured voice had helped calm her frazzled nerves when she scooted in late, was staring at her. Bree could see now his rich brown hair was shot with silver. "You're Paula's brother-in-law, aren't you?"

"I am." He smiled. "Pierre-René Dubois."

Pierre, that was it. Paula's near setup flashed through her mind with an embarrassing twinge. "I'm Bree Lindstrom. An old friend of Paula's." She realized they were holding up the line and quickly moved pineapple and grapes onto the plate, then handed the tongs over. "I was just getting her a plate, since I don't know if she'll be free to eat till it's all gone."

"Really? That's what I was doing too."

She chuckled. What a thoughtful man. "Well, I guess we've got her covered."

They chatted as they moved down the line—might as well keep filling both plates, someone would eat the food. Pierre had recently bought a condo in the area and was starting a new business after retiring from his career job with an international consulting firm.

"I was hoping to spend more time with family now, with my kids, with Paula and Peter." His bushy brows drew together. "And now this. An aortic aneurysm—who would have thought? He seemed so well."

"He did. The epitome of good health." Bree grabbed a cookie and brownie from the dessert tray and stepped out of the end of the line. "I'm glad Paula will have you close by."

"I agree." Pierre hesitated, glancing down at this plate, then at hers. "Well..."

"Go ahead, take her yours." Breeanna smiled. "You're family after all." She'd take this plate to Abigail and Luke, having spotted her own family at a table across the hall.

She left Pierre behind and joined her daughter-in-law and grandson. James was standing in line for food, and Luke kicked his legs in his chair, tired and close to a time-out, by the look on Abigail's face. The sight of Bree's plate cheered him up, and he settled with a chunk of Colby cheese.

"You're a godsend." Abigail gave her a weary smile. "But what about you?"

"I'll get something when the lines thin out." Bree broke a sandwich in smaller pieces for Luke. She glanced across the room to where the Fordsmith family gathered. Paula was still greeting people, but her girls had sat down with their husbands and little ones. Pierre sat with them, holding one of the toddlers on his lap. From the way he bent his head, talking to the little girl, she could tell he enjoyed children.

She could see a glimpse of why Paula had tried to set them up all those years ago. *Don't think that now. This day is about your dear friends.*

"Hey, Mom. Didn't you want anything? I would have grabbed you a plate." James plopped two paper plates down and slid into a chair next to her. "Oh, you got Luke food?"

Breeanna dragged her attention back. "I'll get something later."

"All the more for us, then." James slid a plate across to his wife and bowed his head for a silent grace, then dug in. "So, where's Jessica?"

"She had a job interview."

"And this was the only time she could get it?"

Bree's shoulders tensed at the edge in his voice. "She said so. At least she's following through on the conditions you laid."

"I guess." James paused to sip his punch, then glanced at Bree. "Hey. I'm sorry if I snapped at you the other night."

Bree stared at him, then touched his hand, her tension melting. "That's okay, honey. But thanks. I appreciate it." Apologies didn't come easy to James, so it was all the more meaningful when he spoke them.

"Ryan actually called me yesterday." James took another bite of sandwich.

"He did?"

"He wanted to learn more about the program I'd found for Jessica, said he wants to help. Said he's not sure of the best way, so he thought I might have some advice." James chewed another bite and swallowed, then shook his head. "I was . . . impressed. He's concerned about Jess, about where things are headed. But it doesn't sound like he plans on leaving anytime soon."

Breeanna's throat squeezed, tears pricking her eyes. "I am so glad to hear this." *Thank you, Lord.*

"Yeah, well, we'll see. He's a good guy, maybe a pretty rare one. I hope Jessica can realize that and shape up while he's still willing to stick around."

And there came the criticism again. Did James realize how quickly he fell into that? Clinging to the good news, Bree pushed the thought away and smiled at Luke talking to his grapes.

She visited with them till the crowds started to dwindle and James took his family home, then made her way back to the refreshments table for a sandwich and some fruit. She glanced over to Paula's table—she was finally sitting down and eating. Erin and her husband still sat with her, but Pierre proved nowhere to be seen.

She shouldn't be disappointed by that. Breeanna shook herself and took her food over to join her friend.

"Hey." She squeezed Paula's shoulder. "Glad to see you're finally getting a bite to eat."

"Didn't think I'd feel like it." Paula dabbed at her lips with a paper napkin. "But Pierre was thoughtful enough to get me a plate, and the food actually tastes good."

"I'm glad." Bree slid into an empty chair beside her.

"Everyone is so kind." Paula sighed. "I was a mess before the service, but I'm okay right now. I guess the Lord is holding me up."

Answered prayer. "He's good at that."

"And the service was special, wasn't it? Peter would have liked it, don't you think so?"

"I know so."

She sat with her while Paula finished eating, then helped Erin clear the table of the empty plates and crumpled napkins. The fellowship hall was nearly empty now, only a few children running about while the scattered remaining adults tried to quell their antics.

Breeanna stayed till the end, seeing Paula into the car with Ashley. They'd planned a quiet dinner at home, she said, just immediate family. Bree was glad. Hopefully it would be a time of solace.

She headed to her own car, the January wind icy now even through her woolen coat. After the distraction of the busy afternoon, grief sank over her again like a weighted blanket. *Lord, thank you so much for holding Paula up today. But I know hard days are ahead. I wish I could lift them from her, but I also know I can't. She has to walk through them with you…there's no other way. I just hope I can help somehow.*

She dug in her purse for her keys, fingers fumbling in the cold.

"Hello, again."

At the deep voice behind her, she turned to see Pierre standing at the open door to his car, parked a couple of spaces away.

"Pierre." Bree sniffed and smiled. "I didn't see you there. Are you heading to the family dinner?"

"No." He closed his car door and stepped closer, shoving his hands in the pockets of his black coat. Was it cashmere? "They asked me, but I could tell they'd rather it just be them—Paula and her children. I may be technically family, but, thanks to my years of traveling, I'm still a bit of an outsider."

"I'm sure they don't feel that way." Bree shivered involuntarily at another gust.

"Forgive me." He stepped back. "Here I am keeping you in the cold. Nice meeting you today, Breeanna." He turned to go, then suddenly wheeled back, his brown eyes meeting hers. "I don't suppose you'd want to join me somewhere for a cup of coffee, would you? You'd have to tell me where. I don't know the best spots around here." His eyes crinkled when he smiled.

Bree felt a sudden warmth spread through her despite the bitter wind. This might be risky, but... "As a matter of fact, I'd love to."

Chapter Six

Pierre held the door for Bree. "This is nice."

They stepped inside The Coffee Spoon, the jingle bell attached to the door chiming its familiar welcoming notes.

"It's one of my favorite spots." Breeanna unwound her scarf and breathed in the familiar aromas of roasted coffee beans and fresh pastry, then tried to exhale the tension twisting her insides into butterflies—to thoroughly mix her metaphors. *This is not a date. Relax, Bree. But what if he sees it that way? He won't, probably doesn't even remember that almost setup years ago.*

She realized Pierre was waiting for her to go ahead of him in line and stepped up, her cheeks heating despite the lingering chill from outside. *Get it together, woman.*

The familiar ambience of the coffee shop settled her nerves as she scanned the chalkboard menu, familiar hand-drawn stylized lettering highlighting the special latte of the day. Soft jazz music played below the subdued hum of customers, some on laptops, some quietly visiting with one another. Paper stars left over from the holidays dangled overhead, with delicate cutout patterns letting through the soft gleam of twinkly lights twined inside. More lights ran along the wainscoting just below the ceiling.

Bree ordered a winter spiced latte and a cranberry orange muffin. She really hadn't eaten much at the funeral, and something to nibble on might help settle her nerves. She reached in her purse for her wallet, but Pierre touched her elbow.

"Let me get that."

"Oh, no, it's really—"

"Please."

How to say no to that smile? With a nod of thanks, Bree stepped aside while he ordered black coffee and a Danish.

"You didn't have to do that." She shook her head at Pierre when he joined her at the end of the counter where customers waited for their orders.

"Consider it my thank-you for sharing your favorite spot with me." Again that dazzling smile, one that his heavy brows and the faint scar from one eyebrow to his hairline only made more interesting. "Vancouver is growing on me already."

A young barista called out their names and handed over the cardboard-sheathed drinks and pastries. By mutual consensus, they headed to a pair of overstuffed chairs by the fireplace, near a corner stocked with books by local authors. Breeanna sneaked a peek—yes, her latest Effie Bartlett mystery peeked back at her. She hid a smile. Never got old.

"So, Pierre." She settled into her chair, warming her still-chilly hands on her coffee cup. "Is your family of French origin?"

"*Mais oui.*" He cocked his head. "And actually, it's Pierre-René—as my mother never fails to remind anyone who dares shorten it." He winked. "Personally, I'm fine with Pierre. My parents came over to America in their teens, and so English is my first language. But we learned French at home as well, and I continued with it through school."

"*Je parle a peu le français.*" Breeanna winced at herself. "Wow, I'm even rustier than I thought."

"*Non, non, vous parlez bien.*" Pierre's brown eyes warmed. "You took French in school?"

"Through high school. Obviously far too long ago." She sighed. This was discouraging, with her first trip to Europe finally approaching. "Right now I'm actually trying to learn Italian."

"Really?" Pierre-René took a sip of coffee. "Are you traveling to Italy?"

"Hoping to, with some writer friends in May. It's a long-held dream of mine." The tingle of excitement trickled back in. "We'd talked about it together for years. One from our writers' group passed away from brain cancer a few months ago, and her legacy to each of us was a check for ten thousand dollars." Bree blew out a breath. "Not everyone is able to go, but I'm so grateful I could save it for this trip. She was such a dear, generous friend." Bree fought the tears that did more than lurk at the back of her nose and eyes. Sniffing and blinking sort of worked this time. Too much death lately.

"Cancer." Pierre-René's face shadowed. "It's a terrible beast."

"It took your wife, didn't it?" Breeanna searched his face, hoping she wasn't prying. "Paula's sister."

"Pancreatic cancer, yes." He set aside his coffee and cut into his Danish, brows drawn together.

Okay. Perhaps she should not pursue that topic just now.

"So." He popped a bite of Danish, took a sip of coffee, and looked up, smile back in place. "You say your writers' group. You are a writer?"

"Yes." Bree tried sipping her latte, then made a face and lowered her cup. Still too hot. How did the man down scalding coffee like that? "I write mysteries. Actually, one of my books is right there." She nodded at the bookcase behind him.

"Ah." He swiveled and scanned the shelves, quickly homing in on the Effie Bartlett. He lifted the volume and read the back cover with obvious interest. "Very nice. Are these for sale?"

"I think the coffee shop just keeps those for customers to browse while they're here. But I have extra copies at home—I could give you one if you like." Bree bit her burned tongue. Was that too bold?

"I would love that." Pierre replaced the book with care and turned back to her. "I think now Paula did once mention a friend who was a writer." He cocked his head, pondering.

Breeanna's cheeks warmed. Better to come clean before he made the connection himself. "Actually, I have a confession. Paula tried to set us up on a blind date a few years ago."

"Aha." He wagged a finger at her. "So it was you. And you backed out."

"I didn't back out! I just refused."

"Because that is so much better?" He shook his head, arching his scarred brow.

Why did he have to be so attractive? And that almost-European inflection to his wording at times, though with only a trace of an accent... *focus, Bree.*

"You must forgive me. I'd recently been burned on a blind date—a really, really bad blind date." She shuddered at the memory. "The guy couldn't talk about anything but his health problems the whole evening, and then he started on me, trying to diagnose me with everything from carpal tunnel—because he insisted all writers have it—to osteo-porosis to irritable bowel syndrome, which he maintained was exacerbated by my coffee habit."

Pierre nearly choked on his pastry.

"Yeah. It was bad. Mostly funny now—finally." She chuck-led. "For the record, I now see Paula's setup would have been much more enjoyable."

"Well, at least we are making up for it now." His warm brown eyes met hers.

Bree's pulse kicked up. Did that mean he did consider this a date?

❖   ❖   ❖

He was really liking this woman.

Her frankness, her gentle humor. The way her tailored gray jacket, so somber on anyone else, brought out the gray-blue of her eyes. What a gift to have her company on this grief-laden day.

"So." Pierre-René returned to his lemon cream Danish. "Tell me about your children. I saw you today with your grandchild, yes?"

"Yes, that was my grandson, Luke, with my son, James, and his wife, Abigail. They're expecting another baby the first of June."

"New life, it is the most beautiful thing. Is James your only son?"

"Yes, but I also have a daughter, Jessica. She wasn't at the funeral." Something shadowed those lovely eyes.

"Is she well?"

"Oh, yes." Breeanna tentatively tried another sip of her latte.

The first had burned her tongue, he'd noted. Years in the air force made him alert to every detail, and he kept the habit still.

"She's just…struggling a bit right now. But she had a job interview today, so that's good." She made an obvious effort to brighten her voice.

"When our children are hurting, that is the hardest thing." Empathy squeezed his chest.

"Isn't it?" She met his eyes. "It always has been, of course. But now that they're grown—I feel so helpless to make things better."

"And that is what you like to do, is it? Make things better."

She twisted the simple silver cross at the neck of her black dress. "I suppose it is."

"Here." This was getting too somber. "Have a bite of Danish." He held out a piece on a paper napkin. "They make everything better."

She laughed and accepted the offering, fumbling it into her lap. "Clumsy me." She rescued the pastry chunk and ate it, every crumb. "Now you must try my muffin."

"If you insist." He usually wasn't a big cranberry fan, but this bite was good, with notes of orange zest.

"What about you? You have grown children too?"

"Three. Two married, my daughters. They live back east, so I don't get to see my grandchildren as much as I'd like." He pulled out his wallet to show his bragging pictures— not that he generally bragged about them, just kept them to gaze on the precious faces himself. That he drew them out for Breeanna said something—what, he wasn't quite sure. "That is my grandson Ethan. And Théo, named for our heritage. Then Alyssa, and little Martine." Their curly dark heads and brown eyes smiled up at him, tugging his heart. The visits at Christmas already seemed so long ago, even if the calendar said only a few weeks.

"They're beautiful. I'd pull out my photos of Luke, but you already saw him at the funeral."

"And quite a charming young man he looked to be."

"He's a doll, though he was tired and on the cranky side this afternoon. But you said you have three children?"

"Yes." He tucked the photos away, the familiar confliction in his chest. "The youngest, my son, Jason, lives in Portland."

"Oh, how wonderful. So you moved closer to him also."

"Yes, that was my hope, to see more of him...We lived in Gresham for years. I finally sold the family house and bought a condo after the kids all left home. These last years I've been traveling so much..."

"Umm. And he's not married?"

"No. He...he lives with his partner, Todd, in a loft in downtown Portland. With them I have grand-dogs rather than grandchildren."

"I see."

He dared a glance at her. No judgment in those eyes, neither of him nor of Jason. Only acceptance and interest? Compassion?

"It's not me; I would love to see him more often but he travels for his firm and I was traveling so much..." A pause and a slight shrug.

She watched his face, a cloud passing over his eyes.

He hurried to add, "Now that I am retired—again—I need...er...want to make more of an effort." Another pause. "I love him so much, and have told him so. But I'm afraid he seems to feel, well, judged by me. Because of my beliefs, whether I say anything or not." Often called eloquent by friends and acquaintances, he felt his tongue freeze up when he tried to talk about things so close to his heart. Yet with Breeanna, at least he didn't feel pressured to say words that wouldn't come.

"That must be hard." She reached across the small round table between their overstuffed chairs and touched his hand.

Only a brush, but he felt the warmth of her fingers clear to his elbow. Involuntarily, he pulled back.

Breeanna withdrew her hand, but she didn't seem offended. She sipped her latte again. "My Jessica just can't seem to get her life together. She's twenty-eight, but she didn't finish college, and she's never held a steady job, always bouncing from one thing to another. One user man to another. Right now she's in debt up to her eyeballs. I don't know what it is—unresolved grief from her father, or me being too indulgent, or what. But I've bailed her out too many times, I'm afraid, and she's expecting me to do it again."

"And are you?"

"No—her brother won't let me." She gave a wry smile. "He's right, of course. I suppose it may be partly my fault she's stayed immature this long, by helping her too much before. Not that we're abandoning her; James is helping her get financial counseling. But still..."

"It's the hardest thing in the world, isn't it? To want so badly to help, yet know, at some point, they must figure some things out on their own. So, we pray, learning finally to lean on God's strength, *not* on our own." His chest ached with the heavy truth of the words. "And wanting that for them too."

"Yes." She met his eyes; hers sheened with tears. "The hardest thing."

Their gaze held a moment, long enough for his heart to start pumping harder than it had in years. The crackle of the fire and the soft music blended in the background.

"So." She settled back in her chair, obviously in no hurry to leave. "You said you came here to start a new business? Tell me about it."

Pierre-René drew a deep breath and forced his pulse to calm, a technique he'd used often in the military, especially after—but he wouldn't go there now, not even in thought. Grateful for the shift in conversation, he shared with her his dream. Of making a difference for veterans who had served their country and now found themselves adrift. Of a coffee bar, a little like this one, but one focused on vets— both hiring them, and providing a safe space for them to gather and relax. A space that would also offer services, helping former soldiers learn about and use the benefits due them, which surprisingly far too many never even learned about and thus soldiered along without. And wanting the public and families to also enjoy the coffee and find new friends.

"So many veterans are struggling with health issues, to find jobs, even to keep a roof over their heads." He leaned forward, knowing his passion thrummed through his voice. "I want to change that. Of course, we cannot change it everywhere, not all at once. But we can begin."

Breeanna kept her gaze on his face, her interest evident. "I love that. And you're so right—we were able to get VA benefits for my mom to help with her medical costs before she passed away, because my dad was a World War Two vet. But it's only by chance we found out that was even possible. All the benefits really aren't advertised. I've heard a lot of vets are homeless—it seems so wrong."

He nodded. Of course, PTSD also played into that. But he wouldn't go there.

"Oh, my." Breeanna broke her gaze away and glanced at her phone. "I had no idea it was so late. I need to get home and feed my pets."

"What time is it?"

"It's after seven." She pushed to her feet, gathering her wraps.

"Forgive me. I have been talking your ear off."

"Oh, no. I've loved it." Her voice rang sincere, as did her smile. "But right now I need to use the restroom—that latte, you know."

He shrugged on his own coat while she was gone, then gathered their coffee cups and napkins for disposal. Breeanna came back, winding a scarf over her coat.

"Well." She pulled on her gloves with a tentative smile. "This has been unexpected, and truly lovely, Pierre-René. Thank you."

Despite what she said about her French, she pronounced

his name perfectly, the syllables gently caressed. Impulsively, he snatched at an idea.

"You said you are trying to learn Italian, correct?"

"Yes, I ordered some CDs with travel phrases. It's somewhat similar to French, which both helps and confuses me." She shrugged.

"It is indeed, both Romance languages. I . . ." He hesitated, tongue suddenly unwieldy again. "I know Italian." Wonderful, now he sounded like a complete idiot, or a junior high boy trying to get a date. "That is, I speak it as well as French, if not as fluently."

"Really?" Her brows lifted. "I don't suppose you'd be willing to tutor me?"

Bless the woman for not making him have to offer. Though by the flush now rosying her cheeks, she felt she'd been too bold.

"It would be my most sincere pleasure." He gave a half bow to set her at ease, the gallantry easily drawn from his ancestry. "After all, I need an excuse to have coffee with you again."

"And I want to hear more about this business you plan to start, to help veterans." She'd recovered, her cheeks returning to normal hue now.

"Wonderful. May I have your number?"

She gave it, both of them trying to pretend there was nothing unusual about this. But there his heart went pounding again. He hadn't gotten another woman's number since Lynn died.

They said good night, and after holding her car door for her, he headed to his own, breath blowing clouds in the night air before him.

Well, this had been an unlooked-for ending to the horribly heavy day. *Lord, I certainly hope you were looking before I leapt.*

Chapter Seven

Hard to catch her breath these days.

Breeanna's fingers flew on her keyboard, racing to finish the chapter before she was supposed to meet Pierre-René for coffee and more Italian tutoring, their fifth time in the last couple of months. Abigail had needed her to watch Luke unexpectedly again this morning, as she had a last-minute client for the home organization business she ran part-time, so that had cut into Bree's writing day.

Thankfully the words had finally started to flow again this afternoon, as she'd been struggling with a particularly stubborn villain this time around. The weaselly ex-ringmaster antagonist just wouldn't let her in on his plans. But at last she thought she'd figured him out. And just in time— she had to stay on track to finish this manuscript before the trip.

There. She ended the chapter, saved it, and added a one-line opener to start the next chapter. The next session was always easier to pick back up if she had something already there on the page. Saving one more time for good measure, she shut down her computer and sprang from her chair, nearly dumping poor Cinders on the floor.

"Sorry, kitty." She caught the protesting cat in her arms and cuddled her close, rubbing the soft head under her chin. "Almost forgot you were there."

Affronted, Cinders squirmed to get down, then bolted from the room.

Bree glanced at her watch again. Just enough time to freshen up and grab her coat, then out the door.

She reminded herself to call Paula tonight, see how she was doing. Bree had planned to call every day, but the past couple of days had been so hectic she missed yesterday. Paula in her grief was too important to miss again.

Since she wouldn't be back till late, she dumped kibble in Spencer's and Cinders's bowls, then flew out the door, wheeling back just in time to retrieve her phone. She'd leave behind her feet these days if they weren't attached to her legs.

Seated in her car, she took a moment to breathe and compose herself, then turned the ignition and headed to the highway. Ten minutes later, she pulled into the lot by The Coffee Spoon, which had become her and Pierre's rendezvous point of choice. Thinking of coffee, she should ask him how the business was coming along.

She left her coat on the passenger seat—the weather was finally warming up a bit here in mid April. But she brought her sweater, for it was already four o'clock and would only get colder.

There he was, waiting by the counter, cup of coffee already in hand. He was always early.

Pierre-René's dark eyes smiled at the sight of her, bringing an answering smile to her face and curls of warmth to her middle. Never failed. Grateful as she was for the Italian lessons—it was really helping—she looked forward to these session for more than that. And hoped that was all right, though at the moment she hadn't the time to analyze her feelings too fully.

"*Buongiorno*," she greeted him.

"*Buonasera*," he answered with a tip of his head.

That's right—it was late afternoon, so time for the evening greeting. So much to remember.

She picked up her latte, joined him at the table by the window, and dove into today's lesson. The focus was travel.

Portrei avere una mappa—could I get a map?

C'è un autobus dall'aeroporto alla città—is there a bus from the airport to the city?

Mi scusi, qual è la tariffa—excuse me, what is the fare?

So much to remember. Yet she enjoyed it, the rapid, undulating rhythms of the language, the challenge of twisting her tongue into the unfamiliar syllables and tones. And Pierre...always Pierre. He was an excellent tutor, patient, fun, yet exacting on not only her pronunciation but also her understanding of the cultural mores behind the words.

After admitting her brain needed a rest for the day, she sat back to finish her cooling latte. "How much time did you spend in Italy?"

"I was stationed at the Aviano NATO base for three years—it's about fifty miles south of the Italian border, just below the Alps. They wanted me there because of my languages, of course. Being in Italy really helped with my Italian."

"And what did you do there?"

"It was primarily a weapons training site at the time— only one of three for the US Air Force in Europe. Then in 'seventy-six, near the end of my time there, a six-point-five earthquake devastated the area. The base didn't suffer much damage, but the surrounding communities did. So we helped a good deal with clearing roads and debris, setting up tents in the surrounding villages, and such."

"My. I had no idea. What sort of weapons did you test or train with?"

Pierre-René hesitated, drumming his fingers on the table. "Different types, it varied. We were a site for NATO." He seemed distracted, all of a sudden, avoiding her gaze.

Had she said something wrong? Or did he just need to get on with the rest of his day?

Speaking of which...she checked her phone. "I've actually got to get going. I'm meeting Denise to do some shopping for the trip."

"Ah, yes, it's coming up, isn't it?" The light had returned to Pierre's eyes. "Well, I must not keep my star pupil." He stood as she did, ever the gentleman. "Let me walk you to your car."

"Only if you're leaving as well." As if that would stop him. It never did. Bree held his gaze a moment, trying to penetrate beneath his smiling demeanor, but she could see no trace of whatever had risen to the surface a few minutes before.

Nearing the door, they stepped aside to allow a younger couple to enter. The young woman pulled off her beanie hat, then whirled to stare at Breeanna.

"Mom?"

"Jessica?" Bree started. "Hi, honey."

"Oh, hey." Ryan stepped up beside Jess with an easy smile. "Nice to see you, Breeanna."

"You too, Ryan. How are you?" But Bree couldn't focus on his answer. Her daughter was staring between Bree and the man standing close behind her. Jessica's gaze hovered over Pierre, shrewd and faintly accusing.

"This is my...friend." Bree's scalp heated, her turtle-neck sweater suddenly too tight. "Pierre-René Dubois. He's Paula's brother-in-law, we met at the funeral. He's been tutoring me in Italian, he speaks several languages." She clamped her mouth shut before the babbling went any further.

"Nice." Ryan held out his hand for Pierre's grip. "Helping Bree get ready for her trip, huh?"

"Only a little. But we have a good time." Pierre's dark eyes smiled between the two. "You must be the beautiful Jessica I've heard about. And Ryan, correct? A pleasure to meet you."

"Yes, sorry, I should have said." Bree's tongue and manners were stumbling all over the place. If only Jessica would stop looking at Pierre like...like...as if he were a cockroach that had crawled from under a kitchen sink.

"I'm actually just heading out." Bree gestured toward the door, breaking the strained silence. "I'm meeting Denise for dinner, then shopping." She glanced at Jessica, then Ryan. "You two should come for supper again—sometime soon?"

"Sure." Ryan grinned, obviously trying to ease the tension. Jessica only nodded.

Awkward goodbyes, then Breeanna and Pierre escaped out the door.

"I'm sorry." Bree pressed her fingers to her cheeks. "I don't know what..."

"Don't worry about it." Pierre-René patted her shoulder, but he seemed distracted again. "I'll see you next Tuesday, yes?"

She affirmed and watched him stride away toward his car, then hurried into hers. She clicked on her seat belt. *Lord, I guess I should have told Jessica about Pierre, but what was there to tell, really?* She groaned and leaned her head back against the headrest. *Clearly I should have said something, because that was downright awful.* Ever since Jessica started her second job, they'd barely found time to talk on the phone, let alone get together.

Pushing the scene behind her for now, she made her way through the rush-hour traffic to the mall and inside the food court where she was supposed to meet Denise. No sign of her, though Bree arrived on the dot of when they had agreed. She checked her phone again. Denise's perpetual tardiness did grate on Bree's nerves. And today her usual well of patience had been pretty well drained.

Her cell chimed. "Hey, where are you?" Bree hadn't meant to sound quite that abrupt.

"Sorry, running a bit late." Denise sounded cheery and a bit breathless as usual. "Go ahead and eat; can I just meet you at the store?"

"Okay." Breeanna glanced at her watch, trying to swallow her disappointment. She'd looked forward to a girls' chat while they ate, even if brief. Oh, well. She could use a few minutes to catch her breath.

"See you in half an hour."

Bree scanned the food court for quick options and got in line for some Thai takeout. Sitting down with a recyclable box of pad Thai near the children's play area in the center of the mall, she people-watched for potential characters, a writer's habit she often indulged in when alone. But her thoughts drifted to Italy. Is this how things would be on the trip? Sitting and waiting for Denise, who was always late or rushing off to do her own thing? It would be by far the most time they had spent in each other's company. Denise had always been strong-willed, and Bree worried a bit as to how their personalities might clash. But she was still grateful they were going together.

After finishing the last savory bite of stir-fried noodles topped with chicken, crushed peanuts, and bean sprouts, she threw away her trash and headed to the new store she and Denise had decided to try.

She relaxed a little as she started glancing through the racks outside the door, keeping an eye out for Denise. These styles looked promising—versatile, affordable, yet feminine and with style. Just what they'd need. And they weren't all sized for stick-thin teenagers, either. She didn't want to spend a fortune on clothes.

"Hey." Denise appeared beside her and gave Bree a side arm hug. "Sorry to be late. Found anything yet?"

"What do you think of this?" Bree held out a navy-and-white top and matching jacket.

"Would look nice with white capris." Denise grabbed the tag and checked. "And all rayon, travels well but breathable. Definitely try it on. Is there one in my size?" She raked hangers aside, her graying dark curls bobbing.

"What, you want to be twins?" But Bree was smiling again. She could never seem to stay disgusted with Denise for long.

"No, you're right. I could never pull off that cut as well as you."

"Oh, stop. We need to find some shorts to show off those fabulous knees of yours."

"Nope, I've read Italians don't really wear shorts. They dress up more than we do here."

"Well, good for them. A nice knee-length skirt then."

"Or?" Denise pulled out a red cap-sleeved dress with white pin-dots and checked the tag. "Also rayon."

"Cute."

They gathered possible outfits till Bree's arms ached from the weight, then took turns trying on and modeling in the fitting rooms. Half an hour later, they exited the mall with a couple of bags each, and their credit cards not as taxed as she'd feared.

"Well, new clothes, that's one item off the list." Though night had fallen over the parking lot, Bree breathed easier than she had all day. "I know we've got another couple weeks, but it's been stressing me not knowing what I was going to wear."

"Well, from what I've been reading on travel blogs—I

follow a lot because of photography—we should be covered now, supplementing with what we've already gotten, of course. Lightweight travel blazer, good travel pants, a couple of skirts and tops to mix and match. Nice but comfy shoes for walking."

"Got those. And a nice dress for if we go someplace dressy."

"Oh, we'll have to, at least once." They stopped to look in a window. "Hey, I found a place that teaches Italian cooking, a private home with rooms to rent. Doesn't that sound like a special event?"

"Really? Wouldn't that be fun?"

"It fits in our tour plan perfectly. It's between Rome and Florence. Should I register us?"

"Sounds good to me."

"I'll do that and let you know the cost." They'd reached Denise's car, so she wrapped Breeanna in a hug. "I'm so excited! I can't thank you enough for including me in this. Rachel too, she's over the moon. She was home last night for dinner, and we stayed up late googling places to see in Italy and talking and giggling like a couple of college girls."

"I'm so glad." Bree stepped back with a smile and jingled her keys. Denise's words caught a snag in her heart. If things had been different, she might have been able to bring Jessica on this trip. How long had it been since they'd shared a mother-daughter giggle fest, or even heart-to-heart talk, like that? The closest to heart-to-hearts they'd had lately were teary discussions with James. Not much like Denise and Rachel's relationship, that was for sure.

Bree drove home, weariness settling into her bones. She'd hoped to finish another chapter tonight, but should she put it off till tomorrow? That would set her back from her schedule, and that deadline wouldn't be budged. Especially when she was already under pressure from her publisher to up her sales. She yawned. Overwhelmed was not a good feeling.

She hadn't called Paula. Bree slapped her hand on the steering wheel. She could have done that while she was waiting for Denise. What was the matter with her? She checked the car clock. Almost nine—would it be too late to call by the time she got home? She had to at least text her. *Lord, I'm dropping balls here.* Probably because she was juggling too many, but she didn't see any she could let go.

Breeanna pulled into the garage and let herself into the house. Spencer came loping to meet her, tail wagging and nose nuzzling. She headed to the kitchen door and let him out, checking her phone while she waited on the porch for her dog.

Two unread messages.

From Pierre: *I loved our time together again today. Your Italian is coming along beautifully. I fear too beautifully, lest you not need my services before long.*

Her smile came easily. *Ah, Pierre-René. As if I needed that excuse to see you.* Though it was handy.

Then one from Jessica: *Hey, Mom. Who was that guy you were with today?*

That was it, nothing more. The smile died on Bree's face and fell into her stomach, changing to lead on the way. *Lord, why does everything have to be a battle with Jess?*

She pushed the weight aside for now and texted Paula.

Hey, friend. Just checking on you, sorry it's so late. How are you doing tonight?

She couldn't think of anything more profound, so she hit SEND. Hopefully Paula would at least see it before bed. Good thing her daughter was back with her, although that was about to change in a few days.

Tomorrow she absolutely had to go see her, no matter what else was going on. Paula was walking through those early days of widowhood, when you woke feeling for your husband in bed beside you and the cold emptiness of the sheets still struck ice into your heart each time. No to-do list could be more important than making sure her friend knew she wasn't alone walking this journey. Her daughter was wonderful, but no one could be as helpful as someone who had been through the same agony.

Spencer bounded up the steps and nosed Bree's knee, so she bent to rub his soft, silky ears. They went inside, where Cinders meowed and arched against her legs.

At least her animals loved her. She felt rather a failure as both mother and a friend just now.

Chapter Eight

He needed to get his head in the game.

Pierre-René took a bite of his chef salad and tried to focus on what Ben Gutierrez, his sharp young accountant, was saying on the other side of the café table. Not on the fact that he hadn't heard from Breeanna in a few days.

With his open laptop on one side and a half-eaten corned beef sandwich on the other, Ben's hands flew as fast as his words. Articles of organization, operating agreements, business insurance, LLCs, DBAs, EINs...

Pierre felt a headache building behind his eyes. He might have a business degree and decades of business experience both here and overseas, but starting a business himself was another matter entirely, even if the terms were mostly familiar.

"Any questions?" Ben grinned at him and grabbed his sandwich for another bite.

"Yes, how come you young folks are so much smarter than I?" Pierre smiled back wryly. "So, next steps. We already have the LLC and the EIN, and I've set up the business account at my bank. Are we ready to start looking for a location?"

"Close, I think." Ben wiped his mouth with a paper napkin and made a note on his laptop. "I'd like to run over your funding once more to be sure we know exactly what our rent budget is. And I'd recommend going ahead and starting the process for getting business insurance, and even filing for a food license. That red tape can take forever and hold everything else up if you don't get the wheels turning soon enough."

"Good to know." The food prep industry was one aspect of business he really didn't know much about. Yet. "On the funding, as you know I am using a good chunk of my own savings. I've also applied for a loan through a program that specifically supports businesses started by veterans, and of course, this one will serve them as well. The interest rates and fees are lower."

"Awesome. Then we probably are about ready to start looking for a place." Ben met his eyes, interest and commitment in his gaze. "So, what would be your dream spot?"

That was what Pierre liked about his accountant—he genuinely believed in this project. That, and he knew his stuff. So even if Ben left him behind sometimes with his Millennial speed with technology and such, Pierre was truly grateful for him.

"I was hoping for somewhere in Gresham, maybe in the historical downtown?" Now that he'd moved to that suburb of Portland and Vancouver, he'd love to not have a long commute. Pierre-René took a sip of iced tea. "What do you think?"

"Hmm." Ben squinted. "It's a possibility, but I think you might get more traffic in Vancouver. They're really revitalizing the downtown area right now, and it would be great if we could locate nearer the county VA assistance center. That way if"—he paused—"*when* they refer their clients to us, it's an easy trip."

"That's a good point. As few obstacles to getting help as possible is what vets need. Otherwise it's too easy to just not pursue assistance, tough it out on your own." He shut down that trail of thought and leaned back in his chair. "All right, let's consider Vancouver as well." He'd traveled for business plenty in the past; a half-hour commute shouldn't be that big of a deal. "We'll also want good accessibility for parking, walking, and those with disabilities. That last is especially important."

"So nothing with stairs."

"Definitely."

"That's a tall order downtown. But nothing is impossible. Let me run some numbers and get back to you." Ben tapped on his keyboard. "Have you thought about who else you'll need to hire?"

"A manager, of course, and—what do they call them? Baristas. Also bakers, cleaning crew, et cetera. But I don't think I'm at that point yet, do you?"

"No, not till we have a location locked in and have made any major renovations needed."

Major renovations. He'd hoped that wouldn't be necessary, but of course, for setting up a coffee bar, it would be. Better make sure he'd built that into the budget too.

"I'd also recommend looking for someone to do marketing for you, PR, social media, graphics. Especially with wanting to hire and serve veterans, you'll need to be strategic in how you get the word out."

"Social media?" Pierre frowned. He had a Facebook account but seldom checked it.

"Yep. Can't have a business and not a social media presence these days. You'll need a website too. Know anyone who's good with graphic design, web design, stuff like that?"

"I, ah. No idea."

"I'll check around. Might know someone who knows someone."

"Thanks." Pierre rubbed his forehead against the headache. Another angle he hadn't thought of yet. *Lord, I trust*

*you are guiding in this. The deeper in I get, the less I seem
to know what I'm doing.*

They finished lunch and wrapped up their meeting.
Pierre headed to his car, checking his phone on the way.

A text from Jason, his son in Portland. His heart did a
little leap.

*Hey, Dad. Want to come over for dinner sometime next
week?*

Gladness squeezed his throat, mingled with regret that
he hadn't reached out to Jason in a couple of weeks.
There'd been so much going on with the business, and then
Breeanna…he still wasn't sure what was going on there,
especially after the strange encounter with her daughter.
But his son had reached out to him. How long had it been
since that happened? *Thank you, Lord.*

He typed back. *Love to. Name the day and time, I'll
be there.*

Pierre-René slid the phone back into his pocket. He
would be there, even if he had to change a meeting with
Bree to do it.

✿   ✿   ✿

Breeanna rubbed Paula's shoulder as she wept, again.

"I'm sorry." Her friend sniffled and wiped her eyes with a
wadded tissue. "I need to stop doing this."

"No, you don't. What do you think grieving is?"

"It's just, seeing that note…"

"I know."

They sat on the Fordsmiths' living room rug next to the
sofa, amid a pile of receipts and other papers from Peter's
desk. Her daughter Erin had been helping Paula wade
through the piles of paperwork, legalities, and financial tasks
since Peter passed away, but she'd returned home to tend

her own family. So today Paula had let Bree come and help. After all, she'd walked this same road before.

Paula had already tackled the most urgent items over the past weeks with her daughters' help, paying bills, canceling certain credit cards, handling life insurance and the death certificate. But this desk had daunted her for weeks, Paula said, so Bree had suggested they tackle it together.

The sorting had gone swimmingly for a while, mostly old receipts that weren't needed anymore—Peter had saved everything. But then Bree had found a receipt, dated a few months ago, for pearl earrings with a note in Peter's familiar scrawl—*Ann. gift for P.D.* Anniversary gift for Paula Darling, as he'd called her, though few outside the family would have heard it—Bree being among the few. And that had brought the tears to both of them.

"He was always so thoughtful. Never had to be reminded of anniversaries or other special days, not like some husbands." Paula's eyes brimmed again. "Wonder where he put the earrings?"

"We'll find them." Breeanna ran her hand down her friend's arm and squeezed her wrist. Roger had been more like those "husbands" Paula mentioned...she'd always had to hint a reminder of their anniversary or birthdays. But he would get her gifts at other odd times on his own, not earrings or anything typical, but little quirky items he found in offbeat places and knew would make her smile, like the Sherlock lamp still on her writing desk, or a pair of fuzzy slipper socks with cat faces on the toes. She still had them tucked in a drawer somewhere. Those gifts always made her feel known, and loved.

Bree swallowed back sudden tears of her own. She'd been thinking more of Roger lately than she had for years, probably because of all the memories walking through this season with Paula brought back.

And because of Pierre-René.

Somehow, she felt Pierre would be the kind of man to remember special dates, probably better than she would. What sort of gifts he would buy, she had no idea. But one thing she did know: It was far too soon to be thinking that way. She didn't even know what their relationship was yet, if it could even be called that. Were they just friends? Or something more?

"So." Paula blew her nose once more, then tossed her wad of tissues in the near-to-overflowing wastebasket and tucked the precious receipt in her "save" box. "How are things going with Pierre-René?"

"Ah." Had her friend read her mind? "What do you mean?"

"Come on." Paula nudged her knee. "He told me you've been seeing each other. Italian tutoring, right?" She quirked a brow and smiled despite her red eyes and nose. "I should be miffed that I learned this from Pierre and not from you."

"It's not—I mean, there's really not much to tell." Breeanna gathered up the pile of discarded receipts and stacked them to give her hands something to do. "And I didn't...want to hurt you. The only reason Pierre and I met was because of Peter's funeral, and here you are going through the hardest season of your life..."

Paula shook her head. "Bree, come on, do you know how much I need some fun news to think about? And if it happens to be about two of my favorite people in the world...well, that's only going to bring me bits of joy." She paused and blew out a breath. "Boy, do I need some joy."

Breeanna met her friend's eyes a moment and saw the sincerity there. She nodded slowly. "I understand. And I'm sorry, I should have told you."

"So, tell me now. What do you think of my brother-in-law?"

Bree couldn't help the smile that crept over her face. "He's...kind of amazing."

"I knew it." A light dawned in Paula's eyes. "Told you that you should have let me set you up all those years ago."

"I know, I've been thinking about that. But maybe I wasn't ready."

"And you're ready now?"

"I don't know." Bree sighed. "I sound like a confused teenager, don't I? He is...amazing, like I said. Sweet, charming, so talented, speaks three languages fluently and some German too. When I'm with him, I'm like floating on a cloud. Then later I float down off the cloud and wonder, what in the world am I doing? Am I reading too much into this?"

"He really likes you too, Bree."

"He does?" Bree's heart thumped oddly. So strange to think of Pierre thinking about her...talking about her, to Paula.

"I shouldn't say specifics told in confidence, of course. But that much is pretty obvious."

Bree could tell her cheeks were flaming like that same teenage girl. She didn't know what else to say. She kept making the most organized stack of receipts that had been destined for the trash in the history of humankind, but her hands felt shaky.

"Have you talked at all, about the future? Where this is going?"

"No—no. We're definitely not there yet." Wherever "there" was. "Right now I'm trying to figure out what to do about Jessica."

"What about Jessica? Another something with her boyfriend?"

"No, something with Pierre-René." Bree blew out a breath. "Last week after one of Pierre's and my Italian sessions, we were leaving the coffee shop and ran into Jessica and Ryan. I hadn't had a chance to tell her about Pierre, or hadn't made it a priority—whatever. Again, I wasn't sure there was anything to tell. Anyway, she saw him and seemed really taken aback. Was rather rude, actually." Bree winced at the memory.

Paula nodded slowly. "She probably feels like you're replacing her dad."

"But it's been so long—she was so little when Roger died. Should that really be an issue now?"

"Maybe it makes it more so. Who knows—you'll only find out if you talk to her."

Good point.

They made it through another stack of papers without any more weeping spells and, after multiple assurances from Paula that she would be fine for dinner on her own, Breeanna finally left.

"I'm ready to curl up and stream some of my favorite British cozy mysteries. It amazes me you can write stuff like that."

"Well, I haven't tried writing for TV yet. But I hope you have a relaxing evening, dear friend." She hugged her. "You call me anytime, day or night, you hear?"

"I will."

Bree walked down the street toward her house, enjoying the longer and warmer days, though the spring air still raised goose bumps on her arms without an extra sweater. Such was Washington. She let herself in and Spencer out, then set some leftover chili to reheat for her dinner. With corn bread sliced and wrapped in foil to stick in the toaster oven, she let Spencer back in. Tail dusting the floor, he sat by his dish and looked up at her, looked down at the dish and back up at her.

Bree shook her head. "And they say dogs can't talk. They sure don't know you." She poured kibbles into his bowl and opened a can of cat food.

Within seconds, silent paws padded into the kitchen, and Cinders wound around her legs, meowing.

"You can hear that sound in a deep sleep and a mile away, can't you?" Bree bent to smooth the cat's black ears, then set the dish before her. Cinders hunched right down, quickly decimating the odoriferous pile.

Breeanna rinsed and refilled their water bowls, the scents of chili and corn bread beginning to smooth over that of canned cat food. She needed to set up someone to care for Spencer and Cinders while she was away, as well as water her houseplants, bring in the mail and newspaper, all that. Paula and Peter had always done it before, as she always did for them. But she hated to ask anything of Paula right now so hadn't brought it up.

She certainly wasn't going to ask James and Abigail; they had enough to deal with between one small child, another on the way, plus their jobs—Abigail would take a break from her home organizing business once the baby came, but till then she was packing in as many clients as she could. And Jessica had enough on her plate right now.

Jessica—she should call her to talk about the other night. Paula was right. Right now, before she put it off again. While she waited for the corn bread to finish warming, Bree dialed her daughter's number.

"Hey, honey. Is this a bad time?"

"No, it's okay."

Jessica's voice sounded—stressed? Discouraged? Disheartened? Or did Bree just read that sound into her daughter's voice all the time now? "Are you all right?"

"I was actually just about to call you."

Breeanna's gut tightened. Intuition told her it wasn't just for a mother-daughter chat. "What's wrong?"

"I know you won't want to hear this, but…" Jessica sighed. "I'm getting kicked out of my apartment."

"Oh, honey." Bree pressed her fingers to the bridge of her nose. Just when Jess was making such efforts to remedy her financial situation.

"I have to be out by the end of the month. He demanded that I move, but said he'd help me by giving me three months to pay off my back rent. Mom, it was only this last month. I've gotten the others paid, but like he said, never on time."

Bree could hear the tears clogging her daughter's voice. "I'm so sorry to hear this, sweetheart." Guilt prodded again that she hadn't pitched in something from Jade's gift to at least help with Jess's rent. But no, she and Denise had bought their plane tickets, she couldn't go back. Still, couldn't she have given Jess a little and still gone on the Italy trip, if she pinched pennies? The old arguments circled till Bree clenched the phone hard.

"Anyway." Discouragement weighted Jess's voice. "I guess I'll see if a friend will let me sleep on their couch for a while."

"No, you don't need to do that." She could at least provide a roof over her daughter's head. "I need someone to take care of the pets, the mail, those things while I'm away. You can stay here while I'm gone—house-sit. That would help, wouldn't it? Spencer and Cinders would appreciate the company. And my house isn't too far from one of your jobs. I mean, I'll be gone a bit over two weeks and..."

"Are you sure? What about my furniture and...Mom, I have to be out of here in ten days."

And I'll still be home then. Breeanna closed her eyes and blew out a breath. James was going to yell at her for bailing Jessica out again. "You can come here whenever you need to, and you can stay until you find another place."

"Okay. Maybe I can put my stuff in storage but right now I don't have money to cover that even. I'm paying for gas and food from my tips as it is."

Bree rubbed her forehead, hopefully the better to help her think. She sank down on a chair at the kitchen table, right in front of the window. Dark was sneaking into her yard where the tulips were starting to bloom and the daffodils needed to be deadheaded. So much to get done before she left, and she absolutely had to finish that book.

How could she find time to help her daughter move? She couldn't, that was all there was to it. But turning one guest room back into her daughter's room only meant fresh sheets and towels and moving the winter clothes out of the closet where she had already stored them. So much for being on top of things. Spencer sat beside her, tail feathering the floor and a whine, one of those meant to comfort her. How could he read her so well? She patted his head with her other hand and rubbed his ears. Such a good dog. Having Jess living here while she was gone would be a good thing.

"Anyway, thanks, Mom."

"Ah, um, you're welcome, but..." Cinders jumped up on her lap and settled in for a purr fest. Both animals were used to having someone around.

"For offering me a place to stay. I promise I will do my share of the work around there and take good care of those things you need me to do."

"Ah...thank you." Who was she talking to? What happened to her ungrateful daughter? Maybe this wasn't going to be such a bad thing after all.

"Mom, I hate to ask you this but may I store my things in your garage? I mean, I don't know what else to do."

Either that or I pay her storage. The garage was plenty full already and while she'd planned on cleaning it out when she finished this novel, if Jessica stored her things there, her car would have to be outside again. Bree sucked in a deep breath. "I'll pay for the storage unit."

One more thing to make James irate.

"Mom, I promise, I'll pay you back. I know I've reneged on promises before, but I will pay you. You won't even have to garnishee my tips."

Breeanna choked, then a giggle escaped, chased by a laugh. "Oh, Jessie..." The laugh continued, with Jess finally giggling too.

"I was going to say wages but the tips slipped out."

Breeanna shook her head. Garnishee her tips. Her daughter's world was indeed changing. *Please, Lord, make it so. Or did I jump in without thinking or praying?* Now to deal with James.

Chapter Nine

Bree hated this.

She stood in the parking lot of Jessica's apartment complex, watching her children argue as they attempted to load Jess's sofa into the moving truck James had rented for the day—well, he'd split the cost with Jessica.

"I said grab it closer to the back." James demonstrated, his voice rising. "The back is heavier, it'll tip otherwise. Why don't you ever listen?"

"You think you're the only one who knows the right way to do things. I should have just done this myself." Jessica balanced on the loading ramp in her jeans and work gloves, shifting her weight as they tried to push the sofa up into the van.

"Because you're so great at taking care of yourself?" James gave the sofa an extra-hard shove and lost his grip. The couch slid back down the ramp, narrowly missing his foot, to skid onto the asphalt then flip onto its back.

Bree hurried to stabilize the sofa. "Calm down, both of you. Someone is going to get hurt." She hadn't pulled out her mom voice like that in a long while.

Both her adult children quieted, at least for the moment. Bree blew out a breath, puffing her sweaty bangs from her forehead. She really didn't have time for this, nor did James. But of course, she had caved again. Ryan couldn't get the day off, and whatever she might postulate, Jessica couldn't do it all herself.

Bree marched close to the van and looked up at James and Jessica on the loading ramp. "The only way we're going to get through this is to work together. Got it?"

They both nodded, looking a bit shamefaced. Jessica climbed down the ramp and helped Breeanna flip the couch back over.

James came down next to them. "Let me take the bottom end this time."

Without comment, Jess headed to the other, got a grip, and waited for her brother's call.

"Ready?" James's voice came tight, but at least he wasn't yelling. His sister nodded, avoiding anyone's gaze.

Tension aching her neck, Bree watched them heave the sofa up the ramp once more, this time successfully sliding it into the van. She turned and headed back into her daughter's one-bedroom apartment, thankfully on the ground floor. At least she could carry boxes, though she had to be careful of her knee—she'd wrenched it a couple of months ago, though it had mostly healed.

Rubbing a cramp in her shoulder, she scanned the main room, the kitchenette on one wall, bath and bedroom door on the other. Maybe Jess would find something a bit larger once she got her debts paid off. Working two jobs had to help, right?

Bree hefted a box of books—one thing she and Jessica held in common was a love of reading—and headed back out to parking lot, squinting in the bright spring sunshine. *Thank you, Lord, for a clear day for moving, at least.*

"Thanks." Jessica reached down from the van to take the box.

"When do you have to turn in your keys?" Breeanna shaded her eyes to look up at her.

"By seven tonight."

"And you're sure your landlord isn't going to pursue legal action about the back rent?"

"I told you, he says he'll give me three months to pay it off." Strain edging her voice, Jessica jumped down from the van and headed for her apartment.

Maybe she shouldn't have asked again. But mother-worry was hard to tamp down. The landlord hadn't been willing to work with the credit counseling company, hence Jessica's eviction. But at least he was showing some compassion in giving her these months of grace. He couldn't keep on a tenant indefinitely who failed to pay rent, Bree did understand that. Even if she wished he'd given her daughter a little more time.

They worked the rest of the morning, loading Jess's furniture and stacks upon stacks of boxes—what did her daughter have in them all? Bree certainly knew how stuff could accumulate, after living in the same house for thirty years. But Jess had only lived here for two. Anything that wouldn't fit in the storage unit would go in Bree's garage. Jessica would have to park her car in the driveway while she house-sat—and for however long after that she would end up living back home.

At last only furniture lines on the carpet and dust bunnies in the corners marked the empty rooms. Jessica did one more check through the apartment while James and Bree stood in the shade of the truck and chugged bottled water, catching their breath.

"Thank you for doing this." Bree touched her son's arm. "I know you probably have plenty else to do."

"As usual, Jess's problems respect no one's schedule." James's voice still stretched thin. He pulled off his faded baseball cap and wiped his wrist across his forehead. Though the April morning wasn't hot, they'd all worked up a sweat.

Bree withdrew her hand, a familiar pinch aching her heart. *Lord, what did I do wrong that my children are so often at odds with each other?* If only she could just make them say sorry and hug it out, like when they were little. But nothing was that easy anymore.

"Okay, let's go." Jessica approached. "I'll come back and vacuum later, before I turn in my key."

They drove the few miles to the self-storage, stopping at a drive-through on the way—it was almost lunchtime, and they'd worked up an appetite. Parked at the storage facility, they sat in the open back of the truck to eat their burgers and fries, supplemented with bottles of iced tea.

"Shall we get back to it?" Breeanna said at last, wiping her greasy fingers on a paper napkin. She stood and gathered the take-out containers into a plastic bag.

Her phone rang. She glanced at it. *Pierre.* Should she just let it go to voicemail? Probably, but...She held up a hand to her children. "I'll be right back."

She stepped away toward a little stand of trees in the parking lot. "Hello?"

"Hello, Breeanna." Pierre's richly familiar voice soothed her ears. "Where are you? I stopped by your house but no one is home."

He was at her house? Bree instinctively glanced over her shoulder at James and Jessica, but they seemed deep in conversation. She hadn't had Pierre over for dinner yet, though she'd been wanting to. How did he even know her address?

"No, uh, we're moving Jessica today. We're at the self-storage place."

"Ah. That explains it. Paula mentioned she was moving in today, and I thought perhaps I could help. That was why I came by."

Paula. Of course. Bree had told her about the move when

she took a meal over yesterday. Bree pinched the bridge of her nose, torn between wanting to hug and throttle her friend. "She is. Moving in with me. But I don't have room for all her furniture in my garage. So we rented a storage unit." Well, Bree had rented it. Why didn't she say so? Was she shying away from confessing that to Pierre, afraid he'd judge her like James for doing too much for Jessica? But since when was it a crime for a mother to help her daughter?

"That makes sense. Which storage facility?"

"Pierre, you don't have to do this."

"I know. I want to. Which one?"

She told him, and hung up, chewing her lip. Had she made a mistake? After their frosty encounter in The Coffee Spoon, Jessica might hate her for letting Pierre come help. For Pierre's own sake, she probably shouldn't let him come. But the fact was, they were all tired. Another pair of well-muscled arms would be welcome. And Pierre-René hadn't seemed willing to take no for an answer.

Plus, she wanted to see him. Was that so wrong?

Lowered voices reached her as she stepped back toward the van. Were James and Jessica at it again? Her heart sank.

"Mom shouldn't be having to bail you out again."

"She needs someone to house-sit anyway."

"Yeah, for two weeks. And now how long is this going to last? I know she's paying for this storage unit too. You were supposed to be turning over a new leaf."

"I am. I'm going to all those credit counseling appointments you set up, following their plan. I'm working two jobs, for crying out loud. Mom understands, why can't you?"

"Please." Bree held out her hands to her kids, stepping nearer. "Don't fight. James, do you have to hit your sister when she's down?"

"Seriously." Jessica rolled her eyes, but Bree could tell she was fighting not to cry.

James sighed and got up, slamming his empty drink bottle into a nearby trash can. "Fine. I'm sorry."

If he were five, she would have said, *You don't sound sorry.* But thirty was a bit beyond remarks like that.

"And Jessica, your brother took off work today to help you. I really wish you'd show a little gratitude."

Jessica hugged her elbows and sat stiffly. "Thank you." Her voice could chill drinks.

Bree sighed. She was so tired of playing family referee. "That was Pierre-René—Jessica, you met him at The Coffee Spoon. He's coming to help us."

"He what?" Jessica stared. James turned back to stare too.

"He's being very gracious, offering to help like this. He certainly doesn't have to." She ignored the glance her children shared. Great, this would be the thing that united them. Bree strode toward the storage office. "So let's get your key and find the unit before he gets here."

They did, and Bree left James and Jessica pulling the van into place at the unit while she returned to the parking lot to watch for Pierre.

His black sporty car rolled up shortly, and Pierre-René got out, pulling on work gloves. He smiled at her, that twinkle lighting his dark eyes and lifting the scar from his eyebrow. Dressed in jeans and a dark-blue T-shirt, he looked even better in work clothes than in a suit. How did the man do that?

"You know, you really didn't have to do this." She accepted his hug, savoring the scent of his cologne, then pulled back before she enjoyed it too much.

"But what a nice excuse to see you."

"We're just about to start unloading the moving truck. If you're sure..."

"Lead on." He made a gallant sweep with his hand.

Bree got turned around in the maze of storage units

and identical rolling doors, but they found their way. She introduced Pierre-René to James.

"Great to meet you." James's charm was back. "This is my sister, Jessica."

"Yes, we've met. Lovely to see you again."

Jessica nodded, her shoulders stiff. "Hi." At least she wasn't scowling.

"This is so gracious of you, Pierre-René." Bree slanted a look at her daughter.

"Thank you for coming." No thawing in Jessica's shoulders, but at least she said the words.

"So." Pierre clapped his work-gloved hands. "Put me to work."

James soon had them moving like a conveyor belt, him in the van sliding items forward, Pierre helping navigate the heavier items on the ramp, Jessica and Bree lugging them into the small storage unit. The guys toted in the heavier sofa, stuffed comfort chair, chest of drawers, twin bed, and bookcase. Those along with a floor lamp and folding table and chairs made up the bulk of Jessica's furniture, plus all the boxes. Jess had loaded some boxes into her car to take to Bree's—valuable items or things she'd need in the next few weeks. Her TV and laptop were going to her mother's house too.

Pierre and James laughed and joked like an uncle and nephew. Jessica said little, moving back and forth between the van and the storage. She kept her gaze averted from Bree's searching eyes and didn't interact with Pierre or James much either. But at least she wasn't outwardly rude.

"This is about the last of it. Just a couple more boxes." James handed down a lamp swaddled in Bubble Wrap to Pierre.

"But this is beautiful." Pierre examined the item in his hand through the wrapping. "From Europe?" He glanced at

Jess, clearly trying to make conversation. "I remember seeing items like this in Germany. Where did you get this?"

Bree caught her breath, her chest squeezing. She recognized that lamp now. It was the Little Bo-Peep one Roger had found for Jess at a garage sale when she was tiny—probably only three or four. He had a knack for finding quirky treasures, and it was a family joke that he thought they never could have enough lamps. Carved figurines of Bo-Peep and her sheep held up the sky-blue shade marked with pin-pricked clouds and musical notes. A knob on the base played the nursery rhyme when wound.

"My dad gave it to me." Her voice hard, Jessica stepped close and took the lamp from Pierre, then walked away with the treasure.

Breeanna released the breath, her shoulders sagging. She sent an apologetic glance to Pierre. He met her gaze a moment, then turned to receive the final boxes from James.

So much for building a bridge.

They tucked the last boxes into the unit, then locked it up.

"Is there anything else we have to do?" Jessica still wasn't meeting everyone's eyes.

"Nope." James stripped off his gloves. "The paperwork was all signed when we got here; they said we could just go after we were done. You've got the key."

"That's usually the way it works." Pierre had turned cheerful again. "I've been through plenty of moves and storage units in my time."

"Okay, let's go." Jessica did glance at Pierre then. "Thank you for your help." She turned and climbed into the truck.

"I'll meet you in the parking lot." Bree waved James into the van.

She walked with Pierre-René back out to the parking lot. "I hope we didn't wear you out."

"Not at all." He smiled at her, though sweat stained the neck and back of his T-shirt. "Or are you saying I'm a feeble old man?"

"Never that. You're more fit than I am."

"I don't remember if I told you I had some heart issues a few years back. Made for good motivation to get into shape. I'd slacked off since the military."

"I don't think you did." In fact, for all the time they'd spent together, at times she felt she still didn't know this man very well. "What happened?"

"Nothing too serious, but I had angina and they had to do an angioplasty. My checkups have been good the last several years, though."

"I'm glad to hear that. I don't want to lose you anytime soon." Now, how had that slipped out?

They had reached Pierre's car, but instead of getting in, he leaned against the hood and reached out his hand for hers. "Nor do I want you to."

Hardly breathing, Bree wound her fingers through his. The late-afternoon spring breeze caressed their hair and raised gooseflesh on her arms—or was that just from the warm tingle of his touch?

At the rumble of the moving truck coming from the storage units, their hands slipped apart.

"Thank you again." Bree stepped back. "*Grazie.*"

"*Prego.*" The corners of his eyes crinkled.

"I'd like to have you over for dinner soon." But would that be awkward now, with Jessica staying with her? The thought came after the words slipped out, slicing through the euphoria from Pierre's touch and slamming her back to earth.

"I will look forward to it. Whether before or after your trip. But I will see you before you leave regardless?"

"Definitely." Bree hesitated, wanting to apologize again for Jessica's behavior. *Lord, I don't know how to fix this.*

"Don't worry about Jessica." He met her eyes, compassion in his gaze. "She'll come around."

A lump jammed in her throat. How did he know?

James pulled up beside them, so Bree waved goodbye and climbed up into the cab. She clicked on her seat belt and turned to look over her shoulder at Pierre settling into his car. *Lord, he is such a special man—why can't Jess see that?*

"That was good of him to help us."

Bree nodded. "He's a fine man." She could feel James studying her as he drove.

"We've seen him before at Paula's I think, long time ago. Probably years."

"Really, guess I'd forgotten." She stepped down when the truck stopped at her driveway. "Thank you again." She started to say something more and bit it off and just waved, watching the truck head down the street. Symbolic of a new phase in life? She nodded at the thought. But were they all ready for it? Was she?

James would drop Jessica off at her apartment, where she would vacuum, turn in her keys, and drive her car back to Bree's house.

Breathing in the solace of the last quiet before Jessica would arrive, Bree watered the plants, then showered, relishing the hot spray on her dust-grimed skin. Dressed in a lavender knit lounge set, she fed Spencer and Cinders, then slid a frozen casserole of leftover chicken enchiladas to warm in the oven. It would be different, cooking for more than one person again. Of course, Jessica wouldn't be here for every meal, but still. She'd be back here sometime tonight and hungry.

The worry blanket draped back over her shoulders as she chopped apples and oranges for a fruit salad. Had she been wrong to get involved with Pierre-René right now, when

Jess was struggling still? But she hadn't meant to—it just happened. And really, they hadn't defined their relationship as anything more than being friends. Yet had she been neglecting Jessica because of it? If she'd been checking in on her more, could she have helped prevent this eviction? If James were here, he'd remind her Jessica had made her own bed. Bree couldn't carry the load of all her daughter's bad choices anymore.

Poor Pierre. If Jessica had thawed toward him at all today, it was only by comparison of going from a hard Popsicle to ice cream. And definitely not soft-serve. What was she to do about that man? Her feelings for him definitely were growing beyond friendship, if she was honest with herself. But were his? It seemed so at times, but was he really looking for a serious relationship? And was she ready for that if so? She'd been alone and independent so long.

The front door opened and closed, keys clattering onto the entry table.

"I'm here, Mom." Jessica's voice faded down the hallway. "Going to shower."

Well, alone no longer, at least for now. Bree added a sliced banana to the bowl and stirred the fruit together, poured over a honey orange juice drizzle, and set it in the fridge. The enchiladas were hot, so she turned off the oven and removed the casserole, covering it with foil on top of the stove to stay warm. Then she headed down the hall to the back guest room—once Jessica's room, and now again.

"Hey." Jess sat texting on the guest bed, her blond hair damp around her shoulders, socked feet tucked under her. The air smelled faintly of shampoo.

Bree sat on the bed next to her daughter. "Texting Ryan?"

"Yeah. He feels bad he couldn't help today. But he had to run training for some new employees, couldn't get out of it. I told him we understood."

"Of course we did. He's a sweetheart, Jess."

"You really like him?" Jessica looked up, that vulnerability in her eyes.

"I really do. He's a good guy." Bree waited a beat, then plunged in. "So is Pierre-René."

The wall instantly shot back up in Jessica's eyes. She sat up straighter. "That's different."

"How is it different? Honey, why have you been so rude to him?"

"I haven't been rude." But Jessica's gaze flitted away like a frightened bird.

"Well, you certainly haven't been friendly. He came to help you today, for Pete's sake, and you practically froze him out."

"Did you ask him to? Come help, I mean?"

"Of course not." Bree heard her tone sharpen. Trying to rein it in, she sighed. "Jessica, what is it?"

"I'm sorry." Jessica tossed her phone aside and leaned her head into her fists. "I know I'm being awful, I just can't seem to help it."

"Is there something you don't like about Pierre?"

"No. He seems...perfect." After the grudging word, Jess sat silent a moment, then looked up, the vulnerability back in her eyes. "Do you like him better than Daddy?"

"Oh, Jess." Bree reached to clasp her daughter's hand. "Of course not. How could you think that?"

"I just don't remember you ever being this happy and starry-eyed before. I know I was little when you guys were together, but I've never seen you like this. You haven't called me much since you met him—I feel like you're getting this new life, and I know I should be all grown up, but I still need you, Mom." Her voice trembled. "And I barely even remember Daddy anymore. I'm afraid if you get together with Pierre, I'll...lose him altogether." Jessica's chin wobbled, and a tear plopped down her cheek to land on the comforter. She swiped at it with her thumb.

"Oh, honey." Bree scooted close to her daughter and wrapped her arms around her shoulders. Leaning her damp head on Bree's shoulder, Jessica did not resist.

Breeanna kissed the top of her daughter's head, her heart aching. She'd tried so hard over the years to keep Roger part of her children's lives . . . remembering his birthday and their anniversary, telling his favorite jokes and stories to them at bedtime, looking through family photo albums together and helping each other relive the memories of family vacations, holidays, and funny moments. But of course, it never could be enough.

"No one could ever replace your daddy, okay? I don't know where this thing with Pierre is going, but nobody, no one, could ever do that. You were so little, not even eight when he died, but I had butterflies and fireworks every bit as much with your father as anything that might be starting with Pierre. It just doesn't show as much when you're going through the ups and downs of daily life. But that doesn't mean it's not there."

Jessica let out a deep, shuddery breath and leaned back. "So you promise we won't forget him?"

"I never could if I tried. But yes, I promise. Maybe while you're here, we could even pull out some old photo albums again and help each other remember, like we used to. Would you like that?"

"I would." Jessica nodded with a tiptoe of a smile, then grabbed a tissue to wipe her eyes and nose. "Need help with dinner?"

"It's mostly done. But you can come set the table."

Bree padded down the hall to the kitchen, her heart lighter regarding Jessica than it had been in months. Even if her daughter was living at home again—hopefully temporarily— they had talked. Actually talked. And listened.

Still, the Jessica roller coaster was beginning to wear her out. Thank the Lord the departure for their trip was approaching fast, never mind how much she still had to do—it would be a break from the drama at home.

She checked her phone and saw she'd missed a call from Lizzie. Odd, since quiet Lizzie tended to use email rather than phone. Bree dialed her number.

"Hey, friend, what's up?"

"Hi, Bree." Lizzie's voice came faster-paced than usual, but she didn't sound upset. "I'm sorry to bother you so late, I was just wondering...if it's too late to join your trip to Italy."

"Are you serious?" Bree sat down on a kitchen chair. "I mean no, of course not, we'd love to have you." Her heart leapt at the thought. At least part of Jade's dream for their group going together would come true, and Lizzie's gentle, easygoing spirit would balance out Denise's domineering edges. "But we're leaving in a week; I don't know if you could still get a ticket on our flight..."

"I think I could. You know you gave us your itinerary, and Steve looked and found that a few seats are still open. I just wanted to check with you first, make sure it was okay."

"Are you kidding? I'm thrilled. I mean, I'll check with Denise, but I'm sure she'll be fine with it. We'll just have to make sure the cooking class she set up can take another person." But Bree knew that, for all her faults, warmhearted Denise would include Lizzie with open arms. "This was our group's dream, after all. But what changed your mind?"

"Steve and Elisa both kept encouraging me to reconsider, saying I'd always regret missing it. Then yesterday I found a note from Jade that she'd written to encourage me before I was published, when I was feeling like giving up, telling me not to shy away from my dreams out of fear." She sucked a breath. "I'm so glad I took Jade's advice and kept persevering with writing. And I figured her advice applied here too."

"Amen." Bree's grin stretched her cheeks. "Well, let me double-check a few things, and then get that ticket and pack your bags, my friend. Florence and Venice await us."

Bree hung up her phone and pressed it between her hands. *Yes. Thank you, Lord.* Then she winced as Jessica slammed a door down the hall.

She could hardly wait to escape to Italy.

Chapter Ten

She's late again.

Bree stared at her cell. No message, no call. Did they wait or go on to the travel lounge? They had agreed to meet at the ticket counter, but Denise and her daughter were no-shows. At least so far. Bree blew out a breath and, pasting a smile on her face, joined Lizzie, who waited patiently in one of the chairs lining the wall. "Let's go on to the lounge." Since they were traveling business class, they had decided to use all the perks thereof. And the travel lounge was one of them. "You have the directions?"

"I do." Lizzie picked up her purse and her carry-on, Bree did the same, and they proceeded to the lounge. The uniformed man at the door greeted them, checked their passes, and asked, "You used this service before?"

Both women shook their heads and shared a grin. Adventures for sure.

"Well, welcome again. Please make yourselves comfortable, there's food and beverages, one of the servers will assist you, and we will announce when your flight is ready to board." He glanced at his podium. "Flight to Paris, France, will begin boarding in one hour and twenty-five minutes. So relax and let us make this flight memorable for you."

"Thank you." The two women returned the man's smile and proceeded down a short hall, entering a room with plenty of comfortable seating, even recliners. Uniformed servers were bringing around trays of beverages and personal orders.

Leaving their carry-ons to save their seats, they visited the restroom, then made their way toward the buffet line.

"You can order a full hot meal if you'd like," a smiling woman informed them. "And/or choose from our buffet, both here and in the room right through that doorway."

Bree dug her ringing cell phone from her jacket pocket. Denise. She breathed a sigh of relief and tapped the screen. "Where are you?"

"We got caught in traffic, sorry, but we're nearing the park-and-fly now. We might not make it to the lounge but we'll be there in plenty of time for boarding. Just didn't want you worrying."

"I knew you should have come up last night."

"See you at boarding if not before." Denise clicked off.

Bree rolled her eyes at Lizzie. "Traffic."

"Figures. Glad we came early. No wonder they say you should arrive three hours before takeoff."

"Did I tell Steve thank you for bringing us to the airport?"

Lizzie nodded. "Quit second-guessing and relax like they say." She grinned at Breeanna and wiggled her eyebrows. They settled in their chairs and the servers brought their trays and helped make them comfortable.

"If there is anything else you need, you just wave." The woman's warm smile evoked return smiles.

While she ate, Bree mentally ran through her checklist again just to make sure she'd not forgotten anything—not that there was much she could do about that right now anyway. She sipped the Arnold Palmer drink she'd requested and looked around at the other travelers. An older woman and perhaps her granddaughter sat across from them. A couple obviously on their honeymoon were making love-eyes at each other and off in a world of their own. Several businessmen and -women were hard at work on their laptops, one woman carrying on a phone conversation in Spanish—or maybe Portuguese?

Bree inhaled a deep breath. At least she had finished her manuscript and sent if off a couple of days ago or she'd be hard at it right now too. Hopefully her editor would like it. Through the years she had learned that airports were a great place to write. One time she'd tried earphones but nearly missed her flight when she didn't hear the announcement.

While she'd flown around the USA many times and to Mexico and Hawaii when Roger was living, she hadn't crossed the Atlantic before. "Sure glad we have a direct flight to Paris, no stopping in New York." That had been an option when planning their itinerary but they had opted for a bit higher-priced direct flight. They would change planes at the Charles de Gaulle Airport and continue on to Rome.

One of the attendants stopped in front of them. "Your flight will be boarding in fifteen minutes. Is there anything I can get for you before you leave?"

Bree and Lizzie looked at each other and shrugged. "Not that I can think of." She almost said *Any suggestions?* but didn't.

Her phone sang. She switched it to Speaker and answered.

"We just passed through security and will meet you on the plane. You two all right?"

"We're spoiled rotten."

"Good. See you in a few. It only gets better."

"How can it?" Lizzie asked, her dark eyes dancing.

"Got me. But I'm ready and willing." Bree clicked off just in time for another call. This one made her smile both inside and out. "Hi, Pierre."

"You about to board?"

She nodded, then answered, "Sounds like it. This business class is all right."

"Sure glad you listened to James and me. You're going to arrive in much better shape this way."

"You've flown both?"

"Yes. Many times."

She knew he had relatives in France and had traveled a lot with his profession in international business. He'd told her stories of his grandparents during the war and more about his parents emigrating to America. They wanted to raise their future children in the amazing land of freedom. Tyranny they had known too well.

"They're calling our flight."

"Call me when you land."

"I will." She had signed up her phone for intercontinental calls at his suggestion.

Gathering their carry-ons, they left the lounge and headed to the gate. The well-dressed older woman and her charge waited right in front of them. "This your first time?" she asked Bree.

"Is it that obvious?"

The woman nodded. "I am taking Lisa, my granddaughter, to see where I grew up. I've always wanted to do this, and so this is her graduation present." She offered her hand. "My name is Louisa." They introduced themselves, visiting as the line moved forward and they split to go to the other side of the double-decker plane.

"Are people always this friendly?" Lizzie asked.

"I guess so. James says he thinks I have a sign on my forehead that says, I LIKE PEOPLE SO LET'S CHAT."

Lizzie nodded. "I think he's right."

"May I see your tickets?" a lovely woman with a French accent asked. She glanced at them and pointed to seats in the second row. "You are on the window side of the aisle." She paused. "Is this your first flight?"

"In business class and to Europe." Bree nodded. "How did you deduce that?"

"If you were a seasoned traveler, you'd have known right where to go. I'll be there to assist you as soon as this side is boarded."

"Thank you." They made their way to their seats and Lizzie settled in first to the window seat, picking a zippered packet off the cushion. A plastic-encased folded blanket and a pillow waited for each of them.

Lizzie stared at her, round-eyed. "I think this seat turns into a bed but I sure have no idea how."

Bree knew her eyes were as round as her friend's. She glanced around to see what other passengers were doing. One man had his laptop up and earplugs in place. A young woman or girl was already snuggled under a blanket and kicked back with her eyes closed.

"Hey, we made it." Denise and Rachel plopped into their seats, same row across the aisle.

"I was beginning to wonder." Bree and Lizzie continued to explore the cubbyholes and pockets of their seats. A folder with instructions answered some of their questions.

"I'm still amazed we were able to work it out for me to sit with you, being so last-minute." Lizzie shook her head.

"Me too. God is good."

Small screens on the backs of the seats in front of them lighted up with a voice saying "Welcome aboard Flight Seven Fifteen to Paris, France." The welcome was repeated in French, then German.

They listened and snapped their seat belts in place, making sure everything was stowed away as instructed.

Their attendant stopped beside them. "My name is Maria and I'll be your attendant. So please just settle back and relax. Enjoy the flight." She smiled and continued. "I need to get buckled in so we can take off and then I'll answer any of your questions."

Denise already had her camera out. "Okay, you two, smile sweetly so I can document our journey." She took their picture and did a selfie of her and Rachel.

Bree leaned back. She loved that instant when the plane wheels left the runway and jet power catapulted the plane into the sky. Within seconds they burst through the clouds to a wondrous world of blue above them and a field of puffy white below. Mount Hood looked adrift in that white sea and south, Mount Jefferson, Three Sisters, and others down toward Mount Shasta on the California border.

"Oh, my," breathed Lizzie. "Like a whole new world."

Maria handed them each a warm wet towel, along with a smile. "Be right back."

"This feels so good." Bree inhaled the minty fragrance and felt like wrapping it over her face.

When Maria returned, she showed them how to tip the seats, stow their shoes and handbags, and work the screen; she promised to demonstrate the bed when they desired. "We will be serving beverages and hors d'oeuvres soon, so is there anything else I can do for you right now?"

They both shook their heads and looked over to Denise, who was scanning through photos on her laptop. Rachel was already snuggled down and sound asleep.

"She can sleep anywhere," Denise said. "I wish I had that gift." She deleted a couple of shots. "Congrats on getting that manuscript finished and off. So nice not to have it hanging over your head."

"I know, but I'm so used to working on planes that I feel almost lost. Of course I need to get working on a proposal for that new series my publisher wants, still stuck on that. Lizzie and I are going to brainstorm, you want to join us?"

"Sure. When?"

"How about after dinner." She dug a little zippered pouch out of her purse and waved it at Denise. "Paula gave me this miniature game of Farkle, so we're going to play that now."

"How's she doing?"

"I hated to leave her but her oldest daughter is back for a couple of weeks again, so that will help her with all the sorting she is still doing. Peter kept everything." Bree shook her head. "This was such a shock. Had dinner with them one evening and then blam and he was gone." She blinked back the tears. "I am more certain all the time that life changes in an instant and we have no control over it. No matter how much we think we do."

"So true." Denise sniffed too. "So true."

Course by course, their meal put to rest the rumors of awful airplane food. This was more like the restaurants you saved for special occasions. Afterward they brainstormed for a while until they were yawning, and ideas petered out. Around them people were settling in for the night. Bree was sure she'd not be able to sleep but she did what James suggested, took two Benadryl, and after reading for a short while snuggled down into her very comfortable bed. Still no inspiration for her new series, but maybe that would come in Italy. *Thank you, Lord, we really are on our way.*

❀   ❀   ❀

A gentle tap on her arm woke her. "Sorry, I need to go to the restroom," Lizzie said.

Bree slid her bed back to a seat so Lizzie could get through. Even the restroom was convenient, they'd learned the night before. And it wasn't tiny like the ones in coach.

They'd settled back in their seats when Maria brought

them warm towels again. This time Bree used hers on her face too. What a nice service to wake up to. "Breakfast will be ready shortly."

After collecting the towels, Maria returned with covered trays.

"Breakfast, ladies?"

"This is such good coffee," Bree said when she held the mug with both hands, the better to enjoy it.

"Glad you enjoy it. We try to give our passengers the best."

"And with such class." Bree and Lizzie admired the perfect little salt and pepper shakers, the molded butter bits, the cream pitcher, and the various courses.

"I could get spoiled real easy with this." Lizzie glanced around. "I don't even have a backache from sleeping in a rather unusual bed. I slept all night, and I never sleep all night."

Bree understood. She and Lizzie had shared hotel rooms at some conferences, and Lizzie was indeed a restless sleeper and up often. She had learned long ago to bring earplugs so she wouldn't be bothered.

A bit later, Bree felt the plane begin the descent. A shiver ran up her spine. *Soon.*

"We will be landing at Charles de Gaulle Airport in Paris, France, in about twenty minutes," the voice of the pilot announced.

"We have an hour and a half layover," Denise reminded them. "And then on to Rome. Not sure how far away our next gate will be. This is one huge airport."

"Are you sure we'll be able to communicate?" Bree was already wishing she'd learned more Italian. Pierre had done his best, but she sure didn't memorize as fast as she used to.

✿   ✿   ✿

Waiting in line was the name of the game. Waiting to de-
plane, waiting to get through customs, to exchange dollars
for euros, to locate the boarding gate for their flight to Rome
on a much smaller aircraft. To use the restroom, to get
something to eat. Bree relished the various languages being
spoken all around them. French, of course, German, Spanish or Italian, she wasn't sure which or both. She bought a
package of Swiss chocolate and the four of them shared it.
People-watching in Paris was indeed entertaining.

They were about to board when the woman behind the
ticket counter told them all to relax, their plane wasn't quite
ready. Their flight was delayed for an hour, the announcement said in three languages. An obvious businessman
complained rather loudly to the woman behind the desk. At
least that's what his body language and tone of voice were
saying. Bree had no idea what language he used but she
admired the woman, who spoke softly and with a smile.

When their plane finally took off, Bree watched the
Eiffel Tower grow and recede. She flew over France, the
Swiss Alps showing up a bit later. The land was divided into
small patches of glowing greens and sparkling blue lakes.
She and Lizzie shared a window, both of them sighing and
whispering. Soon they'd left France, and then flown over
the mountains into Italy.

*I'm flying over a land I've only read about. This is real.
I'm really doing this.* Bree pinched herself just to make sure
she wasn't dreaming. The roar of the plane engines changed
as they started the descent into the Rome-Fiumicino International Airport.

"Watch for a sign with my name on it," Denise said later,
after deplaning and heading toward baggage claim. "The
driver will be looking for us too. He'll deliver us to our hotel."

When no sign or driver appeared, they collected their
luggage, then clustered together. "Now what?"

"Surely they checked to make sure what time our flight was coming in." Denise clamped her jaw. "Let's head to the transportation center. Maybe we'll find him there."

Toting all their luggage, they followed Denise, and Bree hoped she knew where they were going. The airport was crowded, and Bree was almost run down twice by people rushing to catch their flights. A man said something she didn't understand, something angry, as he barely dodged around her.

There was still no sign of the driver when they reached the airport exit. Denise frowned. "You all stay here and I'll go check at the desk."

Bree nodded, but she was thinking, *What if he doesn't show up?* The driver had been part of their travel package. Denise had made sure of that, or at least their travel agent had. Denise had worked with this woman several times so she felt secure in all the arrangements.

A middle-aged man approached them, speaking in rapid Italian. "Taxi?" he said, reaching for Rachel's bag. "Come, I take you."

"No, no," Bree said, as Rachel shook her head and held firmly on to her suitcase.

Where was Denise? *Lord, please help us. This feels like that nightmare I had.* Lost in a strange airport, in a strange city with strange languages. She was suddenly exhausted. Her dry throat needed liquid. And it had to be bottled.

Chapter Eleven

Pierre-René drew a deep breath, adjusted the bottle of Pinot Noir in his arm, and rang the doorbell.

Waiting outside the brick building, an old warehouse now turned into prime downtown Portland lofts, he squared his shoulders, then ordered himself to relax. *You're having dinner with your son, not going into battle.* Their dinner date had been bumped a couple of times due to Jason and Todd's work schedules, but finally, here he was.

Jason opened the door. "Hey, Dad."

"Hey." Pierre embraced his son's lanky frame. "Thanks for having me."

"Sure. About time you saw our place now that we finally got all moved in." Jason stepped back into the entryway, his dark eyes shy beneath his shock of dark hair, clean-cut like Pierre's. The couple's two golden retrievers, Monet and Renoir, padded up, fluffy tails swishing, noses nuzzling Pierre's hand.

"Hey, fellas." Pierre bent to let them sniff him as he rubbed their silky foreheads and soft floppy ears. Such beautiful dogs, their breeding rendering their coats nearly white.

"So." Jason shoved his hands into his jean pockets, much like when he was a little boy and hoped his dad would be pleased with a good report card. He tipped his head at the interior of the loft. "What do you think?"

"Amazing." Pierre-René followed Jason farther inside. High ceiling, brick left exposed in the walls. Tall windows that flooded the modern lines of the open living space with light. Jason led him through the entryway into the living area, where a leather sofa and two overstuffed chairs wrapped around the walls with a huge round coffee table on one side. The room flowed seamlessly into a dining area on the other side, where a dark wood table boasted a center-piece of several white pillar candles. Framed contemporary art graced the walls.

"So open and airy." Pierre-René nodded, lifting his eyes to the literal loft that lowered the ceiling over the kitchen area, a partial wall hiding the room above from view. "That's the bedroom up there?"

"And another bath. We have a basement too, a den/TV room plus storage down there." Jason waved his hand at the wrought-iron, spiral staircase that led both up and down, then called toward the kitchen, divided from the rest of the main floor by a half wall of cabinets. "Hey, Todd, get in here."

An equally tall young man with curly brown hair and an easy smile stepped out from the kitchen, wiping his hands on a dish towel. "Hey, Pierre-René. Welcome."

"Thank you." Pierre held out his hand. "Good to see you again, Todd."

"Sorry, my hands are wet." Todd gave them one more rub, then gripped Pierre's. "Thanks for coming."

"And you for having me. Something smells tantalizing."

"He's been chefing away all afternoon." Jason shook his head. "Don't know half of what he concocts in there, but I don't have to know to make it disappear."

Pierre knew Todd was an assistant chef at a popular newer restaurant, but didn't know details.

"Just some pasta carbonara." Todd shrugged and eyed the

bottle in Pierre's hand. "Wait, is that a Domaine Serene? A Pinot?"

"It is." Pierre-René held out the wine. "I wasn't sure what you'd be serving, hoped this would complement it."

"Are you kidding? It's perfect. They're my absolute favorite local winery." Todd took the bottle and examined it with reverence, then handed it off to Jason. "You open and pour. I've got to stir the sauce." He threw the dish towel over his shoulder and returned to the kitchen, followed by a tail-wagging Monet.

It all felt so normal, as if he'd visited many times.

Except he'd met with them only in restaurants up until now. And while Pierre sometimes struggled with his thoughts in the dark hours of the night, he loved his son. And Jason loved him. And for tonight, as always, he was just going to focus on that. They were all his family.

His stomach growled at the wondrous aromas drifting from the kitchen. And enjoy a fabulous dinner.

They ate by candlelight and drank the wine, lingering over plate after plate of Todd's savory pasta carbonara. To the traditional mixture of noodles, peas, and crispy bits of bacon, he'd added delicate pea greens along with plenty of sautéed garlic and onion; to the egg sauce that coated it, a good helping of Parmesan and ricotta cheese. All was supplemented with a mixed greens salad, a round loaf of crunchy bread, and a starter of pancetta-wrapped mushrooms. Pierre wondered if Bree's trip to Italy would even find a meal to top this.

"Santé," he said, lifting his wineglass with a nod to the chef. "Todd, now I see why you are a rising star in the Portland dining scene. Good as any meal I ever ate when I was stationed in Europe. Not that air force men find much time for fine dining. But this was truly *incroyable*."

"My dad uses French a lot." Jason rolled his eyes and

leaned back in his chair. "I've told you he made us all learn the language as kids."

"It's part of your heritage." Pierre cocked a brow. "And knowing more than one language is always an advantage in this world."

"Can't argue with that." Jason exchanged a smile with his partner. "And Todd speaks fluent French so mine is improving."

"So." Pierre-René folded his napkin. "How is work going for you, son?" Renoir nosed Pierre's knee under the table, no doubt hoping some remaining bit of bacon might find its way down.

"Good." Jason folded his napkin on the table and leaned forward. "They've got me doing trainings in web design now, not just doing the designs myself."

"Really." Pierre cocked his head. "That's great." He paused. "You know this coffee bar I am starting. My accountant was telling me I should hire someone who is good with web design and marketing, graphic design, that kind of thing. I don't suppose you would have time?" His heart lifted at the possibilities. Why hadn't he thought of this before? Jason had been a whiz with technology since his teens, created websites for fun, and now he worked for a top company. This might be a way to connect with his son, to work together, on something that could bring them closer...

But Jason hesitated. "I don't know, Dad. I'm afraid I really don't have time to take on another project right now. No matter how interesting it sounds."

"Of course." Pierre's chest deflated. "I totally understand." He rubbed the dog's head still against his knee, drawing comfort from the warm breath, the silky ears. It had been too much to hope for, too presumptuous of him, of course.

"I've just been pretty slammed at work." There was that vulnerability in Jason's eyes again.

"That's a fact," Todd put in. "On the nights when I'm off, I try and make a nice dinner for this guy, and he passes out on the couch almost as soon as he gets home. Some gratitude."

"Not a problem," Pierre assured them. "I'll find someone. Or perhaps...if you think of anyone you could recommend?"

"Yeah, totally." Jason's face brightened. "With all the training I've been doing, I definitely might know someone." Nodding, he continued. "I'll find you a name or two."

"Great." Hope lifted again. "I'd appreciate it. Oh, and someone who knows social media as well."

"So any young person." Todd chuckled. "This coffee bar idea sounds cool, though. Tell us more about it."

So he told them, excitement pricking again through the drudgery of paperwork and red tape that the business seemed to have become of late. Jason and Todd's genuine interest warmed his heart, and they moved to the sofa with their glasses of wine. Todd brought in a tray of individual crème brûlées, the tops just caramelized with a mini kitchen blow torch.

"I told him we had to have a touch of France too." Jason reached for one of the ramekins and passed it to Pierre.

Pierre-René closed his eyes after the first creamy, crackle-topped bite. "Marvelous." He opened his eyes. "Jason, remember when your mom tried to finish crème brûlée under the broiler?"

Jason cackled. "The tops were scorched and the insides still runny. You and the girls refused to eat them, but Mom and I stayed up late in the kitchen that night, scraping every bite so it wouldn't go to waste. Pretty sure we had stomach-aches the next day." He sobered. "She tried, though. Mom always tried."

"Yes, she sure did." But Pierre-René's gut tightened.

Perhaps he shouldn't have brought up Lynn. Memories of her were volatile, too much so for the fragile goodness of this evening.

Todd, bless his heart, changed the subject, and the conversation shifted to French versus Italian cooking styles. When Pierre-René finally looked at his watch, it showed nearly eleven.

"My word." He rubbed the fluffy neck of Monet, who had taken Renoir's place leaning on his knee now, then gently lifted the sleepy dog's head aside so he could push himself up from the leather sofa. His knees creaked as he rose, making him feel suddenly an old man. "I'd no idea it was so late. Do you both have to work tomorrow?" It was Friday night, but he didn't know their work schedules. Probably should.

"Todd goes in tomorrow, but not early. You're fine, Dad." Jason rose too. "Can we send some food back with you?"

"If you really need it taken off your hands."

Todd loaded a heavy-duty paper plate with pasta carbonara and hors d'oeuvres, and Jason covered it with tinfoil, pinching the edges down.

Accepting the offering, Pierre briefly wondered why they didn't use a reusable container. Were they unsure whether he'd want to come back, so didn't want him to feel pressure to have to return it? But he was reading too much into things.

"How's Paula doing?" Jason asked as they walked him to the door.

"Up and down. Peter's death was such a shock."

"For sure. He wasn't that old, was he?"

"No, and he was really healthy. But aneurysms can happen anytime."

"Your heart's okay now, isn't it?"

"Tip-top."

"Good." Jason hugged him. "Thanks for coming, Dad."

"Thank you for having me." Hugging his son's shoulders tight, Pierre-René fought an unexpected clamping in his throat. He released Jason and smiled. "I really enjoyed myself."

"Good." Jason rubbed Renoir's head, who stood leaning against his leg. "Take care of yourself, okay?"

"You too. Both of you."

Pierre-René drove home through the darkened freeways to Gresham, not even listening to his customary classical station. He let himself into the condo, the midnight dark quieter than usual, it seemed. No dogs here, no friendly presence. Only him. Perhaps he should consider a dog, or even a cat. Now that he wasn't traveling all the time, the company might be good.

He switched on a lamp and checked his phone. A text from Bree, sent a couple of hours ago. It would be morning in Italy by now. He smiled at the thought of her. Hadn't mentioned her tonight—hadn't felt ready yet, plus he wasn't sure how Jason would respond. Especially after how Jessica had responded to the idea of *him*. He still needed to figure out what to do about that one. And what their relationship actually was. Should he have talked with Bree about that before she left for Italy? Probably, but the time had flown before he knew it.

Pierre-René showered and slipped on his favorite silk pajamas with a flannel robe, then padded around his place, still accustoming himself to the single-level floor plan. The home he and Lynn had raised their kids in had two stories, as did his home as a boy. But this condo was better, so they said, for this stage of life.

It was nearly one, but he didn't feel sleepy. He made himself a cup of hot chocolate and headed into the bedroom. Sitting in his reading chair, as he privately called the burgundy wing chair he'd set by a small, round table topped with an ivory-shaded lamp, he thought about texting Bree, seeing if she were free to talk. Instead, though, the leather-bound photo album he kept on the shelf under the table caught his attention. He set the phone aside and reached for the book.

As he turned the pages, memories sprang into sharp relief through the faded photos. The girls and Jason at the beach, at family birthday parties, at the petting zoo. And Lynn, her dark curls flying, her smile dazzling, signature hats making a statement in almost every photo. So different from her sister Paula, only their dark, curly hair the same. Lynn gorgeous and vivacious, Paula sweet and steady. Paula devoted to her church and her family, Lynn equally devoted to him and the children... except when she was drinking.

Pierre-René shut the album, the old pain squeezing his chest again. All the times of trying to hide it from the kids, of telling friends at church that his wife just wasn't feeling well, of Lynn finally agreeing to get help and staying sober for months while following one good program after another, only for him to return from a business trip and find that the dreaded nemesis had pulled her down again.

She never hurt the children, not physically, nor him. Mostly she drank on her own, late at night, after Jason, Amanda, and Rosemarie were in bed. She never stopped loving them all, fiercely, passionately. Nor did he ever stop loving her, though at times he felt he was married to a woman having an affair... not with another man, but with the bottle. Till the pancreatic cancer, no doubt hastened by her addiction, took her swiftly, in only a couple of months.

Sometimes he wondered whether Jason's struggles stemmed partly from his mother's problem, or from his own frequent absences when Jason was growing up. A boy needed a father, he knew that, and of course a functioning mother. His older sisters did their best, but they couldn't make up the gaps he knew were there. And the guilt Pierre-René carried over that, and over his failure to save or even truly help Lynn, remained a burden he didn't know if he'd ever be able to release.

Pierre-René replaced the album gently, switched off the lamp, and climbed into bed. He wouldn't call Bree tonight. His heart was too flooded with the past.

Lord, thank you for blessing this evening, for the time with Jason, and Todd. His eyelids drifted closed as he prayed. *Guide me, Father, in all these new things. Bless Breeanna, and keep her and the others safe on their journey...* The weariness of the day dropped over him like a curtain, and he surrendered to sleep.

He was walking in the woods with a teenage Jason, the boy slim and gangly, not yet his current six-foot height. The Oregon woods dappled with sunshine around them, must be the area where he'd sometimes taken Jason duck hunting on a rare fall break when they both were around—but this didn't look like hunting season, the trees still covered in tender spring foliage, yet they both carried hunting rifles.

They chatted as they walked, the kind of easy talk he'd missed with his son. Sharing stories and dreams and hopes, talking about the good times and even the bad.

"You know your mom loves you, Jason. And so do I." He bored his gaze into his son's innocent brown eyes, willing him to believe it.

"I know, Dad."

The words lifted a weight the size of Mount Hood from his chest.

They stopped at a branch of the river where he could see a clutch of mallards near the water's edge. He motioned to Jason for silence, and they crept closer. Pierre-René lifted the duck whistle to his lips and gave a few gentle calls to draw the birds closer. Then he nodded to Jason and showed his son how to hold the gun, barely whispering instructions. The boy lifted the rifle to his shoulder and sighted. Pierre helped him adjust the position...

BAM. An explosion threw them both backward. Flailing, he reached to grab his son, but Jason was falling, falling away from him, shock wide in his dark eyes...

"D-a-a-d..." The scream echoed away.

Pierre jerked up in bed in the darkness, his chest heaving, limbs covered in sweat. He threw the covers aside and swung his legs over the edge of the bed.

Rubbing his hands over his face, he then clamped them over his elbows, trying to still the shaking. His heart pounded so hard it felt to be jumping out of his chest. Could it be the angina back?

Dear God. I thought these—what? Nightmares? Flashbacks?—were finally a thing of the past. But never had Jason been in one. And why now?

He closed his eyes, not that it made much difference in the darkness, and practiced the breathing his counselor had taught him long ago, when he first got out of the service. In and hold for four seconds...out and hold for four. Gradually, his heart rate slowed, and the sweat dried on his arms. He reached for the glass of water on his nightstand and gulped it dry, then pressed his nearby phone to see the time.

Three a.m. And another text from Breeanna, this time a photo of her and another friend—was it Lizzie?—wearing sun hats by some ancient building.

A faint smile touched his face, but he pushed the phone away. He couldn't think about Bree just now. And if she knew what a mess he was, perhaps she'd rather not think of him either.

Chapter Twelve

"I was beginning to think we were never going to get here."

Denise shook her head at her daughter. "Things always take longer than you think with traveling. At least we got to see a little of the city driving in."

"We'll have a different driver next time, won't we?" Lizzie asked.

"Yes, but I think this man was just in a bad mood because he had to come back to the airport."

"Cobblestone streets, too narrow to park a car and let two cars meet—I feel like we stepped back into history."

Denise had found this flat on a list from the travel agent of private residences to rent if you didn't want to stay in a hotel. They had all agreed they didn't want to stay in a hotel if there were other options.

Bree stared around them. Stuccoed walls, three, four stories tall lined the concrete sidewalk, with black metal framed lights on either side of the doorways, all flat in the wall. A scrolled black metal door seemed like others up and down the street. One step. She tipped her head back. There must be a garden on the top floor, because branches overhung the wall.

"How old do you think these buildings are?"

"Several centuries, at least that's what something I read said." Lizzie's eyes were wide, making Bree think hers probably matched. Pictures she'd seen always had tan or cream stucco. And here she could prove it was so.

Denise turned a dial in a box on the wall by the door and pulled out a ring of keys. Her sigh of relief told Bree she wasn't the only one a bit worried. She inserted one key in the lock and frowned.

"It's not turning."

Bree scrunched her eyes. *Please, Lord, let the key work*, she prayed as Denise put more pressure on it. How could so much be going wrong already? Was this how the whole trip would be?

Denise pulled the key out, tried the other similar key from the ring, and voilà, the decorative metal gate/door swung open. She flicked the switch she found on the wall, and white marbled tiles on the floor and the walls gleamed in the light from a black metal hanging chandelier.

Rachel entered first and set her suitcase on the riser two steps up before bringing in the others. "There's a teeny elevator here. We won't have to wrestle our bags up that staircase." She looked to a steep narrow staircase that curved around a corner, her eyes rounded. A sign by the dark wood on their right identified flat one.

"Good thing since we're on the third floor—er, flat."

Lizzie clicked the light on her iPhone to read the instructions posted beside the metal screen door for the elevator. "It says one person with bags in elevator."

Denise took charge. "I'll go on up. Rachel, you load the bags on and I'll take them off. Bree, you and Lizzie come on up with me."

Bree almost saluted but she was too tired. Denise was in full sergeant mode, but her plan did seem the best. The brochure had said the flat had four beds, so they each had a room with shared bathrooms.

Once they and all their bags were gathered in the hallway

of their assigned flat, unlocked by the first key Denise had tried, Rachel was off exploring.

Bree looked around at dark woodwork with off-white stucco walls, high ceilings with cove moldings, a bathroom all in dark woods straight ahead, and a bedroom with a dark wood bed off to their right. They followed the hallway to the kitchen. It reminded Bree of pictures she'd seen of kitchens of the 1950s. Tall cupboards, with a counter that housed the sink under a window on the outside wall. All the floors tile. Stove and refrigerator on the opposite wall and another counter, all railroad-style. Very efficient.

"There are only three bedrooms, the brochure said four." Rachel studied the plan once more.

"What's behind that door?" Lizzie asked, pointing to the inside wall.

Rachel shrugged. "Good question." She pulled it open to find a feather bed filling what could be called a cubbyhole. "Guess this is where I sleep." She studied the brochure again. "Ah, it says four beds, three bedrooms. Guess I missed something."

"Might have been a pantry at one time." Lizzie read from the brochure. "'This building was built in the late seventeen hundreds, has been remodeled and updated, lastly again in the nineteen fifties.' My word, can you believe that?"

"That elevator probably had a crank to raise and lower it at one time." Rachel looked over the tray of packaged foods on the counter. "I'm starving." She opened one of the packages and found crisp cookies. "Would be easier if I could read the labels."

The others checked out the bedroom and bath off the dining room that flowed from the kitchen and the final bedroom off the small sitting room.

"How about I take that bedroom we saw first," Denise asked, "and Rachel and I can share that bathroom?"

"I'd like the one off the sitting area. Lizzie, you okay with the one in the middle?"

"Good, that way I can get up when I have to without waking anyone else. Just look, shutters on all the windows, no glass."

"And all the artwork on the walls." Bree turned in a circle. "This place fascinates me." That bed looked mighty appealing right now.

"So what about food?" Lizzie asked.

Bree grinned. "We're going out for dinner. Our host left us a map with a grocer and restaurants on it. Looks like a good one two, three blocks away." Bree held the map in front of her and turned till she was facing the right direction. "Out the door and turn right, up two blocks, cross the street diagonally, grocer one door to the right and a restaurant across one more street and three doors down."

They set out, Denise locking the door behind them. "Need to be careful on the cobblestone streets. Can someone tell me again why we're not at a hotel with bellboys, or rather men?"

"Because we wanted to do the B and B route, get a feel for how regular people live in this country," Rachel chanted back.

"Right, thanks. You're the one that asked for that, remember?" Denise sent a mother-look at her daughter.

"Well, it sounded like an adventure, you know?"

Bree heaved a sigh. Something else she just remembered. Lots of times she became uncomfortable when the two began this back-and-forth—discussion, rant, she wasn't sure what to call it. Their mother-daughter relationship wasn't so picture-perfect as she sometimes thought.

They trooped up the grade and followed the instructions, pausing for a peep into the grocery store, if you could call the narrow space that.

"Let's eat first and stop here on our way back." Bree smiled at the older man behind the counter. "How late are you open?"

"Eleven." At least he spoke English.

The restaurant had a menu posted on their door.

"Looks pricey," Lizzie whispered.

"I have a feeling they all are." Bree glanced up to see Rachel walking up the sidewalk to check the other.

She waved them on, leaving the one where they were rather reluctantly. A woman greeted them at the second place, nodded at their "four," and picking up menus beckoned for them to follow her. Making their way between tables barely far enough apart for waiters to serve food, let alone guests, Rachel slid onto the padded bench against the wall with chairs for the others. Above her hung a large painting of families working the fields centuries earlier. A classical painting, like several that hung in their flat.

Bree listened to the conversations going on around them, mostly in Italian but she was sure that was German from a table just beyond theirs. She tucked her purse between her knees, obeying the advice the travel agent had included in their packets. She inhaled. If the food tasted anywhere as good as this place smelled, they'd found a winner. Looking around, she figured every iota of space was used wisely.

Reading the menu and translating the prices from euros took some teamwork. The waitress took their orders after graciously answering their questions. Bree had promised herself she would be brave when ordering since she really had no idea what she had ordered, other than the caprese salad of tomato slices and buffalo (pronounced *boo-fa-lo*) cheese, topped with fresh basil and drizzled with olive oil and a balsamic reduction.

"This is so good," she told the others after their food

arrived. "But do you really think they milked buffalo?" The picture in her mind of milking a bison did not compute.

Shrugs met her question.

Denise had the same salad. "Good is right. Delicious fits even better."

When their waitress returned, Bree asked her their question.

"Ours is from the milk of *water* buffalo. Domesticated like dairy cows. Most in this country is from cow's milk, but this is the best so we carry it too. You made a wise choice." She finished setting their orders around. "Now, can I get you anything else?"

Bree shook her head. "*Grazie.*" So far she'd not needed to use her slim knowledge of Italian. But she could be polite at least.

When they'd finished and congregated back on the sidewalk, Bree shook her head. "You need to stay skinny in this country just to eat at the restaurants—and with food like that, how do they stay skinny?" Bree slung her bag over her shoulder, the cross-the-chest-style strap twisting. "What do we really need at the grocery?"

"Breakfast makings. Our host supplied the coffee and tea."

"And those packages," Rachel threw over her shoulder. "I don't think they eat breakfast like we do."

When they filed into the grocery store, all Bree could see was the small size of it, like their flat, long and narrow. Displays lined both walls, and a line of shelves ran down the center.

"*Buonasera,*" she greeted the aproned man behind the much-used wooden counter.

His smile showed a gold front tooth as he nodded. "*Benvenuti.* You are from America?"

"*Si.* Just arrived this evening."

"Any questions, I'll be right here." He pointed to the baskets stacked by the door.

"Grazie." They picked up their cloth baskets and made their way picking up bananas, plums, and oranges from the fresh fruits and vegetables section, cheese and yogurt from the dairy, and some sort of buns from the breads, then gathered at the counter. Good thing they had changed their cash into euros at the airport, as that was what he dealt in.

"All that in such a tiny space," Bree said as they met outside on the sidewalk.

"Sort of like our mini marts, but so much variety."

Lizzie brought out her phone light as they headed back to the flat, for streetlights were rather far between.

Climbing the narrow steps up to their flat made Bree grateful she'd been walking more recently in preparation for this trip thanks to Denise telling her they would be doing a lot of walking in Italy.

✦   ✦   ✦

When they got ready for bed, they all closed the shutters that took the place of windows, although Bree paused to look up the street below her. Lights glowed from windows, and most doors had a light beside them. A neon sign on the roof of one building glowed in the dark. Another building had strings of white lights, potted plants, and bushes along with lounge seats on the flat roof. She'd read in one of their brochures that there were places like that all over Italy, part of the life. She leaned on her windowsill to look straight down. Old, even ancient—people had been living here for hundreds of years. The thought boggled her mind.

Tomorrow they were doing a bus tour of the city of Rome. Rome, she was in Rome. Ah, the ancient history of this place. She, Breeanna Marie Lindstrom, was in Rome. Italy. She pinched the skin on her hand. Yes, she was awake, not dreaming.

She didn't fall asleep gently, she crashed, despite her concerns about having a hard time falling asleep in a strange place. And woke to the sun painting lines on the thick area rug along with voices from the street. She opened the shutters and pinned them back with the peg-metal latches. People on the street hustled along; several schoolchildren, garbed in blue-and-black plaid school uniforms with books slung in a strap over their shoulders, ambled along until one glanced at a wristwatch and announced they were going to be late if they did not hurry. At least that must be what he said, as they all ran off.

She had actually made this happen—well, with help from Jade and God. *Thank you, Father, that I didn't let this dream sink under Jessica's drama.* Bree dressed and joined the others in the kitchen/dining room. The early riser had made coffee, and after pouring herself a cup, Bree chose a yogurt from the refrigerator and a packet of breakfast cookies— more like a cross between cookie and cracker—and sat at the dark wood table. The shutters had been opened, and the light painted squares on the rugs.

"What do you suppose they do in the winter?" She nodded to the shutters. "I think I'd want windows."

Denise shrugged. "Different climate than we have, that's for sure. And no screens for bugs." She raised her voice. "Everyone still on for the Red Bus Tour today?" At their nods and yeses she finished with, "Then can we be ready to leave in fifteen minutes?"

"Twenty?" asked Lizzie.

"We have a bit of a walk to the bus stop for the Red Tour, but we'll get to see the neighborhood since we're walking it."

See it—for sure. Time to stop and appreciate? None. Shade trees lined the streets made of cobblestone or concrete with noticeable cracks. She glanced up at single houses, some with tiny yards, more flats like the one they had hung with window boxes full of red geraniums, and small businesses tucked in between. The Red Tour buses waited in a parking lot with their destinations on a roller board above the windshield. They found the one they wanted and while Breeanna wanted to sit inside the bus, the others climbed to the rooftop seats so she followed. Hat—she'd not brought a hat.

Lizzie sat in the window seat—not that there were windows. It was all open but with metal railings. "There are hats down there." She leaned over and pointed.

A grinning man saw her gesture and waved his wares, rattling in Italian.

Bree poked her. "He thinks you're Italian." No wonder, with her friend's dark hair and eyes and olive skin.

"Great, I don't even speak Spanish." Lizzie rolled her eyes and scooted back for Bree to lean across her. "You try."

Bree racked her brain for Pierre's lessons. *"Possiamo comprare due cappelli?"* She sure hoped that meant they wanted to buy two hats.

"Si, si, take your pick, *signora."*

"Hurry, the bus is about to leave."

"The white one and the tan one." Both were wide-brimmed. Bree gestured in case he didn't understand that much English. *"Quanto costa?"*

He tossed the hats up, she caught them. *"Quanto costa?"* she repeated. Didn't that mean "how much"?

He called something but the bus driver revved the engine and the bus inched ahead. Lizzie threw her money at him and the bus pulled away, the four of them laughing so hard they had to wipe their eyes. Lizzie handed the white one to Bree. "They're fake straw for cool and wide-brimmed to protect our lovely complexions, so away we go."

Bree clapped her hat on her head and tried to study the map and see the city, all at the same time. Giggling made the whole thing more difficult. None of the writers at home were ever going to believe this.

Denise stood up in the aisle, camera poised. "Cheese, everybody." She clicked, Bree grabbed her hat before the breeze took it away, and Denise kept on clicking. With her along, this trip would be well documented.

Despite the sunscreen she'd applied before they left the flat, Bree could feel her shoulders heating up. The sleeveless top might be cooler but the sun shone far hotter in Italy than Vancouver, where it didn't heat up like this until maybe August or September, if then.

The bus stopped and passengers got off to tour the various historical spots and then could catch a different bus for the next leg.

"According to our itinerary, we'll see the Pantheon first, then the Trevi Fountain, and the Colosseum after that." Denise looked up from her iPhone. "Our travel agent suggested this as the best use of time to see what we can of Rome."

"Fine with me," Bree said with a shrug. "Lead the way." She glanced at Lizzie, who nodded too.

They stopped and all the passengers got off at the Pantheon stop to see broad concrete steps leading up to tall columns that framed the entry. Lines of people, many with shade umbrellas, led the way to the biggest bronze doors Bree had ever seen. She'd read about this, but seeing the ancient building made her feel like she should walk around with her jaw agape. So big and so old and it had always been in use. The Apostle Paul had been here.

People looked tiny compared with the columns and the doors. Inside, she had to stop to stare up to the open circle in the top of the dome from which the light moved across the marble-tiled floor according to how the sun moved.

Rachel stood beside her. "That and the doors are the only sources of light."

"How did they build such a dome without all the tools we have today?"

"From what I read, architects through the ages have tried to figure that out. Mom said she'd meet us at the doors in about fifteen minutes."

"Okay." They made the circuit and met at the doors.

"On to the Trevi Fountain." Denise moved her sunglasses from on her head to her face. "I remember how impressed I was when I saw it the first time."

She laughed when they stood at the lower side of the sculptures, a man of the sea, two horses pulling him in a clam-shell chariot. A female statue on either side of him, tucked into the arch of the Roman-looking building behind him. Water flowed off sheets of rock, like natural waterfalls.

Bree could only shake her head, trying to take it all in. Artists had set up easels, trying to catch the magnificence of it all. Denise finished getting her pictures and wandered back to join them.

"He reminds me of pictures I've seen of Zeus and the other gods. Only this is Oceanus, the god of the sea." Bree kept shaking her head. So much to take in.

"Did you throw your coin in the fountain?" When the others shook their heads, Denise motioned. "Come on, we have to do this. You all do it and I'll get the picture. On three."

They did as instructed, Bree fighting to keep from break-ing out laughing. When in Rome...She wondered if the people who lived in Rome did this or only the tourists. Whatever, there were indeed plenty of coins in the bottom of the fountain.

"How about we get something to eat before we board the bus again? Come on, Mom, I'm starving."

Bree mouthed her thanks as they lined up in front of a storefront that sold slices of pizza.

Pizza in hand, they made their way to a Red Bus stop and boarded at the next one that said COLOSSEUM. The bus seat felt far better than the benches they'd sat on at the Trevi.

At the Colosseum, Denise and Rachel said they'd go ahead since Denise knew exactly what pictures she wanted. Lizzie and Bree stayed together, both staring in awe at the high walls built centuries earlier. They entered the huge edifice through an arched portal, the same as the people of ancient Rome would have. Packed sand, walls with dark places, a breeze, voices shouting. Bree ordered herself to breathe. With every step, it got worse.

Animals roaring, people chanting, cheering, screaming. Her mouth dry, hard to breathe…Bree fought to stay with her friend, but her body screamed *Get out of here! Now! Run!* Shaking so hard she could barely talk, Bree staggered; closing her eyes only made it worse. She found her voice. "S-sorry, Lizzie, I-I-I…you go on. I'll wait…for you out-outside."

"What's wrong?" Lizzie's dark eyes widened. "Are you sick?"

"No, no, I…just can't stay here." Bree turned and fled, trying to not bump into other tourists. She'd had this happen before, feeling the agony and horror, hearing the men screaming. Her hands and shoulders tightening now, she still faintly heard their desperate cries, something roaring, chanting. She blinked and nearly bumped into a man standing still, staring upward.

"Excuse me." Outside she found a bench, collapsed head down, and ordered herself to breathe. Breathe! She felt her shoulders drop, her body relax, and her head stopped spinning. Huffing out her regained breathing, she finally heard Lizzie calling her name.

She looked up and waved at her friend, who nearly ran to her side.

Lizzie sat down beside her. "Are you okay?"

Fighting back the tears, Bree muttered, "I...I'm going back to the bus. I need to get out of here."

"I'll go with you." Lizzie had to walk fast to keep up; Bree felt more like running. The people, all those people...she should have realized this might happen. She'd learned to stay away from places where people had suffered—died.

"What happened back there?" Lizzie asked when they found a bench near the buses, away from the flowing tourist hordes.

"I'm sorry." Breeanna dug her water bottle out of her bag. "I should have known better."

"Known what?"

"This, this horrible sense of hearing the screaming, the agony, of being there when it was happening. I felt this way on the *Arizona* in Pearl Harbor, and once when I visited a historic battlefield. Hearing men screaming. Artillery, rifles firing." She swallowed, her throat still dry, and took another sip. "I couldn't get off that boat memorial fast enough." She blew out a puffed-cheeks breath. "I thought I was going crazy. But now..." Another sip. "I know that this sense is just something I have."

"Maybe this helps you be a better writer."

"Well, you notice I never write or read horror or really scary stuff, and I don't go to war movies or creepy ones. I feel like I'm there and scared silly and I can't stand it so I just don't go."

"As I said..." Lizzie watched the crowds for a while, all hurrying to see as much as they could cram into a few minutes. She patted Bree's knee. "You better now?"

"I'm not going back."

"I wouldn't either." She rested her elbows on her knees. "You ever write about this?"

Bree shrugged. "No, too unbelievable, I guess."

"Well, I've seen enough. Why don't we find somewhere to eat?"

Bree nodded gratefully, dug her cell phone out of her bag, and put it on speaker after she dialed. Since Denise didn't answer, she shrugged and left a message. "Oh, well, we're kind of done here. Will wait for your call."

The two made their way back to the lineup of buses. Her phone sang.

"What's up?" Denise asked.

"Just checking if you're ready for lunch?"

"Rachel and I are going to stay here awhile. But you two go ahead and we'll catch up with you later for dinner."

Bree and Lizzie shrugged and stared at each other. "Okay, we'll see you back at the flat."

The two of them checked the time and climbed back on a bus.

"That piece of pizza was good but feels almost like it was yesterday."

"We need lunch *and* gelato and maybe we could just look around." Lizzie's eyebrows wiggled. "I mean, there are places to eat and shop around that parking area where we got on the bus."

"There was a church near there too. We could peek in if we have time. I have always dreamed of seeing ancient cathedrals. And not just the big well-known ones. I know tomorrow we see the Vatican, but I want to see how people live here."

They exited the bus and strolled up a block to find a restaurant where they could sit outside in shade and study the menu. Bree's gaze zeroed in on the caprese salad.

"What is your specialty?" Lizzie asked the waiter who greeted them.

He smiled and pointed at a dish on the menu, which was described in Italian.

"What else do you recommend?"

He pointed to something else on the menu.

The two looked at each other. "Let's each take one and swap?" Lizzie's smile looked daring.

Bree nodded. "I want caprese salad and this one."

Lizzie pointed to the other and added the same salad.

"*Si*, fine choices. Be right back with bread and antipasto."

As he left, the two grinned at each other. "I think he spoke better English than he let on."

A moment later, an older boy set a basket of crusty bread on the table and poured olive oil into a shallow dish, followed by a puddle of balsamic vinegar in the middle. A small plate of various olives was next.

"By the time I eat all this, I'll be full."

"I know. I will always serve bread this way when I get home." Bree dipped part of her bread slice in the oil and balsamic.

✿   ✿   ✿

"We should have just ordered one and split it." Lizzie crossed her eyes to share her feeling of being overly stuffed as they finished their entrées. "But oh my, so very delicious."

"May I bring you gelato, cheesecake, tiramisu?" The waiter grinned at them. "You liked your order?"

"We most certainly did, but *grazie*, nothing else. Your recommendations were *supremo*."

He returned her smile. "Enjoy the rest of your day."

"Wait, what around here do you recommend we see next?"

"If you like flowers, one block over." He pointed. "Market is very popular."

"Is that church up the street open?"

"Always."

"*Grazie.*" They settled their bags across their shoulders and headed down the block to find an outdoor market with stalls, much like farmers markets at home. The fragrance made them stop to just inhale. Hanging baskets of pink and white fuchsia, geraniums, purple and variegated petunias, combinations of every kind and a profusion of color.

Bree felt as if she'd died and gone to heaven. Such beauty. Buckets of gladiolas, daisies, lilies—she had to bend over to inhale the lilies. Never had she seen such variety. One booth had a lovely young woman braiding daisies and some other blooms into crowns. She set one on a little girl's head and the child blinked and rolled her eyes up to see.

"*Si, Mama.*" The little girl, her dark eyes dancing, touched the flowers. The mother nodded and paid. "*Tu, Mama, anche tu.*" As the two walked off with matching headdresses, Bree had to blink a few times. Like there was a glow around them as they walked hand in hand.

She focused her camera and clicked several times. "I sure hope that turns out." She listened to a conversation as she drooled over the flowers. If only she understood more Italian.

When they reached the other side, they found a bench and sat down, flower fragrances still drifting over their shoulders.

"Give you more ideas what you'd like to do with your yard?"

"Oh my, yes. I go crazy in nurseries at home, but nothing like this. Have you noticed all the flower boxes at the windows, even those high up on a wall? So many geraniums especially. I'd like to be able to talk with people who live here."

"I know. Right now I'm grateful for that breeze too. Let's go do the church next and then I saw a bookstore."

"Right next to the gelato place?"

"Uh-huh."

They mounted the wide concrete steps to the one open door where a black-frocked young man nodded a greeting. "Welcome." He handed them a brochure and motioned them inside. It took some time to adjust to the interior dimness after the brilliance from outside. They paused at the door to the nave and Bree felt like she was inhaling centuries past. Lit candles at the altar, lemon cleaning wax, a mustiness of ages. The stations of the cross lined the walls under and between the stained-glass windows. Bree slid into one of the rear pews so she could look up without getting dizzy. This had been built in the fifteen hundreds and rebuilt from the destruction of the war. Some of the windows had panes of glass that were plain but colored, though obviously not aged.

A woman wearing a black shawl over her head knelt at the altar rail and crossed herself. When she finished, she stood and lit a candle, mopping her eyes as she turned.

Oh, to know her story. I've seen so many stories. Just then a priest joined her and together they sat in one of the pews.

She glanced at Lizzie, who nodded. If only they were closer to eavesdrop.

"Ready?"

Bree nodded. She dug into her bag and brought out some money to drop in the box on their way out. Such a sense of peace and awe cloaked them as they stepped back out in the sunshine. "I felt like I could hear centuries of chanting, tears, a child crying, and yet such silence, reverent silence. Like if I sat there long enough, I might hear God Himself."

"Ah, such a gift of words you have, my friend. I think the age of this place has a lot to do with that. So many thousands of prayers offered up. Incense that floated up to those carved wooden beams so high above."

They stopped at the bookstore, where tourist guides and coffee table books with pictures of Rome took up most of the front. But they had plenty of books in English, others in Italian, and Bree found a section in French. If only she had an idea what Pierre might like. She had no idea what books he even had at home, since she'd not been to his condo yet. What would it be like to be with him touring here?

"You ready for gelato now?" Lizzie asked.

"I can't believe I'm saying this, but yes. And then let's hail a cab."

They returned to the flat to find Rachel passed out asleep and Denise taking pictures of the flat and out of the windows.

"Where were you guys? I was getting worried."

"I found a bookstore." Lizzie sighed. "Good thing I brought an extra suitcase."

"After that, I found a gelato bar. We saw the most incredible flower market and visited a relatively small cathedral, after a superb lunch, so we had a grand time."

Denise nodded. "Good for you. I hope you took pictures but next time you might call."

"We did and left you a message."

Denise checked her phone and shrugged. "Guess you can't always depend on cell phones here."

❖   ❖   ❖

The next morning, the same driver from the airport fiasco arrived to take them to the Vatican.

"*Buongiorno*," he greeted them with a smile. "You are all ready, fine. Good. And you have your tickets? Please, may I see them?" He nodded approval and held the doors of the black SUV, assisting them in and with seat belts before climbing into the driver's seat. Bree sat in the front passenger seat, something she always requested so she wouldn't get carsick.

Their driver pointed out the sights as he drove, a far different man from the one who'd picked them up at the airport. "You have one of the better guides for your Vatican tour," he announced as they drove along a three- or four-story-high wall. "And this is the Roman Catholic Church Vatican." He kept on spewing information.

Bree craned her neck to stare up the stone and cement wall, at the people, looking doll-size next to the wall, lining the sidewalk. She'd seen the Vatican in movies and on television, but now she was seeing the incredibly amazing fortress in real time.

Roger had always wanted to see the Vatican. He had been raised Catholic but turned Lutheran thanks to a young man who understood the difference grace makes and helped Roger see the same. But the Vatican still captured his imagination as Michelangelo's masterpiece did hers. She and Roger had dreamed of a honeymoon in Italy, long ago. They'd started going together their senior year in college and by graduation, knew they would marry. Which they did in June two years later, but the honeymoon money set aside went for the down payment on a house instead. Years passed as she taught in a local high school and he gained experience in hospital management, the dream of seeing the *David* and the Vatican slumbering but not forgotten.

And now at least Bree was here to fulfill it. Maybe Roger knew and was smiling up in heaven. *I hope so, Lord. And Jade too, bless her.*

"Those are all visitors waiting to get in. Because you purchased tickets for a personal tour, you will not have to stand in that long line." He pulled the SUV off to the side of the street and stepped out to assist them. Once they were gathered on the sidewalk, he brought a petite woman over to meet them. "This is Claudia, she will be your guide for your tour of the Vatican. I will meet you back here about three."

Their guide smiled and nodded and said something in Italian, speaking so rapidly Bree caught only a couple of words, *grazie* being one of them.

Claudia smiled and nodded at each of them as they introduced themselves. "*Bene.* Now make sure you have all your things, please check, as we will be going through several lines and you must—you must keep together. Once we are through all the inspections, we will sit so I can prepare you for what all we will see." She looked at each of them and smiled again. "You are ready, *si?*"

She herded them across the street and wove through the crowds, making sure they kept up with her. "*Allora, allora.*" Beckoning them faster, she waved them up to windows, through turnstile gates, and finally to a line of tables with chairs in the shade. "Everyone all right?"

They nodded and with relief sank onto the folding chairs.

She introduced herself by her full name. "Claudia Regio. I grew up in Bologna and was always fascinated by history. I earned my bachelor's at the University of Bologna and got my master's in European history from University College Dublin, then did my doctorate at Cambridge." She shrugged gracefully. "Now I've been a tour guide here at the Vatican for some years. This is the place I can use my knowledge and love of history the most." She laid a coffee-table-size book on the table in front of them and opened the cover. "Now you can have an overall view of what you are going to see." Her smile invited them to join her. "*Si?*"

"*Si.*" They all nodded.

Despite the shade, the sun was heating up their shelter and Bree took out a handkerchief to dab at her forehead.

When Claudia closed the book and finished answering their questions, she announced, "We'll make a rest stop now since we are near one and then begin the tour. Remember no flash is allowed. Photography yes, but flash no. *Si?*" After everyone nodded their understanding, she smiled and led them forward.

Their guide answered all their questions, telling them the history of the sculptures and statuary collected from all over the world. World maps from the 1400s, tapestries restored by scores of needlework experts, restorations that took years. Tapestries that had hung in castles, now safe and guarded from the elements that caused decay. Restoration so future generations could continue to see these treasures as they were right now. History made visual. Beside every piece hung a plaque listing the supporters who paid for the restoration, many of which were organizations in the United States. A feeling of pride in her country made Bree nod and file the thought away.

Tour guides with large groups took up most of the wide passages speaking an array of languages: German, French, Italian, Spanish—at least she somewhat recognized those—and perhaps Russian, Polish. Some folks had audio guide earphones pressed to their ears, children, obviously bored, tagging along.

When they filed into the Sistine Chapel, Bree stood in awe at the people studying all the paintings and then the ceiling, before looking up to the ceiling herself.

Claudia tapped her shoulder. "Come, there's a place to sit." Bree followed where her guide beckoned and sat down, feeling relief and joy that now she could look up, really look up without cricking her neck. To think all that expanse had been designed, drawn, and painted by one man, lying on scaffolding for those many years till he finished it. As her attention moved from section to section, tears welled and overflowed. She sniffed and mopped, losing track of time and space. The murmurs of those present faded away as she saw the Bible laid out in paintings. On an arched ceiling. The colors, the richness, the Word for the world to see.

A tap on her arm jerked her back. "Come, the others are waiting."

Bree nodded. "Thank you, I totally lost track of time." They made their way out the exit door, following the constantly moving crowd. "Thank you for waiting," she said to her friends.

"Are you all right?" Lizzie asked her.

Bree nodded. At least she had finally quit crying. Using back stairs they moved to another section and finally out through the sea of chairs in front of the papal balcony from which the pope spoke to the people. Since he was not in residence this day, he would not be offering mass for those who gathered. Claudia waited at the far side and gathered them up to return to the SUV by the appointed time.

"Thank you, *grazie*, this has been my pleasure to share with you at least a portion of this housing of world history."

"All this and we only saw a small part of the Vatican?" Denise questioned.

"That's right. And there are crowds like this all the time, from all over the world. That map that you have identifies other parts of this amazing place."

After they took pictures of and with her, she led them back out to the street where people were still waiting patiently in line for entrance. Their driver and the SUV waited at a curb on a nearby side street.

"*Grazie molto* to you all." Claudia smiled up at their driver. "I think they are nearly worn out, well, we all are. Where will you take them for supper?"

"Ah, can we find a gelato bar first?" Lizzie asked.

"Ah, *si, si.*" He smiled wide, nodding. "I will take you to the best gelato in Rome." He tipped his hat to Claudia. "*Arrivederci.*"

They waved goodbye to their guide and stared at one another. "I am so glad and so grateful we did this." Bree puffed out a breath. "What an incredible adventure. The only thing I regret..."

"Regret, what could you regret?" Denise stared at her in shock.

"We didn't have any time to sit and people-watch. You have to admit, there were plenty of fascinating people in those crowds. I mean, think of the stories..."

    ❖   ❖   ❖

That night after gelato, seeing more of Rome, having a marvelous dinner at a restaurant owned by a relative of their driver, and staggering up to their flat, Breeanna closed herself in her room and punched in Pierre's cell number.

"What time is it there?" she asked after the greeting.

"Almost noon. About nine hours behind you. What did you think of the Vatican?"

"It is beyond words."

His chuckle warmed her ear. "The second time I toured it, I was even more in awe."

Bree nestled into her pillows. "I'll have pictures of all we've seen and our flat when I get home."

"That was brave to go with the flat rather than a hotel."

She told him a bit about their frustrating time at the airport. "Made me wish I knew the language well, would have made that easier."

"Ah, yes. Are you in Rome one more day?"

"Yes, one more day in Rome. Then Denise is picking

up our car the following morning and we're driving to Tuscany."

"She's driving?"

"*Si*, she's been here several times."

"You better get to sleep."

"How do you know?"

"Your voice is telling me?"

"And you must need your lunch. Hard to believe we are really on opposite sides of the world and we can still talk on cell phones. I think the thing that amazes me the most here is everything is so old, ancient. And I am here."

His chuckle made her smile. "*Buonanotte, amica mia.*"

"*Buonanotte.*" She had to think, *What else had he said? Ah, "my friend."* But they had clicked off by then.

Her cell phone lying on her chest, Bree stared at the painting hanging on the wall at the foot of her bed. All they had seen in this one day. What adventures lay ahead of them?

Chapter Thirteen

"That ought to do it." Pierre-René gave a final turn with the wrench on Paula's kitchen sink faucet.

"Thank you so much." She shook her head. "I'm realizing how helpless I am with fixing things. Peter—he could do everything, it seemed." Her voice trailed off, wistful.

"Well, I'd never aspire to that. But thankfully a leaky faucet is within my realm of possibility." He smiled at his sister-in-law and washed his hands, then turned off the water and waited a moment to be sure. No drips.

"Thanks for bringing dinner too. You don't know how lovely takeout sounds when I've been forcing myself to cook for one all week. As does the prospect of someone to actually eat with, now that Erin isn't here."

"Actually, I do." The loneliness of widowhood—or widowerhood—gentled with time. But it never got easy.

The corner of Paula's mouth tipped sadly. "Of course, you do. I'm sorry." She stepped to the kitchen table and peeked inside a foam food box. "Greek food, yum."

"I got some gyros, kebabs, several different sides. An assortment since I wasn't sure what you'd like."

"It all smells wonderful. Let's eat."

Over savory chunks of chicken and lamb with rice and

tabouli, they chatted, the camaraderie they'd had since Pierre and Lynn married still easy between them.

"So." Paula dipped her pita in the fresh-made hummus. "What do you hear from Bree?"

"Not a great deal—they're keeping pretty busy. But she texts me once in a while, and has called me too."

"Really?" Paula's eyes bored in. "That's some pretty steady communication for being gone less than a week."

"I suppose." Pierre-René shifted in the kitchen chair. Were his ears reddening? He hoped not. He wasn't used to having his love life—if one could call it that—as the focus of conversation. He changed tactics. "Anything else I can help you with this evening?"

Paula paused and sighed. "I was wondering if you'd look through Peter's closet with me." Sadness shadowed her blue eyes again, and he almost wished he hadn't changed the subject. "I shouldn't just leave his clothes in the closet forever, but I haven't known quite what to do with them. I hate to just send all his things to a thrift store, you know?" She shrugged. "I wondered if there might be any items you'd like...I know you and Peter weren't exactly the same size, but not too far off, either."

"I'd be honored to take a look." Peter had been a bit taller and lankier than he. But hopefully there would be something, if only as a comfort to Paula.

After finishing dinner, they headed upstairs to Peter and Paula's bedroom.

She paused in the doorway and drew a breath. "It's still hard coming in here. Sometimes I still see him, lying there on the rug by the bed...it happened so fast. S-some nights, I chicken out and sleep in the guest room. Other times, it's not so bad." Another shrug that reeked of sorrow. A sigh. "Having Erin here helped."

Pierre wanted to wrap his arms around her but squeezed

her shoulder, wordless. Such was grief. And he didn't have anything to make it better, not that anyone did, save just being there.

"Well." Paula sniffed hard. "Let's do this."

They turned on all the lights and spread Peter's wardrobe over the queen-size bed and a couple of chairs. Dress shirts, polo shirts, slacks, ties, jackets. A good suit or two.

The more tailored items wouldn't fit Pierre-René's broader shoulders, but a couple of the casual jackets did, and a V-neck charcoal wool sweater. He took several ties and shirts too. Peter had good taste, conservative but nice quality.

"I'm so glad. It will help knowing these items are with you. Do you think Jason would want anything? He's built a bit slighter than you are. Or—what is his partner's name?"

"Todd. I can ask. We had a good time together the other night. Having dinner again next week." Paula and Peter knew all the ups and downs of his family over the years, more than most.

Paula's eyes warmed. "I'm so glad."

She and Pierre headed back downstairs a short while later, arms laden with the clothing he was taking. "Well, that's a weight off me, to have tackled that closet." She nodded. "Thank you."

"You are most welcome."

"Hang on, that's my phone." She handed him the hangers of the clothes she was carrying and hurried away into the kitchen.

Left in the entryway, Pierre-René stacked the clothes neatly over his arm. He'd head home now, have time to find space for these and shower before calling Bree. He liked talking to her as the last item of the day, when he was in pajamas and comfortable in his room. And with the time difference, late night here was early morning in Italy, usually a good time for her too.

Snippets of Paula's phone conversation reached him from the kitchen.

"Oh, honey—it's that bad?...No, I think it's too late...let me ask Pierre, hang on a minute."

Paula appeared in the doorway, holding her cell phone against her shoulder, her face a mingle of apology and concern. "It's Jessica, Bree's daughter. She's staying at Bree's house, you know, and she's got a terribly stopped-up toilet. It's too late to call a plumber, and I know you are just about to head home...but do you think—?"

Pierre was already nodding. "Let's go."

❖   ❖   ❖

Utter mortification. That's what Pierre-René read in Jessica Lindstrom's face when she opened the door.

"I'm so sorry to bother you guys." She stepped back into the entryway to let them in, twisting the end of the blond braid that hung over her shoulder. She wore pajamas, mostly hidden beneath a pink fleece robe, making Pierre picture what she must have looked like as a little girl.

"This seems to be my day on call as a plumber. I already battled Paula's faucet, victoriously, I might add." Pierre-René smiled, trying to put the young woman at ease. "Where is this culprit?"

Jessica turned and led the way to the smaller bathroom. She stepped to the side of the toilet, gripping her elbows.

"Aha." Pierre peered at the brimming water in the toilet bowl. "Looks like a problem, all right."

"I've already tried the plunger a bunch of times."

"Any idea what stopped it up?"

Silence.

He glanced up. Jessica twisted the tie of her robe and bit her lip, her cheeks scarlet.

Pierre glanced at Paula. Did she have any clue what was going on here? She shrugged and lifted her hands at her sides.

"It's, um…" Jessica's face crumpled as she snatched a cardboard box from the counter and thrust it at Paula, then fled from the bathroom.

What on earth? Pierre sat back on his heels. Despite having been married twenty years and having two daughters, sometimes he felt there was no way to understand the female sect of the human species.

"Oh." Paula looked up at him, understanding dawning. "It must be a tampon that's stuck in there."

Pierre bit the inside of his cheek, fighting a sudden urge to laugh. He bent back over the toilet. "Well. I suppose that explains…a lot."

"Bless her heart. I'll talk to her. Do you need anything to get started?"

"Some rags, please. This could get messy. You know where they are?"

"I do." Paula disappeared down the hall.

Pierre-René turned back to the errant toilet. A mercy Paula knew the house—and Jessica—so well. Rubber gloves would also be good, but he'd make do. First thing was to check the drainage. He removed the tank lid and lifted the flapper valve slightly to let a little water into the bowl.

The water immediately rose even farther, threatening to overflow. He dropped the flapper valve back into place. All right, then. Completely blocked.

Paula appeared in the doorway with an armload of rags that she set on the bathroom floor. "Here you go. Holler if you need help, but I'll be back." She disappeared again.

Pierre spread the rags on the tile floor, girding the toilet on all sides, then gripped the plunger. *Okay, Lord. You've got a sense of humor letting me be the one here tonight. Help me get this cleared.*

He started plunging. Jessica had already done it, but he'd have more strength—and the experience of many a clogged toilet during his family's growing-up years.

While he tried not to intentionally eavesdrop, he could overhear the women's voices from the adjoining guest room.

"It's just been an awful day." Sounded like Jessica was in tears. "My boyfriend, Ryan...he says we need to take a step back, that we're going too fast. And maybe he's right, and he says he's not going away, but I just can't help being afraid it's the beginning of the end. I thought he would be different from all the other guys, but now it feels like déjà vu all over again. And then this stupid thing with the toilet..."

More tears. Murmured comfort from Paula that he couldn't quite make out.

Poor girl. And given her history with Pierre the past few weeks, having him as the knight in shining armor must be a genuine nightmare. Pierre allowed himself a rueful smile and tried flushing the toilet—then jumped back as the toilet well and truly overflowed.

"Need a hand?" Paula was at the door again.

"Not sure what you could do. More rags, maybe?" Pierre grabbed a still-dry one to wipe at his shoes. Great.

"Be back." His sister-in-law hurried away.

Pierre-René pushed the rags around the base of the toilet, soaking up the worst of the overflow. He tamped down rising frustration and refused to think how late it was getting or about his meeting with Ben to go over business stuff in the morning. If he ever was going to build a bridge with Jessica, he needed to persevere through this now.

Fortified with more rags, Pierre resumed plunging again.

He'd never given up on a battle with a plugged toilet before and didn't intend to start now.

But dozens of plunges, two more flush attempts, and one more slight overflow later, he was beginning to think there was a first time for everything.

Jessica appeared in the bathroom doorway, tearstained but relatively calm. "It's really nice of you but please don't put yourself through this anymore. I'll call a plumber in the morning."

"Let me try a little longer. I thought I heard something promising on the last plunge." Though it might have been wishful thinking.

"No, it's not worth it." Jessica leaned against the doorjamb, twisting her braid again. "I've been researching online, and plunging doesn't usually work when the clog is caused by…this." Her voice dropped off at the end. "It said you have to use a plumber's snake to try and get hold of it and pull it out."

Pierre rubbed an itch on his forehead with a still-clean part of his wrist. "I actually have a snake at my condo." He hated to think of making the twenty-five-minute-each-way drive to Gresham and back tonight, but if that's what it took…

"Peter had a plumber's snake." Paula, who had been in the kitchen, popped in again beside Jessica. "Let me run over and get it. I saw it in the garage the other day."

"Please, I don't think it's worth it." Jessica shook her head. "Apparently sometimes even that doesn't work, and you have to take the whole toilet off and reach into the pipes…I'll just get a plumber tomorrow."

"Get the snake." Pierre-René nodded to Paula. "We'll try that, and if that doesn't work, I promise I'll give up." He hesitated. "If that's all right with you, Jessica." He waited till she met his eyes.

Jessica gave a tiny shrug and nod, and Paula headed off, more energized than he'd seen her since the funeral. Well, if a clogged toilet was what it took...he wasn't complaining.

Pierre leaned against the counter to catch his breath while they waited. Plunging could be surprisingly good exercise. At least when one did it for, what had it been? An hour or two at a time?

"It's really nice of you to do this," Jessica said again. He was faintly surprised that she stayed, with Paula gone. "You didn't have to."

"I know. And Jessica, you're not the first one this has happened to. One of my daughters clogged our toilet once with not a tampon, but a whole pad."

Jessica made a slight choking sound. "She flushed a pad?"

"In her defense, she was only fourteen. Still new to the whole...periods thing."

Jessica's ears flushed, no doubt from hearing that word fall from his lips. But she met his eyes again. "I didn't know you had daughters."

"Two of them. Both married with children of their own now, though they don't live close. But I'm blessed to have a son nearby, in Portland."

"How many grandchildren do you have?" Jessica hugged her robe tighter around herself. The temperature in the house had dropped, though after Pierre's toilet-battling exercise, it felt good to him.

"Four. Aged eight months to six years."

"That's nice. My mom just has one so far, Luke. He's a cutie. He'll be a big brother in a month, maybe less." She hesitated. "But you probably already know that."

"Your mom has mentioned it, yes." Should he say more about his and Bree's relationship? But what was there to say? Probably best not to risk this fragile truce that seemed to be forming.

"Here you are. Reinforcements." Paula held out the plumber's snake, slightly out of breath from the walk three doors down and back.

"Bless you. And now, sir," Pierre-René addressed the toilet sternly, preparing the snake, "I'd advise you to surrender peacefully, before you regret it."

A faint snort and giggle from Jessica. Probably nerves more than anything, but the sound warmed Pierre's chest.

He hadn't used a snake in several years, but the process came back to him. Before long he felt a promising resistance. He cranked the handle a couple of times to try to work the head into the tampon, then slowly, painstakingly began to pull the snake back out. He was almost holding his breath as the end emerged from the toilet's depths—with the soggy culprit attached.

Paula and Jessica, leaning in close to watch by this point, broke out into spontaneous cheers.

"Pierre-René, you're a hero." Paula hugged Jessica.

"I'll agree with that." Bree's daughter was smiling now, only traces of embarrassment left on her face.

Pierre pressed the toilet handle, the resounding flush music to his ears. "*C'est parfait.*" He could feel the grin stretching his cheeks. Hadn't felt this victorious since advancing in rank back in the air force.

"I'll clean up in here," Jessica said as he washed his hands. "And can I make you both some tea before you go?"

Half an hour and a cup of chai later, Pierre-René bid the ladies good night and headed home. He checked his car clock as he started the ignition—after eleven, good grief. Weariness weighted his shoulders as he drove, but it was a good fatigue. Not an expected turn for the evening...at least, not for him. But maybe it had been exactly what the Lord had in mind. He chuckled as the sparsely lighted freeway passed by his windows. He never would have thought a clogged toilet could be the means of reaching Jessica. *Father, you never cease to amaze me.*

Not that he would assume the road would now be smooth. But they had made a start. How else might he reach out to Bree's daughter? Something about her tugged at him, with a tenderness he usually knew only with his own children.

Pierre turned into his condo parking lot, got out of the car, and headed inside. He dropped his keys into the caddy on his dresser and shucked his clothes, putting them all into the laundry hamper, given his activities this evening.

After a quick hot shower, he thought about calling Bree, but it would already be past 9:00 a.m. there—she would probably have headed out for their activities of the day.

He'd call her in the morning. Pierre fell into bed and slept dreamlessly.

He nearly slept past his meeting with Ben in the morning, but made their eight o'clock just in time. Afterward, he got into the car and checked the time on his phone. Seven p.m. there—hopefully she would be back from the day. He should wait longer but... he didn't want to.

Still sitting in his parking space, he tapped in her number.

"*Buonasera.*" Bree's voice smiled into his ear.

"You sound happy today. Or rather, tonight for you." Pierre leaned his head against the car headrest, a smile spreading across his face. How did she do that with only a greeting?

"It's been a lovely day, and we're heading to Tuscany tomorrow morning. Well, Perugia actually, on the Tuscan border. We'll be staying at a private house where a lady teaches Italian cooking. But enough about me, how are you?"

"I'm well. I had an interesting evening with your daughter."

"With Jessica?" Her voice lifted an octave.

"We had an eventful battle with a clogged toilet." He told her the condensed version.

"Oh, my word, I'm so sorry you had to get involved in that. But you're an angel."

"Certainly not. But if Jessica has taken the first steps toward forgiving me, I consider the evening well worth it."

"Forgiving you for what, for Pete's sake?"

"For being...quite taken with her mother." Pierre-René swallowed. He hadn't meant to say that, not now. The whole topsy-turvy night seemed to have loosened his tongue.

"I see." Bree fell silent. Or was it just the bad foreign connection? No doubt she didn't know what to say either.

Did Bree have any clue how deeply he felt about her? After all, he hadn't even kissed her, despite seeing each other so much these past few months. And now here she was on the other side of the world, hardly the time for defining their relationship.

Pierre cleared his throat. "I'd like to connect with Jessica more, if she'll let me." He thought of mentioning what he'd overheard about Ryan but figured that was Jessica's to tell. "I've been thinking, I know some people at the local community college. Has Jessica ever considered going back to school, taking classes there?"

"I've suggested it, and so has James. She just gets so overwhelmed...so hopeless, somehow, to make real changes. I don't know why." Bree sighed. "But I'd love to see her actually pursue a career she'd enjoy, one that would have more promise for the future than being a waitress or cashier."

"What are her gifts, her bent?"

"Well, she's always been good at art. In college, she was interested in graphic design, something like that. But she hasn't done anything of that sort for years."

Graphic design. An idea clicked in Pierre-René's mind, but he wouldn't bring it up yet. Needed more pondering, and some research. "Well, I should let you go. But it's all right with you—if I reach out to Jessica?"

"If she'll let you." Bree sighed again, the sound harsh with static. "She can be stubborn, I'll give you fair warning."

"She's a special young woman, Bree. I saw that tonight. Struggling right now, yes. But there's a strength there too. I want to help her."

"Thank you." Bree's voice caught, and not just from the connection. "That means so much. She's…she really has struggled, Pierre."

"Well, I know something of struggling." He pinched the bridge of his nose. "Between Lynn's issues and my PTSD…" His mind stuttered to a halt. Had he just said that?

"Your what?"

Pierre-René stared at the windshield, his breath coming fast. He hadn't meant to say that. Not at all. His mind blanked, heart picking up speed.

"Pierre-René?"

"Sorry." His voice croaked. "I've got to go." He ended the call, then dropped the phone on his car console.

What had he just done?

Chapter Fourteen

He hung up on me.

The thought pounded through her mind like boots marching as Bree hauled herself out of bed on their final morning in Rome. Her sleep had been fitful at best. Why in the world was she letting this bother her so? So what if he hung up. Really that was no big deal.

She dressed and tucked her morning things into her suitcase, glancing at her watch. An hour until their ride back to the airport to pick up their rental car for the drive north. After applying her makeup—she needed extra to cover the ravages of missing sleep—she packed the case and her hairspray and zipped the case closed. Immediately her mind skipped back to her question. What made Pierre hang up on her?

Perhaps they had just been cut off. That happened often with cell phones. Of course that was it. But surely he would have called back or texted.

Wheeling her suitcase to the entryway, she joined the others in the kitchen.

Lizzie stared at her. "What's wrong, Bree?"

"Oh, nothing. My overactive imagination needs to be corralled, that's all."

The look Lizzie sent her shouted, *I don't believe you for a minute.* "How about I fix your coffee? That should help."

She rose from the table and turned to the kitchen before Bree could answer.

"Ah..."

"Here, have the last banana." Rachel handed her the fruit. "There's one more yogurt too. I'll get it."

"For Pete's sake, do I look like I'm dying or something?"

"Not quite." Denise handed her the creamer. "We have some biscuits left. How about cleaning those up too? The rest of us are all packed, and we'll get the baggage down as soon as we finish eating. By the way, everyone, we need to leave a tip here." She held up an envelope. "Just put it in here?"

Lizzie pulled out her wallet. "How much is appropriate?"

Amazing how caffeine could lift one's spirits. Bree dipped the biscuits—the British term for cookies—in her yogurt, alternating with the banana too.

"I'll do a run-through to make sure none of us left anything." Denise laid the now-completed envelope in the middle of the table and pushed herself to her feet. "No idea why I'm stiff this morning but..." She puffed out a breath.

"Couldn't be all the walking we did yesterday?" Rachel teased her mother, earning herself a mother's rolled-eye look. Giggling, she left to move suitcases to the elevator.

By the time they were all loaded into the taxi, with a driver disgruntled about their luggage, so they held their carry-ons on their laps, Bree could tell that Denise was not happy. She was the one who had dealt with the driver and rolled her eyes at Bree when she looked over her shoulder.

He drove fast, even for Italy.

When they arrived near the car rental place at the airport, he almost threw their luggage on the sidewalk, snatched the tip from Bree's hand, and did not bother with a farewell of any kind. The women looked at one another and shook their heads.

"Come on, Rachel, let's go get the car." Denise sucked in a deep breath, and together they headed up the street.

Lizzie and Bree moved all the luggage into one space and looked around for some shade. "Back there by that building is the closest." Lizzie nodded toward the shadows.

"They should be here any minute. We won't melt."

"Are you sure?" Lizzie asked, twenty minutes later. She lifted her hat to mop her forehead.

Bree dug the paper fan that Denise had suggested she bring from her bag and fanned her face, then handed it to Lizzie. "If we stand closer together we can share." She punched in number three for speed dial to Denise. The phone rang and clicked over to messages. "What's happening?" She clicked off.

Patience is a virtue. Her mother's voice didn't need a cell phone. Bree never had liked that platitude. Nor another favorite, *Money doesn't grow on trees, you know.*

Her mother had passed away four years ago now, but Bree could hear her voice plain as the sun doing its best to melt them.

"We should have followed your suggestion, sorry."

"Oh, well. I should have brought a water bottle too but...hindsight is always twenty-twenty."

"Thanks. My mother used to say that one too." She saw a black SUV turn a corner onto their street. "They're finally here."

"About time."

"Sorry about that," Denise said as she stepped out. "The vehicle they tried to give us was a Mini, not a full-size SUV so we had to wait until they finished cleaning this one. In case you've not noticed it yet, Italian time is different from our time." Her tone said she was less than happy too.

They reloaded three times to fit the luggage all in and closed the hatchback before finally hearing the click. Lizzie and Rachel climbed in on either side of a suitcase on its side like a dividing wall.

"Okay back there?" Denise asked as she pulled out into the street, the GPS provided by the rental agency on the dashboard. She had already tapped in their destination.

"Mom, can we stop and buy more water?" Rachel asked.

"Can you wait until we get up the road a ways?"

"Of course," Lizzie answered.

Bree looked over her shoulder and mouthed, *Thank you*, which earned grins from both Rachel and Lizzie.

"You better drive carefully, Mom. If you have to hit the brakes, we'll be dead meat back here."

"Thank you, Rachel." Her tone was just slightly sarcastic.

Bree chuckled inside. She'd already figured out on this trip that driving in Italy lived up to all the rumors she'd heard. None of the drivers were careful—they were more like Indy race car drivers only on streets and expressways rather than a racetrack. A service van, at least that's what she thought the signage meant, cut so close in front of them, Bree figured he took the front bumper with him.

Denise muttered something better not said aloud and increased their speed. "Got to keep up with the traffic."

By the time they stopped, Bree's hands were cramping from being clenched. She stepped down, grateful to be on terra firma. They located the restrooms, bought drinks and snacks, not sure what they were but figured anything chocolate or crunchy ought to be good, and climbed back in the SUV.

Sometime later, following the instructions on the GPS, they exited the expressway to a two-lane road. Bree sucked in a breath of relief as they drove the lay of the land. Up hills to see a town capping another hill in the distance, around a curve to ancient grapevines with sun-glinting hints of the harvest to come, farmhouses protecting flocks of scratching hens and hounds asleep under the porch. Lakes in the distance and shores of lakes sparkling in the sunlight. Cattle and horses grazing and flocks of sheep lying in the shade of trees, chewing their cuds.

"Mom, I'm starving." Rachel sounded like a kid again. "There's a town right on the lake up ahead. Maybe we can eat there."

"Everybody want to stop?" Denise checked the time on the dashboard clock. "After three, no wonder we're hungry." Denise followed the instructions on a road sign and they slowed to the ordered speed. All of them watched for restaurants.

"That one up on the left looks good," Bree offered.

"It's closed." Denise frowned. Two more had been closed also. "Is it some kind of holiday—oh no!" She slammed her palm on the steering wheel. "That's right. Siesta time and everything closes up."

Bree stared at her. "You mean that really does happen? Not just in books?"

"No, it's real. Wait, one up there looks open, there are cars in the parking lot at least." She swung into the parking lot.

"Mom, they charge for the parking here."

"Are you sure? Oh great, there's the meter machine. Anyone have any change?"

Rachel was out and checking while the others gathered purses and stretched muscles weary of sitting. "They only take credit cards," she reported.

Denise stalked over to the machine and inserted her card. And waited for the machine to do something. And waited. When nothing happened, she pulled at her card to try again. "The card's stuck." She pinched the edge of her credit card between thumb and finger and tried again. Nothing. "So now what?"

"We could ask inside the restaurant, they at least have

their doors open." Lizzie pointed across the crushed gravel
area.

The four crossed the lot and climbed the three wooden
steps to the screened door. Delicious smells of garlic, fish,
and tomatoes invited them to enter.

The woman behind the desk looked up from her paperwork and smiled. "Ah, welcome, welcome, four of you,
good, good, right this way." She scooped up four menus as
she passed and showed them to a window booth that overlooked the sparkling lake. "Please be seated." She nodded
to the side. "The restroom is back there. Room for one
at a time."

"*Grazie*, you read my mind." Bree kept on walking down
a short hall to the door decorated with an outline of a
woman. She'd been warned to be careful of unsanitary restrooms but hadn't time for an inspection. The woman was
still at their table when she returned and Lizzie left.

"Ah now, what would you like to drink?"

"Iced tea, if you have any?"

"Not wine?"

Bree tried to answer in Italian but all the words she'd
learned fled from her brain. "No, thank you." She slid into the
bench seat and looked at the others. "You having wine?"

Denise shook her head. "Not while driving."

"I'll be right back. The specials of the day are on the
menu."

"Did you ask her about your credit card?"

"She apologized and said I'd have to call my bank. The
maintenance man was out of town till tomorrow. My card
will be destroyed."

"But..."

Denise raised both hands, palms out. "I know, but there
is nothing I can do other than report it." Thunder sat on her
forehead.

"So you'll be without a credit card?"

"How can they send you a replacement?"

The questions overlapped. "I'll give them our address in Florence, have it delivered." Denise blew out a breath and settled her shoulders. "Now we order our lunch." She snatched up a menu and, jaw tight, studied it.

Reading the menu in Italian took focus. Pierre had worked with her on word recognition for this. *Come on, memory, wake up and get busy.* "What are the rest of you having?" One item caught her attention. Caprese salad.

"Do you have buffalo cheese for this?" she asked when their server returned.

"Ah, no, sorry."

"I'll order that anyway, and I want fish of some kind."

The woman pointed to one on the menu. "Caught right out there this morning." She pointed to the azure blue water with white bits of frosting. "My husband is our fisherman so we never know from day to day what we'll have on the special. Everything else comes from our supplier but all still fresh."

The others put in their orders and they settled back to sip their beverages.

"You suppose their water is safe to drink?" Lizzie asked.

"No problem, we're in Italy, not South America. Not to disparage other countries, of course." Denise tipped her head from side to side. "I was so looking forward to doing the driving leg of our tour but right now..."

"I don't know how we didn't see ten accidents on that expressway. My word, they drive like speed racers here." Bree glanced at her watch. Surely it didn't take more than fifteen minutes to make their salads? Thirty minutes. They were running out of small talk. Her stomach grumbled a complaint.

"Is she the chef too?"

"Got me." Denise pushed against her raised fingers on the table to stretch her hands. She looked around. "At least we're the only ones here."

"Yeah, everyone else is enjoying their siesta." Rachel dug out her phone, and her thumb danced on the keyboard.

The waitress brought their salads on a big tray she carried with one hand and set a basket of bread in the middle of the table, then set each of their plates down. "The oil comes from our own olive trees and the balsamic is local. Good for dipping your breadsticks or the crusty bread. Had to wait for it to come out of the oven."

"Still hot. Worth waiting for." Lizzie retrieved a slice of bread and dipped it in the low bowl of oil with red-brown balsamic vinegar puddled in the middle. She closed her eyes in delight after the first bite. "I think this was worth the trip."

"Forget the rest of the food, just bring on more bread." Rachel broke her breadstick in half and dipped.

Lizzie purchased a bottle of their olive oil on their way out. "I've never had bread or breadsticks like that. And that grilled fish. What did she call it again?"

"Got me," Bree answered. "I kept wanting to ask her to slow down when she talked, so I could keep up." They climbed back in the SUV with Denise glaring at the card machine. "Any idea how long before we get to where we're going?"

"Supposed to be two hours. Doesn't look too complicated."

❖   ❖   ❖

"You think we can come back here and go inside some of these places?" Rachel asked after about the third "sorry, can't stop now," from her mother.

"We'll find plenty of little towns like these in the next

couple of days. I promise we'll stop and go exploring after we do our cooking lesson."

Bree tried reading the signs along the road, wishing she'd learned more Italian. That drew her mind back to Pierre and the teaching sessions. He was such a good teacher. *If only I could have learned more! I promised myself I'd get language lessons earlier. Why did I hesitate so long?*

And why did he hang up on me last night?

What would traveling with Pierre-René Dubois be like?

Now, where had such a crazy thought come from? She pulled her water bottle out of her bag and drank several glugs. Focusing on the passing scenery, she realized dusk was sneaking over the hills and settling in the valleys.

"We should be pretty close to Raffaela's now, shouldn't we?"

"Yes, by the clock, but I've been watching the GPS and it seems to be sending us in circles or at least not where we should be. Read me the instructions again." Denise paused. "Please." She handed several typed pages to Bree.

Bree scanned the list, trying to figure where they were. "If we're on that road..." She held up the instructions.

"We are. And we've passed the last town before the area Raffaela lives in."

"Then we turn left on supposedly the next road."

"Okay, watch for a gas station on the right." Denise raised her voice so they all heard her. Lights were coming on in some of the houses they passed, and the lights on businesses were being shut off.

"Okay, there's a gas station up ahead and a road off to the left." Bree pointed. "We're almost there."

Denise slowed down and made the turn. "Are you sure this is the right road?"

Bree looked for signs but saw nothing. The road passed

so close to a house on the right that she thought they were driving in the yard.

"This can't be right. None of the numbers fit. I think we better turn around and try again. We must have missed a turn." They turned around in the next driveway. By now dark had overtaken dusk and they couldn't see anything beyond their headlights. They finally stopped in an open area, half shrouded by a huge old tree. The headlights had shown them that.

"Do we have a phone number for her?" Lizzie asked.

"We do." Denise took back the papers, found the number, and inputted it. And waited. "Nothing, maybe I dialed wrong." Shaking her head, she slapped her hand against the steering wheel. "No service."

"You think that would mess up the GPS too?" Rachel leaned on the front seat and patted her mother's shoulder.

"I don't know." Denise stared out the windshield. "Can you believe how dark it is out here?" She had shut off the headlights but left the interior lights on.

Quiet in the car but night singing outside. *Sounds like frogs and insects*, Bree thought, enjoying the little breeze coming in the open window. *But we certainly can't spend the night here. Lord, what are we going to do?* She humphed to herself. Four American women lost in the Tuscan countryside.

Car lights were coming down the road in front of them. *Should we blink the lights and ask for help?* The thought blew away when the vehicle slowed and turned into the clearing where they sat.

Leaving his lights on, a man got out of his car and walked slowly toward them. He seemed to be asking a question, but his Italian came too fast for Bree to catch any of the words. At least he was smiling, his voice friendly.

"Do you speak English?" Denise asked hopefully.

He said something else in Italian, tipped his head, and half shrugged. Apparently not.

Bree leaned over Denise to show him the map. What was the word for "where" again? "*Dove?*" she asked, pointing to where they were trying to go.

His smile broadened. "*Si*," he said. Then something else; she caught "*Perugia*" this time. He made a number of gestures, then headed back toward his car, beckoning.

"I think he wants us to follow him." Denise looked at each of them.

"He seems really nice. What are our choices?" Bree offered, though her middle tightened. *Lord, is this of you?*

The man pulled back on the road and waited for them, then drove on. Within minutes they were back at the same gas station. Both cars stopped and he came to talk to them again.

"*Grazie. Molte grazie.* We've been here before." How Bree wished she knew more Italian.

He pointed across the street to another road, then made a shape in the air like a sign.

"I think he means follow that road till we see a sign."

"Maybe Raffaela's sign for the cooking class?" Lizzie piped up.

"Hopefully. Looks like we just didn't go far enough."

"Looks that way." Denise lifted her hand at the man. "*Grazie.*"

"*Prego, prego. Ciao.*" The man waved and drove off.

The four looked at one another. Lizzie half shrugged, a giggle starting, and shook her head. Bree rolled her lips together, trying to stop her response.

Denise heaved a sigh and, shaking her head, rolled up the windows again and drove out of the station. They crossed the street and turned down the road now visible only in the headlights.

It felt like ten miles up hills, down hills, around curves

until they finally found the Y with a sign to the right. Not far beyond that a white sign with black lettering announced COOKING CLASS.

Bree heaved a sigh of relief. "I think that man was an angel God sent to bail us out of trouble."

"I won't argue with that." Denise turned into the driveway and parked between a house with blooming flowers on trellises and a block wall with more trailing plants.

A dark-haired woman with a ready smile came out to greet them. "*Buonasera*, I am so glad you made it." While she had an accent, they could understand her.

"Sorry we're so late," Denise answered. "My cell phone didn't even work wherever we were. Some nice man guided us."

She nodded. "That happens here. Come, I will show you to your rooms."

Bree drew a breath of gratitude, hoping the beds were comfortable. Not that anything wouldn't be better than the car seats. She stretched her legs once out of the car. That knee she'd injured those months ago still managed to stiffen and cramp up.

Chapter Fifteen

The next morning, bed felt so good Bree hated to move.

Finally finding this place last night was cause for exuberant rejoicing. She'd fallen asleep thanking God for sending the angel, dressed in man form and driving a car, to rescue them. Even without speaking the same language. Light pollution wasn't a problem in at least parts of Italy, Perugia specifically. Surely there must have been stars, but...

She heard Lizzie in the bathroom, the door opening, and Lizzie's grin evoked a return one.

"What a day we had." Bree yawned.

"Now, that's an understatement if I've ever heard one. You better get moving. I'll fix the coffee right now and you might have to fight me for more of that cake, bread, whatever Raffaela baked for us." She did the two-fingers-to-the-lips signal for "superb."

Bree threw back the covers and stood to stretch. Grabbing the clothes she had laid out, she took the six steps to the bathroom and closed the door. No time for a shower this morning, so she washed, amazed at the instant hot water coming from a hot-water heater, unlike anything she had ever seen. A nine-inch-cake-pan-size unit on the wall, no holding tank, an invention that should have made it to the USA by now. But it was not something she'd ever seen advertised or in an appliance store.

"You better not eat all of that cake." She didn't have to raise her voice much—this entire apartment might fit in her living room at home. No wonder this two-story building did not have to be very big to house six separate units. And the way the building fit into the side of the hill. She was looking forward to seeing the place in daylight.

After fixing her bed she joined Lizzie, who was standing on the little balcony off the living room, sipping coffee while she admired the scene spread out before her. "So this is their place?"

"Guess so. Look at that garden, fruit trees, olive too, and I love the rows of grapevines. So green and peaceful. See the chickens scratching wherever they please. I love this."

A knock at the door turned Bree around to answer it. "*Buongiorno.*"

Their hostess smiled back at her, nodding. "*Buongiorno, amica mia.* Class will start in fifteen minutes, through that door right there." She pointed to the house behind her. "Don't bother knocking. Did you sleep well?"

Bree nodded. "*Si. Bene. Grazie.* We'll be there." She was already wishing they were staying longer than two nights.

She left the door open since there was a screen door too and fixed herself a plate of cake bread, cheese, rusks—similar to what she'd fed her babies—and an orange. With a cup of coffee, she took one of the chairs at a two-person table. The kitchenette was the picture of compact efficiency yet still charming. She'd have to remember to thank Denise for finding this incredible place for them.

Since the apartment building was set into a steep bank, Denise and Rachel climbed the steep stairs between the house and the rentals, tapping and peeking in the door.

"Come on in. What a place! You outdid yourself in finding this, my friend. Where are you guys?"

"Lower level and two doors in. There's a parking area down at the other end of the building. I got some pictures of the buildings and the place. I'm blown away, their brochures and website don't begin to do this justice. And we've not learned to cook yet."

"We better get over there, ladies," Rachel said, pointing over her shoulder.

"*Buongiorno*," their hostess greeted them as they trooped into a spacious room that included a large dining table and a living area, decorated for comfort with family treasures in Italian country style. "Welcome to my home and my cooking class. I am Raffaela Brucellio. So now please go around and introduce yourselves as we have another guest here, also from the United States. Your name, where you live, what you do for a job, and what you like to cook." She smiled to Denise to begin.

"I'm Denise Chapman, I live in Eugene, Oregon, the USA, I'm a photographer/writer, a single mother, and not really much of a cook. I love doing photo shoots of food, and my daughter loves to cook. I think she's hoping this might make me more willing to at least join her in the kitchen." She nodded to Rachel.

"I'm Rachel Chapman, live with my mom, just graduated with my master's in illustrating children's books, so this is kind of my celebration trip..."

"Congratulations." The others might have practiced their responses.

Rachel ducked her head a bit, pink creeping up her neck. "Thank you." She swallowed and continued. "Let's see, oh, I started cooking when I was maybe five or so, self-defense, you know." She raised her eyebrows at her mother.

"I think she wanted to eat something besides Pop-Tarts and peanut butter and jam for the rest of her life," Denise arrowed back.

"And I always dreamed of attending a cooking class in some other country, especially Italy, and here we are."

Her smile and shrug made Bree want to hug her. She knew Denise did *not* like to cook but had never heard more of the story. After all, part of motherhood meant feeding your family. No wonder they ate out or did carryout so often.

"Oh, you poor kid." Sometimes Bree spoke before she thought. "Sorry, that wasn't nice."

"And here I thought you were my best friend!" Denise adopted a woebegone look, setting them all to laughing.

Grinning, Bree continued with her name and the rest of the information. "I love baking. Pies and breads especially, cinnamon rolls. I asked my mother to teach me how to make her bread and the best pies in the world for my home ec project. You know, we used to have home economics classes in high school and we had to have a project. I've been baking ever since."

"But not Italian food?" Raffaela asked.

"Nope, Norwegian foods but not Italian, and that's why I'm so excited to be here." She nodded to Lizzie. "Your turn."

"I'm Lizzie Porter, a former schoolteacher turned writer and I live not far from Bree. I like cooking adventures so I watch lots of cooking shows. My mom is from Mexico so she taught me many of her old family recipes that I still make for mine. Once I attended a cooking class at the local college for several semesters and had a great time. But this is my first time to take a class like this." She smiled at the woman next to her. "Your turn."

"Hi, I'm Maizzie Miller from Irvine, California. I love to travel with my husband on his business trips *and* I love to cook so he saw an ad or something about cooking classes in foreign countries and he did more research to find this for me."

"What do you like to cook?" Raffaela asked.

Maizzie shrugged and thought a second. "I like making

unusual things for breakfast—well, I guess for all meals. When I see something that strikes my fancy, I make it."

Rachel stared at her. "You really do that? How?"

"I record most of the shows I watch so I can go back and get the ingredients and all." She shrugged. "And then I just do it. Saving shows so I can watch them again really is a big deal for me."

Denise and Bree stared at each other, grins lighting their eyes. "What a character she'd make," Bree breathed. As would Raffaela. Maybe she would find some inspiration for her new series here.

"What an interesting group you are." Raffaela picked up a stack of red fabric from behind her. "Thank you for coming here." She handed out a red apron to each of them. "This will help keep your clothes cleaner at least. My grandmother always used an apron, and my dream is to pass on my grandmother's way of cooking in Italy."

"Do you mind if I take a lot of pictures?" Denise asked as she tied her apron.

"Not at all. So we will begin."

I can't believe this, Bree thought. *I am in Italy, in Tuscany—er, Perugia, in a cooking class with a teacher who speaks English with a charming accent in her home. And we will get to eat the results for lunch. Wait till I tell Pierre-René Dubois about it all.*

Pierre sure was popping up in her thoughts a lot. Bree refocused.

Raffaela held up a wooden board about twenty-four inches square. "Every cook needs a pasta board. Mine is made of hardwoods but you can use plywood too. Today some are using silicone but I prefer wood and the more well used, the better. I use this only for making noodles, and I keep it right handy. I scrape it clean after making noodles like we will today. It is heavy enough. This bar underneath it"—she turned the board over for them to see—"keeps it from sliding around when I am rolling out dough, and yes, I make all my own. In the handouts I will give you, you will see various kinds, and I will demonstrate others too."

Bree felt dumbstruck. "And you still do this?" slipped out.

Raffaela nodded with a smile. "And I never make it ahead. That is why our food is so good. Fresh flour, fresh eggs make the best pastas."

Lizzie and Bree exchanged wide-eyed looks.

Their teacher held up each of her utensils, a scraper, rolling pin, saltcellar, and food scale, along with some other things, many of which had been handed down in her family, all with stories behind them.

"Today we will make our dessert, a chocolate pear cake, first as it takes longer." She assigned them each a different part of the process.

When they slid the cake pan in the oven, she asked as she had after each step, "Any questions? None? Good, we will now begin our pasta." Back they went to the covered table in the main room, a combination dining/living area.

On her instructions they each weighed their flour out of a container that they handed around the table, first sprinkling flour on their board and then mounding the remainder in the middle.

"Now make a hole in the center and break an egg in the hole." She pointed to a wire basket of beautiful brown eggs. "From those hens you saw scratching in the vineyard and all around." She demonstrated each step, how to fold the flour over and over with their hands and begin kneading the dough.

They all followed her instructions, and the kneading began. Fold, push with the heel of her hand, turn, fold, push, turn, fold, push.

The kneading seemed to go on forever. Bree had made

hundreds of loaves of bread and other doughs but none that required this much work.

"You are kneading elasticity into the dough, and adequate kneading will make a great deal of difference in the finished pasta." She smiled at them. "*Allora, si, allora.*"

One by one she approved the others' dough, but when she came to Bree, she smiled and whispered, "Let me finish this for you."

Bree stepped back, wishing she had some Advil with her; her upper arms and shoulders were in misery.

The next step was to roll the dough, again following her careful instructions. "*Si*, push it clear out of the edges of your board. Push hard, out to the edges, good, now turn it and roll some more." All her pupils diligently pushed and flipped and turned and kept on.

Bree's arms and shoulders grumbled at her. *Push harder*, she told herself. She glanced up at their smiling and nodding teacher. *No wonder she stays so slim and strong. If she makes pasta every day, or even a couple of times a week, how does she get anything else done?* The thought of buying a pasta maker was more appealing by the moment.

"All right, now we will cut the dough into strips. Dust your dough with flour, good; now fold your dough in thirds, dust it like this, and fold it again. Good, good, now we will cut it in strips with a sharp knife. A good cook always keeps her knives sharp. Make your cuts about this wide." She held her fingers about three-quarters of an inch apart. "And then shake out the strips."

Bree cut the first strip and shook it out. Whew. She finished and looked around at all their piles of noodles. They must have made enough for a week. The thought almost burst into words, but this time she kept it inside.

"Now you see your pile of noodles—that is what will make your dinner today, an average serving."

Bree looked up to see Denise taking pictures. Had she been doing so all along? Talk about focusing. She turned to Lizzie, who looked as round-eyed as she felt.

"Now we will let our pasta rest while we make the sauce." Again she assigned them each a job. Bree's was chopping the onion.

"Remember, you *never* cut onions or any vegetables or fruit on your pasta board. You have other boards for that."

Again they followed all her instructions, carefully observing what everyone was doing.

Raffaela nodded and led the way back to the table. "Now while that simmers, we'll clear off the table and I'll show you how to fold the napkins." Again, she demonstrated and they all folded the napkins.

"Bree, you slice the bread, Rachel, you and Maizzie set the table, Denise and Lizzie, you lay the place settings. *Grazie.*" She paused. "How many of you would like wine with your dinner? The grapes were grown here on our farm and then we have a small local winery that finishes the process. Our grapes turn into a basic red wine."

Bree hesitated for only a breath, then agreed to join the others. When she drank wine, it was usually white on the sweet side. She'd heard European wines were different from American, something to do with government requirements, so now she'd find out for herself.

"Good for you." Denise sent her a smile of approval. Through the years they'd had discussions of wines, not that either of them was a connoisseur but this was part of the Italian adventure.

Rachel studied the finished table. "That is so lovely. Mom, we need to set our table like this sometimes too."

"Hardly. We don't have all the fancy stuff to do that."

"Now." Rachel's forehead wrinkled. "I just bet I can find neat stuff to do it."

"Not quite so easy, I think." Bree motioned to the table. "Most of these things have been in her family for years. Traditions." She could hear Tevye from *Fiddler on the Roof*, singing, his voice powerful and deep. "Tradition! Tradition!" She'd need to look that up, now that her curiosity had been piqued.

"Well, then I guess we can start some traditions of our own."

Denise shrugged. "I guess."

Raffaela poured the wine and set the bottle in the middle of the table. "Please be seated and I will bring in the food."

When the serving dishes were all in place, Denise raised her glass. "I think we need to toast our adventure together." The others raised their wineglasses. "To Raffaela, our hostess and teacher. Thank you." They clinked their glasses and swallowed their first sip of the lovely purple wine.

Raffaela nodded and smiled. "Just remember, you cooked this meal here, and you can do so again at home."

Bree took her first bite of the pasta and closed her eyes the better to savor the flavors. *Delicious* seemed such an anemic word. Garlic, butter, onion—she tried to remember what spices and herbs they'd added. "And to think we helped make this."

"I know, I think I've died and gone to heaven," Denise said. "If I cooked like this, I might even do more of it, or at least enjoy it more."

"M-o-m, I tried to tell you..."

"Hush, child, I'm euphoric."

Bree glanced at Rachel, who grinned back at her. "I'll come down and we'll do this together."

"We'll come up—it would take a fortune to stock our kitchen with all the stuff we'd need to create a masterpiece like this."

"When you said our noodles were just right for an average person, I about choked." Lizzie motioned to her empty plate. "And I don't feel like I'm about to explode. What's the secret?"

"No secret. Just good, wholesome food, made with natural ingredients, grown right here as much as possible. People ask me how come Italians don't have weight problems like you do in the States and I think that's why. Nothing prepared in advance, no canned or frozen. And we eat relaxed and not hurrying." She looked around the table. "I do hope you have room for our dessert. I'd hate for you to miss out on anything." She set the cake, fresh out of the oven and still in the glass dish, at the end of the table. Rich chocolate—they'd used cocoa—with pear halves baked right in. She cut it into six pieces and passed the plates around.

Thinking she'd just have a bite or two, a bit later, Bree looked down at her empty plate. "That was one of the best cakes I've tasted and I sort of doubted the combination when you said chocolate and pear."

Raffaela smiled, her whole face taking part. "You're not the first one to say that, but this too is one of my grandmother's recipes. It is a rather dense cake but so flavorful; I feel sorry when some people turn it down without tasting it."

"So you say you are making a recipe book of your family recipes? Will it be for sale?"

"That's what I'm planning. I'm including family stories, bits of kitchen lore, etchings, pictures, and the recipes, of course. I believe I set myself a big task."

"Yeah, you did," Bree agreed. "So it will be available for future classes?"

Raffaela nodded. "And for the public also—someday."

"Then I hope we're all on your mailing list. I would love to purchase one for myself and others for presents." Bree nodded. "Especially after being here."

"*Grazie.*" Raffaela stood. "You have been *bravi* guests and I hope you all go home with good memories of Italy and Umbria in particular."

"*Grazie* many times over." Nodding, Bree smiled and felt her shoulders settle back where they belonged. "This has been such a marvelous day. So much better than I had any idea…" She glanced at her friends, who were all nodding too. "You said we need to be out of our rooms by ten tomorrow."

"*Si, per favore.* I'm glad you came. *Buongiorno* and may the remainder of your trip be all you dreamed of."

Back in their room, Bree flopped back on her bed. "I am whupped."

"Me too." Lizzie did the same. "Makes me wish we'd planned to stay one more day."

"Florence tomorrow."

"*Si.* Florence. A whole week there."

Bree checked her messages. Oh blast. A missed call from Jessica. She heaved a belly-deep sigh. Now what?

Chapter Sixteen

He had a place.

Pierre-René got out of his car and stood gazing at the building a moment, fingering the just-received keys in his hand. Not much to look at from the outside, just a simple corner storefront with two windows that covered most of the front wall, split by an unassuming glass door. A dark-brown awning drooped on one side. A driveway led to a parking lot and another exit on the side street, which would make having a drive-through window a possibility if they wanted to add it down the road.

But it was his.

He surveyed the downtown Vancouver street, lined with trees and pedestrians, businesses to the left and right. This wasn't old-town Gresham close to his condo, as he'd first dreamed of, and he wasn't thrilled about the commute to get here. But this seemed to be where the Lord had led—and what his budget could afford. And as Ben had noted, he was extremely fortunate to find a corner location downtown at all, with lots of foot traffic and reasonably close to the VA office. Plus, no stairs up to the door, so he wouldn't have to add an ADA ramp. One item crossed off his to-do list. His next job would be to find out if there were more of those kinds of requirements.

Thank you, Lord, he said to himself as he walked over

and fitted the key in the lock. He'd met with the landlord and signed the lease only an hour ago. The man believed in his vision and had agreed to wait on charging rent until they actually opened—another miracle answer to prayer.

The door shrieked on opening, one more for the list, but Pierre could imagine a friendly jangle, like that from the bell at The Coffee Spoon—not that he wanted this place to be a mirror of that one. This would be a place where military vets would feel comfortable, where they could be themselves, whether working here, finding connections, or merely getting a good cup of coffee.

Pierre's throat tightened at the thought. He scanned the interior space that had been a candy store. When it went out of business, the owners left a counter and display case, a good start. But he needed to add another sink and floor drains, cabinets, not to mention a couple of ovens and all the coffee equipment, a rather daunting list from the research he'd been doing. Coffee grinder, coffee brewer, espresso machine, plus toasters, microwave, refrigerator, blender, ice machine—it went on and on. But perhaps now that he had a space, he could start hiring some help.

The windows needed some kind of attractive shades or blinds. New paint, of course, and new light fixtures. The checkered tile floor would definitely have to go... he studied it further. Perhaps not.

His phone chimed. JASON. "Hey there, son."

"Hey, Dad. You sound in a good mood."

"Well, I just got the keys for my coffee place." He craned his neck to scan the space again, a grin creeping back.

"That's awesome. Congratulations."

"Thanks." Warmth seeped through his chest. "What can I do for you?"

"Just wanted to let you know I talked with Michelle, that friend I thought might be able to help you with marketing and a website? She said she could meet with you this afternoon, if you're free."

"This afternoon? Okay." Pierre-René checked his watch. Already eleven. "I have some contractors coming to give estimates today, but I'll find time."

"If you can. She seems really gung ho to get started."

"Well, great." No time like the present. "Can you give me her number? I'll give her a call."

"I'll text it to you."

They said goodbye, and Pierre hit Michelle's number. They arranged to meet at a smoothie place a few doors down at 1:00 p.m. That way he could show her the location if she wanted. She might as well get a feel for what they were dealing with.

Two hours later, time Pierre had filled by making phone calls to more potential contractors, he sat at an outdoor café table sipping a mango smoothie across from a young woman with fiery orange short hair. Several earrings in each ear. She'd grabbed his hand while introducing herself and her company all in one breath, ordered her smoothie, sat down with her phone and laptop, and hadn't stopped talking since.

"So what's your, like, vision for this place?" She slurped her pomegranate açai smoothie and typed on her cell, fingers flying so fast Pierre felt he was watching through a time-lapse camera.

"My vision." He rubbed his forehead, forcing his attention away from the texting blur. "Well, I want it to be a safe place for veterans, where they can get their feet solidly under them again. Where they can find—" He cleared his throat. "But—but not only veterans. This shop is for everyone who loves coffee. All ages since I'll have some things kids like too, like several kinds of hot chocolate, just thinking kiddie cups..." His mind barreled off in that direction. "Perhaps a kiddie table?" He felt her watching him and nodded. "Interesting, I'd not thought about such things before." *Veterans need kids around—this could be good for whole families. Thank you, Lord, something more to ponder.*

"Cool, cool, I like it. Do you have a name yet?"

"No, not yet."

"You need to do some kind of play on words, something creative, you know?" She tapped her phone on her chin. "Something you said, about the vets and their feet, what was it again?"

"I, ah, that they could get their feet on solid ground again, I believe."

She pointed her finger at him. "That's it. Solid Ground—get it? Like coffee grounds? That's your name. Clever, huh?"

"Hmm." Possibly a bit too clever?

"You don't like it?" She tapped away on her cell again.

Making notes? Or texting or...?

"It's creative." Pierre shifted in his seat. "I just don't want any of this to feel...forced. I want it to be a place where vets can feel comfortable and be themselves, not like we're trying too hard or that the focus is on them and their problems."

"But I thought it was." She slanted a glance at him from heavily mascaraed eyes.

"Well, it can't be too obvious."

"Solid Ground isn't obvious. It's subtle and sophisticated." She showed him her phone. "So much so that three other coffee shops are already called that." With a disgusted sigh, she tossed her phone on the table and turned to her laptop. "So scratch that idea." Here again, she typed so fast her manicured nails blurred. "Keep thinking on the name, you'll come up with something."

Or she would, no doubt. Pierre-René caught himself

rubbing his knuckles, an old nervous habit. He stopped and tried to ease the tension in his shoulders.

"Hard to come up with much of a website without a name," Michelle said after a few moments of what seemed like haphazard clicking. "So I'm using Solid Ground for now; we'll change it out later. What do you think of this?" She turned her laptop toward him.

"What is it?"

"A mock-up for your website."

"Already?" He craned his neck to see better. He didn't know much about web design, but he had to admit his first impression was positive. Deep blues and browns, evoking both military and coffee hues. Artistic lines. Attractive, professional font. For the first time since meeting Michelle, Pierre felt a frisson of respect overriding the fear. Maybe Jason had known what he was doing in recommending her, after all.

"So . . . how soon could you have this running?"

"Once you have a name? A couple of days, max. I work fast."

And no qualms about patting herself on the back either. Pierre mentally kicked himself for his critical attitude. "Well, I'm grateful for your expertise here. I do realize I won't get much business without a website."

"Or without social media. You on Facebook, Instagram, Twitter?"

"Facebook. But I don't check it too often." It had been months, but somehow he couldn't admit that to this techno-whiz young woman.

Michelle shook her fiery head. "Ya gotta establish a social media presence." She pointed a finger at him. "Post something every day, multiple tweets a day if you can, especially once you're up and running." She studied his face. "You know Twitter? It's the only way to grab an audience today." She slumped a bit, obviously disappointed in him.

The only way? Surely that wasn't true, especially in the close-knit world of veterans. Pierre's shoulders tensed up again. The mere thought of trying to wade into the murky waters of social media…

"Couldn't you do it?" he blurted.

Her shaped eyebrows arched, then she nodded—hard. "Totally, if you want me to. I'll need access to your Facebook account—no, wait, I'd just set up a separate page. Again, we need a name, see if you can update me on that by tomorrow. Then I'll get you on Twitter, Instagram, oh, and LinkedIn…"

"Wait." He held up his hands. Any moment now, his shoulders would start full-on twitching. *Come on, Pierre-René, you're a seasoned businessman. You can handle one slip of a girl.* "On second thought, let's wait on the social media. Since this is an initial consultation, we don't need to move too fast. I need to choose a contractor first of all, that comes before Facebook. Why don't you just work on the website for now, and we'll touch base in a few days?"

"Fine." Michelle's mouth flattened, but to her credit she didn't argue. "I have a questionnaire for new web design clients; can I send it to your email? It'll help me to fit the site to what you need and want."

"Certainly." Pierre-René gave his email, then watched her pack her laptop, empty and toss her smoothie cup, and head for her car, all with the energy she seemed to put into every movement she made. When Michelle's bright-colored head finally dipped into her tangerine-hued sports car—orange must be her favorite color—Pierre leaned back in his café chair and blew out a long breath.

She's clearly good at what she does, but…wow, Lord. He rubbed his hands over his face. *What have I gotten myself into?*

He wondered the same thing after the third contractor

toured the space and gave an estimate even higher than the previous two. Pierre leaned against the bare counter and rubbed weary eyes, a headache starting to pound. He'd had no clue that this space wasn't rated to handle the amount of water and electricity that a coffee shop would need, since their utility demands with actually making coffee and baked goods would be so much higher than for the previous store that merely sold already-made candy. It could be upgraded, but it wouldn't be cheap. He thought he'd planned well for the funding, even left a decent buffer. But now this was one worry stalking other worries creeping up his spine.

Someone knocked at the door. Pierre pushed himself up from the counter and turned. *Did I schedule another—oh, good. Paula.*

He smiled wearily as he let his sister-in-law in. "What are you doing here?"

"Came to see your place, of course. And bring you these, since I don't believe you're set up for baking yet." She held out a plastic container of cookies, gazing around the bare walls with obvious delight. "Oh, Pierre, it's wonderful."

"You really think so?" He pulled off the plastic lid and sampled a cookie. Chocolate chip, Paula's signature recipe. The brown-sugary sweetness and melting chocolate chips blessed his tongue with homemade comfort. "Thanks."

"Of course I do. I mean, I know it's rough right now, but look at the potential. The windows, the natural light, the counter and bakery display already there. And such a good location, easy access, handicapped parking right outside and extra in back." Tears sheened Paula's eyes. "It will be such a welcoming place."

His sister-in-law cried easily these days, but still. Her enthusiasm helped him remember his initial exhilaration at finding this spot.

"Have you applied for your food license yet?" Paula set her purse on the counter.

"Ben Gutierrez got it going for me. But he says I've got to take some sort of online food safety certification class; employees will too." One more hurdle he hadn't known about. Well, nothing came easy or without the unexpected—he ought to know that after over six decades of life.

"So what renovations are you having done?"

He told her, including the problem with the utilities. "I think I'm going to go with the second contractor I met. His price is the lowest, but more than that, he was very straightforward about everything, no beating around the bush or trying to sell me any kind of spiel. I liked that."

"You know, I can help too—once the remodel is finished, I mean. Painting, curtains, decorating." Her eyes lit. "It would be so nice to have a project to work on. Oh, and I know Bree will love to help too. She has a good eye for that kind of thing."

"Mmm." Pierre gave a half nod and stepped into the back room that held a sink and cabinets—one of the biggest renovations would be turning this into a fully functioning and up-to-code kitchen.

Paula followed him. "Have you talked to her lately?"

"Not for a few days." He bent to study the plumbing under the sink, trying to look as if he were inspecting something important.

"I did, last night. They're about to head into Florence— that's where the *David* is, I think. Bree must be so excited. Did she tell you it's been a lifelong dream of hers to see him in person?"

"She did." Pierre-René straightened, fighting irritation. Kind of Paula to stop by, but he had things to do beyond chitchatting about Breeanna and her Italy trip. "I think I'm going to head home. I've got a number of calls to make still. Was there anything else you wanted to see?"

"Oh—no, I don't think so." Paula looked slightly taken aback, but stepped back into the main front room. "I just wanted to see your space and congratulate you."

"And I appreciate it." Pierre mustered a genuine smile. "The cookies are *très délicieux*. Okay if I stop by and see you later this week? Your faucet holding up okay?"

"Good as new." Paula turned to go, then back again. "You haven't been in touch with Jessica again, have you?"

"No, I haven't." It wasn't like he had Bree's daughter's phone number. He had meant to reach out again after his late-night plumbing rescue, but there would be plenty of bridge-building still before they could be counted friends. And the business had simply been taking all his time and attention for the past week. "Why?"

"I'm worried about her—she's working so much, she's hardly there. At least, whenever I walk by the house, she's hardly ever home, or I just see her rushing in and out to and from her jobs." Paula sighed. "Well, hopefully she won't have to keep this two-job thing up too long. Bree has told you about her financial issues, I imagine?"

"Somewhat." Pierre really needed to get going. "Can I walk out with you?"

He accompanied Paula to her car, then made it to his. He leaned his head back against the seat, guilt twisting in his chest for being impatient with his sister-in-law. All she had done was push out of her own grief to come by and encourage him, bless her heart.

And talk about Bree.

Pierre-René closed his eyes and rubbed at the now-pounding headache. He still hadn't called her. Not since that night several days ago when he'd—abruptly ended their call.

Hung up on her, man. Call it what it is.

He should call her, needed to call her. But what would he say?

Pierre glanced at the car clock. Five p.m., so 2:00 a.m. in Italy. Too late to call now. He hated himself for the relief that expanded in his chest.

Why couldn't he just call her and pretend nothing had happened? Maybe she hadn't even heard what he'd said. Or if she had, she might have forgotten amid all that was happening with her trip. She might not even be wondering why he hadn't called. Or if she was, be too polite to say anything.

He would call her late tonight, once it was morning in Europe. Or tomorrow morning, evening for her, maybe that would be better. Soon, anyway.

And if she asked about what he'd said, or why he'd hung up, he'd find a way to smooth it over, let her know it wasn't a big deal, that he was handling it, taking care of himself. She didn't need to worry about him, not at all. He was, quite truly, fine.

A car backfired down the block, jolting Pierre straight up in his seat, heart jumping in his chest, hands strangling the steering wheel. Cold sweat broke out over his forehead and limbs.

He breathed deeply, in through his nose and out through his mouth, for a few minutes till his pulse calmed sufficiently, then relaxed his clenched jaw and started his car.

Driving back toward his condo, Pierre called himself every kind of fool.

Who was he kidding? If this lovely, beautiful, wonderful woman who had come into his life was worried, she had good reason to be.

Chapter Seventeen

"Wish we could stay for another class, even just another night."

"I know the feeling." Bree smiled at her friend. "I would love to stay longer at this place, so peaceful." The two exchanged smiles, sitting on lawn chairs in the yard right off their room. One heavy red hen scratched in the grass near the wall, a barred gray one with a flop-over red comb chasing bugs. Bougainvillea sweetening the breeze, the bright magenta splashing down a wall. She glanced at her watch. Denise said they'd leave in fifteen minutes but she was off shooting pictures somewhere and Rachel had yet to show her face. No matter, this way she had written postcards to send to Jessica and James, Paula and Pierre. She huffed a sigh. Three days now and she'd not heard from Pierre, not even after she left a phone message for him. Not that she should have expected to hear from him, but...

Bree and Lizzie had finished off the delicious jam cake bread their hostess had left in their rooms, along with the cheese and outstanding coffee. The recipe for the cake bread was safe in Bree's collection folder, along with the recipes and instructions from the day before. Bree ran her finger over the plate to collect a few more delectable crumbs. She wished she'd managed to connect with Jessica, after that missed call. The time difference made it hard; though Bree had tried twice, once again first thing this morning, she only got Jessica's voicemail. Surely if something were really wrong, she'd have heard from someone else, wouldn't she? Paula or James? So much for carefree travel and leaving her worries at home.

"Yesterday was fun, wasn't it?" Lizzie sipped the last of her coffee.

The afternoon before the four of them had driven into a nearby town to be greeted by three- and four-story-tall brick and stone buildings, as if they were driving into a fortress. Navigating the narrow streets caused more than one sucked-in breath when they met a car coming toward them. No wonder the Italians drove such small cars. Their SUV took up more than its share of the street, feeling like it was almost scraping the walls.

"I hope I never forget that window way up on that wall with a window box of bright-red geraniums." Bree blew out a breath. "I wanted a tour of the apartment behind that window. Those blank walls seemed more like prison walls than for homes and businesses."

"The pizza was good too." Lizzie chuckled. "I love hearing all the conversations in Italian."

"I wanted to know what they were saying." This speaking bare-minimum Italian was not enough for this nosy author. Body language here was fun to watch, though. "If I ever write an Italian character, I will know how dramatic they can be." She mimicked those they watched, waving her arms while she talked. Such a whole new world was opening up to her here. Hopefully it would open up her writing too, eventually.

Lizzie chuckled. "Surely there is a story for me in there somewhere. My young readers would love Italy too, right?" She tipped her head back to stare up at the glistening blue sky through the leaves. "I think we should make a rule for while we are here: Gelato every day."

"Sounds good to me." Bree grinned back. "And I have decided to have caprese salad at every restaurant. Fresh mozzarella cheese here beats what we get at home."

"Raffaela said it's really easy to make."

"Sure, if you have fresh milk and…"

Denise brought the car in the upper driveway. Stepping out, she called, "You two ready to go?"

The two rose from their chairs, nodding. "Suitcases are there by the back door."

Rachel climbed out and hefted them into the back. Since another class was going on that morning, they had said their goodbyes the night before. Raffaela had smiled as she hugged each of them. "Next time stay longer."

"Next time" sounded so…so inviting. Wouldn't that be delicious? Another trip to Italy. Staying in touch to build friendship? Enjoying Raffaela's cookbook. They'd even talked about a possible West Coast book tour for her. And maybe, if Bree could start a new series set overseas, that would give her an excuse to travel more. Ah, so very many exciting possibilities. Who could have ever dreamed all this in advance? Pushing home worries aside for now, she tucked her card-writing paraphernalia in her bag, checked to make sure she had a bottle of water, and followed Lizzie to the car.

"And so we are off to Florence," Denise announced as they exited the driveway.

The excitement tickled Bree's middle again. At last.

"You said we could stop at some of the shops in a village like we came through before," Rachel reminded her mother.

"That I did. I'm sure we'll be going through other villages, we're not going the expressway, so when something looks interesting, sing out." She glanced at her daughter in the rearview mirror. "We did some yesterday afternoon, sort of."

"Right."

Bree detected a slight tone of sarcasm in Rachel's voice. "Do we have a map?"

"Nah, we have GPS, don't need a map."

Bree shook her head. After getting lost the other night? "I'm buying a map when we stop."

"How will you read it when we don't speak Italian? At least with GPS we can make it give instructions in English."

"Good question. We need Pierre here." Bree swallowed. Where had that come from? She felt Denise's questioning look and heard a chuckle from Lizzie.

"Oh, really?" Denise asked. "You think he could read an Italian map?"

"He was stationed someplace in the northern part for a few years. Said he spent part of that time working with Italian soldiers too. At least that's what I think he said." Hearing the trill of her phone, she dug it out of her bag. Jessica, finally. "Jess. What's wrong?"

"Mom, what made you say that? I just wanted to hear your voice. What time is it there?"

Bree swapped surprised looks with Denise. "Ah, it's almost eleven." So nearly 2:00 a.m. at home. "What are you doing up so late?"

"Just got home from stocking shelves."

"Bless your heart. Everything's all right there?" A silence stretched. "Ah, Jessica, is something wrong?"

"Um, Cinders quit eating and James took her to the vet because I had to be at work and the vet said that it was a blockage and surgery need to be done right away, and so they did it and how do I pay for that and I'm sorry, Mom, but she got into garbage and I thought I had closed the door and..."

"Whoa, slow down." Bree fought to breathe without gasping. "Now, Cinders needed surgery for something and the rest of it doesn't make sense. What happened? Is she okay?"

"Yeah, Dr. Benson said she'll be fine—she got into the garbage and ate something that caused a blockage, but I'm so sorry, and now there's this big vet bill..."

"I'll call Dr. Benson in the morning and give them my credit card number, which I should have left with them anyway—just in case." Bree closed her eyes. She should have known something would happen with Jess house-sitting. Thank God her kitty was all right. "Jessica, stop crying. It's not your fault, cats just sometimes get into things. Good, now—now breathe." She took her own advice, sucked in a deep breath and held it, then felt her shoulders relax as she slowly let it out.

"I'm really sorry, Mom."

"Don't worry, Cinders will be fine or Dr. Benson would have told you. Just get some sleep, and I'll talk to you tomorrow."

"Okay, thanks, Mom. Oh, and by the way, I think Pierre is a really nice guy."

Where had that come from? "Well, I think so too. All right, bye now."

She clicked off her cell and dropped her head against the headrest.

"Will Cinders be all right?" Rachel asked. She had pet-sat for Bree on several occasions through the years.

"Sounds like it, although I'll know more when I call the vet. Let's see, it's about two a.m. there, so when can I call to be nine a.m.?" She paused and figured. "About six p.m. here, right?"

"They open at eight, so five tonight. That's not so bad." Lizzie used the same vet Bree did. "You signed one of the permission forms for while you're gone, right?"

"I did, but it didn't have a space for my credit card number. I should have left the number at home."

"Uh, uh, nope. Bad idea. Not with Jessica house-sitting."

"You're right." Years earlier Jessica had "borrowed" her mother's credit card for an "emergency." She'd never done so again, but why put temptation in her way?

"Mom, time for lunch and I think this village is a good stopping place. It talks here about a really good restaurant and specialty shops."

"Fine with me. Tell me when to stop."

"They have caprese salad, Bree, so easy for you."

Bree rolled her eyes. *"Grazie, mia amica." Lord, please calm me down so I don't concern the others. I trust you to take care of the situation at home and especially Jessica. I trust you, Lord, help me trust. But should I really have left for the other side of the world? What if something else happens?*

Denise slowed to the posted speed limit and they all watched for the restaurant.

"There it is, up on the left," Lizzie crowed.

"Good for you." Denise slowed even more and turned into the parking lot. "I hope this one doesn't charge for parking. Missing that credit card is a pain. I'd planned on putting all my expenses for this trip on that one to make income tax easier."

"Let me pay for this one," Bree said. They had agreed to split all mutual expenses four ways at the end of the trip, supposedly to make it easier for everyone's book-keeping.

Inside, Denise asked their waiter, "So, what is your specialty?"

"Every morning we make the pasta right here." The man pointed to the shelves behind the counter that displayed various pastas, sausages, cheeses, and breads. The fragrances made their stomachs rumble.

"Are you the owner?" Rachel asked.

He nodded. "Third generation. We serve the best. Travelers, they come from all around the world to enjoy a meal here. All our vegetable and herbs grow in the gardens, our chickens lay eggs—we, what you say, one-stop shop."

"And you make your own cheeses too?"

He nodded, his face creasing in a smile. "*Si*, from goats and cows."

"Not water buffalo?" Bree asked.

His laughter shook him all over. "I want water buffalo, my wife she say no, no water buffalo. No sheep either. We smoke our own sausages too, from our pigs. She like pigs."

"One-stop shop is right."

"We ship all over, to America too, you buy salamis, get to your home before you do." He licked the tip of his pencil. "Now what we get for you? Start with *vino*? Bottle of Chianti. Now..." He collected all their orders, answering their questions, nodding all the while. When finished, he set a basket of breadsticks and crunchy bread in the middle of the table and poured olive oil and balsamic in two low bowls. "You share." He gestured to each side of the table. The next time, he returned with wineglasses and a just-opened bottle of Chianti, filling each glass half full. "Now, you enjoy."

"He is the picture of any Italian waiter, owner, whatever." Rachel leaned over and pulled a pad of paper and pencil from her bag; the drawing took place before their eyes.

"What things did you draw at the farm?" Bree asked. She leaned over the table, trying to relax into enjoyment of this trip again after the phone call. "You even gave him that mole." She shook her head. "And eyes, such life."

Rachel flipped the pages up over the wire binding, showing her farm sketches.

"You got the chickens—and the flowers." Lizzie tapped the paper. "You draw so fast."

"Sketching has to be fast or I'd run out of time when I

see it. Later, I go back to the sketches and fill in the ones I like best."

"For folks who start out the day knowing the destination but not the journey, we sure do find great places," Lizzie noted with a smile.

"We are going to the candy store next door before we leave." Bree emphasized the "are." "They advertised chocolates from Vienna. I had some once and I've never forgotten it."

Denise rolled her eyes. "If you insist."

Their waiter, Angelo, set the salads before them. "Enjoy!" He looked to Bree and pointed at the mozzarella. "Better than buffalo." He touched finger and thumb to his lower lip in the gesture of perfection. "Made yesterday. And tomatoes and basil out of our garden."

"*Grazie, grazie.*" Bree grinned at him. What a character! She promised herself she would find a way to include him in a book someday, somehow.

By the time they finished, Bree felt like she needed someone to roll her out to the car. "Good thing we get to walk a bit," she moaned, rubbing her abdomen. "Right now even the best chocolate in the world doesn't sound appealing."

They were past the midafternoon mark when they climbed back in the SUV and slammed the doors.

"No more stops until Florence," Denise announced. "We have a hundred miles to go. And in the arrangements I made with the owner of the flat we've got for the week, we'll be there about six. He said to call him if we'd be late."

"Going to be pushing it, just pray all goes well. First drop the SUV off at the rental place, then catch a taxi to . . ." Denise looked to Bree, who read off the address.

"Sounds simple," Lizzie offered.

"Yeah, right."

Bree sure hoped the hesitant tone in Denise's voice didn't prove prophetic.

"You have the instructions so read them to me slowly," Denise told Bree. "What am I looking for now?"

Bree studied the GPS, trying to hear the instructions, but the accent in the voice made following it more difficult. Once she located where they were, she repeated the instructions for Denise.

Traffic had increased the closer they got to Florence. Half an hour past the time they should have been at the rental place to drop off the SUV, the GPS said they were there. But they weren't.

Denise pulled over next to a curb and sucked in a deep breath. "Okay, now we call the rental company, and they'd better give us clear instructions. How about you write them down for me?"

"Of course." Bree dug in her bag for her notebook and pen. "Ready."

Denise put the phone on speaker. When they answered, she asked for someone who spoke fluent English and told them where their GPS had taken them. The man apologized and asked if they were ready.

"Please slow down," Bree said as she wrote down the directions.

"Sorry." He slowed. She read the instructions back to him. He agreed and said it would take them about fifteen minutes with traffic heavy as it was.

They pulled back out into the lane and waited at the next stoplight. Traffic inched ahead. They waited again.

Bree glanced at the clock on the dashboard. Five fifteen. "I better call our host and explain our situation."

Denise drummed the steering wheel. "If we only knew alternative routes."

Bree tapped in the number and waited. No answer. She left a message detailing their situation. "We'll be there as soon as we can."

When they finally parked at the car rental lot, Denise and Rachel headed for the check-in while Bree and Lizzie unloaded the luggage and made sure nothing was left in the vehicle. With their luggage now in a heap, Lizzie took the first turn at the restroom while Bree guarded the luggage. People-watching made the time pass more quickly. They swapped places and on the way to the restroom, Bree saw Denise and Rachel standing in line. Denise saw her and shook her head.

At six forty-five the two of them rejoined the two waiting. "The taxi said at least fifteen minutes before they could be here."

"I wonder if that's fifteen minutes American-style or Italian." Bree sat down on her suitcase.

Denise rolled her eyes. "Who knows."

"Did you or they tell the driver we have a lot of luggage?"

"I hope so. But since I couldn't understand the language..."

       ✿   ✿   ✿

They again held their carry-ons on their laps. The driver was not smiling as he pulled out on the street. He spoke some English but even so, Denise had given him the written address.

Denise and Bree swapped looks. She'd always heard how delightful Italian cabdrivers were, answering questions, pointing out special buildings. This man reminded her of the driver they'd finally met in Rome. So much for a helpful attitude. Since she was sitting in the front seat, she couldn't really whisper with the others.

Lord, please get us to the right address and help our host be understanding. She had left a second message on his answering machine. What if he wasn't there to let them in?

Her neck was tensing up again. She had the original written instructions from him on how to find the wrought-iron gate, then enter the code for the building. The flat was on the third and top floor via an elevator.

The driver slammed on the brakes as she braced herself on the dash. Seat belts were necessary this trip.

Dusk crept over the buildings and streetlights lit up. So many one-way streets. She heaved a sigh of relief when he swung over to a curb in front of a ten-foot wall with a black wrought-iron gate. He checked the numbers against those on his instructions, muttered something in Italian, and swung open his door. Instead of opening their doors, he raised the rear door and started pulling out luggage to set on the sidewalk. The four looked at one another and climbed out.

"No tip?" Bree whispered.

"I'll tip him, but very little." Denise dug into her leather zippered pouch. She counted the euros, handed them over, gave him a forced smile—but a smile—and said, *"Grazie, signore."* They all watched him pull out and drive away.

"Well, that was an interesting experience," Denise muttered. Bree looked to Lizzie, whose eyes were dancing. Within seconds a chuckle snorted out, then a giggle, and within a breath, they all suffered a laugh attack—together.

Chapter Eighteen

A distant ringing pulled Pierre-René up from the depths of sleep.

An alarm? Morning reveille? No, he wasn't at the Aviano Air Base anymore.

His cell phone. Groggy, Pierre groped on his nightstand, noting the time that lit on his phone along with the caller. Paula, at 3:00 a.m. Not good.

"What's wrong?" He sat up in bed, fumbling to switch on the light.

"Pierre, the fire department is at Bree's house. I'm outside with Jessica, we can't reach James or Ryan. Can you come?"

"Of course." Adrenaline rushing, Pierre flung back the covers and shoved his feet into his slippers by the bed. "I'll be there as quickly as I can."

He sped down the darkened highway, resisting the worst-case scenarios threatening to flood his mind. *Stay calm, wait till you know more. Jessica is safe, that's the important thing.* But what had happened? Was the fire still going? What about Bree's pets? His gut clenched—he knew how she loved those animals. How bad was the blaze, and was it Jessica's fault?

Memories flickered at the edges of his mind as he turned at Bree's exit, however he tried to quench them. The Christmas

Jason was five, he'd been gone on business for several weeks before returning home late on Christmas Eve. He'd entered the house to the ominous odor of smoke. Rushing into the living room, he'd found that the Christmas garland on the mantel had ignited from candles left burning, flames licking downward at the children's stockings hanging there. Lynn lay passed out on the couch by the Christmas tree, a near-empty bottle of whiskey on the coffee table beside her.

Pierre had dashed to the bathroom, filled the mop bucket with water from the bathtub, and extinguished the blaze. But the stockings were charred, along with memories from that Christmas. Lynn woke in time to stumble through Christmas breakfast the next morning for the kids, albeit with reddened, shame-laced eyes. He'd made up a cheerful story for the kids about how Santa came down the chimney so fast their stockings caught on fire, the telltale garland and candles safely bundled away in the outside garbage bins.

It had been years before he could enjoy Christmas candles again.

The flashing lights on Bree's street shoved the memories from Pierre's mind. He parked down the block then jogged toward her house, panting by the time he reached the neighbors clustered beneath the pulsing red beacons of the fire truck and ambulance. He was in good shape, but anxiety always sucked the oxygen from his lungs.

The emergency vehicles' engines were still running, but given the way the yellow-coated firefighters were replacing the hose and chatting comfortably by their truck, whatever conflagration there had been must be out.

Pierre sucked a lungful of air and relief. "Paula? Jessica?" There they were, talking with the fire chief by the front lamppost. He wended his way through the crowd.

"I'm here." He gave Paula's shoulder a light squeeze, not wanting to interrupt.

"Thank you for coming." Paula turned and hugged him. She tipped her head for them to step back a bit, letting Jessica keep talking with the chief. "The fire is out, thank God."

"What happened?"

"A kitchen fire. Something on the stove—I haven't gotten the full story. The chief says there's no structural damage, though."

Something else to be thankful for. But what had Jessica been doing cooking in the middle of the night? Pierre-René glanced at the young woman.

Wrapped in an oversize jacket a neighbor must have loaned her, Jessica stood gripping Spencer's leash and nodding at whatever the fire chief was saying. She appeared to be holding it together pretty well, but even in the low lighting, Pierre could see the lines of strain on her face. A cat carrier sat at her feet. So she had gotten both animals out safely.

The fire chief tipped his hat to Jessica and headed back to the engine, signaling his crew, who began climbing back aboard. The ambulance, thankfully not needed, had already left.

Just as the fire truck pulled away from the curb, James came jogging up, out of breath.

"What on earth happened? I just got all your messages." He angled a glare at Jessica. "What did you do now?"

"Is that all you can say?" Jessica grabbed at Spencer's leash as the dog lunged toward James, wired from the excitement. From within the cat carrier, Cinders let out an unhappy yowl.

James scrubbed a hand through his hair. "I mean, you're all okay, right? You, the animals?"

"Yes, I got them out straightaway, right after I dialed nine-one-one." Jessica's voice held ice as she wrestled to control Spencer.

"You should have done that first, before calling. Basic protocol, you get to a safe place and then call." James's voice sharpened.

"Hey," Paula broke in, lifting her hands. Neighbors were dispersing around them. "How about if you all come over to my place for a bit? It's warm in there, we can talk. Jessica, did the fire chief say it's safe to go into your mom's house?"

"He said yeah." Jessica drew a breath. "They've disconnected the water, gas, and electricity in the kitchen for now till it can all be inspected, hopefully tomorrow. But he doesn't think there's damage that will mean I can't stay there."

"Well, at least come to my place for a little while. I'll make some tea, or better yet hot chocolate."

"Okay." Jessica shivered. "Just let me put the animals inside. I'll shut them in mom's room for a little while; that'll help them calm down."

"I'll come with you." Pierre stepped up and lifted the cat carrier. Jessica shouldn't see the damage inside for the first time by herself. He should know.

They entered through the front door, avoiding the streaks of mud and water left by the firefighters' boots in the entryway. Jessica headed straight upstairs with Spencer, Pierre following with Cinders.

"You can just set her over there." After closing the bedroom door, Jessica nodded to a corner with an overstuffed, rose-upholstered chair and unclipped Spencer's leash. She knelt beside the quivering dog, running her hands over his head and ears. "There's a good boy. It's okay, Jessie's got you."

Pierre set the cat carrier down and unlatched the door. He peeked inside. "Hey, kitty kitty." A decided hiss came from the darkened depths.

Pierre pulled back. He'd never claimed to be a cat whisperer.

"She'll come out when she's ready. They're both pretty upset. And she had surgery a couple of days ago, poor baby." Jessica sat cross-legged on the floor, Spencer leaning his head on her shoulder while she fondled his ears.

Pierre wondered who was comforting whom. "Surgery for what?"

"Some kind of blockage from something she ate. She got into the garbage. I just brought her home from the vet yesterday. It's been one thing after another lately." She sighed and unfolded herself to stand. "Guess we better go over to Paula's. My brother is sure to have a prime lecture ready for me." A woeful look fell over her face.

"The main thing is, you are all safe." Pierre-René had plenty of questions himself, but this wasn't the time for that. Instead, he reached for the door handle. "Will they be all right shut in here?"

"Spencer peed while we were outside, and I'll bring up their water bowls and kibble. Not that they'll probably want to eat, but just in case. And my mom keeps an extra litter box there in the bathroom already."

"Sounds good." Pierre headed downstairs at Jessica's gesture, then accompanied her through the kitchen with a flashlight so she could get the pets' food and water bowls from the pantry. He was glad, for even in the dim beam of light, they could see—and smell—the devastation in the room. Jessica was shivering again by the time they came out.

"I can't believe I let this happen." Without waiting for a response, she headed upstairs with the bowls, then returned a moment later. "Okay, let's go." She reached for her jacket on the coatrack by the door out of habit, then stared stupidly at the oversize one she still wore. "I don't even know who gave me this."

"We'll figure that out later." Gently, Pierre-René took her arm and led her out the door.

In Paula's cozy rooster-themed kitchen, the four of them sat around the table with the promised cups of hot chocolate. Despite the warming mug in her hands, an involuntary shudder shook Jessica every few seconds. She huddled over her cup, avoiding everyone's gaze. From the fairly levelheaded young woman talking to the fire chief, now she seemed a lost little girl drawn into herself. James, by contrast, sat glowering in his chair, no doubt only holding back on said lecture because of Paula and Pierre's presence.

"Jess." Paula touched Jessica's sleeve, her voice gentle. "Can you tell us what happened?"

"I don't fully know."

"You don't *know*?" James seemed to be fighting to keep his temper.

"I got back really late, from my job stocking the shelves at the grocery store. And I hadn't eaten, so I opened a can of soup and put it to heat on the stove." Jessica scrubbed her sleeve over her eyes.

For the first time, Pierre noticed that under the borrowed jacket, she wore a green polo with a grocery store logo on the pocket, along with her jeans. A work uniform.

"I sat down at the table and put my head down to rest my eyes a minute. And the next thing I knew, Spencer was whining and barking and I could smell smoke. I jumped up and the stove—there were flames everywhere. I think the soup boiled over and got in the flames and somehow it reached a pot holder I had left nearby and it spread from there, but I'm not sure. At first I ran to get water from the sink, but it was spreading to the curtains and I didn't think I could put it out. So I grabbed my phone and called while I ran to get the animals." She glared at James. "*While* I ran."

James leaned his forehead into his fist, shaking his head. "Never, never leave something unattended on the stove, and especially with anything cloth nearby. How many times did Mom tell us that?"

"I know, okay?" Jessica was near shouting now. "I know it was stupid, and horrible, and this is awful. But I didn't mean to fall asleep! I can't help it that I'm so tired all the time I can barely see straight. I'm trying to do everything you want me to do, work two jobs and work with the credit counselor and pay off my debts and somehow get my messed-up life in order, but I just can't seem to do it all, and I'm never going to be the perfect adult you are, so if you can't accept that, then maybe you should just give up and leave me alone!"

Pierre and Paula exchanged glances.

Paula laid a hand on the young woman's arm. "Jess. Exactly how much are you working?"

"Four full days a week at Applebee's." She leaned her head into folded arms on the table. "Then five nights a week stocking the shelves, after I get off from waitressing. Usually my shift goes till midnight there, sometimes one a.m."

"Good grief." James set down his mug. "You can't keep doing that."

Jessica huffed a laugh into her arms. "I have to."

"Seriously, Jess. I mean, you could have been hurt tonight, or worse."

"You said it yourself, this is my chance to prove I can be a responsible adult. If I screw up again this time, you and Mom will probably give up on me altogether." Her voice muffled, but Pierre could hear the tears in it.

James stared at his sister's bowed head a moment. "Is that what you think?"

Silence.

"Jess." He scooted his chair closer. "We're never going to give up on you. Yeah, we had an agreement, but nothing is worth risking your life. We'll figure it out. I want you to get your life back, not kill yourself. You know that, right? Jess?"

James waited till his sister lifted her head to meet his eyes. "I love you, for crying out loud."

Jessica's face crumpled in earnest this time. She plopped her head back down, her shoulders shaking. "Thanks."

A lump lodged in Pierre-René's own chest. James awkwardly patted his sister's shoulder.

At last Jessica drew a long breath and lifted her face, tearstained but more at peace. "I'm so sorry, you guys. Sorry about everything. I'm just—" She shook her head in slow motion. "So tired."

"Well, first thing, you need to get some sleep." James scooted his chair back up to the table, in-charge mode back. "And then, you'll need to call Mom."

Jessica winced. "Do I have to? Tell her right away? I don't want to ruin her vacation."

"You can't keep something like this from her."

"I know, I know, but maybe we don't have to tell her right away. Can't we see what the damage is first?"

James sighed. "I guess I could call the insurance for you."

"I don't think there's any harm in finding out a bit more before we worry Bree." Paula glanced at Pierre. "What do you think?"

Pierre hesitated. He didn't want to step on family toes here, but…"I think you need to tell her, Jessica. Talk to the insurance first, sure. But don't wait too long." He took another sip of his chocolate, then plunged ahead with the thought that had been tickling. "May I make another suggestion? I've been needing some help with this business I'm starting. I don't know if your mom has told you two about it." *Lord, I hope this idea is from you.*

"She might have said something." James leaned back in his chair, attention now on Pierre.

"It's a coffee shop, with a community focus, especially on veterans—but I can tell you about that later. The thing is, I've been running around like a chicken with my head cut off trying to stay on top of everything. The renovations are underway, but I need help with cleaning, painting, decorating, buying, and figuring out how to set up all the coffee and food prep equipment, marketing—I've frankly been getting more than a bit overwhelmed." He turned to Bree's daughter. "Jessica, do you think you could quit the shelf-stocking job if I could match your pay with two full days of work for me?"

She stared, then nodded slowly. "I guess. I mean, I only get minimum wage there anyway."

"What days are you off from waitressing?"

"Tuesdays and Thursdays, and usually Sundays. I fill in for others whenever I can."

"Perfect." Pierre-René met her eyes, hoping she could see this wasn't just charity. "I genuinely need help. I'm realizing that no matter how much I love it, I know very little about coffee."

"I did work as a barista for a while." Jessica sat up a bit straighter. "Last year. I liked it a lot, I only stopped because..."

"Because she got fired thanks to one of her loser boy-friends." James lifted his hands when Jessica shot him a glare. "What? You don't deny Dereck was a loser. He's a big reason you're in this mess. Not like I'm talking about Ryan."

"I met Ryan when I worked at that coffee place." A wistful smile touched Jessica's face; then she grimaced. "He's not going to be happy to hear about tonight."

"But he will be happy to hear about your new job." Paula reached over and patted her hand. "You told me he didn't like you working all these late nights."

"Yeah." Jessica drew a long breath, then let it out, the sigh holding relief, even hope, Pierre hadn't heard from her before. "Well then, if you're sure, I guess I'll give the grocery store my notice tomorrow?" She quirked a brow in his direction, evidently giving him an out if he didn't want to take a chance on her after all.

Pierre-René smiled at her. "I'm sure."

"I'm not sure how long I'll have to work there, you know, after giving notice."

"That's okay. We have a plan in place."

They finished their hot chocolate, then left a yawning Paula to go to bed. James headed back to his family—the sky was lightening from black to gray-blue—and Pierre walked Jessica to Bree's house. On the way, he promised to give her the number of the contractor he was using, since major repairs were needed in the kitchen before it would be functional again.

"You sure you're okay?" He stopped on the front porch, hands in his jacket pockets against the early-morning chill. A mockingbird trilled in the spring air, scented now with the first of the lilacs from the bush by the door, rather than smoke.

"I'll be fine." Jessica paused, hand on the doorknob. "Thank you for coming tonight, and for the job offer, and everything. You really don't have to do all this."

"But I want to." Pierre hesitated, then pushed forward. "I care about your mother, Jessica. And I'm coming to care about you too. Is that all right with you?" He found himself holding his breath.

Jessica stood silent a moment, then nodded. "I wouldn't have said this a month ago, but yeah. It is. And—I'm sorry I was rude when I first met you. It wasn't anything personal."

Something released in Pierre's chest. "Thank you." He would have turned to go, but Jessica still stood there, as if she weren't finished.

"I realized something tonight." Jessica released the doorknob and took a step closer, the porch light glinting on her blond hair, so like Bree's, only longer. "I want to go back to school."

"Really." He hadn't seen that coming.

"I don't want to live like this anymore." She gestured, hands to her sides. "Maybe working myself to exhaustion would be worth it if I were doing something I loved, but I'm not. I'm just getting by, sometimes not even that. I don't want this, not for me, not for my family—the one I have now, or the one I might have…someday." Her cheeks colored faintly.

"I think that sounds very wise." He looked up at her, tenderness warming his chest in the same way, if to a lesser degree, as it did toward his family. "I actually have some connections at Clark—you know, the local community college—if you're interested."

Jessica's mouth tipped. "You have an answer for everything, don't you?"

"If only." Pierre bid her good night and headed back down the walkway toward his waiting car, stars fading toward dawn overhead.

If only.

Chapter Nineteen

Bree sucked in a deep breath. *Please, Lord, let the gate open.*

The wrought iron swung in, and they hefted their luggage along the brick path leading to steps on the right wing of a U-shaped, cream-colored building with window boxes of red geraniums. Lighted palm trees and shrubs, more walks and green grass, all welcomed them in.

Bree looked around, shaking her head. "This is not what I expected." She motioned to the wall with bougainvillea in pink and magenta softening the upper edges. "Of course I had no idea what to expect but…Wow, this is amazing—looks almost medieval." Bree set her suitcase down, the better to study the scene. "All this behind that high wall."

"I sure hope our host is waiting for us." Lizzie blew out a breath. "I don't know about all of you, but I'm hungry."

"I have Vienna chocolate," Bree offered.

"That's okay, I'll wait." With the luggage now piled on the concrete-and-brick steps to the entry of matching wood-framed, etched-glass doors, Bree raised her iPhone flashlight to better see the code numbers in the dim light. She read them off while Denise pushed the buttons on the lighted panel. They all heard the click. Three steps and marble tiled floor with mahogany paneled walls reminded her of a fine, classic hotel with an elevator in the middle.

"Oh, my word." Bree could feel her eyes widen. And

they were spending a week—at this flat—in Florence, Italy. Upstairs, Bree knocked on the mahogany door. A click and the door of the flat opened.

"Hello, sir, I'm Bree Lindstrom. I'm sorry we're so late."

"Welcome, please come in." He extended his hand. "I am Adriano Ricci and I was getting very worried about you." He smiled to the others. "Please, all of you, come in and bring your luggage."

"I called and left several messages." Bree introduced the others. He shook hands with them all.

He shook his head. "Did you call the house phone or my cell?"

"I called the number listed on all the paperwork."

"The house phone. I asked them to put my cell number up too. You see, we live south of here now so our flat is available year-round." He led the way to a table in what might be called the sunroom. "Please have a seat so I can show you our book to make your stay easier and more pleasant. I'm sorry to rush you but I have a meeting to attend."

You can look later, she reminded herself, already enamored by the twelve-foot ceilings in all but the step-down sunroom, marble floors, the comfortable-looking furniture, all classic with beautiful woods and fabrics.

Signore Ricci opened a three-ring binder with all pages laminated in clear plastic. "Here is the floor plan. A bit of history—this building was built in the fifteen hundreds and our family has owned this flat for five generations; we are the fifth so our children will be the sixth. There has been major remodeling several times, the most recent in the fifties. We updated this flat as needed, the kitchen being the most recent."

He pointed out the page of contact numbers, another of local restaurants. Sights and contact numbers, and various instructions for all the appliances. "We have several rooms that are reserved for larger parties locked. My wife and I were hoping to show you around. She had another commitment today, but she will be here too, the day you check out."

He glanced around at all of them. "Do you have any questions before I begin the tour?"

Denise nodded. "Yes, what nearby restaurant do you recommend?"

"Our personal favorite is two blocks from here. You turn left at the street and it will be on the third block. The food there is always fresh and the staff is so friendly. We told them you were coming and to be extra nice to you."

"*Grazie.*" Denise smiled. "I just want to say too how much I am enjoying your accent." She glanced around. "And your home. This is so much more than we dreamed."

Bree added. "Yes, the online pictures do not do it justice."

He stood and they followed him on his tour. They had access to two bathrooms, three bedrooms, and all the general living area. And the two levels above, accessed by a narrow stairway at the end of the sunroom. As in their flat in Rome, shutters hung at the windows.

He made sure they had the two sets of keys and bid them happy touring.

"*Ciao.*" With a smile and a wave, he was gone.

Bree closed the door behind him, then turned and leaned her back against it. "I am in awe. To think I found this through our timeshare by looking up Florence, Italy. I never dreamed such a thing was possible."

"I know. Let's get our luggage into our rooms and then I'm all for heading down the street." Denise grabbed the handle to hers and led the way.

"How about Lizzie and I share this room that has two beds, and Denise, you take the master bedroom. Rachel, that one by the bathroom?"

"Are you sure?" Denise asked. "After all..."

"Lizzie and I have roomed together before. We do great."

"Perfect," Rachel added. "Mom snores."

Bree got the feeling Rachel was more than ready for some space from Denise.

Down on the sidewalk they turned left as instructed and picked up the pace.

"I'm surprised they're still open," Bree said when they saw the sign ahead.

"No, no, this is the time Italians eat. They do the siesta, then work a few hours and have a late dinner."

"And we eat early dinners. I could just crawl in bed if I weren't so hungry," Lizzie commented.

"Me, too, but we have to make the beds first. The linens are all laid out at least."

Rachel shrugged. "No biggie. I probably won't need a blanket anyway. You having your standard, Bree?"

"If you mean caprese salad..."

"Me too. Especially when they just picked the basil. Makes me want to grow some at home."

"You? Garden?"

Rachel shook her head at her mother. "Just a pot or two, surely we could handle that."

"Yeah, we." They stopped to read the menu in a lighted wall box.

"I still need more lessons in pasta," Bree sighed. "How come even reading the menu sounds delicious?"

A waiter stopped right behind them. "We try to make that happen. Will it be four?" At their nods, he motioned to a table right on the sidewalk and handed them menus when they sat. "I will be delighted to answer any questions but in the meantime, what can I get you to drink?"

They ordered their beverages, then a boy set a basket with various breads and the standard olive oil with balsamic puddled in the middle. His grin welcomed them. "You from the Ricci flat?"

"How did you know?"

"Signore Ricci called to say four American women were coming here, so..." His shrug was so Italian, Bree almost chuckled. There was a reason for stereotypes for sure.

"I have to quit chowing down on the bread and salad so I have room for the entrée." Bree spoke softly, which probably wasn't necessary since one of the other tables was growing louder with each refill of their wineglasses.

Signore Ricci had not stretched the truth when he said this place had great food. No one managed to clear everything off their plate by the time the waiter, wearing the required black apron double-tied around his hips, asked if they'd like dessert.

"What are you most known for?" Denise asked.

"Tiramisu, of course, but we make our own gelato and..."

"One dish chocolate and vanilla, four spoons."

They all groaned but no one ignored the dessert.

"Now you're going to have to roll me up the street," Lizzie said at the final spoonful. "Perfect, we got our gelato in for today."

Back at their home for the week, they helped one another make the beds and crawled in. Bree had opened the shutters on the window before they left for dinner to lean out and see the area. "You mind if we leave these open? Gives us a breeze at least."

"Or we could close them and turn on the A/C." Lizzie motioned to the unit sitting on the chest of drawers.

"I'd rather keep the window open."

"Me too."

*   *   *

When their room lightened in the morning, Bree looked up the wall to the ceiling. "Look, those dark dots on the wall are mosquitoes."

Lizzie stretched and yawned.

Stretching her arms, Bree caught herself scratching one. A field of red dots. "Oh, no. they all dined on me. And I never thought to bring bug repellent. Did you?"

Lizzie shook her head. "Mosquitoes never bother me. I guess these all figured you have better blood or some such."

They found Denise and Rachel at the table in the sun-room, eating.

"Hey."

"I got up early, grocery store two blocks away. Plenty for all. I bought a bottle of Chianti too, thought perhaps tonight we could do drinks up on the second floor and enjoy the lights of Florence."

"Now, that's service." Bree chose a yogurt and a banana and after pouring herself a cup of coffee sat down, automatically clicking on her cell phone.

Messages from Jessica, James, and finally one from Pierre. She didn't realize she'd been holding her breath until she saw his name. She started at the first. Cinders was back home. The bill was paid. James wrote the baby was doing well, but looked like it might come earlier.

Please, Lord, not till I get home.

Another from Jessica. Pierre was a really nice guy. And yes, she was tired but so far so good.

Pierre: *Sorry I've not been texting, let alone calling. We have a location for the coffee shop, the web master Jason found me is rather unusual, to say the least, but knows her stuff. Jessica is trying hard. I think she plans to call you soon. P.*

"Everyone okay?" Denise asked.

"I guess."

"And you heard from Pierre."

"How did you know?"

"Your face tells a thousand stories."

Great. At least she'd finally heard from Pierre, but no apology for hanging up on her. Had she misinterpreted that? And he said Jess was going to call, but not that he would. Had she just read more into their relationship than he did all along? But then why had he said that about being "taken with" Bree? She laid her phone down with a sigh.

"I'm calling the Accademia Gallery to make reservations, the sooner the better." Denise flipped to the proper page in the three-ringer. "Those people sure know how to host a vacation rental." She tapped in the number. "Yes, can I please speak with someone who speaks English, *grazie*?" When she clicked off, she raised her arms with a "yes!"

"When?"

"Day after tomorrow. First thing in the morning. Our choosing to come before tourist season is in full swing is paying off. I thought today perhaps we could just take it easy, walk around here, absorb daily life in Italy. There's a park not far away, interesting shops next street over, the grocery store is worth seeing, and the clerk this morning told me about a great restaurant about six blocks away. What do you think?"

Lizzie nodded. "Before we go out, I want to give that washing machine a try. Although hanging my clothes on those lines out the window..."

"When in Rome, do as the Romans do."

"Right. Or in Florence, do as the Florentines do. Anyway, what if something falls off and I have to go to that mini yard down there and pick it up..."

"There's no dryer here?" Bree asked.

"Nope. Book says hang 'em outside."

"Another adventure." Denise pushed over The Book, as they now referred to the binder the Riccis had put together for their guests. "You all oughta look through this. Lots more places to see than I realized."

"Does Florence close down for siesta time too?" Lizzie asked. "If so, we need to work around that." ·

By the time Lizzie had washed a load of clothes and very carefully either draped or pinned them to the lines on rollers and outside the windows, with the others holding their breath, Denise had taken pictures of the entire flat and the views from the windows, Rachel had filled more pages in her sketchbook, and Bree had written postcards to those back home. It was well past noon.

"Okay, we're out of here," Denise announced.

"Just a minute, I need to answer another email." Bree looked up from her laptop.

"Do it on your phone."

"Takes too long. This is from Paula."

"What has she to say about her brother?" Lizzie wiggled her eyebrows.

"Brother-in-law. And nothing. But she did say Jessica is burning her candle at both ends and in the middle, so she's been visiting the pets every day. Made her decide to get another dog, but probably not a puppy."

"Hey, there's a bakery on that street we're going to. This gives it five stars." Rachel looked up from studying The Book.

"Oh, oh, we're in trouble now," Lizzie muttered.

"Okay, done." Bree slammed her laptop closed. "You know what? Maybe I should just stay here. I've got to get in some brainstorming for this new series, and this could be a really creative place to work. Especially with all of you out of the flat."

"You'd rather do that than go sightseeing and…" Denise

dropped her voice to a whisper. "And visit the bakery and have caprese salad for lunch and…"

"You ever realize your middle name might be Temptress?" Bree slung her bag over her shoulder, stuffed her postcards in the outside pocket, and headed for the door. She'd just try to get back early and brainstorm before dinner. "Have you already taken pictures of this…" She motioned around the elevator landing. "And the courtyard, or whatever they call it here."

"Done but for some with all of us in the pictures." Denise herded them into the elevator. "I can do that another time."

"We need to find a drugstore." Bree scratched one of the bites on her arm. She looked like she'd stuck her arm in a mosquito swarm. "How come neither of you got bitten?"

Rachel and Denise both said they kept their shutters closed.

"Amazing there weren't blood splats on the wall from where I mashed some."

"When they're full, they leave, right?" Rachel asked.

"You think I need a transfusion?" Bree chuckled when they all rolled their eyes.

Bree found a drugstore for salve to stop the itching as well as repellent. She shook her head. "Seems so strange to buy something when you can't read what it is." The woman behind the counter smiled back, and Bree had her write which salve was which on the package. She gave directions, and a second recommendation, for the bakery and coffee shop combination. "You'll see the tables two blocks down. *Arrivederci.*"

Floating fragrances announced the bakery before they'd walked a block. Bree paused, inhaling and trying to identify the scents drawing her like a magnet. "Rich coffee."

"Almonds, yeast…" Lizzie's brow furrowed. "Not sure what the other might be."

"I don't care what they are, I am now officially starved." Rachel gave in and tipped her head like the others. "Sweet something. The Book said this bakery excels in both breads and pastries."

Together they picked up the pace, and Rachel held the door for all of them. They halted just inside and stared. Breads of all shapes and sizes filled shelves on the walls, and the glass-fronted display cases were divided by pastries, cookies, baked desserts, buns, and croissants.

"Someone pinch me, I think I must have died and gone to heaven." Bree, who loved to bake and was known for her cinnamon rolls, had no idea what most of the offerings were. "How are we going to get a taste of everything?"

"Easy. Well, sort of." Denise ignored the camera hanging from her neck. "We divide up the display cases."

"How about I get the beverages and the croissants?" Rachel offered. "Coffee, everyone? I know there are choices but..." They all nodded.

"Make mine a vanilla latte, the largest," Bree responded. "And while I'm sure there are various croissants, how about plain ones for today?"

"Bree, you and I'll do the pastries and such because we already lost our sergeant." She nodded toward Denise, who was already off in camera land.

The other two shrugged and away they went. "Let's get two each of an assortment, and that way we can cut them in half."

"*Buongiorno.*" A smiling woman, with her long hair in a bun of more salt than pepper, greeted them.

Both Lizzie and Bree returned her greeting.

"Can you please tell us what things are?" Lizzie asked.

"*Si.*" A smiling nod. "*Molto bene.*"

"Point," Bree whispered, trying to read the little card with (probably) the name, which meant nothing to her.

While she'd had lessons in speaking, Pierre Rene had not covered reading.

Lizzie pointed, motioning for two.

"*Si, si, cannoli.*" Neither of them understood what else she said.

"There's several kinds there," Lizzie whispered.

"Let me try." Bree racked her brain. "*Cos'è questo?*" What is it?

"Ah." The woman nodded, then began labeling the flaky pastries in the case for them.

"Let's take two of two, whatever flavor. She thinks you're Italian." She swallowed a giggle. After all, Lizzie looked the part.

"*Bene, bene.*" The woman's smile, showing off her gold tooth, grew wider.

Some looked similar to doughnuts. Bree pointed and held up two fingers, and the woman happily added them to their order.

Bree recognized the biscotti and chose two of each of the three. "I get these in the coffee shop in Vancouver, though ours don't look quite like this."

They chose two kinds of filled buns, and several other things that just looked intriguing.

"*Bene, bene.*" The lady pointed to the cashier and nodded more. "*Grazie, grazie.*"

"Well, we might like some better than others but I can't wait to taste them all." Bree paid for their two boxes and they followed a smiling younger woman who carried out a tray with coffee mugs, cream and sugar, and two plates of croissants and focaccia bread.

She set the tray down on the table under a shade umbrella where Rachel was already seated. "*Buongiorno*, welcome. My name is Anna."

"You speak English?"

"*Si*. We learned in school. Our second language. My mother did not, though, as you saw. You all did very well. *Bravissime!*"

"*Grazie*." Bree nodded. "You certainly speak better English than my Italian."

"I would most likely have trouble in America." She opened their boxes.

"Could you please identify our purchases? I want to write them down." Bree dug out her notebook and pen.

"Bree is a wonderful baker already." Lizzie leaned forward enough to inhale the aromas. "This looks too good to be true."

Anna nodded. "You know the biscotti, and the cannoli?"

"She might, but I don't," Lizzie answered.

Denise sat down at the table. "*Grazie*"—she smiled at Maria—"for letting me take such pictures. What a fascinating story you have here. Besides the delicious..." She motioned to their table with one hand, sipping from her coffee mug held in the other.

"You missed out on the fun." Lizzie and Bree grinned at each other.

"So what is this?" Bree pointed to a pastry that sported thin slices.

"That is *sfogliatella*, one of the most popular pastries in Italy. You will find a dark cherry filling in a flaky sweet dough." She deftly cut them in half. "I know you should start breakfast or lunch or whatever you are having with croissants and focaccia, but I want to watch your faces."

They all took a bite at the same time. Bree closed her eyes, the better to appreciate the flavor. "Oh, my word. So delicious but looks difficult to make."

"Not one of the easiest but..."

"But worth every effort." They all used their napkins, and

Denise shook her head. "I never tasted this one on my other Italy trip. Incredible."

"It has a different flavor…" Bree said.

"Instead of butter, tradition uses lard. And while some use other fillings, this dark cherry is the traditional. Now, how about this one. Looks like one of your doughnuts but here it is *bomboloni*."

"And that one?" Rachel pointed to a beautiful golden pastry.

Again, Maria cut the two in half. "This is *zeppole*; we use butter, eggs, and lemon for both the dough and the filling."

The lemon flavor exploded in Bree's mouth. As soon as she swallowed, she nodded. "This one I can learn to make. We took a cooking class in Perugia and made pasta with a meat sauce, and a delicious chocolate and pear cake. I'm sure there are pastry cooking classes here in Florence."

"Oh, yes, many. And some excellent illustrated cookbooks too. I've heard of several places that do online classes."

Bree and Denise swapped looks.

Maria identified several others then turned when someone called her name. "I better get back to help. If you have more questions, feel free to come again. We're happy to have you here."

They waved as she headed off. "What a fantastic waitress." Denise reached for a croissant. "I think we should come back."

Bree held up one of her half buns. "I want to learn to make these at home. There is something different in the crust too."

"Google it." Rachel spoke with a mouth half full. "Sorry, we need to have a cooking party when we get home. Bree, you already make such good bread and rolls, this should be easy for you."

"I'm planning on getting an Italian cookbook when we find a bookstore. Surely they have them in English too."

"Like Raffaela is dreaming of with all her grandmother's recipes?"

"Yes, just like that. Shame it wasn't ready."

"We shoulda taken this to the park."

"Nope, this is too perfect." Denise flagged one of the other waitresses. "Can you take a couple of pictures of us?"

"*Si.*" Their waitress took the camera and did so, handing it back to Denise who clicked through them and nodded. "Good job."

"So, do we buy pastries now to have with drinks up on the lanai, or patio, or whatever they call it here?"

"I suggest we buy some and then instead of more sight-seeing, join the siesta practice."

"You suppose my clothes are dry?"

Bree nodded. "Think I'll do a load before crashing." She stretched her neck, leaning her head from side to side. Maybe after that, she could manage to write. "We were supposed to stop at the grocery on our way back."

"Later." Denise covered a yawn. "You know what Lizzie said: 'When in Florence, do as the Florentines do.'"

Bree stood and pushed her chair back in. "I'll get some breakfast rolls."

"And I'll get the goodies for tonight."

❀   ❀   ❀

That night after dinner, the four of them made their way up to the lanai, where padded chairs flanked an iron table and a lounge sat off to the side.

"We can stop here or we can go up to the top of the building." Rachel pointed to a very narrow and steep stairway.

"The view across the city is lovely from here." Bree set

the plate of *dolce* on the table. She crossed to the railing where she could lean and gaze at the lights. A cathedral and several other very old lighted buildings made her wonder if they'd see them up close.

"You have a three-sixty view up those stairs, but there aren't any chairs up there."

"Then how about we save that for another night and enjoy our repast here?"

"Fine with me, heights and steep stairs aren't my favorite anyway." Lizzie sat down at the table. The others joined her.

"I didn't know you're afraid of heights." Bree pulled out her chair at the table.

"Not really afraid, let's just say I'm cautious."

Denise poured the wine and they all lifted theirs for a toast. "To seeing as much as we can and yet taking time to just enjoy each, including this lovely place we are staying."

The glasses sang the same note, and they each sipped.

"I am actually in the city in Italy where the *David* is on display. A city of such amazing history." Bree nibbled on a biscotti.

"Did you get any brainstorming done?" Lizzie asked.

"I did. Not as much as I would've liked, but some ideas are stirring." Felt good to have at least some of them jotted down, even if she had kept getting distracted wondering about Pierre and worrying about their relationship. Maybe she should just decide they were friends and leave it at that. No biggie if a friend hadn't called her back for a few days, right?

Her phone chimed the number she had for Jessica. "Hello, dear daughter."

"You sound happy, Mom."

"I am." She described where they were and what they were doing. "So you see, it would be a real shame to not be happy. And what's going on with you? How are you managing the two jobs?"

"Well, I wasn't managing too well, actually. But I've quit the grocery job now and started working for Pierre."

"Really?" Bree frowned. "How did that happen?"

"Before I bring you up to date, just know everything has turned out for the best."

Alarm bells rang in Bree's head. She blew out a breath. "So what happened?"

"I didn't want to tell you but Pierre said I must."

"Really." So Pierre was now involved in her daughter's life? What did that mean?

"Well, the night before last I came home from stocking shelves and put a can of soup on to heat, but then I sat down and fell asleep because I was just so tired. Then Spencer woke me and the stove was on fire. I called nine-one-one and grabbed Cinders and Spencer and we tore out of the house. The firemen put it out and said it could have been a lot worse and we are all right and Pierre showed up and offered me a job and James yelled at me and Paula had us come to her house and—" Tears halted her monologue.

"But you're all right?" Bree closed her eyes.

"Yeah, we're all right."

Oh, Lord, it could have been so bad. Thank you, thank you. You saved my daughter and my furry kids and my house too.

"So you're not working those kind of hours anymore?"

"No, even James said I couldn't keep doing that," Jessica continued as Bree tried to slow her pounding heart.

"But no one told me. You all texted me this morning, and not one mention. How could none of you have called me?" *How could they keep such a secret from me?*

"Everyone said I had to let you know, that they wouldn't tell on me, and I just...well, I didn't want to tell you I messed up again. I wanted to talk to the insurance company first. But now I'm going to need your input on working with the insurance and stuff; they'd said they'd need to talk to you so you can sign off on the repairs. But don't be mad at anyone, please—"

"I-I'm not mad at anyone, Jessica," Bree interrupted gently. "I'm just so grateful you weren't hurt."

But oh, Lord, I wondered if it was okay to leave Jess at home and now look what happened while I'm in Italy having the time of my life.

Chapter Twenty

With the cacophony of hammering and drilling coming from his kitchen-to-be in the coffee shop, Pierre-René was surprised he heard his phone.

He walked over to the far side of the room to hear better. "Hello?"

"Hey, Pierre. It's me, you know, Michelle."

"Hello, Michelle." Had they had an appointment to talk this morning? Not that he recalled, but so many to-dos kept adding to his list lately, he could have missed one. Though that wasn't like him. "What can I do for you?"

"Sorry to bother you, I just wanted to ask you something." Since it was still hard to hear over the ruckus, Pierre stepped outside. Even so, her voice sounded different from her usual confident rattle, more unsure, vulnerable. "I was just wondering, are you still looking to hire veterans for that place you've got?"

"Well, yes, I am." He hadn't expected that one. "I only just posted flyers at the VA, I was waiting till the renovations were underway."

"Cool, cool. Well, I might know someone who would be interested in, you know, interviewing. He has, what do you call it, managerial experience."

"Well, great. Could you give me his name and number, so I can contact him?"

"I can pass along the message. His name is Terrence Blaine. He's my cousin, actually." Michelle hesitated. "Do you think you could maybe interview him this week?"

"Well." Pierre stepped into the shade of a tree along the sidewalk. The spring sun beamed warm today. "I'm not quite ready to hire anyone yet. We're not finished with renovations."

"I know, I know. You wouldn't need to hire him or have him start working yet or anything. I just really feel like it would be good for him if he could meet with you soon, you know?"

"Why is that?" Something was going on here.

"He's just…had some issues, you know, and he really needs a better job. He's a veteran, that's what you want, right?"

"Yes. But Michelle, we're not a counseling facility. This would be a job, with responsibilities. Especially if he's interested in the manager position." He'd need someone he could count on, and right now experience and wisdom waved multiple red flags.

"I know, I get that, and so does he. That's why he doesn't even want to try—he's too hard on himself. But I just know if you would meet with him, like if I could tell him he has an appointment with you, he might not have enough time to talk himself out of it. And maybe if you met him, you'd, you know, actually give him a shot." Michelle's words almost tripped over one another, nothing new with her. But the urgency in her voice was new.

And for that reason, Pierre-René sighed and went against his better judgment. "All right. See if he could come to the location around five p.m. today. The construction should be finished for the day by then." At least he hoped so.

"Thanks, gosh, thank you, I really appreciate this."

"Can you at least give me Terrence's number so I can reach him if needed?" But Michelle was gone.

Pierre blew out a breath, the French exhale of frustration he'd picked up from his father, and pocketed the phone. He'd hoped to hire a steady manager to helm this operation, not one loaded with baggage. *Lord, give me wisdom in handling this.*

He headed back into the shop, where the noise level had risen even higher, if that were possible.

"What are they using in there, a jackhammer?" Raising his voice above the clamor, he crossed to the far corner where Paula and Jessica stood, comparing paint color cards with potential fabric swatches for the window shade. The grocery store had been able to release Jessica to start working for him right away, so she'd arrived bright and early an hour ago. A good sign.

"You'd think. But I believe they're just cutting into the wall to connect the plumbing for your additional sink." Paula held out two cards. "What do you think, Crème Brûlée or Buttered Toast?"

"Are those paint colors or items for our bakery?" Pierre bent closer. "They both look brown to me."

"No, no, no, not brown." Jessica shook her head, her ponytail flapping. "They are warm earth hues for your walls, to draw customers in and make them feel cozy and welcomed. I'm still partial to Mocha Latte myself. I mean, how perfect of a color is that, for your coffee bar?"

Pierre-René chuckled. "You really think the customers will care what shade is on the walls?" But he loved seeing light in Jessica's eyes. Only her first Tuesday working here, and already he could sense a new spark in her. Or maybe it had been there, but he'd just never seen it before—or it had been buried by recent cares. Something released in his chest, despite the worry from his phone call with Michelle.

Thank you, Lord. Inviting Bree's daughter to work here had definitely been the right thing.

"Subconsciously they will care. They'll know whether this place appeals to their senses, as well as their hearts. They'll know whether it makes them want to come back. Oh, and we're thinking either slate or a navy-blue print for the window shade." She waved fabric swatches at him like the flags of a conquering battalion. "Which makes you want to sit down for a cup of coffee rather than grabbing it to go?"

He was beginning to feel rather swarmed with enthusiastic women. But Pierre-René Dubois had never backed away from superior numbers. He grabbed the waving banners and studied them in the window's natural light. "I'd go with slate. We don't want our customers to feel like they're actually back in the military."

"Now you're getting the idea." Jessica beamed at him and pulled out her phone.

"You make notes on your phone?" Whatever happened to dependable pen and paper?

"I found an interior design app that's helping me organize everything and not miss any aspects we should be thinking about." Jessica looked up. "For example, have you thought about having a stenciled border below the ceiling molding? That could add a homey touch."

"Ah, no. I hadn't. But feel free to come up with ideas, and we'll see." Pierre scanned the space, already seeing new possibilities. "You know, I believe Michelle was using blues and browns in our website design also. You ladies must think alike."

"I know. I mean, about the blues and browns she's using." Jessica slid her phone back into her jeans pocket and went back to comparing the paint color cards, holding them up next to the window frame. "We've been emailing."

"You have?" He'd given Jessica a contact list of the people

on his business team, short as it was thus far. But he hadn't expected her to already be using it.

"Yeah, she seems really on top of things."

"She is." Except, perhaps, when it came to this cousin of hers. But that remained to be seen.

"Michelle said she really needs you to decide on the coffee shop name, though. Had any more thoughts?"

"I've been struggling over that one." Pierre scratched the back of his neck. "I am not sure why, but my brain simply refuses to cooperate with me on it." Perhaps because the project meant so much to him. "Though I have a basic corporation name, of course—had to for filing the initial paperwork."

"Oh, we can help with names." Paula turned from tucking dozens of fabric swatches back into an envelope. "Tell us your ideas so far."

"Michelle suggested Solid Ground, but I'm not sure I like that. Plus, apparently several places already have that name. I was thinking of just something simple, maybe The Coffee Place."

"That's a little plain." Paula cocked her head.

"Well, I don't want anything too fancy." Irritation prickled Pierre-René's neck. Why was this so hard? "I want vets to feel comfortable here, as well as families, kids, really anyone."

"Okay, so let's just brainstorm a bit." Jessica sat down in a metal folding chair Pierre had brought in and clasped her hands over one crossed knee. "Um, The Coffee Place...The Coffee Bar..."

"You want community—what about The Coffee Crowd?" Paula put in.

"The Coffee Commune." Jessica's mouth tipped.

"No." But Pierre felt a chuckle replacing the irritation. "Cups for All."

"The Grind of Life."

"Brew for You."

"A Cuppa GI Joes." Jessica snorted a giggle. "Sorry. How about Hope Brews Eternal? A little Shakespearean allusion."

The chuckle became real now. "Let's keep working on this."

But the laughter carried them through the rest of the morning of brainstorming and planning. By the time she and Paula left at lunchtime, Jessica had a paint order to place and they'd chosen a window shade from the online catalog she also pulled up on her phone. It seemed the younger generation nearly could exist in actuality off those devices these days.

✿   ✿   ✿

Late that afternoon, Pierre stood at the still-shadeless window, keeping a lookout for Terrence Blaine. He glanced at his watch. Five p.m. on the dot. If the man didn't show up on time, he'd know to trust his misgivings.

Behind the newly refurbished counter, Jessica was working to unpack the just-arrived coffee grinder from its carton, with Paula's help. Pierre felt guilty taking so much of his sister-in-law's time—she'd helped this morning already, after all—but Paula insisted she liked being busy.

Certainly work could be a balm for a grief-laden heart. He knew that well.

Pierre checked his watch again. Several minutes past five now. He shook his head and started to turn away. Might as well help the ladies with the unpacking.

Wait. He didn't always sense the heavenly whisper so clearly. Pierre turned back to the window.

A man in his late thirties approached along the sidewalk,

scanning storefronts. Medium muscular build, straight-shouldered bearing. A slight limp favoring his left leg. It was him.

Pierre-René opened the glass door. "Terrence?"

Relief lit the man's face, even-featured but for a scar that dented his nose. "That's me. Mr. Dubois?" He reached out his hand.

"Pierre-René Dubois." Pierre shook it. A firm grip. Good. "Come on in."

Once seated across from Pierre at a second metal folding chair, a card table set up between them, Terrence seemed to have trouble holding still. His hands rubbed his thighs or folded in and out of each other.

"I want to thank you for taking the time to see me." Terrence ran both hands over his head, his hair still cropped military-close. Some vets never broke that habit. "I know you're just starting to look for hires, Michelle told me. I told her she shouldn't have asked what she did, not for me. I apologize."

"No apology necessary." Pierre clasped his hands between them on the card table. "So, Terrence, tell me about yourself. Michelle says you have managerial experience."

"Yes, sir, I do." Terrence shifted forward in his seat, then back. But his dark-brown eyes held Pierre's. "I was a manager in an office store for a while, then most recently in a frozen yogurt shop. Here." He pulled a folded résumé from his shirt pocket and slid it across the table.

Pierre studied the document. "I see. And can you tell me why you left these jobs?"

Terrence hesitated. His gaze flicked away, then back to meet Pierre's once more. "I'll be honest with you. I was fired."

"And why was that?"

The vet laid his hands on the table. Pierre noted that his

beefy fingers were trembling—also that the thumb and two fingers of the right hand were badly scarred.

"I have PTSD." Terrence's voice came surprisingly steady. "I did three tours in Iraq and Afghanistan, had an IED blow up right in front of my vehicle during the last. I'm dealing with it, doing better now, but sometimes I still have flare-ups. And back then, when I was working those jobs, it was bad. I was good at my job, anyone there will tell you that. But once in a while, I'd have a bad day, and yell or snap at somebody, a co-worker, couple of times even a customer. Or something would trigger me, and I'd space out and miss something important I was supposed to do. So yeah, I understand why they fired me."

"I see." Pierre fingered the paper. "And why do you think you would do differently at this job, Terrence?"

"I'm in a different place now. I'm not over it, not totally, I won't lie to you. But it's better. Back then, I dipped in alcohol, I was a mess. Now I'm in AA, and in counseling. I haven't had an episode where I flipped out in over a year. And even when I did, I was never, you know, violent or anything."

"And right now you're working at"—Pierre glanced down—"a drive-through?"

Terrence nodded, his hands rubbing each other again. "Yeah. It's not much, just flipping burgers. But I haven't had any episodes there, you can check."

"You married, Terrence? A family?" Pierre folded the résumé.

"Married ten years now." Terrence dug a photo from his wallet and held it out. A beautiful, auburn-haired woman. "She's amazing, my Sarah, stuck with me through it all. Not that it was easy—lots of times I thought we weren't going to make it, you know. But we're in marriage counseling too now, and things are better." A shy grin crossed his face as he stuffed his wallet back in his pocket. "Expecting our first baby this fall. Finally."

"Congratulations." Pierre smiled at the younger man, hoping the genuine warmth he felt showed on his face.

Terrence sobered. "That's another reason why I could really use a better job. Flipping burgers doesn't really do it to raise a kid."

"Well, Terrence, I appreciate your honesty. I don't have to tell you most men starting a business would feel you were too high a risk to hire on, especially in a leadership position. And that's what I'm looking for, an onsite manager for this place."

"Yeah. I understand." Disappointment washed over Terrence's face, but he schooled it back to neutral and pressed his hands on the table preparing to stand. "I really appreciate your willingness to meet with me."

"Wait, I'm not finished." Pierre held up his hand. "I still want to call your references, confirm what you've told me. But I think it fair to tell you I'm seriously considering you for this position."

"Seriously?" Terrence stared at him.

"I don't know how much Michelle told you about this place, but while it will have a broad audience, military veterans are a big part of my heart for what this business will be." Pierre hesitated. "I am one myself, you see."

Terrence nodded slowly. "I see." Something in the keenness of his gaze made Pierre wonder just how much this man did see. "But I wouldn't blame you if you, you know, didn't want to take a chance on me. For a leadership position, like you said."

"Well, I'm not promising you the job just yet. But giving folks a chance is a big part of what I want this place to be about." He stood and offered his hand.

Terrence pushed himself up and gripped it. "Thank you." His throat worked.

The sudden whiz of a motor made both men jump and look toward the counter.

"Sorry." The sound switched off, and Paula and Jessica glanced over, their faces guilty. "We just tried plugging in the coffee grinder, didn't realize it was on."

"Not a problem." Pierre's pulse settled back.

"Looks like it's going to be a great place." Terrence shoved his hands in his pockets and glanced around. "You got a name yet?"

That again. Pierre shook his head with a touch of chagrin. "Afraid not. Terrence, this is Paula, my sister-in-law, and Jessica." How to introduce Jessica? "She's my first employee, helping us get set up here."

"Right now for names we're between The Coffee Place, The Gathering Place, and A Cup of Hope." Jessica bent to peer under the shiny new machine, adjusting some setting. "What do you think, Terrence?"

"I like The Gathering Place." Terrence gave a nod. "Seems to fit what you're doing here, gathering folks together, wherever and whatever they might be from." He glanced at Pierre as if fearing he'd overstepped. "Just my opinion, sir."

"At ease." Pierre gave him a brief smile. "I'll think on it. And I'll be in touch, Terrence."

"Thank you, sir." With goodbyes all around, Terrence headed back out to the street.

"He seems like a nice young man." Paula flipped through the instruction manual. "Ugh, I can never make heads or tails of these instruction thingies."

"Here." Jessica took the pamphlet. "It doesn't look that different from the one at the coffee place I worked before. Should be pretty straightforward."

"Thank God for your experience, Jessica." Pierre-René

leaned on the counter. "I don't know what we'd do without you."

Jessica's ears pinked as she bent back over the grinder's settings. Was she that unused to praise? "I'll need to get some coffee beans to really try this thing out."

"I can place a preliminary order once all the business paperwork goes through. Some of it I'll need a name to finalize. But maybe we finally have that. For now, I'll bring some beans from home."

"Or I can." Jessica straightened, one hand on the machine. "I've been coming up with some ideas for different drinks you could offer too—if you're interested."

"'If'? I am forever grateful." Pierre opened his briefcase on the counter and tucked Terrence's folded résumé inside. "And how are things going with the repairs after the fire?"

"Better than I could have hoped, honestly." Jessica sighed. "I was lucky to get a meeting with the insurance company's inspector right away, and the damage is less than we thought at first. He thought the insurance company would cover most of the repairs. I'll pay my mom back for the remainder, of course, since it was my fault. But she's giving me whatever time I need. I really appreciate you sharing that contractor's name. I'm meeting with him tomorrow."

"And what do you hear from your mother?" He hoped the question didn't sound as awkward as it felt.

"She's doing okay. So excited to finally see the *David*, was it today? Maybe yesterday, I get confused with the time difference."

"They're in Florence already?" Pierre frowned. Had the time passed that fast?

Both women looked at him as if he'd grown another arm.

"Bree didn't tell you?" Paula cocked her head, a thousand questions in her eyes.

"Ah, no." Because he hadn't talked to her in almost a week.

Pierre's neck started to flame. What had possessed him to bring Bree up right now, with two of the women who knew her best? He bent back to his briefcase, shoving papers into place with uncharacteristic disorder. "I'll have to ask her the next time we talk." Which had better be soon. But she hadn't called him either, so it wasn't entirely his fault. Yes it was, he was the one who had hung up, for Pete's sake.

With Jessica's and Paula's stares boring into the back of his head, Pierre mumbled something about needing to go call these references and made his escape out the door.

It wasn't till he arrived back at his condo and sat down alone at his desk that he finally admitted the truth that had been niggling at him since meeting with Terrence today.

That younger veteran, with his wounds visible and invisible, yet all acknowledged, was a far braver man than he.

Chapter Twenty-One

None of them let me know.

Bree hated waking in the middle of the night stewing about something. A fire in her kitchen big enough to call 911. Jessica asleep at the table. *Thank you, Lord, that Spencer woke her up.* She knew how deeply her daughter slept when she was exhausted.

Bree sat up in bed and grabbed her wrap from the foot. *Paula knows me well enough to know how I needed to know what's happening.*

She could see her kids keeping something from her, to protect either her or them.

The marble tile felt cool on her feet. Ramming her arms in the wrap sleeves, she found her glasses and her iPhone on the dresser and left the room. At least she could let Lizzie sleep. While it was still star-studded dark outside, the night-light in the hall guided her to the sunroom. Looking out over the city, Bree could see the lights still dotting the darkness like land stars. *Three a.m. What time at home? Six p.m. Yesterday.*

Jessica would be at Applebee's at the busiest time of day. Would today be her first day working for Pierre? James might be home with his family by now, in the midst of dinner. Paula—she might be at Bible study, if she'd gone back since Peter died. Pierre. Working on his coffee shop plan, maybe eating alone in his condo or with Jason.

Why do you care what they're doing?

Someone should've called. If I can't trust them, how can I dare to be gone again? So much for my new ideas of traveling more.

She paced. She moved into the living room and sank into one of the stuffed chairs. Tipping her head back, she stared at the ceiling.

Call Paula.

I don't want to call Paula. She has enough to handle with the grief. Her daughter had gone home by now. She was alone.

Lord, I trusted you with all my family and look what happened. She felt a tear trickle down her cheek.

What happened? that familiar voice whispered.

Jessica could have been burned, died.

Could have but she didn't. Spencer did his job, the firefighters took care of their jobs, and you planned on repainting that kitchen anyway. Now the insurance will pay for it.

A chuckle seemed to float on the still air.

You're mad because they didn't let you know. As if you could have done anything from halfway around the world.

. . . *But stew.* Bree nodded. And that's what she did . . . get all angry and worried and . . . and trust flew right out the window. So long she'd been the one in charge, the one who took care of everyone and made everything happen. *Did you bring me to the other side of the world to show me it's really not all up to me, Lord?*

Back out in the sunroom, she could see the band of yellow white fading the indigo to azure. Should she make a cup of coffee? Go back to bed? She'd lie down on the sofa, lots of throw pillows. And so she did. And promptly fell asleep.

"What are you doing out here?" Lizzie asked. "Are you all right?"

Bree sat up and yawned. "What time is it?"

"Seven. Are you all right?"

"I am now." Bree yawned again. "Woke up all angry that no one called me or even texted me about the fire at home."

"Oh. But Jessica called you."

"Yeah, a day later."

"I see. And I was lying awake worrying that Steve and Elisa will be getting on each other's nerves at home without me there to be a buffer between them."

"Does that happen a lot?" Lizzie didn't talk much about her family life, her heart.

"Probably not as much as I think it does. I was so reluctant to even get involved with Steve when we first met, worried over how it would affect my daughter. But overall, even though they clash at times, it's been good. I need to remember that."

"Mm. Sometime I might want to pick your brain about..." She hesitated. "Starting over, you know. With a new relationship. Later in life." Her face heated. Not that she even knew what this thing with Pierre was.

But Lizzie gave her an understanding smile. "Anytime. It's not all easy, for sure, and definitely not simple. But it can be very, very worth it."

"Thanks." Bree drew a breath.

"You want to go for a walk? I need to wake myself up so I'm ready for the Accademia. Today you get to see your *David*."

"I know." A fresh frisson of excitement ran down Bree's arms. "And then soon, you'll get to see your Venice."

"I can hardly wait. You think you'll do okay there? I know you and boats..."

"I think so." Bree shook off a niggling fear. She hadn't

been on a boat since Roger died on one, but surely that was long enough ago. "I always used to dream of taking a gondola ride. You'll be right there with me, right?"

"Every step of the way."

By the time they returned with fresh calzone, Denise was in the sunroom, going through photos on her camera.

"You've been to the bakery. Smells heavenly."

"And the fruit market. Guess this is one good thing about city living. Shops are in walking distance."

"At least in Italy and in the right neighborhood." Denise followed them into the kitchen. "I made another pot of coffee."

"Did Lizzie tell you our adventures yesterday?" Bree poured herself a fresh cup. "You know, after you two left so early to walk down the Ponte Vecchio to the Pitti Palace for Rachel's book idea, Lizzie and I brought another of my dreams to life. We found this corner café open and people-watched. We filled our pages with observations of life in Florence. I just wish I could understand the conversations around me. While I picked up a word now and then, they all talked so fast and in other languages too..." She shook her head. "I took pictures of some characters. As you know, cameras are so much faster than writing. After a while we caught a taxi to an open-air market where we strolled, shopped, and ate lunch. You should have seen the stall of leather products from Turkey, I think."

"So, do you know where you were?"

"I wrote it down. Should have taken a picture of the sign." Shaking her head, she rolled her eyes. "Just didn't think of it. I finally bought a leather shoulder bag for Paula and a small leather horse for Luke, along with a new wallet for James. At least I have some of my gifts taken care of."

"We better hustle, that taxi should be here in twenty minutes or so."

Their taxi arrived for the Accademia Gallery, getting them there in plenty of time for their 10:00 a.m. tickets. The line was already long, waiting for the doors to open.

Denise waited in line to pick up their tickets at the ticket window and the others went to the back of the line for the entrance. Once inside, their line continued down a hall where they chose to tour the amazing display of the earliest string instruments: violins, pianos, and many with only Italian names, Stradivari being the only one she recognized. Once again she was reminded how old the history was in this city of Florence. Many of the arts had grown here due to the wealth of the families that could support it. Great artists had walked these streets and lived in many buildings still in use. What treasures were hidden behind courtyard walls. Slowly the line moved down another hall, where Renaissance paintings in ornate frames, etchings, smaller statues on pedestals lined the walls.

That hallway broke into a huge hall called The Tribune. Bree stepped back from the moving crowd to look to the far end where the *David* was lighted from all sides and angles. She caught her breath. *I'm really here. Even this far away, he's larger than I thought and…and…* The beauty made her sniff and blink. *This is so much more than I dreamed.*

Denise huddled them together. "How about we all spend as long as we want here? No rush, we've got all day if you want."

Bree nodded. "Good idea." She sniffed again. "I've always dreamed of sitting looking at him and now there's all this other stuff too. Pierre said he liked the *Prisoners* even more than the *David*."

What would it be like to see a place like this with Pierre? The thought caught her by surprise. Various tour groups moved through the throng while Bree and Lizzie stopped to see each piece, read every sign, learn all that they could. All the sculptures were by Michelangelo. The *Prisoners* lined both sides of the hall, each an unfinished male statue, each emphasizing a different part of a man. The hand and arm showed every sinew, every scar, every callus. One powerful leg showed a gash.

Studying each piece made her even more aware of the complexity of the human body. These were not noblemen, soft and waited on; these were workingmen, laborers, fishermen, carpenters. Back and forth across the room, Bree and Lizzie moved to keep them in order. One man created all this and painted the Sistine Chapel. They paused at the statue named St. Joseph, which reminded Bree so much of the *Pietà* at St. Peter's Basilica, which they had toured another day. This time Mary was holding the baby, and Joseph's cloak surrounded them. In the *Pietà,* Mary held the broken body of her crucified son. Bree ignored the tears streaming down her face.

She turned to Lizzie. "That makes me think more of God protecting them than Joseph."

Lizzie nodded and mopped her eyes.

Still back from the *David*, Bree turned to finally look at him. Yes, larger by far than she'd realized, seeming so alive. Could he see Goliath? The sling and small stones. Lights surrounded the marble statue, behind and above. Visitors could walk behind him, all around him. Slowly she drew nearer, pausing, trying to think like the genius who had brought this perfect figure from a block of marble, chiseling away. After moving around him studying his hands, his feet, his head, she pulled away to see the whole again.

Statistics and his history were listed in books she knew would be available at the gift store, but that could not begin to describe the power that emanated from him. And yet the challenge ahead.

David, the boy who felled the giant Goliath with three small stones and a sling.

An artist who chipped away at a piece of marble to reveal this trapped inside it.

What eyes and mind it took to see that.

Never had she thought there could be life in marble. *Oh, Jade, thank you. I wish you could be here with me.* She could just see how her friend would smile, watching Bree right now.

Bree moved back and found a seat in front of a carved pillar, grateful to be able to sit down for a while. Words were not enough. She slipped into people-watching mode. Selfies being taken all around her. A young couple, maybe twenties, posing with their backs to the *David*, and the woman taking the photo. Applying lipstick, fussing with her hair, the man simply waiting. Did he even end up in the picture? Did she care? Bree could feel her head shaking without her volition. She thought about taking out her camera and taking the photo she saw but decided to not waste her effort.

The woman sitting beside her called a man to task for using an unlawful flash. Signs everywhere warned that no flash cameras were allowed. Bree watched her, obviously an employee or perhaps volunteer of the Accademia. *Classical* was the word she chose to describe the woman of some years, but aging beautifully, thick shoulder-length hair that turned under just enough to frame the Italian face, dark eyes, set in high cheekbones, sculpted nose and chin, an arresting face, and a carriage that matched.

"Do you do this every day?" Bree asked her.

The woman nodded. "*Si*, several of us take turns."

"You must see all kinds." Bree motioned to the constantly moving crowd.

"*Si*." Her voice was rich, flowing honey. "You are from America?"

"Easy to tell?"

The woman nodded, a slight smile moved from her mouth to her eyes. "I hope you are enjoying yourself here."

"Oh, I am. Living a lifelong dream to see the *David* in person. Not in a book or on a screen, but real."

"Is he all you imagined?"

"Far beyond what I ever dreamed." She looked around. "I did not consider crowds like this."

"You were wise to come before the tourist season really begins. We have to monitor the numbers that come through here." She rose to admonish another flash taker.

"With all the incredible lighting in here, why do they use a flash?"

She shrugged, a Gallic shrug, giving Bree a picture to go with words she'd read many times. "I've been at this position for several years and yet...yet I am still in awe. They just don't understand that flashes will eventually damage the marble. We have all special lighting that keeps that from happening. We warn them once, then we call for the guards to take them out of the entire building." She shook her head. "Most people comply with the signs, though."

"*Grazie*, you have made my time here even more delightful. May I take your picture?"

"I—I see no reason but if you would like, of course." She smiled and one eyebrow raised slightly. "Without flash, of course."

After she left there, Bree wandered back to where they came in and started over again, to refresh her mind on each of the works. Which one of the prisoners did she like best? Why did she have to choose? She stood in front of *St. Matthew*. How could that man get so much feeling from a block of stone? She looked at the paintings but it was easier to keep on moving. She found Lizzie sitting at another column in the hall adjacent to The Tribune.

Bree sat down beside her. "Have you seen the others?"

"Last I saw Rachel she was sketching one of the *Prisoners* and I've not seen Denise." She scooted over to make room for Bree. "I'm just enjoying watching the people right now. Talked with an older man and his adult son, here for the first time. The son brought his father, in a wheelchair. Such love between the two. The son said his father made many of his dreams possible and now he wanted to do the same for his father. The look between them made me about cry."

Bree told her about the woman she'd been visiting with. "So many people with so many stories."

"I think I'm ready for lunch." Lizzie stood and rolled her shoulders. "I am so grateful that I got to come and to see all this. I wonder what year this building was constructed. Or probably years. Everything has so much history."

Rachel caught up with them. "Perfect timing. Mom just texted and she's in the gift store by the exit."

"Did you get as much as you wanted?"

"Probably not if I was here every day for a week."

They glanced at many of the paintings as they followed the line through several other rooms with walls of paintings.

"Do we have a time limit here?" Bree asked as they entered the store.

"When my stomach grumbles loud enough to be heard?" Rachel shrugged.

"Are you starving?"

"Oh, I'll live. I mean, I'm used to trying to pry my mother out of a bookstore, or rather gift shop. Oh and she said, remember we have to wrestle our own luggage sometimes."

"Good point." Bree made herself stay away from the big coffee table books of the gallery and of Michelangelo's works. Instead she picked up a small, paperback biography of him. She read a couple of pages, and it was like stepping back a few hundred years to life in his day. After hitting the postcard racks, she lined up to check out. Her attention kept drifting to the big books. *You can find them all on the internet*, she ordered herself. Easy to call them up there.

She'd almost picked up a DVD that she could show her family when she got home but refrained from that too. It couldn't begin to re-create her time in The Tribune.

Instead of searching out another place, they decided to eat at the Ristorante right where they were. When the waiter seated them, they all looked around and then grinned at one another. *Good choice*, Bree thought. She'd been surprised when she checked her watch. Already after three. No wonder they were hungry.

"What if we order a pizza and individual salads?" Rachel suggested. "I've been watching their pizzas go by. They look really good."

"Sounds like a winner to me." Bree laid her menu down and inhaled. "So many delicious smells. Feels like the hardest part of this trip is deciding what to eat. I want to try everything." She gave a definitive nod. "And this time I'm not going to order caprese salad." The others applauded.

Later as they stepped back out on the sidewalk, Denise asked, "So what would you like to do next?"

"What are our options?" Lizzie asked.

"We can go back to our flat, or walk around this area and see what we can see, or..."

"Sit at a café, drink caffe, and people-watch or..." Bree looked down the street. "Or go see that fountain." She pointed. "Surely there's a café on that square."

"Gelato vendor ahead," Lizzie intoned.

"I had to make decisions at lunch and now again. I'm tired of making decisions." Bree laid the back of her hand to her forehead. "Oh, woe is me."

"I'll tell you what to order," Rachel teased. "I'm having pistachio if they have that."

"You ordered that before," observed Denise.

"I know, I like it." She grinned at her mother.

They found a bench overlooking the fountain and sat, licking their cones. "Is there any rule that says we can have only one gelato a day?"

"For you it's not a problem. For me, gelato likes me so well it takes up residence. I should be more cautious." Denise moaned.

"There you go with the 'shoulds' again. Remember Thou shalt not should upon thyself? Excellent commandment." Bree licked a runaway gelato melt. "Look at those little kids."

"Bet that splashing feels good today, plenty warm."

The boy splashed the girl and, giggling, she splashed him back. Two women sat on another bench talking, but one was keeping an eye on the two.

Bree glanced down to where Rachel sat cross-legged on the brick courtyard, her pencil flying across the paper. First the fountain, then the splashing children. Bree pulled her iPhone from her bag and, bringing the focus nearer, clicked pictures of the children. She took several shots of Rachel drawing, of hand and pencil moving across the paper. The growing sketch. Lizzie wandered over closer to the fountain.

Rachel flipped the last page over.

"Do we need to find an art store?" Bree asked.

"I have another back in my room. But if you see one, sing out. I always try to keep at least one new pad ahead." Rachel smiled up at her.

"What will you do with all these sketches?"

Rachel shrugged. "I use them sometimes as a basis to finish creating the scene, to remind me of where I've been.

To keep getting better at sketching. I've always wanted to create a picture book with both illustrations and text."

"You got your master's in illustrating, right, so what's happening? Like that Halloween book."

Rachel shrugged.

"I thought you really liked it."

"Profs said it wasn't good enough for publication."

"Really? Did you ever show it to an agent?"

Rachel shook her head.

"How many of them have sold picture books?"

Another shrug.

The line that sang through Bree's mind was *Those who can, do; those who can't, teach.* Too often she'd seen the wisdom of that in action. Something that made her careful who she was taking classes from.

"So where is the book now? Did you finish it?"

Rachel nodded. "That one I did. I have a couple of others started."

Bree looked up when she heard a scream. Just in time to see someone running away and Lizzie falling, arms flailing, hitting the edge of a curb. Crumpled in a heap.

Chapter Twenty-Two

"*Aiutare a vigili, un borseggiatore!*" a man near Lizzie yelled. He crossed to kneel beside her, concern etched on his face.

"Lizzie, oh Lizzie," Bree muttered as she dashed to her friend.

The man looked up and asked something.

"I'm sorry, I don't—I can't understand you."

A *vigile*, one of Italy's patrolling policemen in uniform, blew his whistle and arrived at about the same time.

Bree knelt at her friend's head. "Lizzie, can you hear me?"

"Someone pushed me and tried to take my purse." Her voice was soft but coherent.

"You see this person?" the *vigile* asked.

Lizzie started to shake her head, then thought better of it. "No, but he didn't get anything." Her one hand was still clenched on the strap across her chest.

The man turned to the *vigile* and spoke rapid-fire Italian, pointing. The *vigile* nodded then jogged off, apparently in pursuit of the thief.

"Can you tell me where you're hurt?" Bree asked Lizzie.

"My face."

"Uh-huh, you're bleeding. Do you think you can turn over?"

"No, no." The man made a gesture, pressing his palm

toward the ground and shaking his head. Bree caught the word *ambulanza* in his rapid Italian.

"I think he's saying not to move, there's an ambulance coming," Denise said.

"Or is he saying we need to call one? How do we call?" Rachel asked.

Denise pulled out her phone. "The travel agent gave me some information on what to do in an emergency. I think I still have the email somewhere."

Bree dug in her bag and pulled out a packet of tissues. "Here, let me put this on your forehead. See if we can stop the bleeding."

"Can you tell if you're injured anywhere else?" Rachel asked.

"Move your feet?" Bree suggested.

"Something wrong with the right one."

"Okay, your hands."

"Left works, still lying on my right one but not good."

They heard the growing *wee-waa* scream of an ambulance in the distance. Someone must have called for them. *Thank you, Lord.*

The *vigile* returned—empty-handed.

Rapid Italian between the man and the returning policeman.

"We searched but lost him. He was a young man, quick on his feet. This man gave a description but all the thief had to do was shed his coat and he could disappear in the crowd."

The ambulance shut off the siren as it braked to a stop.

Two men grabbed medical bags and strode to where Lizzie still lay, the stack of tissues blood-soaked.

"Anyone see my glasses?" Lizzie asked.

"Here they are." Rachel picked them up. "One lens is gone, but I have them." The three friends stepped back to let the medics take over.

"*Parla italiano?*"

"*Solo un po*," Bree answered. "We're American tourists. *Parla inglese?*"

One man said yes, the other shook his head.

"Do not worry, *signora*, we will take care of you. Now you tell me where you hurt."

"Does all over count?" Lizzie asked.

"*Si*, I understand. But where specifically, *per favore*."

"My face, my right foot, and perhaps my right arm or shoulder?"

"Your neck?"

"No."

The older medic examined Lizzie's foot. Said something, and felt up her legs.

"Your paperwork is in your bag?"

Lizzie nodded and grimaced.

"How is the pain?"

"Getting worse." She shivered.

"Getting shocky?" Bree asked the young medic.

"I do not understand."

"Is she going into shock?"

"Ah." He nodded. "Not surprising. We need to get her in the ambulance."

"May I go with her?" Bree asked when they lifted Lizzie onto the gurney.

"You are family?"

"No, a close friend."

The man shook his head. "Only family in the ambulance. You can follow."

"Where are you taking her?" Denise asked.

"The Ospedale Santa Maria Nuova."

"We'll be there as soon as we can." Bree gave Lizzie's hand one last squeeze, then released her as the men hefted the gurney, her heart screaming to go with her friend.

Denise, beside Bree, hugged her arm as they watched Lizzie loaded into the ambulance, then the siren wailed again as it started up and rumbled away through the narrow, winding streets.

"I wish they would have let me go with her." Bree fought the urge to cry.

"We'll be back beside her before you know it." Denise's in-charge voice had returned. "Come on, let's hail a taxi. And we'll be praying all the way."

※   ※ . ※

It seemed like hours before Bree found Lizzie on a gurney in the emergency room at Santa Maria Nuova. Denise and Rachel had to remain in the waiting area.

"Hey," Lizzie muttered around the ice packs on her face.

"How are you feeling?"

"They gave me a pain med in the IV in the ambulance, it's helping."

A nurse stopped by to check on her.

"Do you speak English?" Bree asked.

"I do."

"How bad do you think this is?" Bree asked.

"She will need stitches on her forehead. Her eyes will be bruised, scrapes, and we must check for concussion. They will x-ray her right arm and foot, I am sure. Do not worry. We will take good care of her." She smiled reassuringly and stepped away.

"Bree, I'm so sorry."

"Sorry for what? You didn't cause the accident."

"I know, but..."

"Not your fault someone chose to be a pickpocket. You followed all the warnings."

"Except I was by myself. A sitting duck."

"That's why things like this are called accidents, Liz." Bree squeezed her friend's left hand. "We'll get through it."

Bree was allowed to wait by the gurney in the ER to speak with the doctor. Lizzie was fighting to stay awake but the meds were doing their job.

When they brought Lizzie back from X-ray, the same nurse returned to translate for the doctor. "He says we should keep her overnight for observation. We will keep ice on her shoulder and foot, then cast that foot in the morning. The shoulder has been put back in place so she will need a sling on that arm. After the cast, she must stay off that foot for at least a week if not longer."

Bree focused hard to understand with the accent. "But there's no sign of concussion?"

The nurse translated to the doctor before replying, "None. Her face will look bad but nothing is broken."

"Would the best thing be to fly her home?"

"I believe so, yes," the nurse translated.

Bree nodded. *"Grazie,"* she said to the doctor. "I'll tell the others."

"We will move her to a room now," the nurse said as the doctor departed.

"Can we see her before we leave? I could spend the night here."

"You could. But we will monitor her pain levels so she will be sedated. If nothing else shows up, we will transport her to the airport."

"I will deal with the flight arrangements and let you know what flight."

"Yes, I am sorry your visit to my country has been disrupted."

"And you will explain all this to her?"

"Si," in the morning when she will be aware again. I will come for you when we have her settled."

"Grazie."

An aide showed her back to the room where Denise and Rachel waited.

Sinking down in a chair, Bree started to tell the others when a tear that ambled down her cheek was chased by a horde of others. "Great, now I'm being a baby." She mopped her face with the tissues Denise handed her. "She'll have to be off that foot for at least a week, so they'll transport her to the airport when we have a flight for her tomorrow." She sniffed and blew again. "She was looking forward to Venice especially, and now she's getting shipped home."

"But no other damage?"

"Dislocated shoulder, badly bruised arm, broken right foot will be casted when they get the swelling down; she has stitches in her forehead and her face will probably look like hamburger. But none of that is major, for which I'm so thankful."

Denise and Rachel both nodded. "So we call or text our travel agent and she will deal with the flights and let us know."

"Really?"

"Really. That is one of the things included in her fees. One less thing for you to stew about."

"Yes, but what if she has to change planes? She can't walk," Bree said.

"Maybe one of us needs to go with her?" Rachel suggested.

"Let's ask the travel agent for advice," Denise suggested. "I'm sure she's had experience with this."

"I need to call Steve." Bree blew her nose and mopped the now-dripping tears away. "Let's see, seven p.m. here means it's ten a.m. at home, right?" At their nods, she dug out her phone and clicked Lizzie's home number.

Her husband answered. "Hi Bree, is something wrong?"

"What makes you ask that?"

"You're calling, not Lizzie."

"You're right, I have bad news." She went on to tell him what had happened.

"But she's all right?"

"Yes, but the doctor here said since she has to stay off that foot for at least a week, the best thing is to send her home. Denise is talking with our travel agent now and she'll make the arrangements."

"Oh, my poor Lizzie. When can I speak with her?"

"She is sedated now and being moved to a room. If she is alert at all, I will call you back so you can talk with her." Bree felt the tears renewing. "I'm so sorry, Steve."

"Me too. Would staying longer in the hospital there be better? I could fly over there and…"

Bree blew her nose and mopped again. "I think this way might be for the best."

"She wanted to see Venice the most."

"I know. She was so pleased the pickpocket didn't get her bag. She was hanging on to it so hard, the medics about had to cut the strap to get it away from her."

"That's my Lizzie." Bree could tell he was choking up too. "But she'll be all right?"

"Yes, she will." *Please, Lord, let that be so.* As she clicked off, she saw a nurse coming toward them.

"We have her settled and she is somewhat awake. Please follow me." She started to turn. "I am so sorry this will disrupt your time in Italy." She shook her head. "Pickpockets are…" She mumbled something in Italian that Bree had an idea she should just ignore.

Once they were in the room, Lizzie's eyes fluttered open when Bree took her hand. "I—I'm sorry."

"Me too. I just talked with Steve and…" But Lizzie was out again.

"Keeping her sedated for a few more hours will be easiest for her," the nurse said with a nod.

"I know. Perhaps when she wakes up, we will have more information for her."

"We will be in contact with you."

"*Grazie.*"

"Come," Denise said. "We'll go back to our flat and work on all this."

"I feel like I should stay with her."

The nurse shook her head. "We will monitor her and call you if there is any change."

        ❖   ❖   ❖

Back at their flat, Denise poured them all sparkling Italian soda from bottles in the refrigerator and they took their drinks up on the sunporch. Shade covered much of the deck as they settled into the padded chairs around the iron table.

"So the guided tour of Florence is on the schedule for tomorrow?" Bree looked to Denise.

"That's right. We're booked with an agency our travel agent worked with many times. They pick us up at ten, return at four."

"You two can go ahead on that and we'll see about me."

"I can tell you're thinking you'll fly home with Lizzie."

Bree nodded. "I mean, I saw what I wanted most. Lizzie was the one who wanted to see Venice."

"So, let me think this through. Lizzie had an accident so you should give up a third of your trip..."

"Look, I keep thinking about what I would want if I were in her place. Would I want to fly home alone?"

Denise stared at her, one eyebrow wiggling. "Perhaps we should let Lizzie make that decision."

"Right, Lizzie who is sedated for the night and…"

"Who will probably be in her right mind tomorrow morning and able to make her own decisions."

They all stared at Denise's phone as it began to chime.

"Travel agent." She clicked on. "Okay, what did you learn? You're on speaker."

"I got her a nonstop out of Paris tomorrow night. She will leave Florence on the six p.m. flight, which means she must be at the airport around three. There will be a two-hour layover in Paris and someone will be with her all the time. I've talked with the hospital and this is clear for them. She will be in a wheelchair with her foot elevated and crutches to keep the weight off her foot going to the bathroom. There will be aides at all three airports to get her on and off the planes."

"Bree thinks she should fly home with Lizzie."

"Why? The hospital said she would have pain pills but a clear head to ask for any more needed assistance. The airlines will provide ice for her foot too, if needed."

Denise nodded and looked at Bree.

"Besides, I got the last business-class ticket on that flight. It's full up."

"Okay, but what if I fly with her to Paris, then fly back here after she's on the plane to Portland?"

"I'm sure I can arrange that, but why?"

"Just to calm my worrying, I guess. I mean, you hear tales and…"

"And they're always the negative ones. We've always had very good service for a client with medical emergencies, especially with this airline."

Denise gave Bree another eyebrow-wiggle look.

"If this seems all right to you, you want to call her husband or should I?"

"Give me all the flight numbers and I'll call him so

he can be at PDX." Bree wrote all the information down. "Thank you."

"Yes, and I will call you back."

"Thank you."

Denise hit the OFF button. "I hate to say *I told you so*, but..."

Bree tipped her head back to stare unseeing at the sky. *Lord, you must be orchestrating all this because I am certainly in over my head.* She blew out a puffed-cheek breath. "Is there any more of that Italian soda?"

❀   ❀   ❀

"You will certainly not give up the rest of this trip because I have to go home early." Lizzie stared at her friend the next morning. "Even though perhaps I should wear a bag over my face so I don't frighten children."

"Actually, it could be worse. At least you can open your eyes and the bandage covers your forehead."

"Ice is amazing." She touched her cheeks with the fingertips of her left hand, since the sling held her right arm clamped to her side. "I'm afraid to look in a mirror." She tipped her head back against the pillows. "All because some thief wanted my money. I didn't even have much in the bag, most was in the pouch around my waist like the instructions for travelers said. Happened so fast—and to do a face plant by a fountain in Florence, Italy. Now, that will be a story for my grandchildren someday."

"Glad you can make jokes about it." Bree hadn't heard her friend talk so much the whole trip. "Makes me want to cry. You wanted to see Venice like I wanted to see the *David*."

Lizzie shook her head and flinched. "Ouch, not a good thing to do. Perhaps I'll do another trip someday. After all, I found out I can do this—you know, fly over the United

States and the ocean and parts of Europe. Maybe Steve and I will travel more."

Bree shook her head. "Now, that would be a miracle, considering his views about flying."

"You never know. I've always wanted to see Israel, to walk where Jesus walked. Perhaps he will do that. Now that I've spread my wings. It could be good bonding for us, don't you think?"

"I do. I brought your luggage. If I missed anything, I'll bring it."

"Thanks." Lizzie yawned. "I'm getting mighty sleepy. You go on that tour with the others and…"

"And you just go to sleep and I'll be here when you wake up. I might just kick back that chair and do the same."

✿   ✿   ✿

Later that afternoon, she rode in the transport van with Lizzie to the airport. Denise and Rachel greeted them at the door, and the three followed the woman pushing the wheelchair. Once seated before the security checkpoint, where only ticketed passengers could go, they told Lizzie and Bree about their tour.

"The domed cathedral I wanted to see the most is closed for repairs but our driver took us so we could see it from every angle and we walked part of it. The whole thing is a major work of art, the different colors of the marble green and pink and white and granite used in almost a checkerboard pattern. What an engineering feat, and done so long ago." Rachel had studied the architecture of the region one semester in art school and was thrilled to be able to see the magnificent building in real life.

"We need to go through," the woman pushing the wheelchair announced.

They said their goodbyes, with Lizzie promising to call them from Paris and when she landed in Portland. They stood waving as she passed through the checkpoint before turning to make their way back to the driver waiting for them.

"I sure hope we made the right decision," Bree muttered.

"It wasn't your decision to make. It was Lizzie's."

"True, but..." *Lord, keep her and us safe.*

Chapter Twenty-Three

Pierre woke sweating and gasping for breath.

He lay back in the familiar darkness of his bedroom, willing his breathing and heart rate back to normal. Why were these nightmares happening so much lately?

When his pounding pulse finally slowed, he rolled onto his elbow and gulped down the glass of water at his bedside. He punched the light atop his alarm clock to see the time. Almost 5:00 a.m. Well, that was it for sleep tonight.

Pierre-René hauled himself out of bed and into the bathroom. He brushed his teeth, thankful for the cleansing spearmint on his tongue. Would that he could brush away the tentacles of the dream as easily.

It had been one about Lynn again, but set back in Italy at the Aviano Base, though he hadn't met her yet when he was stationed there. In the dream, he'd been on a day's leave, and they'd been strolling through the village, laughing and carefree as in their dating days, when the earthquake hit, burying Lynn under the ruins of a crumbling building. He'd dug and dug to get to her, clawing at the stones, but as soon as he cleared one, several tumbled in to take its place. When at last he reached her, not Lynn's face but Bree's stared up at him, pale and lifeless.

Pierre shuddered, scrubbing his hands over his eyes. *Lord, please lift this darkness away. What's wrong with me?*

Am I subconsciously worried about Bree being in Italy?
That doesn't make sense.

It wasn't like he'd completely ignored what happened so long ago and its effects on him—he'd done some counseling, worked through what he needed to at the time, he'd thought. He still used the breathing techniques. But lately, they didn't seem to be enough. And he really didn't have time for this, not with Bree returning in mere days and the coffee shop grand opening bearing down upon him in only two months.

He drove into Vancouver just as the sky began to gray, mostly ahead of the traffic on the 205 bridge. Definitely a perk of traveling this early. The commute was already getting to him, and the coffee shop hadn't even opened yet. Maybe he should consider moving closer. He tipped his head from side to side, trying to stretch out the tension.

"You don't have to deal with that right now." Sometimes verbally ordering himself worked.

When he approached the coffee shop, keys in hand, through the still-bare window he saw Jessica already there, bending over behind the counter.

He let himself in. "You're here early."

"Hey." She straightened. Her long blond hair was pulled back into a braid, her face pensive. "Yeah, thought I'd get an early start. I'd like to get this espresso machine figured out so we can start experimenting with different drinks—it could take a while to get them just right. And I want to be ready to be able to train your baristas with them once you start hiring."

"That sounds good." Pierre set his briefcase on the card table. He'd ordered café tables and chairs, but who knew how long those would take to ship. He needed to find booths too, and the kiddie table they'd discussed. "I've got some interviews scheduled this afternoon for the baker position. I told you I hired Terrence as manager, right? He'll start next week but agreed to sit in on interviews today."

"Okay." Jessica turned back to the machine.

Pierre sat down in the folding chair and opened his laptop, then hesitated and glanced back at Jessica. He hadn't made it through the air force, several different cultures, a difficult marriage, and a career in international business without learning to read people. He didn't feel particularly up to dealing with others' problems today, but...

Pierre cleared his throat. "You okay?"

"Yeah." Jessica glanced up, then back down.

He'd heard that before; he had two daughters. Pierre-René closed his laptop. "What is it?"

Jessica sighed and flipped switches on the espresso machine. "I was all excited about this going back to school, but then I looked at the tuition and fees. I thought community college was supposed to be cheap, and I guess it is compared with a four-year school, but it would still be hundreds of dollars to take even a couple of classes this fall. And once you register, you have to pay by the next Monday. I can't do that at this point, not with all my debt. So I guess I just have to give up on it for now."

Pierre leaned back in his chair. "Don't they have financial aid?"

"Yeah, but I think it's too late to apply with the FAFSA, not for this fall. Maybe I could try for the spring semester. I was just feeling excited about it, you know?" She tucked a stray strand of hair behind her ear.

"I do. Well, let's not give up hope yet."

"Then I'm supposed to meet Ryan later, my boyfriend. It's been a while since we really talked, and last time we did, he thought we needed to take a step back. I'm scared he's going to break things off." Jessica's chin quivered.

"You don't know that." Hardly stellar words of encouragement, but Pierre didn't feel very inspirational today. *Lord, some help here.* "Try to hear the man out. It sounds like he really cares about you. I'll be praying for your time together."

"Thanks." She sniffled but smiled a bit. "That means a lot."

His heart easing slightly, Pierre checked his email. Michelle wanted to swing by this morning to drop something off, if he would be there. He typed back a quick response in the affirmative. He had several new email applications for positions at the coffee shop, in addition to the interviews he'd already lined up for today.

"Sheesh, you two are up and at it early," Michelle noted when she breezed in the door, bringing a wave of energy and the scent of something sweet and bready. She slapped a paper bag onto the card table.

"What's that?"

"I grabbed a latte at The Coffee Spoon on my way—no offense, you guys aren't open yet, you know—and thought maybe you could use a little pick-me-up, since you don't exactly have ovens going yet." She shoved the bag closer to him.

"How thoughtful. Thank you." Pierre peeked in the bag, the aroma of blueberry muffins setting his stomach rumbling. Breakfast hadn't even crossed his mind this morning. He stood and pulled a warm, fat muffin from the bag. "Jessica, here."

"Thanks, Michelle." She stepped over and took it, biting in right away.

Pierre pulled out another for himself, his spirits lifting with the first bite. Amazing what food could do, and drink. One more reason for this place.

"No prob." Michelle waved her hand, then dug into the voluminous batik satchel she seemed to use as a briefcase or at least a catchall. "Here are the flyers—just proofs, of course. Let me know which one you like and we can get this advertising train on the road."

"Or on the tracks." Jessica smiled behind her muffin. "At least out of the station."

A smile, that was a good sign. Pierre studied the flyers, some sturdy postcard size, others big enough to post on bulletin boards and the windows of willing shop owners along the street.

The Gathering Place

Opening July 12!
Your neighborhood spot for coffee and community
Families welcome
Veterans resources available
Hiring now!

"These look great." Pierre rubbed his thumb over one. "I especially like the postcards. Would we send them out as a mailing?"

"That's the idea." Michelle snagged a muffin herself. "You could include a coupon good through your first month, or on your first visit, either way." She swallowed a bite. "Jessica did most of the designing, you know."

"Really?" Pierre-René raised a brow. "When did you manage that?"

"We met up a few times and Michelle showed me how to use the program." Jessica shrugged, but her ears pinked. "It's not that hard."

"Well, I wouldn't know where to start." Pierre noted the tasteful design, varying slightly between the versions, but all in the same theme of soothing slate blue and warm coffee brown. "You definitely have a gift for this."

"That's what I keep telling this girl." Michelle whacked Jessica's arm with one of the flyers. "Did you sign up for those classes yet?"

"No." Jessica's brightened face fell. "I don't think I can afford it."

"Oh, please." Michelle pointed a finger at her. "That's just an excuse."

"Is not. Have you seen those tuition prices?"

"And have you seen the entire financial aid section of their website? Sure, it might be too late for the FAFSA for this fall, but there are other possibilities." Michelle grabbed Jessica's shoulders and plopped her down in the remaining folding chair, then snatched her phone from the bottomless bag, her fingers flying over the screen. "Let me show you right now. There are even work-study options, if you're interested."

"Really?"

Pierre watched. *Lord, you are full of surprises.* Who would have thought Michelle would be the one Jessica needed most of all?

❊   ❊   ❊

A couple of hours later, Pierre hung up after a string of phone calls and blew out a long breath. He should know something by this point about the red tape involved in getting a business licensed and running, but whew.

"Sorry if we were loud." Jessica looked up from sketching something out on a large pad of paper propped on the counter. Michelle leaned nearby, her visit having extended long beyond "dropping off flyers." "Guess we got a bit caught up in menu ideas."

"Don't worry about it." The young women's chatter *had* been distracting, but his irritation eased now he was off the phone. He definitely needed them out of here before the first interview, though. "How is the menu coming along?"

"Going to be awesome, is what it is." Michelle grabbed the huge pad of paper in front of Jessica and turned it for Pierre to see. "Ta-da. Isn't she fabulous?"

"It's just a sketch, some ideas." Jessica twiddled her lower lip between her teeth.

Pierre stood for a closer look. Not just ideas, Jessica had sketched out a whole sample menu design, like for the large chalkboards he'd seen behind the counters in other coffee shops. Attractive lettering, yet friendly and legible...clear divisions that made the sections easy to scan...curving lines of leaves and berries to embellish the corners...a "Kiddie Korner" of the menu in childlike printing. The food and drink selections were incomplete, but seeing the names of the lattes, teas, espressos, and hot chocolates made it all suddenly real. And Jessica had labeled a special portion for "Bree's Cinnamon Rolls."

"My mom said she'd let you use her recipe, right?" She reached to fix a wayward *s* with her pencil. "Her cinnamon rolls are amazing. They'll bring in the crowds."

"She did. As long as we can find bakers to hire who will do them justice. I love using her name like that." Pierre-René shook his head, the joy buried lately under paperwork and construction seeping to the surface again. "I agree with Michelle, Jessica. It looks wonderful."

Jessica's ear pinked. "Cool."

"Well." Pierre glanced at his watch. "I've got Terrence and our first potential baker coming soon. Are you ladies going to work here awhile still?"

"Not me, I've gotta vamoose, stayed too long, having too much fun." Michelle grabbed a handful of art supplies that must have been hers. "But you're going to look into all those financial aid options, right?" She aimed her finger at Jessica again.

"Right." Jessica smiled back, determination in her face this time.

"Remember, they've got different directions you could take, graphic design, digital media. Find a couple of introductory classes in whatever looks interesting—you don't have to figure it all out yet. Isn't that right, Pierre?"

"Absolutely. A business class or two wouldn't hurt either."

"True." Michelle's finger jabbed in his direction now. "Very good point. Well, I've gotta run, got other clients too, you know. See ya, Jess, see ya, Pierre." She blew toward the door like a flame-topped twister, then turned back, her hand on the door.

"Hey." Her voice came softer than usual. "Thanks for giving Terrence the job."

Pierre met her gaze. "He seems like a good man."

"Yeah, he is." Michelle swallowed. "I'm really hoping that, you know, this is a new start for him. And for Sarah and the baby and all. They're kind of all the family I've got."

"I'm praying it will be."

"Yeah." Her gaze flicked away, then back, a rare vulnerability in her black-lined eyes. "Well, I better go."

The door banged, and Pierre watched her leave, heels clicking down the sidewalk, batik bag bouncing on her shoulder.

"I'm going to grab some lunch. You need anything?" Jessica picked up her purse.

"I'm fine." After she left, Pierre sat back down on the metal folding chair, surveying the gathering place that was slowly growing out of the mess and chaos. Moments like that one with Michelle, he caught a glimpse again of what made all this worthwhile. Suddenly he missed Bree, wanted to tell her all that was developing here. Though she'd been gone less than two weeks, she seemed a world away. Or was, at least half a world.

He should call her. He'd just been so busy, and she was always hurrying off to one amazing, ancient place or another. Was that just an excuse?

He glanced at the clock. Eleven thirty, so 8:30 p.m. in Italy. He could squeeze in a quick call before Terrence arrived at noon. He hit her number and held the phone to his ear, thankful Jessica had left. Dry mouth, sweaty palms. Was he in junior high?

"Hello?"

"Hello, Breeanna." He swallowed to give some moisture to his tongue. She sounded tired; perhaps he'd chosen the wrong moment. "Is this a bad time?"

"No, sorry, it's just been quite the couple of days. Lizzie got attacked by a pickpocket, thrown to the ground and injured. We had to put her on a plane back home today."

"Oh, my." Pierre sat up straight. "Is she badly hurt?"

"Not as bad as it could have been, thankfully. Broken ankle, dislocated shoulder, other minor injuries. I so hated for her to miss Venice, but there was no choice. She's been a good sport about it all." He could hear the exhaustion in her voice.

"Well, I'll let you go sleep. But I'm glad to know. I'll be praying."

"Thank you. How are you?"

"Fine. Busy with the coffee shop, things have been a bit hectic. Jessica has been a wonderful help, though."

"Really? I'm so glad to hear that. No further catastrophes?"

"Not so far. She's a good worker and has quite an artistic streak. Did she tell you she's thinking of going back to school?"

"She mentioned it but then the finance side killed all hope . . . for now anyway."

"Maybe not. Michelle, my web assistant, told her about some financial aid options and such. But I'm sure Jessica will tell you more."

"It sounds like you've made a big difference in my girl's life in these short weeks. Such a gift to hear some good news about Jessica. Thank you."

"I hardly did a thing. But quickly, tell me about you. Aside from the injury, you are having a good time? You saw the *David*?"

"We did, just before it happened, actually. It was… incredible, Pierre. Everything I'd dreamed and far more."

"I'm so glad." It wasn't often a dream actually came true. A sudden longing to take her in his arms made his chest ache, drying up his words. The silence hung.

"So…your return date still stands?" he said at last.

"Yes, the rest of us will return as planned. You can still pick me up at the airport?"

"Planning on it." He checked his watch. "Well, I must let you get to sleep, and I have a meeting with a potential new hire."

"All right. Thanks for calling, Pierre. I miss you."

"Miss you too." They ended the call, and he drew a deep breath. Not exactly their free-flowing conversation of before Bree left, but it had been better. *Thank you, Lord.* He paused. *She said she missed me.* That brought on a smile.

Terrence arrived, dressed in a button-down shirt and pressed slacks. He shook Pierre's hand. "Hey, Mr. Dubois."

"Pierre, remember?" He noted that Terrence's hands seemed steadier today. "Thanks for your willingness to be here."

Terrence gave a firm nod. "Glad to be."

"We've got quite a list lined up, mostly for the head baker position, a couple for the assistant. I'll appreciate your input on the interviews, since you've been a manager before."

Terrence met his eyes. "Thanks for trusting me to be one again. I won't let you down."

"I called your references, everything you said checked out." And he'd sensed God's finger in their meeting. Pierre laid a hand on Terrence's shoulder, careful not to startle. "Grateful to have you on the team as we launch this place. A new start in many ways, no?"

His new manager's Adam's apple bobbed. "For sure."

The bell jangled that their first candidate had arrived.

The next few hours passed in a blur of résumés and standard interview questions and responses, of trying to gauge work ethics and who might fit well into the ethos of The Gathering Place.

"Whew." Terrence leaned back in his folding chair after the fifth potential hire left. "Brings back memories."

"Want a drink of water?" Pierre got up to grab one of the extra bottles he had stashed behind the counter and held another out for Terrence.

"Thanks." Terrence caught the bottle and took a swig. "Anyone else coming in today?"

"One more for the head baker job. Should be here in a few minutes. What do you think of those we've interviewed so far?"

"Some good possibilities." Terrence drummed his fingers on the card table, nodding.

"I agree." Some candidates had solid commercial baking experience. At least a couple Pierre was sure could do the job well. He hadn't felt that gut rightness yet like he had with Terrence, but he couldn't expect that with every employee. He took another swig of water.

"I think she's here." Terrence stood to open the door. "Come on in. I'm Terrence."

"Jayla Washington." The slender young woman stepped inside.

"A pleasure to meet you." Pierre extended his hand. "I'm Pierre Dubois. I received your application."

"Thanks for meeting with me." Jayla's voice was quiet, but she met his gaze and grip directly. A turquoise blouse and black slacks set off the warm brown of her skin, her cornrow braids pulled back into a bun.

"Please, have a seat." Pierre gestured to the folding chairs set around the card table. "Hopefully we'll have some actual furniture here in a couple of weeks. I've placed the order, but these things take time."

"Doesn't everything?" Jayla sat in one of the metal chairs, Pierre and Terrence taking the others.

"So, Jayla, how did you hear about us?" He glanced at the résumé and references before him. All in order, but they didn't tell him much about her.

She folded her hands on her lap. "Well, I was in the VA office the other day, checking on something with my husband's disability benefits. And I saw your flyer."

Terrence leaned forward. "So your husband is a vet too?"

"He is. We were both in the army, met while deployed in Afghanistan. He was more on the front lines than I was, got half his leg blown off by an IED."

Pierre felt more than saw Terrence flinch. "I'm so sorry."

"We're making it through. The benefits help, though he'd really like to find a job he can do despite it. I've been working security the past few years, but we've got a little girl now, and those shifts are all over the place. I've been looking for something with better hours so I can spend more time with my baby girl."

"Of course." Pierre's heart went out to the young mother. "How old is your daughter?"

"She's two." A smile warmed Jayla's face. "She sure knows her own mind, but lights up our lives."

"I know the feeling. So, what draws you to this position specifically? Do you have a long interest in baking?"

"I always loved it, was how I relaxed growing up—I'd take over my mom's kitchen, or better, my grandma's. She, my grandma, taught me most of what I know about baking— pies, cobblers, cookies, quick breads. Even in the army, I'd find my way into any kitchen I could. I bake at home when I can, but it's hard to find the time with working like I do. But I bake for my church, I've organized big church events baking for hundreds of people. I know how to use a commercial kitchen. I've looked into other baking jobs before, but they all want two to three years of experience. And I don't have the kind they're looking for, you know what I mean?"

"I do." Pierre tapped his pen on his knee. "It frustrates me in the hiring world, how employers want several years of experience, but how is anyone to get that if every job expects you to have it already? Especially for veterans. If you ask me, making it through the military is experience employers shouldn't take lightly."

Jayla offered another smile. "I'm glad someone finally said it."

"That's what I like about this guy." Terrence leaned back and folded his arms. "He actually gets it, what we vets are up against."

"Well." Pierre tapped his fingers on his knee. "I'll admit you don't have the 'experience' some of our other candidates do, but as you say, working in your church's kitchen makes a difference." He thought a moment. "Would there be any chance we could try a sample of your baking? I'd pay for the ingredients if you would whip us up a batch of something, your choice."

"Oh, you don't have to do that." Jayla pressed her hands together. "Pay me, I mean. I love any excuse to get back to that oven. When can I bring something by for you to try?"

"Anytime in the next few days should be fine. I'll give you my number; you can give me a call when it's ready and we'll set a time to meet back here." Pierre rubbed his chin. "Actually, I do have to make a trip to the airport to pick up my—a friend, this coming Tuesday. So any day except that."

"Or I can come, if he's not free." Terrence raised his hand. "All the more for me."

They all chuckled.

"We'll be seeing you again soon, then." Pierre stood and extended his hand.

"Sounds good." Jayla stood also and shook it, then lifted her purse to her shoulder. "You have all my paperwork?"

"I do." Pierre tucked it into his briefcase. "I'll call your references and review our other applicants, so we can be ready to make a decision. Thank you so much for coming in, Jayla."

"No, thank you. This has been a real encouragement."

Jayla's step did indeed seem lighter as she headed out the door.

"I like her," Terrence said almost as soon as the door swung closed.

Pierre-René held up his hand and waited till he was sure Jayla was out of earshot down the sidewalk. "Do you? Why?" He did, too, but wanted to hear Terrence's thoughts without undue influence.

"She's straightforward, tells it like it is. Actually loves baking. Some of the other candidates seemed like it was more just a job to them." Terrence shrugged and rubbed one hand inside the other. "Mostly a gut feeling, I guess. But my wife says I can tell about people—good judge of character, you could say."

Pierre nodded. "I see that. And I agree, I liked Jayla too. It's too soon to make a decision, but we'll see." He did sense that similar heart in Jayla that he'd found in

Terrence and Jessica and Michelle. A love for the job and desire to make a difference, not just a paycheck. But he still needed to find baristas and a cleaning crew. Pierre blew out a breath and opened his laptop. *Lord, July is coming awfully fast.*

"Gives a good feeling, doesn't it?"

"Hmm?" Pierre glanced through his email. No more job inquiries, but a message from Michelle with some attached business card proofs for him to choose between.

"Helping people, like this."

Pierre looked up.

Terrence leaned against the counter. "Giving folks like Jayla and me a chance. Here I just wanted a better job— I didn't know I was going to get to be part of something bigger." He swallowed, then looked away, but not before Pierre caught the sheen of tears in the younger man's eyes. "Kinda makes me believe in God again."

Pierre-René shut his laptop. Email could wait. "I'm glad to hear you say that. He definitely makes me believe in Him, all the time."

"Even with all that's so messed up in this world?" Terrence dashed a knuckle against his eyes. "I used to believe in God, you know, as a kid, Sunday school stuff. But over there in Iraq, Afghanistan...it kinda pounded it out of me. Seeing what people could do to each other."

"I've struggled with that too, though I haven't seen all that you have. But our God came down into our messed-up world, into our strivings and evil and pain. He experienced it with us, took it on for us. That helps me."

Terrence nodded. "That's good. Thanks." He drew a deep breath through his nose. "Well, you don't need your manager crying his eyes out. What else is on the agenda for today, boss?"

"That about does it." Pierre slid his laptop into its sleeve and then into his briefcase. He'd reply to Michelle's email later. "Why don't you get home to that beautiful wife of yours. Once you officially start next week, we'll need to buckle down on what needs to get done this month. Lay out a strategy before Breeanna gets back."

"Your friend, huh?" Terrence waggled his eyebrows at him. "Afraid you'll be too distracted once she's back on the same side of the world?"

"Watch your tone with your superior, soldier." Pierre waved a finger at him.

"Yes, sir." Terrence saluted with a lopsided grin.

Chuckling, the two men headed out, Pierre locking the door behind them. They walked toward their cars on the tree-lined street, parked only two spaces away from each other.

"Thanks again, Terrence." Pierre-René gave him a nod and reached for his car keys.

"Sure thing."

Crash.

At the thunderclap of sound, Pierre sprang behind his vehicle. He ducked and covered, gripping the door handle and side-view mirror, head down.

His heart slammed in his chest, darkness swam in his vision. *Keep down, head down.*

"Pierre? Boss? Hey, man, it's all right. You're okay."

Vaguely he became aware of Terrence's voice, his hand on Pierre's shoulder. Slowly he pushed to his feet, his vision clearing. His breath came in erratic gasps.

"You're good, man, you're safe. Okay?" Terrence kept his hand on Pierre's shoulder. "A garbage truck just dropped a dumpster real loud, I think. That's all."

"Keys." Pierre croaked. He felt at his empty pockets.

Terrence bent to the ground and popped up, keys in hand. "Here you go. Safe and sound."

Pierre took them, hands trembling. He forced his breathing to slow. In for four—out for four. In—out.

Terrence shoved his hands in his pockets. "Maybe this isn't my place, but listen. You know you've got a problem, right?"

Sudden anger burned Pierre's throat. He turned and jabbed the unlock button on his key remote, then flung open the car door and tossed his briefcase inside. It jarred on its end in the passenger-side foot well.

"Hey. I'm sorry."

Pierre turned, still glaring.

Terrence backed away, hands in the air. "Like I said, maybe it's not my place. But I know PTSD when I see it, man. If you ever want to talk, I'm here. Just saying."

Pierre stared at the younger man, and for a moment, something in him reached out, almost pushing forth the words *Yes, yes, I want to talk, to someone who will listen, who might even understand*.

But instead, shame pressing his shoulders, he got into his car and drove away.

Chapter Twenty-Four

"I think you should take the tour we took yesterday."

Rachel nodded in agreement with her mother. "I can call our guide from yesterday and see if he can take you. He really knows and loves Florence."

"But what are you going to do?"

"We're going to the Bardini Gardens."

"But I want to go there too." Bree stared at the other two. And kept one eye on the clock. Lizzie had promised to call when they landed in Portland. They had left Paris on time last night, and that would put them in Portland at 8:00 a.m., Florence time. It was now seven thirty. She could be calling any minute.

Denise looked up from her phone. "They're supposedly on time."

Bree's phone chimed.

"We're on the ground," Lizzie reported.

"You sound rummy."

"I am rummy, I slept really well, been taking my pills, they've taken marvelous care of me and we're taxiing to the gate where a wheelchair will meet me. Steve borrowed a wheelchair to get me out to the car." She paused. "Thank you, Bree, for all your help. Tell Denise and Rachel too."

"You're on speaker."

"Good. I pray God's blessing on the remainder of your trip and watch out for pickpockets."

"We will. Tell Steve hello from us."

"I will and see you when you get home."

Bree clicked off her phone. "Thank you, God, all went well." She got up to pour herself more coffee. "Anyone else?" She opened the refrigerator door. "Anyone want a juice or ..."

"We need to finish things off, so bring out the rest of the cheese and crackers."

"And fruit too."

Bree set the food on the tray and brought it to the sunroom. "I think I do want to do the Florence tour."

"Good." Rachel laid a business card on the table and clicked in the numbers. When someone answered, she asked if their same tour driver would be available again. "Oh, sorry to hear that." She shook her head to the others. "Do you have any other drivers? Oh, okay." She laid her phone down. "They're calling us back."

Rachel held up her hands. "I have both fingers crossed."

Bree cut the ham-and-cheese-filled breakfast roll in half. "Anyone want to share this?"

Rachel's phone rang, and she clicked it on speaker. "Yes, thank you."

"Marco exchanged with another driver so he'll be available to take your friend at eleven a.m. He doesn't have time for the full six hours but promises to cram in as much as he can in three hours."

"That will be marvelous," Bree answered. "I'll see him at eleven then. *Grazie.*"

Rachel clicked off and grinned at her mother. "I think he liked us."

Denise nodded back. "Another God thing?" She heaved a sigh. "Kind of makes up for the time you spent helping Lizzie."

Bree nodded. *Thank you, Lord, another blessing. Lizzie is home safe, I get to see Florence after all.* "You know what I'd like to do tonight?"

The others shrugged. "Have another caprese salad?"

"How about back at that restaurant down the street and then go up on the roof for a while and just enjoy."

Bree packed while the others left for their tour of the Bardini Gardens. When she realized she was humming, she nodded. *Thank you, Lord, for working today out for me, for getting Lizzie home safe.* They had already set up with their flat owner to check them out at 9:00 a.m. He had made a point that this was his process, and they would leave for the Santa Maria Novella train station after that. As she wandered from room to room, saying goodbye in her own way, she admired anew this lovely place they had been given for their Florence week. *Forgive me, Lord, for trying to run things again. Both Denise and I are so good at that.* When eleven neared, she locked the door behind her and took the elevator to the entrance.

She came out on the street at the same time her tour guide parked at the curb. He came around the front of the SUV and smiled at her. "Now I get to meet the real author. You have interesting friends to be traveling with. They spoke so highly of you, I was glad we could move things around so I can show you Florence. I am Marco de Rossi."

She shook the offered hand. "They were so pleased with their tour that we were all excited you could take me. I'm Bree Lindstrom."

He opened the front passenger door. "Unless you'd rather…"

She laughingly shook her head. "No, I'd much rather sit in front." Dark curly hair, a face used to smiling and laughter, and so eyes that smiled too. "Denise said you're so knowledgeable and that your love of Florence glows when you talk."

"Tell her *grazie* and *si*, Florence is the diamond of Italy, history that influenced all the arts, the architecture, the life of the world. Yes, Rome has the Vatican and Paris, the Louvre, but we are the birthplace, the growing place of the Renaissance. You can't be a student of Italian history without Florence." While he talked he had helped her in, closed the door and gone around to the driver's side, and settled in his seat. "So, do you have places you want to see the most?"

"How about you show me the things you think I should see and learn of?"

"I am at your service."

By the time they returned to the wrought-iron gate to her flat, she understood why Rachel was so enamored by the stunning Brunelleschi's domed cathedral, how much of an influence remained of the Roman days, the amazing old homes fenced and gated, many dating back to the thirteen and fourteen hundreds, or the fifteens like the flat she was about to leave, gardens and places that overlooked the city, and always his love of Florence's history shining through.

"I am constantly amazed at how old things are here. America is so young. Two hundred years is nothing compared with the centuries here. You have made those people real to me, along with this city. And your own family history." She nodded to the family ring he had shown her, something to be passed to his son. "Thank you." He came around to open her door. She handed him his fee with a healthy tip.

"*Grazie*, and I hope you return to Florence someday," he answered. "All of you." He passed her his business card. "There is a lot more of Florence that I would be honored to show you."

"Blessings, Marco."

He waited to see her through the gate before he drove off.

Bree inhaled a deep breath and slowly let it out. Two o'clock. She was mostly packed and again had a handful of postcards to write and send.

The next morning they finished cleaning the kitchen and had everything set back in order before Signore Ricci and his wife rang the buzzer.

"We cannot begin to tell you how much we have enjoyed your home here." Bree smiled as she shook his hand.

"And you found your dream?"

"I did and the *David*, that entire Accademia was beyond belief. The *St. Joseph*, the *Prisoners*…" She slowly shook her head. "Incredible. I think I liked the *St. Joseph* even more than the *Pietà*." So grateful I could spend as long as I wanted there. I never felt rushed through."

He nodded. "I'm glad for you." He looked to the others. "Wait, aren't you missing one?"

They told him what had happened to Lizzie and he sighed as he shook his head. "I am so sorry to hear of that. No matter how hard our *vigili* try, too many tourists are not as careful as they need to be and the pickpockets are getting even better. But to knock a woman down like that…"

"We're grateful she was not injured worse. But she said to tell you how much she enjoyed staying here. Such a different experience from a hotel."

"Perhaps you might return someday, and I would be honored if you chose to visit us again. We lived here so many years and now we are grateful we can share with others, especially artists like all of you." He smiled to each of them.

"Your book"—Denise laid her hand on the binder—"was invaluable. We all read through it and appreciated your maps and instructions."

"And you visited our restaurant down the street? Not that we own it, but we are part of the family."

"Several times. They greeted us like family thanks to you. And the bakery and the grocers." Denise shrugged. "I don't know how you can not live here."

"Sometimes one must go where the work lies." He signed off the contract and slid it over to Bree. "And you are now on your way to Venice?"

"*Si*, via the speed train, although the older kind might allow us to see more of the country."

He nodded. "It would but that silence of the Alta Velocità is an experience too."

They shook hands, said goodbye at the door, and, being last, Bree gave him a hug. "*Grazie, signore, buongiorno.*"

"*Si, buongiorno* and *Dio ti benedica.*"

They met another SUV at the street, with Denise taking more pictures as normal. This driver did not greet them or offer to point out anything; he unloaded them at the station, took his payment, and left. The three stared at one another, then broke out in chuckles.

"After the wonderful people we've met here, he sure won't be on the list." Denise grabbed the handle to her suitcases, smaller hooked on the larger, and led the way to the ticket window.

Thinking on the man's sullen look, Bree shook her head. "Perhaps he is just having a bad day."

"More likely a bad life," muttered Rachel, who seemed on edge today.

"Three to Venice." Denise pushed her new credit card, thankfully arrived at last, under the window. Tickets in hand, they followed the arrows down halls, paused at an escalator, found an elevator, and finally stepped out on a long, elevated train platform and waiting area. Bree sat down on a bench to people-watch again. Rachel plopped down next to her with a sigh.

"Your mom off with her camera again?"

"Where else?" Rachel opened her sketchbook but sat idle, unusual for her. Her hands and pencil seemed always in motion.

Bree angled her a glance. "You okay?"

"Yeah, I guess. Mom and I had a fight this morning. Nothing major."

"Mm." Should she say anything else? Bree didn't want to interfere in Denise's family, but… "I know a little of how that can be. Jessica and I clash at times too." Though probably for different reasons.

"It's just hard sometimes. I've finished school, got my degree, but I'm still stuck living at home, no idea when I might get a real job and be able to move out on my own. I didn't exactly choose a surefire lucrative career. And Mom, she's great about it, but it's her house, her rules."

"Or anywhere *not* her house." Bree cast her a grin.

Rachel snorted. "Guess it's no wonder we finally got on each other's nerves over here, being together almost twenty-four seven. At least at home we can escape to different parts of the house and jobs. Maybe the wonder is that we haven't come to blows."

Bree patted Rachel's knee. "Have you tried talking to your mom about it all?"

Rachel pushed back her dark braid and started sketching the open-sided shelter and the people around. "Not really. I guess I should." She penciled in her mother as Denise drew near taking photos.

"Communication helps, they always say." Maybe something Bree needed to practice more herself. How was Jessica feeling about having to move back home, at least for now? Bree hadn't really asked.

The bullet-looking train pulled into the station with a whoosh rather than screeching wheels and brakes. They boarded, found two facing seats with a table, and put their small bags in the overhead, the large ones on racks by the door.

A voice announced something in Italian then English and German as the train left the station, picking up speed without a jolt or any noise. None. Low conversations among other passengers but no train rumblings and roarings or swaying from side to side. Smooth and silent.

Bree and Rachel had window seats and within a few minutes, Rachel had snuggled down into her hoodie and fallen sound asleep. Bree opted to watch the scenery rushing by. They had almost two hours to Venice. After a while she took out her biography of Michelangelo and continued reading. When a *cameriere* stopped at their table, they chose sandwiches, salads, and drinks for lunch along with some snack items, not really knowing what they ordered since their waiter spoke English with such a heavy accent. They shrugged it off as another adventure.

"Was this here when you visited Italy before?" Bree asked.

"No, these have come into use in the last ten or so years, I think. Sure is different from the train from Eugene to Portland or Vancouver. There, driving is much faster and easier."

The trip took just under two hours, amazing for 160 miles, and that included several stops. They watched the info flashing in several languages on the drop-down screen to know when to gather their things together to disembark, then followed the crowd through the Venice station to the taxi area.

Denise reread the instructions on how to get to their hotel. "Okay, I just talked with the woman from the hotel, who will meet us at the boat dock where we get off. Instead of taking a commercial water taxi, we're scheduled for a private boat." She studied some more. "Okay, now we board one of those buses to the Grand Canal."

Bree was glad she was wearing one of the sun hats from Rome, as perspiration already trickled down her back. Each day was feeling hotter than the day before. "A gelato sounds mighty good about now, and/or iced tea."

The others agreed. "Once we get settled in our hotel, we can ask how to find the nearest one."

A smiling woman in uniform stopped beside them and their pile of luggage. "May I assist you?"

"Oh, good, *grazie*, you speak English." Relief washed over Bree. Not that she didn't trust Denise, but she didn't feel up to struggling with her limited Italian right now. Or getting lost in Venice.

Denise read off their information.

"May I see that, *per favore*?" Denise handed her the paper. The woman nodded and handed it back.

"This way, *per favore*." They grabbed luggage handles and trekked after her.

Eventually—it felt like a five-mile hike, with backpack— their angel pointed to a number on a dock. "You will take that boat to your hotel." When Denise tried to tip her, she shook her head. "Just enjoy your stay here. From your instructions, someone will meet you."

"*Molte grazie*." Bree wished she could say more in Italian but instead she switched back to English. "You are an angel sent to guide us."

The woman smiled and shook her head. "Enjoy your stay and come back again."

They walked out on the dock at a man's bidding. A boat with a lovely wood finish and benches along the sides, some under a canvas, bobbed in the swells created by all the boat traffic on the Grand Canal. Boats of every size and type crowded the water, from gondolas to small freighters, and ferries to tour boats. The dock rose up and down on the swells also. One man took their suitcases and stacked them aft. Another stood in the boat and held up his hand to assist the passengers.

Bree's mouth dried. The dock rode the swells, the boat bobbed both up and down and in and out. Rachel hung on to the rail of the deck, took the man's offered hand, and stepped from the dock to the broad step on the side of the boat.

A boat. She had thought she'd be all right. All these years since Roger died, she had often promised herself she'd go out in a boat again on a lake or the Columbia River. But had she done it? No.

And now Lizzie wasn't even here to help her through.

Denise followed Rachel and the two turned to encourage Bree.

"Come on, easy peasy."

The boat rose on a swell, pulled as far as the moorings allowed from the dock, and settled back in the trough.

She could feel her heart pounding, sweat dripping off her chin. Trickling down her spine.

"Just take my hand, *signora*, you'll be safe."

If I fall in that boat and break my leg, the rest of this trip is over. It will mess it up for everybody. I can't do this, Lord. I can't.

Chapter Twenty-Five

Frozen, that's what she was.

Bree stared down at the gulf of water that rose and fell and widened with the swells created by all the boat traffic on the Grand Canal. The boat she was supposed to step into was never still.

"Come on, Bree, you can do it." Denise waited for her, seated on the opposite side of the bucking boat.

She shook her head. "Is there no other way?" *Tears even, Lord. What is the matter with me?*

"Don't worry, *signora*, we are here to help you. Here, take my hand."

She clutched his hand like a lifeline, but her feet would not move. No matter how firmly she ordered them to do so, they stayed bonded to the dock. *Lord, help me. I have to do this.*

Mortification tasted bitter like plain cocoa.

Another man on her other side. "We won't let you fall."

As if they had control over that tumult she saw beneath her.

Please, Lord, please help me. Her head felt like the water looked, swirling and cresting. Could she get seasick when not even in the boat? She worried she would throw up—*please no.*

She now knew what terror felt like. Feet superglued

to the dock. If she watched that swaying any longer…her stomach drowned in acid.

A thought, a brilliant thought, fought through the haze of her mind. She let go of the hands trying to help her and sat down on the dock, dangling her feet over the edge. The boat captain smiled at her and nodded. "Very good, *signora*." He extended his hand again and she slithered into the boat, sitting on the *traghetto*'s edge and then standing to stumble to a seat, clutching his hand for balance. Her descent to the seat across from Rachel and next to Denise could in no terms be called graceful, but she didn't care. She'd made it. To the applause of those around her.

Bree banked her tears of relief and smiled, despite her quivering lips.

They pulled away from the dock, and the boat picked up speed. A guide pointed out the buildings as they passed. She'd been warned this was a city of waterways, used like streets in other cities. Venice had been built right on the water with many of the buildings on landfill, braced by pillars. It had the dirtiest water anywhere since sewage and garbage were still being dumped there. Despite governmental efforts. The tide marks on the buildings attested to the reality of an open sea.

As the boat eased into a dock on a side canal without the swells and roughness of the Grand, the captain set the steps in place and assisted them up to the dock. "*Grazie*," she said. "This was not nearly like the other."

"*Si, signora*, glad you made it."

A woman waited for them and introduced herself as their guide for the days in Venice. They each did the same, and she flagged a man with a luggage carrier who swung their suitcases up on the wood flooring, spoke with their guide, and headed off, pushing the load.

"We will follow him to your hotel." She smiled and within

five paces was ahead of the others. Denise and Bree swapped wide-eyed looks and tried to pick up their pace. But there was so much to see. Restaurants that beckoned with aromas of tomato, basil, sausage wafting on the breeze, gift stores with glorious paintings, glass lamps, vases, dishes in the most incredible colors, travel books from pocket-size to full-color coffee table editions, carts with open flaps selling sunshades, sunscreen. Postcards, packets of postcards, fans both powered and folded, phone cords, adapters, thumb drives of all sizes and varieties, candy, bottled drinks, mementos of Venice, of Italy, gifts for men, for women, for children, and even rubbery toys that said VENICE for the family pooch. A fiddler entertained at one spot. A mime at another.

"*Allora, allora!*" Rosita beckoned anytime Bree slowed to look.

Rosita held the door for them to an old but small and classy hotel. Used to the sizes of lobbies in American hotels, Bree was caught by surprise. She and Rachel stared around at the beautifully carved woodwork and vaulted ceilings. A dining area with stiff white tablecloths off to the left, hallway to the elevators and another exit on the right, comfortable seating in groups with potted plants. Their travel agent had chosen this for them, mainly because it was in the middle of the places they had said they wanted to see.

Rosita, their guide, motioned for them to sit in one of the seating groups and brought out papers with their itinerary for Venice. "You have a gondola tour tomorrow morning at ten to return at two. On the third day we have a boat to take us to Murano and Burano Islands to see the glassblowing and the lace making, two arts that have grown through the ages, adding to the history of the area. I am sorry to say that Saint Mark's is closed for repairs but you will see much in the square surrounding it. You have one day free and then you leave for the airport."

The thought of getting back in a boat made Bree swallow hard. Of course, if the only way in was by boat, leaving would be the same. Dread clenched her stomach.

"Your luggage will be up in your rooms by now and the bellman will show you the way. I will be here in this room again at nine thirty to take you to the gondola. Any questions?"

Denise nodded. "Recommendations for a good place nearby to eat."

Rosita smiled. "You have several good choices if you exit by that door, turn left, and keep to the left. You'll see places you'd enjoy within the next block." She pointed to the maps she had given each of them. "I have marked several exceptional restaurants on your maps. If you have no more questions, I will be off and see you in the morning. If you do have any questions later, you have my number." Her business card was clipped to the top of each map. "*Ciao*."

They waved her out the door and, nodding, Denise suggested, "Let's check our rooms first and then meet in the hallway. We're only two doors apart."

When Bree walked into her room, the small size surprised her. Two double beds, a chair, chest of drawers, suitcase stand, and a tiny bathroom. Warm European fabrics in the ornate drapes, pulled shut, but very little floor space. She had to walk sideways on the outsides of the beds to find a plug-in. Good thing she had an adapter. Her phone would be needing a charge before evening so she plugged it in, put her toiletries in the bathroom, stepped back out into the hallway, and closed the door carefully behind her.

Rachel and Denise were doing the same.

"A bit crowded with two?" Bree asked.

Rachel rolled her eyes. "And Mom snores." Apparently the tension hadn't eased yet.

"I have an extra set of earplugs."

"Good, I might take you up on that."

"Remember, we're on the third floor, and I think that's as high as this building goes." Denise pushed the elevator button, looking down the hall to a lace-draped window at the far end. "No waste of space here, that's for certain."

Outside they only slowed at the gelato bar on their way to choose their restaurant. "We'll be back," Rachel told the smiling man behind the glass display freezer case.

They strolled past a small stone chapel, with plantings of shrubs and a spray of white blossoms on either side of the closed wooden door. As at all the other churches they had seen, the carved wooden door, while worn and faded, was a work of art. An etched inscription in Latin arched over the doorway.

Bree typed a note into her phone reminding herself to return and explore later, hoping that carved door might be open. A drinking fountain spouted in the middle of the tiled courtyard.

Just up ahead they saw two corner restaurants divided by a narrow street, shadowed by the buildings.

"Things sure are close together here," Rachel commented.

Bree stared up at the windows with carved gargoyles and floral frames and balconies with wrought-iron railings, all arched and curved, no posts and squares. A carved marble male head and shoulders sat on the shelf on a wall by a wood-framed glass door. *Next time, I'm bringing my sketchbook*, Bree promised herself. She had mentioned to Rachel her desire for drawing lessons sometime. Watching her created an itch Bree never knew she had.

"*Si*, saves space." Denise nodded to her daughter.

"Now, how do we choose which restaurant?" Bree stopped to read the menu of the restaurant left of the apex of the streets. "This sounds great."

"Smells better." They took the lone empty iron table with four chairs.

Rachel pointed to the menu. "No caprese?" Her eyebrows arched.

"Well, guess we better move along." Picking up her menu, Bree grinned, her eyes dancing.

Once their waiter described what each of the plates included, they ordered and sat back to look around. An American family sat at two tables pushed together and greeted them when they heard the language. *Interesting how easy it is to open conversation here*, Bree thought as they shared experiences, where they lived, and some hints about Venice. *It's never like this at home.* The father had been to Venice before and was delighting in showing his family around.

By the time they finished their meal and did a bit of wandering, they stopped for their gelatos. "We'll be back," they promised the charming server and returned to the hotel to crash.

As soon as Bree slid into sleep, she jerked awake. She'd been back on the bucking dock and the bobbing boat. Heart pounding, she bolted upright and blinked herself back to the present. *Breathe!* Leaning back on the pillows against an upholstered headboard, she reminded herself it was only a dream, albeit a nightmare, and she was fine now.

Except she wasn't. She was still trembling, her mind fuzzy and disoriented. *Lord, what is the matter with me? I thought Roger's death was long enough ago...and now I have to get on a gondola tomorrow that's even smaller than the boat today. I always thought that sounded so romantic; now I don't know if I can do it. I was just so terrified.* Her throat closed again.

Pierre...she wanted to talk to Pierre. Suddenly so much she could taste it. Before she could reason herself out of it, Bree sniffed hard and dialed his number. He answered after the second ring. She could hear hammering in the background. Four o'clock here meant 7:00 a.m. at home.

"Bree, are you all right?"

"I'm fine." Bree fought the lump that rose again at the concern in his voice. "I'm sorry, you're already at work. I shouldn't have called."

"No, no, it's fine. Construction got an early start today. Let me step outside where it is quieter. Now, what is going on?"

"It's nothing, I just—" Bree lost the battle with the tears. "We got to Venice today, and…and…I couldn't get on the boat. I tried and tried, but I couldn't do it." She snatched a tissue from the bedside to soak up the running from her eyes and nose. "I don't know what was the matter with me. And now I had a nightmare during a nap and I just…wanted to talk to you. I'm so sorry, I'll let you go."

"Oh, my dear one." The warmth, the caring in his voice sent Bree grabbing for more tissues again. "Venice, of course. The boats and water, and Roger's accident."

"Yeah, I guess. Hang on." Bree set the phone down a second to blow her nose, then sucked a long breath and picked back up. "Sorry. It had occurred to me, but I thought I'd be fine. I was positive I'd be fine. After all, that was more than twenty years ago." She massaged her forehead. "And now we're booked for this lovely gondola trip tomorrow, and I— I just don't know if I can do it." The memory of the rocking water flashed through her mind again, and she shuddered.

"Well, you don't have to."

"But we've already paid for it. And I've always thought a gondola ride sounded like a dream. I'd be so mortified to skip out on it—I already had to sit on the dock and scoot into the boat like a toddler today just to get to our hotel." An almost-chuckle tickled her chest.

"See, you found a way to do what you needed to do. But the gondola isn't something you have to do, if you really don't want to. It's okay to be human and need grace sometimes." Bree heard a wry note in his voice. "Even if we overachievers have a hard time admitting it."

"Well, I'll think about it." Bree sighed, the tension in her limbs flowing out. "Thank you, Pierre. I'm so sorry to bother you. It helps just to talk."

"You are never a bother, *amica mia*. Never."

Bree leaned back against the headboard, her heart a mingle of emotions. What a dear he was.

❀   ❀   ❀

The next morning, after a rough night, Bree joined the others downstairs in the dining room, half of which was outside. They opted for the buffet, delighted with the variety of choices, the displays each a work of art.

"Not a food bar and coffee on the go, that's for sure. I wanted one of everything." Bree sipped her coffee, just poured by a smiling waiter, then drew a breath. "I better tell you now so you're not surprised. I am not getting in that gondola, not after yesterday."

Mother and daughter stared at her, but even Denise did not say a word.

"I hope you have a marvelous time but let me know when you're back and I'll meet you for lunch." The words were still hard to say, but she knew this was right.

"But what are you going to do?"

"Ah, find a comfortable place, write some cards, read my book, and people-watch, besides wander through all these carts. Brought my sketchbook out too; Rachel made me want to practice drawing. That little chapel we passed has grabbed my imagination."

They finished their meal and the other two headed for their gondola ride while Bree settled her sunglasses, shady hat in place, and ambled. *You always dreamed of a gondola ride and you backed out.* The voice insisted on being heard, no matter that she was studying ties in the hope of finding one for Pierre. She was seriously behind in gift shopping. *What kind of a wuss are you? All the money you spent to come here—you paid for that gondola ride. You wasted that money.*

Teeth clamped, she ignored the voice. She paid the vendor and tucked the paper sack into her bag. Her phone showed three more hours until the others returned. After dropping her postcards in the box by the hotel desk, back outside she turned left and smiled to herself when she saw the open door at the chapel. Inside, the front pews were occupied and the cassocked priest faced the altar, chanting in Latin. Grateful she was wearing her hat, she slid into the worn back pew. Bree closed her eyes and let the voice swirl around her, like music. Ancient words in an ancient tongue, in an ancient chapel. At the "amen," she opened her eyes. The cross with the crucified Christ hung between two stained-glass windows, one of Mary and the other of Mary holding the baby Jesus. Candles flickered along the altar rail. Peace settled into her soul, and silent words of worship and praises floated upward with the flickering of the candles. At the end of the service, she let all the others leave before she followed them.

"*Grazie,*" she said with a smile at the man whose face wore the peace he shared with her.

"*Benvenuta nella nostra chiesa.*"

Bree caught a couple of words—he must be welcoming her to the church. She shook her head. "*Parla inglese?*"

"Some. *Grazie* for joining us. Come again." He bowed and made the sign of the cross in front of her. "May you be blessed as you bless others."

She swallowed and nodded as she realized what he had said. "And you also."

Someone else came up so she started to leave, stopped to pick a couple of the brochures from the rack, and dropped some cash in the slotted box. *Lord, help me to always bless others.*

Grateful for the shade of the buildings, she turned in between the two restaurants and followed the street past a pharmacy, a leather repair shop, another restaurant, turning corners whichever way seemed appealing. Seeing a hanging sign caught by a shaft of sunlight, she stopped to stare in the two lighted front display windows. Masks of all kinds, some full faces, others feathered, all colors, costumes of medieval times, glorious brocaded silks, golds and greens, blues of all shades. Threads, laces, myriad notions.

The woman watched her and smiled and nodded at Bree's delight.

"I've never seen anything like this," Bree said after the greeting.

"I collect the unusual."

"And you make the garments?"

"*Si*, and I have help. Making masks for *Martedì Grasso* is an art of its own."

"I've never been to Mardi Gras in America but I know the traditions started here."

"*Si*. I ship masks and some garments all over the world." She greeted a group of tourists who wandered in. "Can I help you find something?" she asked Bree.

"I'd like that black feathered mask with the sequins."

The woman lifted it from the wall by the handle and laid it on the counter. "Good choice."

"Do you have a brochure or something? I'm an author, I write mysteries, and your shop is giving me some very exciting ideas." If she did make her new detective a travel writer...

The woman reached behind the counter and handed her several different brochures. "This is a bit about the history of masks and this one..." She identified the others. "Do you have a card?"

"*Si.*" Bree handed her a business card and a bookmark. "If you like mysteries."

The woman nodded and read her card. "Breeanna?"

"I go by Bree. Thank you so much for your time and the adventure you provide for dreamers like me."

"I hope you can come again."

"*Grazie*, me too." Bree signed the receipt and nodded again. Oh, such a delight. She couldn't wait to tell Rachel and Denise.

Glancing at her watch, she realized she should probably start back. Hopefully she'd find her way.

When she saw a restaurant with an older woman making ravioli, her hair in the old way of bouffant or rolled high above the forehead, she knew she'd gone wrong somehow. The woman rolled the dough, just as Bree had in the class, and then marked the squares with something like a big cookie cutter, dropped a spoonful of filling in the middle of each square, then after laying dough over that, used another tool to press the dough together. When she cut them all apart, Bree felt like clapping. Instead she stepped inside to the counter and told them she needed to get back to her hotel. As the young man and a bit older woman laughed along with her, she inhaled again.

"This place smells heavenly. What do you do, have a fan to blow your advertisement down the street?"

They laughed and gave her directions, the woman writing them down.

"*Grazie.* I'll bring my friends back for dinner here."

Her phone rang as she passed their favorite gelato place. "I'm almost there," she answered.

"I'm so sorry you missed the gondola tour," Denise greeted her as Bree walked up to them.

"Wait till I tell you about my adventures too. But what did you like best?"

"What I learned is that I like yards with green grass and flowers, and fresh air, but the waterways amid straight-up walls are intriguing."

"You know, Mother, the upkeep here must be continuous. And you don't usually mow the lawn at home." Rachel gave her mother one of those looks. "Where are we eating? I'm starved."

Guess their tiff is still in operation, Bree thought. *Ignore them* sounded in her mind.

"How about across from where we ate yesterday. That looked good." Bree gestured over her shoulder to the folks behind the counter. "And they recommended it."

Once they were seated and had ordered, Denise leaned forward. "You have to go to the islands tomorrow. You have to! Rosita said she talked with her friend who owns the boat she uses and he told her not to worry. That he will make sure you're safe."

"And she meant it." Rachel nodded. "She was really sad you missed today."

She's not the only one, Bree thought. The memory of being frozen on that dock still tried to stop her heart. *But you got around it*, the other voice answered. And she had—embarrassing or not, she'd made it. Surely God could get her through tomorrow.

"On our free day, I want you two to see the mask store, and I want to eat some of that ravioli the old lady was making."

"Sounds good to me," Rachel said with a smile. "So much to see and do."

✿   ✿   ✿

Dry mouth attacked after a rerun dream woke her in the morning. *You have always wanted to see the glassblowing, you and Lizzie. You have to do it for Lizzie. And besides, Rosita promised.* Bree knew she drooled over the pictures of blown glass art in the brochures. She forced herself out of bed to get ready and met the others in the dining room.

"It'll be okay," Rachel whispered when Rosita joined them. Bree nodded. *Please, Lord.*

"We'll start with the glassblowing on Murano Island, then over to Burano for the lace making. While there are no longer lace-making factories here, we'll see demonstrations of several methods, all of them centuries old. So many women made, and still make, their lace at home since it doesn't take big machines and lots of space." She tucked her brochures back in her bag. "You ready?"

The closer to the dock, the slower Bree's feet moved.

"*Buongiorno, signoras.* We have great weather to be on the water today." The captain, Miguel, greeted them after Rosita did the introductions. He turned to Bree. "I'm sorry you had such a difficult time. Those others..." He made a throwing-away motion while shaking his head. "Here, let me show you." He held out his arm. "Not hands but this way." He took her hand, laid it inside along his lower arm. "Now you hold on to my elbow and I will do the same for you. *Si?*"

Bree swallowed and nodded. "*Si.*" He felt solid as the proverbial rock and looked that way too. His T-shirt fit over well-muscled torso and shoulders. "Now." He put one foot on the dock and the other on his boat. "Hang on and you step in." She sucked in a deep breath and followed his instructions, his smile making her feel even more secure.

She stepped from the dock down to the step on the hull of the boat then down onto the flooring as if she'd been doing so all her life.

Blinking rapidly, she grinned at him. *"Grazie."* She sniffed. *"Molte grazie." I did it, we did it. And I'm not even shaking.*

"Shame those others didn't do it like that," Denise muttered. "Would have saved you near heart failure, let alone bad dreams."

Bree slid into one of the bench seats along the hull of the boat. *I did it. Thanks to Miguel, it was easy. Thank you, Lord.* She looked up to catch his smiling nod. *"Grazie* ten times over."

Sitting beside her, Rachel gave her a one-armed hug and a big smiling nod. "Yes!"

Miguel and Rosita both pointed out landmarks as they cruised out to the islands, along with Bree's myriad questions about the area and Venice in particular.

Miguel made getting out of the boat as easy as getting in. They followed other tourists into what seemed like a dark cave but was really an ancient building that grew hotter as they entered a cavernous room centered on a white-hot fire maw with men in hooded masks at various steel tables. Following their guide's instructions, they settled into tiered seating and focused on the man standing on the floor of the firing space in front of them.

Bree sat enthralled as he gave a brief history lesson and demonstrated dipping a long pipe into molten glass, inserting the tip into the flame, and both turning and blowing into the pipe at the same time. Breath by breath and turn by turn, the blob became a glimmering pitcher with a handle and a lip in glorious reds and blues…the process one of patience and skill acquired by intricate and extensive training. When he cut the piece off the pipe and set it to cool, they all applauded.

"Ooooh, I want one," Rachel breathed.

Bree realized sweat was trickling down the sides of her face and how focused she had been. While she'd seen videos of the process at one time, being here and seeing it for real made her all the more grateful for Miguel. Their group filed out of the firing room and made their way to the showrooms, where salespeople were available to answer any questions and show the wares. Lighted shelf after lighted shelf, pieces grouped by function, by style, and by the plethora of colors. Each piece a thing of beauty, from simple bowls and vases of all sizes with swirling colors to incredibly intricate horses and other animals and sea life, all kinds of statuary, all created in the same way they had watched.

The people demonstrating assured them any piece they desired could be shipped safely, rather than carried home in a suitcase. Even though Bree lived somewhat by an edict she'd learned early in her writing career—*If you have to dust it, water it, or feed it, you don't need it*, especially the *dust it* part—today she ignored that inner voice. Instead she purchased a pair of ten-inch vases, one in reds and blues for her and one in reds and yellows for Lizzie. Lizzie, who had dreamed of seeing this place on an island in the Adriatic Sea, most of all.

Several hours later, in what seemed like several minutes, they boarded their boat again and headed to the lace island of Burano. Houses and buildings were dressed in hues of reds, blues, yellows, many with pots of plants and wash hanging out to dry. With no automobiles allowed on the island, only walkers and bicyclists with an occasional dog used the narrow streets. They stopped at an outdoor café for lunch and then ambled the streets, stopping in the shops that featured a wealth of laces and women with pillows on their laps, with pins in the desired design and spools of thread, their fingers flying as they picked up a spool, wove it around a pin, and picked up another, using both hands. Others used lace-making needles, and one used a crochet hook in the tatting method.

Bree had tried lace making with pins, pillows, and bobbins, realizing quickly that this was another skill learned only through hours of focus and patience. She'd also tried tatting, an old skill that was regaining popularity. All yielded beauty that appeared fragile, yet lasted if properly cared for. Handmade, a thing of lovely grace and beauty, and easily packable. Surely there was a life lesson here. Bree succumbed and carefully placed the flat packages in her bag.

"I think you'll like this memory." Denise showed her a picture she'd taken of Bree lost in the lovely land of lace.

Bree nodded. "I will indeed." *And to think I almost missed all of this because of fear. Thank you, Lord, for providing a way out or perhaps through.*

As they ambled back to the waiting boat, she marveled at the variety of colors of the buildings, the tiny gardens using every inch of space, and the flowers, bougainvillea of brilliant pinks and reds burgeoning over walls and trellises. Various palm trees, big-leafed banana clusters, and tropical fruit trees including mango and coconut palms. Fragrances of the sea, flowers, and yeast, undergirded by delectable foods, baked and simmered.

"I now know what people mean when they say fresh-caught fish is best." She'd had fish and chips for lunch, Rosita assuring her that the fish had been caught in the early hours of the morning. Fishing, glassblowing, and lace making, all passed through families who'd lived on these islands for centuries. Again, the age of it all, the history.

"I can never thank you enough," she told both Rosita and

Miguel as she stepped off the boat. "What an incredible day. *Grazie*."

"My pleasure. You are welcome." He nodded and smiled. "Come again."

Back at the hotel, they said their goodbyes to Rosita as the next day they had no tours planned, their free day. "*Buonasera, vieni di nuovo*." How they would love to come again.

That evening after another delicious dinner and a gelato at their favorite place since they'd visited it every day, she settled against the padded headboard of her bed and called Pierre.

"You sound tired," she said after their greetings.

"I suppose I do although I hoped I was hiding it well. And before you ask, there have been no more tragedies or scares, just lots to do. I had no idea opening a coffee shop would be so intricate." He almost caught a yawn.

Bree did the same. "How can a yawn be contagious even over the phone?"

"I'm sure I don't know. So how are you and Venice getting along?"

"Well, I did skip the gondola ride. But today I made it to the islands."

When Bree described Miguel and his solution, Pierre chuckled along with her. "Wise man. And yes, I did visit Murano and the glassblowing. It did not make me want to try it. But Bree, I am so proud of you. You conquered that fear."

"Thanks to Rosita and Miguel. But I missed the gondola tour."

"I didn't think that was so great. Those waterways stank to high heaven, especially when the tide was out."

The two shared a chuckle.

"Sleep well," he said a couple of minutes later. "I'm heading into Vancouver, and you know how traffic is."

When they clicked off, Bree snuggled down in the comfortable bed. So good it felt, talking with Pierre like this, leaning on his warmth and strength a bit—even across the globe—when her own were lacking. She'd sensed her heart yearning toward him, her feelings deepening in new ways, just the last couple of days. But what did it mean? How did he feel? Soon she would be home, and then…what?

✣   ✣   ✣

"Our last day here," Denise announced the next morning. "What do you two want to do?" She nodded to the waiter to refill her coffee. "I need every drop of caffeine I can pour in today."

"You could have stayed in bed longer," Rachel answered with a matching nod to the refill. "I'm going to pack, for one thing."

"And have more gelato." Bree nodded. The tension between mother and daughter seemed eased today, another thing to be thankful for. "I know you'll love the mask place, and we can eat at that restaurant."

"I wish we could tour Basilica di San Marco; the pictures I've seen are awesome. You have to admit we've seen a lot of CLOSED FOR REPAIRS signs in every city we've been in." Denise forked a piece of mango from her dish of cut-up fresh fruit. "A fruit bowl is something I'd love to have every day, but…" She shrugged. "I'm too lazy to fix it."

"Hey, we can't even get all these fruits and berries," Rachel reminded her.

Bree agreed, both about the foods and that they'd seen plenty of scaffolding, chutes from buildings to trucks, and billowing-in-the-wind canvas to keep construction debris from falling on the pedestrians.

Rachel and Denise were as enthralled with the mask shop

as Bree, and after they found the restaurant, and watched the woman making ravioli, they enjoyed their meal.

"I think that was the best ravioli I've ever tasted," Denise said as they headed back to their hotel to finish packing.

They all three packed boxes to be mailed home and took them to the hotel desk on their way out for their evening adventures.

They found a bookstore, where Rachel bought a small but well-illustrated cookbook in English.

"Okay, Bree, we'll make this at your house." She pointed at a pasta recipe. "We don't want to wait too long, or we'll forget. And we have our notes from Raffaela." She flipped a page. "See, here are all the special tools we'll need." As her mother groaned, Rachel flipped to the back. "And here are sources to buy them."

"I'll do the cleanup," Denise promised.

They crossed several bridges arched over the waterways, the arches high enough so gondolas with their standing gondoliers and other smaller craft could have passage. The sun was setting, so scarlets, vermilions, and yellows painted the sky. The peaks and decorative cornices of the roofs of several ancient public buildings blacked the skyline as they arrived at their destination.

They entered the Piazza San Marco from the south side, with Doge's Palace on the right. The basilica had originally been the chapel for the rulers, the doges, so their guide-book said.

"This is huge, I had no idea..." Bree studied the architecture, the people, the deepening sky. "Don't wait for me, you two go on. We'll meet back here whenever."

"Thanks, call me if..."

"I know. Same here."

Lights blinked on everywhere around her but failed to hold back the darkening. Deepening blue took over the western sky, showing off the evening star poised on one of the pinnacled parapets of the marble building. When did she ever take time at home to watch the evening come calling? Above Doge's Palace, the azure deepened to indigo.

An eight-piece string ensemble set up at an outdoor restaurant with white-draped tables and chairs and lines of extra chairs for just drinks or for folks who wanted only to enjoy the music. When the opening bars of the Alleluia beckoned, she sat down, awe bringing tears at the haunting music. How could it be, even one of her favorite songs amid all this glory? She closed her eyes, the better to absorb. When the final notes faded away, she sniffed, mopped the last of the tears, and decided to amble on.

Vendors showed a toy that flashed lights when tossed in the air, looking almost like stars come down. A little boy stood by one young man, watching every motion then giggling when the light flashed. A family of two parents and three kids watched, and the children talked the father into buying one.

Bree stood enjoying as the children attempted to get the gadget to perform as it had for the vendor. Soon, those watching were smiling and giggling along with the kids. The two youngest, a boy and a girl, got it to working on about the second toss, making her think of James and Jessica. She thought back to when they were small. Most of their vacations had been places they could take their boat, waterways of the Pacific Northwest.

Here the father struggled, much to everyone's delight. The young vendor couldn't have had better advertising as several other spectators tried it too. Bree thought of taking one home for Luke but decided to amble on instead.

How was her family doing at home? Was Jess really

doing as well as Pierre said? How were James and Abigail managing without Bree around to help with Luke?

The musicians swung into a new song—"I Could Have Danced All Night." While her feet wanted to answer the call, she watched another young family with the woman dancing her little child, dipping and turning. The father and his camera followed them, all of them laughing. Bree wished she knew how to video the scene like the man was doing. Would Pierre dance with her like this? The thought made her pulse patter faster.

A bit farther on a photographer was taking pictures of a young woman in a hoop-skirted wedding dress with a sweetheart neckline and an abundance of lace. A young man in a black tuxedo exchanged adoring looks with her, the woman following the instructions from the man behind the camera. Another woman made sure the dress, the hair, the positioning were perfect. A guy moved the reflectors on demand.

"*Finito*," called the photographer. The young woman picked up her hooped skirts, her red high-topped tennis shoes flashing as they strode away.

Bree laughed to herself. Models or real life, no matter. What a hoot.

The music followed her.

Out in the main square, lighted fountains splashed, cameras flashed as visitors recorded their adventures. Bree checked the hour on her iPhone. Perhaps it was time to head back. Sitting on a bench, she let her mind roam back through the Venice segment of their trip, the time of the greatest fear and the greatest victory. *Lord, you knew it all in advance. Had I trusted you earlier, might it have been different? Or was the freezing fear necessary?* She pondered. Why might it have been necessary? She tipped her head back. Too much light to see all the stars, but she found

Orion's belt. Years ago her father had often said that she had more nerve than sense. True, she'd tried anything, without fear. Then, when Roger died, she found fear—but she had taken on all the challenges, faced them down, cared for her kids, and built a career, all with just her and the Lord. Or maybe too often in her mind, just her. *Is it the pride, Lord? That I can do it. And if I can do it, why do I need you?*

Did I have to come to visit Venice to learn these lessons? When Roger was killed, I had nowhere to turn but to you. My security died with him. She blew out a breath. That's when she learned what anger at God truly felt like. Who else could she blame?

She studied the people around her. Did she miss Denise and Rachel?

Back then was when she truly began the lifelong lesson of learning how much God loved her. And now she'd had another of those soul-deep lessons. Trust. How often had she heard Him in her heart saying, *Bree, are you going to trust me?*

Yes, Lord, I trust you, but do I have to get in trouble for you to teach me that, over and over again? She glanced up to see Rachel waving at her. As they chattered on about all they had seen this evening, despite all the people and the goings-on, she recognized gratitude bubbling up and running over. Rachel had confided in Bree that she and her mom had a good talk yesterday, after one of their clashes came to a head through sharing the hotel room. And it had helped. Another lesson Bree could take home to her own family, perhaps.

She slipped her arm around Denise's shoulders. "Thank you for all the time you put into booking this trip for us."

Denise nodded. "You're welcome. My privilege. Talk about a host of adventures that we had no idea were coming."

"True. I wish I could thank Jade in person for this incredible gift she gave me."

"You will one day. Just don't be in a hurry to make it happen, okay?"

Bree grinned and nudged her friend. "Hopefully we get to the airport, on the plane, fly to Portland, and get home without more *adventures*."

"Agreed. But plenty of amazing memories."

Chapter Twenty-Six

He wasn't sure he should be here.

Pierre-René hesitated on the steps of Bree's front porch. He could hear voices inside, and Jessica's car was parked in the driveway—of course, since she was still staying here— along with a family SUV on the street that must be James and Abigail's. A real family gathering.

Surely he didn't belong...at least not yet. Maybe not ever. He'd become more certain of his feelings these past couple of weeks, but a lot would depend on how things went when he picked Bree up from the airport this afternoon.

Still, Jessica had invited him to come over, before she left the coffee shop this morning. He'd given her most of the day off, as well as himself. Thankfully Terrence would supervise some workers this afternoon.

"We're going to finish fixing up Mom's kitchen today before she gets home," she'd said, her face shy. "You can come over, if you want."

So here he was.

Berating himself for his lack of courage, Pierre lifted his hand to ring the doorbell just as he heard the lock turn. The door swung inward, revealing Paula and her smiling face.

"What are you standing there for, silly?" She pulled him into a hug. "Come on in, we're about to eat lunch."

Lunch? He hadn't meant to barge in on a meal. Pierre-René followed her through the entryway and dining room into the kitchen.

"Hey, Pierre." Abigail looked up with a smile from placing bowls of soup on the kitchen table. Her ponderous belly looked as if she were about to drop the baby right there on the kitchen floor. "You're just in time, pull up a chair."

"I didn't intend for you to feed me." Pierre held back. "I had a sandwich in the car. You all go ahead."

"Come on, you can't pass up Abby's taco soup." James waved him in, adding a bag of tortilla chips and a carton of sour cream to the table. "At least have one bowl."

"Yeah, come on, Pierre." Jessica brought dishes of grated cheese and chopped tomato, then sat down beside Luke. She tucked her hands under her thighs, a tense gesture Pierre had noticed in her before.

Jessica might be the only one more nervous about her mom's return than Pierre. Or at least as much. Overruled, he gave a nod of acquiescence and drew out a chair next to Paula. "Thank you."

Luke, now almost three, grinned and waved at him across the table, then bounced in his booster seat. "Mo' cheese, Mommy."

"What's the nice way to ask?" Abigail cocked a brow.

"May *pease* have mo' cheese?"

"Yes, you may." Abigail sprinkled cheese on Luke's soup, then placed both hands behind her hips to arch her back before sliding into her seat with a sigh.

James touched her shoulder. "You okay, honey?"

"Yeah, just a lot of low back pressure today." Abigail gave a tired smile. "Once Bree is safely home, I am more than ready for this baby to come."

"Gamma's comin' home," Luke informed the table, attempting to stand his spoon up straight in his soup. It fell to the side and clattered out of his bowl, spattering reddish broth.

Abigail sighed, removed the spoon, then nodded at James. "Would you pray, please?"

"Sure. And son, don't play with your food." James extended his hands. Everyone grasped hold, completing the circle.

Gripping Paula's hand on one side and Jessica's on the other, Pierre closed his eyes, his throat tightening. Not often lately had he been wrapped in a family circle like this.

"Lord, we thank you for this food, and for bringing us together today. Thank you for Paula and Pierre-René and the blessing they have been to our family. Please bring Mom safely home on the plane and help us finish getting the kitchen ready for her. In Jesus' name, amen."

"Amen." Luke piped up.

Chuckles mingled with the amens around the table as everyone released hands.

"So, what's the plan for this afternoon?" Pierre dipped into his soup. Savory tomato broth, with chunks of tender ground beef, bell peppers and onions, black and kidney beans, all topped with sour cream, cheese, and fresh avocado. "Abigail, this is delicious."

"The ladies are going to hang the curtains." James nodded to the bare, open kitchen windows, the springtime sunshine and breeze streaming through. "I put the rods and brackets back up before lunch. And some of the new cabinet doors are sticking, I'm going to tackle that next. Might need to reset a couple. You good with a screwdriver or drill?"

"Both, but I didn't bring my tools." Pierre-René kicked himself.

"No worries, I did. What time do you have to leave for the airport?"

"By three. Her flight is due at three thirty, and it's a short drive. I want to get parked and be there in plenty of time."

"I can't wait to hear about her trip." Abigail caught Luke's elbow from knocking over his milk cup.

James nodded. "She'll have to go through customs too, right?"

"That's correct." Pierre scraped up the last of his soup. Turned out he'd still been hungry after all. He sat back and gazed around the restored kitchen. New pine cabinets by the stove that almost matched the old, undamaged ones. Freshly painted light-green walls, a new stove, and several new tiles in the floor near it, a muted terra-cotta that made him think of Italy.

Jessica followed his gaze around the room, twisting her hands in her lap. "I sure hope she likes it."

Pierre-René gave her a reassuring nod. "She will."

Bree's daughter smiled faintly, but he saw the trepidation in her eyes. Still, what progress they had made these past two weeks, for them to even be sitting here together today. Something released in Pierre's chest. So easy to forget all they had to be grateful for. *Thank you, Lord.*

A short while later, James crumpled his paper napkin and reached to stack the dishes, Paula helping. "Well, let's get to those cabinets."

Abigail attempted to stand, then bent forward, hands on the table. "Oof."

"You all right?" Paula laid a hand over hers.

"I think so, just a cramp." Abigail breathed deeply through her nose a moment, then relaxed. "Better now." She straightened, shaking her head. "Goodness, this baby is having a field day with me today."

"You should rest while we clean up." Jessica ran water in the sink.

"I agree. Jessica and I will load the dishwasher." Paula picked up a dish towel. "And you men get started on those cabinets."

"Yes, ma'am." Pierre grinned and feigned a salute.

His sister-in-law snapped the dish towel at him.

"Fine." Abigail sighed. "I'll go read to Luke a little while on the sofa. With any luck, he'll conk out for a nap. You know, even that's hit-or-miss now; some days he skips it altogether. But with this new baby coming, I want to encourage naps as long as I can." She blew out another breath, twisting her upper body. "Come on, honey, let's pick a book from Grandma's shelf." Luke's feet pattered down the hallway toward the living room, Abigail following slowly.

Pierre found himself on the kitchen floor, holding a cabinet door steady while James attempted to reset it. He didn't seem quite as competent with tools as Pierre would have expected, but he held his tongue. After all, James hadn't grown up with a father past age eleven.

The drill slipped, stripping a screw, and James exhaled in frustration.

"You guys okay?" Jessica looked down from the sink.

"Fine." James's voice stretched tight.

"Maybe you should let Pierre do it. He's really handy with tools."

"Thanks, Jessica, I've got this. Though these definitely don't seem as good quality as the other cabinets. Which is why Mom was going to just repaint those, not replace." James set a new screw. The drill spun again with a shrill whine. "Until, of course, they caught fire."

Jessica scrubbed the soup pot, silent.

Pierre glanced up at her face, seeing the apprehension and guilt written there again. His heart hurt for her. The tension between her and James had been better lately, but family wounds didn't heal all at once, as he knew too well.

"Overall, I think it's looking great." Pierre moved his grip to make room for James. "Where are the curtains you ladies are going to hang?"

"In the living room." Jessica handed the clean pot to Paula and rinsed her hands.

"I couldn't find an exact match for the fabric that burned. But they're a pretty yellow-and-green print, kind of European," Paula said. "I love them, and I think Bree will too."

"Let's go get 'em and check on Abigail." Jessica's voice brightened, and the two women left the room.

"I think that does it." James scooted back and tested the cabinet doors. They didn't stick now, at least not much.

Pierre-René clapped him on the shoulder. "Well done."

"Thanks for your help."

"Anything else that needs doing?"

"I was going to clean my mom's car, have it ready for her. It's been in the garage, but I wanted to vacuum it out, wash the windows. No pressure for you to help, though."

"I'd like to, if you'll have me. I have another forty minutes or so."

"Sure." James shot him a grin that warmed Pierre's chest.

He'd never felt the resistance with James that he did with Jessica at the beginning, but he sensed a new camaraderie springing between them. Which would be just as important as his relationship with Bree's daughter, should they...if their relationship...well, it was a good thing. And perhaps for James too, if he was reading the younger man right. After all, he'd carried the burden of being the sole "man of the family" for a long time.

They pushed themselves up from the kitchen floor, Pierre-René's knees creaking more than he chose to acknowledge, then stepped back as the ladies reentered the room, chattering and with arms full of yellow-and-green Provençal print curtains.

"Luke asleep?" James asked his wife.

"He's out on the sofa, thankfully." Seeming reenergized, Abigail laid her armload of curtains over the back of a chair.

"Jess, you think you can climb up and lift those curtain rods down?"

"Sure." Jessica clambered up a step stool with the nimble legs of youth.

James nodded to the door. "Let's leave them to it."

He backed Bree's car out of the garage, and Pierre used the squeegee James handed him on the windshields and windows while James hooked up the vacuum for the interior. Somehow the pull and push as he washed and wiped lifted Pierre's heart, despite the nerves that clenched his stomach as the afternoon ticked by. But it was good to be doing something for Bree.

He rinsed the squeegee off at the outdoor faucet and checked his watch. A quarter to three—he needed to get on the road.

"Anything else I can do before I head out?" He raised his voice over the roar of the vacuum.

James switched it off and poked his head out of the car. "You leaving?"

"About to."

"Go right ahead. And thanks for picking her up, by the way."

"I wanted to." Pierre stuck his hands in his pockets, suddenly feeling a vulnerable schoolboy.

"Yeah, I figured." James studied him a moment. "You like her, huh? My mom."

"I do." Pierre-René swallowed. "I really do."

James nodded, a slow smile spreading over his face. "Well, then, you better go get her."

Did he intend a double meaning in that? But Pierre nodded, holding James's gaze. "I'll do that."

"James!" Behind them, the screen door slapped, and Paula charged out. "You better get in here, I think Abigail's in labor."

The vacuum clattered to the ground. James slammed the car door and sprinted toward the house.

Well. Nothing like adding more excitement to the day. His own adrenaline kicking up, Pierre grabbed the vacuum and replaced it in the garage, then pressed the garage door button and headed in through the interior entrance. In the kitchen he found Paula and James bent over Abigail, who leaned both arms on the kitchen table, moaning softly, hips swaying side to side.

Jessica stood back, worrying the cuticle of her thumb. She looked up as Pierre entered. "We were hanging the curtains, she was reaching up to hand me one, then she just doubled over. Do you think it hurt her or the baby?"

"I don't think so." Pierre gave her shoulder a quick squeeze. "She's likely been going into labor all afternoon, by the signs I've been seeing." He'd been through this three times with his wife, after all, then in a way more recently with his grandchildren. "She probably was trying to push past it, get everything done before your mom comes home."

"I guess." Jessica nibbled her nail, her eyes widening as Abigail's groan escalated.

Paula leaned near Abigail's ear, murmuring soothing words while gently rubbing the mother's lower back. James dashed into the entryway, then returned with keys and Abigail's purse in hand, stuffing his phone in his back pocket.

"Okay, she seems to be progressing fast, we're heading to the hospital." His words tripped over one another. "Jess, Luke is still asleep, can you stay with him?"

She nodded hard. "Of course."

Paula spoke up. "I'll stay too. You guys just get on the road and don't worry about a thing."

"I'm sorry, everyone." Abigail straightened and gingerly

rubbed her belly, blowing out a long breath. "I was really hoping this little one would wait till at least tomorrow. Guess I was in denial."

"Babies come when they want, and second babies often quickly." Paula gave her a side hug. "He or she will be in your arms before you know it, and then that's all that will matter. You have a bag for the hospital?"

"Been in the car for weeks." James reached for Abigail's hand and tucked it into his arm. She leaned on him, her other arm supporting her belly, as they made their way to the door. "Pierre, can you bring my mom straight to the hospital? I'll text her to let her know."

"Absolutely." He gave a firm nod. "Go with God, we'll all be praying."

After the door closed, Jessica pressed her hands to her cheeks. "Whoa. That was intense."

"It gets a lot more so." Pierre-René chuckled, memories of his children's births flooding back. "But it's all worth it." He checked his watch. "And now I'm the one who's got to hit the road."

He got into his car and drew a deep breath as he turned the keys in the ignition.

A lunch with the family. A baby on the way. And soon, Bree would be waiting.

❖　❖　❖

Bree waited with her luggage at baggage claim, craning her neck to search the faces of the people streaming in and out of the automatic doors to the outside.

Pierre was always so prompt. Where was he?

My man. Or is he? After these last strange couple of weeks, she didn't know what to think. Not to mention her brain was fried, jet-lagged, and sleep-deprived from the tumultuous last days of the trip, the flight from Venice to Paris, then the long one from Paris to Portland.

Bree moved her big black suitcase, bound with the luggage strap her literary agency had given them all at a writers' conference some years ago, to keep it out of the way of traffic. It fell on her foot.

"Ow." She shoved it upright again with a bit more force than necessary, then grabbed her smaller bag just before it hit the floor, this one filled with gifts and goodies from Italy. Her shoulder sagged as she hefted it. How had it gotten so heavy? And she'd not brought back near as much as she could have. Of course, she had shipped some things home.

Impatience trying to distract her, she scanned the milling crowds again. She should check whether Pierre had texted; she hadn't since deboarding, though she hadn't heard any dings or rings.

Propping her luggage against a nearby bench, she dug out her phone. Nothing.

Shoving it back into her purse, she looked up to search the area again.

And there he was.

Just stepping through the double doors, in a dark-teal polo shirt and gray slacks that set off his silver-threaded dark hair. Pierre-René paused just inside the entrance and scanned the crowd, hands in his windbreaker pockets, his brow pensive. He hadn't seen her yet.

"Pierre." With a sudden surge of joy, she scurried toward him, narrowly missing several passengers with her careening luggage. "Pierre-René! Over here."

He looked toward her, and their eyes met. Then he was hurrying toward her too, both of them laughing, weaving through the crowds. They skidded to a stop by one of the big white pillars near the exit, then stood still a moment, only a foot apart, breathing hard.

Bree's heart skittered as she looked up at him. What was she, in high school again? And here he was just staring at her without saying a word. "Well, don't I get a 'welcome home'?"

Pierre-René took the heavy bag from her hand, setting it beside his feet. Then he pulled her into his arms and kissed her, with an urgency that made her gasp, a tenderness that made her slip her hands up to his shoulders and return the kiss.

He pulled back, chagrin in his dark eyes, and released her. "I'm sorry. I shouldn't have—I didn't plan on that. Please forgive me."

"Forgive you?" Bree pressed her hands to her hot cheeks. "Well, I didn't plan on it either, but that doesn't mean I didn't like it."

"You did?" A vulnerable look came into his eyes, making her want to hug him again.

"I didn't say that either." She gave him a mischievous smile. "But maybe we could talk about it more later?" She shrugged at the surrounding crowds.

"Right." He nodded . . . firmly. "Definitely more important things to think about right now." He lifted her bag again, then took the handle of her big suitcase and set the smaller one atop to pull both together.

"I can take one of these." Bree tried to pry one handle or another from his grip.

"Ah-ah-ah." He waved his hand at her, his familiar charm returning. "You are the lady of the hour—let me serve you, madame. Now, ready to go be a grandma again?"

"What?" She stared at him, her stomach sinking. "I missed it?"

"No—I don't think so, not yet. Wait, didn't you get James's text?"

"No." Bree snatched out her phone again. Empty home screen. "Nothing." She typed in the passcode and opened her messages to be sure. "Nothing at all. What happened? Tell me."

"Perhaps he forgot, in the rush." Pierre craned his neck to see. "You remembered to take it off airplane mode?"

"Oh, my word." Bree did so, then palmed her forehead as a string of messages from her son appeared. "I can't believe I did that. Now of all times—oh, poor James. What happened, when did she go into labor, can we go straight there?"

"This afternoon, when we were all at your house working on the kitchen—Jessica invited me to join them. They left for the hospital just before I came to get you, and yes, I'm under orders to take you straight there." He smiled, that grin she loved lighting his eyes and circling warmth into her heart despite her angst. "This baby may be in a hurry, but never fear. I fully intend to get you there in time."

The next thing she knew, Bree was sitting beside Pierre in his car, zipping over the 205 bridge toward the Vancouver hospital. Thankfully the traffic was clear—it should only take them about fifteen minutes. She still couldn't believe she'd left her phone on airplane mode. Thank heaven for Pierre.

She glanced at him, sitting beside her for real, no dream, after these weeks of being so far away. Those days wondering what he was thinking, why he'd hung up and never called, then finding him so dear when she called and was struggling, new feelings deepening for him, still not knowing how he felt. But now...*he kissed me, Lord. What does that mean? And oh, Lord, please be with James and Abigail, strengthen her to give birth, bring this little one safely into the world. He kissed me...Pierre-René kissed me.* And not a polite, casual, French air peck to both cheeks either. A real, honest-to-goodness kiss.

She shook herself and pulled out her phone again to text James.

We're on our way. So sorry, phone was on airplane mode. Praying and see you soon.

Bree pressed her phone between her palms and drew a steadying breath. So many emotions swirling at once.

"It's new every time, isn't it?" Pierre clicked his turn signal to change lanes, starting to move over for their exit. "A little life coming into the world."

She nodded, her throat too full to speak. Except—she had a sudden thought. "Where's Luke?"

"With Jessica. Paula stayed too." Pierre turned off the freeway.

"So you really were all there together at my house? And Jessica invited you?" Hard to wrap her mind around.

Pierre-René chuckled. "A lot happened while you were in Italy."

They arrived at the hospital and headed to the maternity floor waiting room. Pierre sat in one of the padded chairs, but Bree couldn't. Pacing, she texted James again.

We're here now. In the waiting room.

Her phone dinged almost immediately.

She's ten centimeters. Shouldn't be long now.

Bree headed over to Pierre. "She's fully dilated. Oh, Lord, be with them and help her." She pressed the phone to her chin.

Pierre reached for her other hand and tugged her down into the chair beside him. "Come. Let's pray for them together."

Bree closed her eyes, grateful for the warm grip of his fingers pressing hers. She didn't have words, but Pierre prayed, his voice strong and sincere, and her heart echoed the prayer with him. She found herself still able to sit when he finished, leaning back in the chair, gazing at the calming pictures on the walls as the minutes ticked by. Ten minutes, twenty. Forty.

Her phone rang. Bree jumped, sending the device clattering to the floor. She snatched it up again to her ear. "James?"

"Mom." The grin in her son's voice shone through the phone. "You have a beautiful little granddaughter."

Chapter Twenty-Seven

Bree swayed gently side to side, gazing at the miracle in her arms.

"We are so glad you are here, sweet baby girl," she murmured, brushing her fingers over the faint fuzz of blond hair and gazing into those penetrating dark-blue eyes. So like Jessica's as an infant. "Thank you for waiting till Grandma got home, little Cynthia Marie." Marie—they'd taken the little one's middle name from Bree's own. The tightness in her throat threatened tears again at the thought.

Abigail sat in the nearby rocking chair in her and James's bedroom, watching Bree and the baby with new-mother adoration. She and little Cynthia were doing so well, the hospital let them return home the very next day. Bree had come over straightaway this afternoon, though she'd had her first quick visit in the hospital room right after the baby was born yesterday.

Cynthia Marie squirmed in Bree's arms, tiny fists waving, miniature puckered mouth rooting at Bree's sleeve. She chuckled.

"I think she's getting hungry again." Bree laid the tiny warm bundle in her daughter-in-law's arms, watching as Cynthia started to nurse. "She's an old pro already, isn't she?"

"I'm so grateful, after how Luke had such a rough start." Abigail relaxed in the chair, one hand smoothing her daughter's tiny head. "This one has been so easy by comparison, the birth, the feeding. But the wonder and the love are just as fresh and new, aren't they?"

"That's for sure." Bree squeezed Abigail's shoulder. "Thank you for letting me come over again so soon. What can I do to help before I leave?"

"You must be exhausted yourself." Abigail raised tired eyes. "You only got back yesterday afternoon. Don't worry about us—we'll be fine."

Bree gave her a look. "I'm not leaving till you give me a job. What will it be—dishes, laundry, dinner in the oven?"

Abigail gave a laugh of acquiescence. "There's lasagna in the freezer. If you could get that warming and make a salad, I'd be grateful. James is skilled in many areas—the kitchen not being one of them."

"I know. I blame myself, as his mother." Bree shook her head. "I'll do that, and I hope you'll let me take Luke for a while tomorrow."

"That would be great. James is trying to give him extra attention, but he definitely goes between being smitten with his baby sister and miffed that she's taking over his perfect life."

After getting dinner going and saying goodbye to James and Luke, who were building a block fort in the living room, Bree drove home. Jet lag weighted her eyelids even on the short trip. She set some of Abigail's taco soup to warm— bless her heart, providing meals for her mother-in-law right before having a baby herself—and fed her pets, who certainly knew how to make her feel welcomed. Spencer bounded joyfully into the kitchen, tail thumping a yahoo- you're-home tattoo on the new cabinets, while Cinders twined around Bree's legs till she could barely move about to set their dishes on the floor. She had to admit Jessica had done a great job supervising the kitchen restoration—

it looked as good as when she'd left it, maybe even better with the fresh paint and new stove. Even if she missed her old curtains a bit.

"I missed you more, babies." Squatting beside the animals as they munched their kibble, Bree scratched behind Spencer's ears and smoothed her hand down Cinders's back. "Are you feeling better, poor kitty?" A vet surgery, a fire, a tampon-plugged toilet…she shook her head. If she'd known how many disasters Jessica would cram into two weeks, she'd never have left the country. But that was why the Lord didn't let her know the future, or she'd never learn to trust Him. Or see how He could take care of everyone and everything, whether Bree was around to supervise or not. She chuckled wryly. Had she really thought herself so invincible? Venice had certainly blown that notion out of the water, no pun intended.

She pushed herself to her feet, every muscle aching, and dished up her soup. Lacking the energy to fix anything more, she set the bowl on the kitchen table along with some chips and raw baby carrots and sank into the chair.

Footsteps pounded down the hallway, and Jessica blew into the kitchen to fill her water bottle.

"Off to your shift at Applebee's?" Bree had nearly forgotten her daughter was here. "Did you eat?"

"Running late, no time now. Bye, Mom." Jessica tossed her a kiss and whooshed out the door, hair flying.

Bree shook her head as the door banged. What had Jessica been doing in her room all afternoon, so that she ran out of time to eat? Of course, she could have been doing work for Pierre on the computer—she said she'd been spending a lot of time on that. *You better give your daughter the benefit of the doubt*, Bree admonished herself. They'd hardly had time to talk yet, and they were both getting used to sharing space with someone again. Maybe she'd eat something at Applebee's.

She ate, set the dishes in the dishwasher, then called Lizzie to see how she was doing. Steve answered and said Lizzie was mostly sleeping, but doing as well as could be expected. Promising to call again tomorrow, Bree forced herself to her office to open her computer for at least a little while. Only 7:00 p.m. and she felt like she could sleep for days, but she must have a gazillion emails to catch up on. She'd checked occasionally during the trip, and done a brief dip this morning after sleeping till nearly ten, but only enough to be overwhelmed.

Five hundred unread messages in her inbox. She winced, then gave a quick scan through. Mostly promotionals...one from Denise with some initial photos attached from the trip. How did she do that so fast? One from her editor that had come in late morning today. Bree sat up straighter. Their response to her latest manuscript, turned in before she left.

Her heart rate picking up as it always still did, Bree clicked it open.

Dear Bree...were glad to receive your latest manuscript for the Effie Bartlett series...always a pleasure to work with you...enjoyed the story's premise; however, there are some plot elements we feel need to be addressed...

Bree read through the eleven and a half single-spaced pages of notes, her stomach sinking lower with each paragraph.

Blast. They wanted a major rewrite. And pronto.

How was she going to get it all done? She almost opened the manuscript right then but shook her head and closed the computer.

She'd look at it again—tomorrow.

The next morning before lunch, Bree sorted her laundry from the trip into piles on her bed, mentally wrestling with the plot issues her editor had brought up. As if it weren't enough to have to come up with a new series, now this latest book was a problem too. Jessica blasting music from the guest room didn't help. How could her daughter think with that racket?

She considered asking Jess to turn it down, but she'd be leaving to work at Pierre's soon, and Bree didn't want to rock the boat more than necessary. She bit her tongue and closed the bedroom door. If Jessica was going to keep living here a number of months still, which seemed likely, since she was nowhere near finished paying off her debts—at some point they'd have to talk through ground rules for two adult women sharing the same house again. Like she'd told Rachel, *communication* . . . but easier to preach to someone else than do it herself.

She pulled another armload of dirty tops and underwear from her emptying suitcase and glanced at the clock. Almost eleven thirty. James had texted this morning asking if Bree could take Luke this afternoon so he and Abigail could get some rest, so they would be here in an hour. Hopefully tonight she could get some revision done on her manuscript. *Lord, help me come up with decent ideas by then. And be able to stay awake long enough to write them.*

Bree threw one load of laundry in the washer and headed to the kitchen to start lunch. Tomato soup and grilled cheese, that was easy and always a hit with her grandson. She poured the soup and milk into a saucepan to heat and laid sandwiches of whole-grain bread in the frying pan, with slices of cheddar as filling.

Jessica clattered downstairs just as Bree slid the second finished grilled cheese on a plate to keep warm.

"Hey." She rushed in and gave Bree a quick hug, then reached for a sandwich. "Can I take one of these? I'm running late to go help Pierre."

"Again?" Bree's voice stretched tight. "I was making these for Luke; he'll be here any minute."

"Fine." Jessica returned the grilled cheese to the plate and backed away, hands in the air. "Sorry."

"No, it's fine, take it." Bree slid the sandwich into a plastic baggie and handed it over, then grabbed the spatula to flip the next grilled cheese before it burned. "I just wish—we need to talk about when you're going to be here for meals and when you're not."

"You barely got back, Mom. Just chill a little, okay?" Jessica snagged an apple from the fruit basket. "I'm meeting Ryan for dinner, so you don't have to worry about me for that."

"Oh, good. That you're seeing Ryan, that is." She'd been meaning to ask Jessica how things were between them, but her daughter was already heading out the door. "Say hi to him for me, and Pierre," Bree called. The door shut.

Bree sighed. Jessica was seeing a lot more of Pierre these days than she was. They'd barely talked since she got back.

A knock and then a key in the door announced that James was here with Luke. Putting on her best grandma smile, Bree went to welcome them.

A reddened, grumpy little boy's face greeted her from James's arms.

"Thanks for doing this." James slid Luke to the floor in the entryway, exhausted lines around his eyes.

"No." Luke immediately started to cry, dancing in place and reaching his arms up to James. "Don't go, Daddy."

"Hey, sweetheart." Bree crouched down to her grandson's level. "You and Grandma are going to have some fun this afternoon, okay? I got out your train."

"No." Luke pressed his face to James's pant leg.

James sighed and tousled his son's hair. "It was a rough night for all of us, been a rough day. I know you're still tired too..."

Bree waved him off. "We'll be fine. Just go. Luke, honey, let's go get some grilled cheese." Her grandson whimpered again when she picked him up, but once James was out the door, the little boy relaxed his head on her shoulder, arms around her neck and growing-so-long legs monkey-style around her waist.

"Gilled cheese?" He sniffled, a grin trying to sneak past his sadness.

"Grilled cheese." She pressed a kiss to his hair and carried him into the kitchen.

Over tomato soup and some one-on-one attention, Luke's usual sunshine emerged from behind the storm clouds.

"Look, Gamma." He held up his grilled cheese with a hole bit in the middle. "I see you."

"I see you too, sweet boy." Bree ruffled his hair. "So, what do you think of your new baby sister?"

"Baby Cyn-dah ree?"

"Yes, baby Cynthia Marie."

"She cry all time. Mommy hold her *all* da time." Luke studied the hole in his toast.

"I see. You know, when you were a little baby, your mommy held you all the time too."

"She not hold me now." He poked his finger into the cheese, his mouth drooping again.

Bree's heart tugged toward him. "That's because Mommy is tired, and little babies need extra attention. But your mommy loves you just as much as ever, and she'll hold you again, honey."

"Pwomise?" He looked up at her, blue eyes serious.

"Promise."

Luke stayed content the rest of the afternoon, at least as long as Bree gave him plenty of attention. She managed to fold some laundry on the sofa while he was absorbed in the train on the living room rug. The problems with her novel circled her mind like buzzing bees. How had she missed such huge issues? Was she losing her touch? Her sinking book sales might say so...but her publisher hadn't threatened to drop her yet, just pushed for a new series. She'd counted on Italy for inspiration, but she hadn't had time to even glance at the notes she'd jotted down. Or had she just been too distracted this spring with everything with Jessica, not to mention Peter's death and the upcoming trip and Pierre...it always came back to Pierre. Her stomach knotted again. He'd been so sweet, picking her up at the airport and staying with her at the hospital—and that kiss when they met; the memory still weakened her knees. But then, since they said goodbye that night, nothing. Not a call or even a text. She knew he was busy with his business, but still...it had been the same when she was in Italy. First hot, then cold. The man was on the way to driving her crazy.

"Daddy!" Luke jumped up and ran for the door.

Bree shook herself and pushed to her feet. She hadn't even heard the knock. That's what you got when you combined writer's brain with jet lag and men problems.

She said goodbye to a slightly-more-rested James and watched their SUV drive off.

Paula called a greeting from the sidewalk before Bree could head inside.

"Just wanted to come say hi." Her friend came up the walkway. "I've missed being able to stop by and do that."

"And I've missed you." Bree gave her a hug, breathing in the familiar comfort of their long friendship.

"You doing okay?" Paula stepped back and examined Bree's face, concern in her eyes. "You look exhausted."

"Oh—you know." Bree shrugged, fighting a sudden need to cry.

"No, I don't." Paula looped her arm through Bree's and led her toward the house. "But you're going to tell me."

Sitting across the kitchen table from Paula, cups of tea in front of them, Bree mopped her face with a tissue again.

"I'm sorry. I didn't mean to fall apart like this."

"Oh, hush. How many times have I cried on your shoulder these past months? How many times have both of us over the years? Now tell me, what's going on? Something with Jessica again?"

"No, actually. She's doing surprisingly well at the moment, though who knows how long that will last." Bree leaned her forehead on her fingertips. "I just—I don't know, the trip was wonderful, amazing. But the end was hard, with Lizzie getting hurt and I had this thing happen in Venice that I'll tell you about. Then I got content edits back from my editor, and they want a major rewrite, in only two weeks—just when I was trying to get going on ideas for this new series. And I'm trying to help James and Abigail with Luke and the new baby, but I've still got jet lag and haven't even finished unpacking, and Jessica's in and out of the house so fast I can't even sit her down to find out how she actually is, and—and Pierre k-kissed me at the airport, but now he hasn't called, and he hung up on me while I was gone, and I just don't know what's going on there, and how am I going to get everything done?" Her voice cracked into tears again. She needed another tissue.

Paula pressed one into her hand. "You poor darling. You can't be everything to everyone all the time, Bree. You're not invincible, you know."

Bree sobbed a laugh. "Yeah, that's what I learned in Venice. At least, I thought I did."

Paula quirked a brow. "Sounds like a story I need to hear. And maybe your family needs to learn that as well. I'm half inclined to call up that brother-in-law of mine and give him a piece of my mind too." She laid her hands over Bree's. "But first, let's pray."

❀   ❀   ❀

Pierre bit into the warm cobbler and closed his eyes in bliss. Tender, flaky pastry crisscrossed over juicy chunks of fresh peaches, all flavored with just the right amount of brown sugar, cinnamon, and lemon.

"Jayla." He opened his eyes to see the young woman biting her lip where she sat across from him and Terrence at one of their newly arrived café tables. "This cobbler is—delectable."

"Really?" Her dark eyes lit, a shy smile spreading across her face. It reminded Pierre of the look on Bree's face when talking about one of her stories. Which made sense—both women were artists, in their own ways.

"Oh, yeah." Terrence dug into another bite, nodding hard. "Amazing."

Pierre finished his piece, then laid his fork aside. He and his manager exchanged glances, and Terrence nodded. Folding his hands atop the table, Pierre smiled at Jayla. "I've talked to your references, and they all gave solid support. I did the same for our other candidates, but Terrence and I have agreed, you fit the best into our ethos here. So Jayla, we would officially like to offer you the job of head baker at The Gathering Place. If you'll take it."

"Oh, my gosh." She clapped her hands to her mouth, tears starting to her eyes. "That is just the best news. Thank you."

"No, thank you." Pierre nodded to his empty plate. "I was hoping for a competent baker, didn't know we'd be blessed with someone with passion like yours. Let us know when you can start, as we'd like to develop a solid menu before we open. I'd love if you can incorporate some of your own recipes into our menu, and my—and Bree's, as well. We'd especially like to feature her cinnamon rolls. She loves baking too, though writing is her career. I think you two would—will enjoy each other's company."

"I'd love to meet her and get some of her recipes." Jayla lowered her hands to her lap and drew a deep breath. "As for when I can start, I'll need to give notice at my security job. They'll probably require two weeks, but I could go ahead and start doing some work in my spare time before that, if you need me."

"Why don't you talk to your current workplace, and we'll go from there. Terrence will get our contract and paperwork to you in the meantime." Pierre glanced at his manager, who nodded back. "We look forward to working with you, Jayla."

"I can't wait to tell my husband and baby girl." Jayla left shortly after, still smiling.

"Well, that gets our bakery off to a good start." Terrence walked up to the counter and drummed his fingers. "But we still need to hire, what, four or five more people?"

"Maybe six." Pierre ran the numbers through his mind. Perhaps an assistant baker, or at least someone to help Jayla and make sandwiches, two or three baristas, whom Jessica could train. A cleaning and maintenance crew of possibly a couple people. "I'd like you to take over more of the hiring process from here, if you're willing. By the way, did the exterminator come by yesterday?"

"For the mouse evidence we found? No, thought I told you." Terrence shook his head. "Nobody ever showed. I called to reschedule, had to leave a message."

"Hmm, that's not good. I'll follow up on that." Maybe they needed to try a different company. He had to be absolutely sure any rodent problem was eliminated before the health inspector came through. "Would you be willing to make some calls to the job applicants I've gotten through the VA and our online listings? Weed through them a bit before we set up in-person interviews?"

"Absolutely." Terrence nodded hard. "I can do that."

"Thanks." Pierre-René clapped him on the shoulder, still mindful to be gentle. "I'm grateful for you."

He drove home a short while later. Still a long way to go, but this dream had already come so far, and now he could see it taking shape. Like Bree and her trip to Italy. Her eyes and smile swam through his mind, beckoning. He needed to call her, talk to her—really talk, like they hadn't since before she left. He needed to hear about her trip, but even more, he needed to be real with her. Honest about why he hung up that time, about the PTSD. The thought sped his pulse, but he drew a deep breath and managed to slow it. He owed it to her to be open about where he'd been, and where he was now.

He glanced at the car clock as he neared Bree's exit. Almost six—would she have had dinner yet? On impulse, he pulled off at her exit rather than continuing on over the bridge.

Wasn't like him to be spontaneous, and yet, there had been that kiss at the airport. His neck heated at the memory. Perhaps he was setting new patterns.

He'd stop by and surprise her, see if he could take her to dinner. At a nice restaurant too, perhaps that French one over the bridge in Portland that Jason and Todd had recommended at their now-weekly dinner last week. Good thing he was still wearing business casual from the meeting with Jayla, his good blue button-down shirt, navy blazer, and gray slacks. He'd give Bree time to dress up if she wanted, let her feel pretty, take her on a real date. Had he ever done that? Pierre-René kicked himself. Coffee shop tutoring sessions in Italian certainly did not count, or he'd be betraying his heritage as a Frenchman.

He parked in front of Bree's house and hurried up the walkway, his steps light as a schoolboy's. Pierre paused on her front porch to straighten his collar, then knocked.

Nothing. He waited, then knocked again and rang the bell. Perhaps she wasn't home, or in the bathroom.

Pierre's shoulders deflated. This was what he got for not planning ahead. A silly impulse this had been, especially when she'd just returned from being out of the country.

He'd turned to head down the walkway when the lock clicked. He wheeled back to see Bree opening the door.

Her eyes were red, her face blotchy from crying.

Pierre's heart sank. He was right. This had been a terrible idea.

Chapter Twenty-Eight

Take-out Chinese was definitely not how he had seen this evening going.

Pierre sat across from Bree at her pine country kitchen table, sharing Styrofoam containers of orange chicken, chow mein, and broccoli beef.

"I'm so, so sorry, Pierre." Bree, dressed in a lavender lounge suit, shook her head again and twiddled her wooden chopsticks. "You had the sweetest idea, and I ruined it."

"Breeanna, please." He laid his hand over hers on the table, savoring the warmth of her fingers beneath his palm. "You have no need to apologize. We will plan it for another time. It is I who should apologize, catching you off guard like that."

"No, I want you to feel free to stop by anytime. I just seem to be a mess ever since I got home." Bree's eyes reddened again.

He caressed her fingers. "Well, you have had a few things to deal with. Such as a brand-new grandbaby and a major book rewrite, all on top of jet lag. It would be strange if you weren't overwhelmed." He hesitated, then pressed forward. "And we are all a mess, Bree. In our own ways. I want to apologize to you, for hanging up that time on the phone, while you were in Italy. I must have hurt and confused you badly."

"Why did you?" She met his gaze.

"I..." Pierre-René withdrew his hand, the familiar dry mouth encroaching. But she deserved to know. "I don't usually talk about my—PTSD." His heart hammered, perhaps seeking a way out?

"I thought that was what you said, right before we got cut off—or you hung up. But I wasn't sure, with the connection." Her blue eyes were direct but gentle now, despite the lingering tearstains. "Is it from something that happened when you were in the military?"

"Yes. An accident, when I was stationed in Italy. I'll tell you more—someday." He swallowed, fighting to keep his breathing even. "I dealt with it at the time, got some counseling. I've managed pretty well over the years." Something or Someone nudged within that he was understating the truth, but Pierre pushed forward. "But it wasn't fair to you, to just drop off like that. I hope you will forgive me."

"Of course." It was her turn to squeeze his hand, her voice steady now that she had someone else to focus on. Bree was like that. "Of course you are forgiven, dear man."

He swallowed hard, this time not against the dryness but a lump rising in his throat. He hadn't wept since Lynn died. He wouldn't do it now, not here, not in front of Bree.

"But." She withdrew her hand. "You did confuse me a lot. Frankly, I'm still confused. You call me faithfully, then hang up on me. You comfort me from the other side of the world, kiss me at the airport, then I don't hear from you for days. I mean, what is this? Are we friends, are we dating, what?" She stopped for breath.

"Well." Pierre sat back. "You've wanted to say that for a while."

She nodded, looking self-conscious but determined. "I guess I have."

"And I apologize. Again. I hadn't realized how much I've

left you guessing...but now I see I have. Forgive me. My father would be ashamed of me."

"For pity's sake, stop with the French courtesy, Pierre. I'm ready for some American directness."

Italy had made a warrior out of this woman. Pierre fought a sudden urge to laugh, quickly subdued by the sobriety of the moment. He reached for Bree's hand again, and though she resisted for an instant, she let him take it.

"Well, how is this?" He laid his other hand atop hers, the touch of her fingers sending flutters through his chest. "Yes, I would like to date you, Breeanna Lindstrom. Officially. If you are willing."

She stared at him, the warrior melting away with a woman's flush in her cheeks. "I—well. That is, yes. I'd like that."

A grin stretched his face, exhilaration pumping through his veins. "Well. I call that reason for another kiss." And he leaned over the mound of Styrofoam to give it.

Several moments later, their chairs drawn considerably closer, Pierre reached for another take-out container and drew a long breath to steady his pulse. "So, this supper must have you wishing for the delicacies of Italy once again."

"Actually"—Bree bit into an egg roll and shook her head in pleasure—"at the moment, this all tastes amazing." She smiled at him, curling warmth deep into Pierre's gut.

Never mind just dating her, this woman would have him proposing marriage any minute if she didn't watch out.

＊　＊　＊

She needed to do this.

Bree reminded herself for the fourth time as she headed downstairs to answer the door a few evenings later. It would be James, stopping by to pick up the load of diapers Bree had washed for Abigail. Jessica was in the living room, relaxing with a bit of well-earned Netflix. A chance to talk to both her kids.

Hopefully they would listen.

James had let himself in by the time Bree reached the entry.

"Hey, Mom." He reached for the bag of clean laundry, waiting near the door. "Thanks so much for doing this. We really appreciate it."

"You're welcome." Bree almost said *Anytime*, but stopped herself. "Did Abby's parents get in okay?"

"They did, landed late morning and got here around lunch. They dove right in to help; her mom was fixing dinner when I left."

"That's wonderful." Maybe the extra help would smooth the way for what Bree needed to share. "Can you come in the living room, talk a minute?"

James frowned, laundry bag in hand. "Well, I should probably get back..."

"I won't keep you long." Bree fought back a twinge of guilt and pressed forward. *Paula will never forgive you if you back out now.* "There's something I've been wanting to share with you and Jessica, and there never seems to be time. Can you let Abigail's parents take care of things for half an hour?"

Something in her voice must have reached him, for James set down the laundry and nodded. "Guess I can stay a few minutes."

Bree led him into the living room, where Jess lay on the sofa typing on her phone, an episode of something playing in the background. What was the point of having TV on if you weren't going to watch it? Bree had never understood that.

"Hey, honey. Can we talk a minute?"

"Okay." Jess finished her text and sat up, then frowned. "Hey, James. Is something wrong?"

"No, nothing." Bree didn't want this to be a bigger deal than it was. "I just wanted to talk to you two, and James stopped by for the laundry. Could you turn off the TV a minute?"

Jess did so, and Bree sat down on the sofa by her daughter.

James took a nearby chair and leaned forward. "Mom, you're starting to worry me. What's going on?"

"Nothing's wrong, I told you." Bree folded her hands, noting that they were trembling. Good grief, if the thought of setting boundaries with her family did this to her, she definitely had a problem.

Jessica brought her hands to her mouth. "Wait—is it something about you and Pierre?"

"Ah—no." Bree hadn't seen that coming. Her cheeks heated, and she pushed back her hair. "Although, now you mention it, we have decided we are, ah, officially dating."

"That's great, Mom." A grin broke out on James's face. "I'm really happy for you."

"Me too." Jessica's voice was quieter, but her smile seemed genuine.

"I was going to tell you both, but that wasn't the main thing on my mind tonight." Bree drew a breath and pressed her hands together. "I had such a wonderful time in Italy, you know, and you all did a great job of handling the crises here. I really appreciate it."

"I'm so glad you like the kitchen okay." Jessica's face beamed.

"I do. But while I was over there, I realized some things. My own limitations, for one."

Her children were silent.

Why was this so hard? Bree pressed on. "Maybe because of being a single mother, maybe just because of…me, I've tended to think I can fix anything, handle any crisis. Always be the one to step in when either of you needs help. And

I've realized I can't, not all the time. It's not healthy for any of us."

"Right." James nodded and slanted a look at Jessica. "We've talked about this. And yet here Jess is staying with you again."

Jessica started to protest, but Bree held up her hand. "I'm not talking about that, not just that, anyway. I'm talking about you too, James."

"Me?" He stared.

"You know I love taking care of Luke, but sometimes you call me so last-minute, it really messes up my writing time. I try to make up the time at night, and I do, but my career has been struggling."

"You hadn't told us that. And I always ask whether you have time to watch him." James's defenses were up.

"You do, but the expectation is there—and I don't want to say no. Right now it's different; you've got a brand-new baby—I understand that. But it's been an issue for a while. Once things settle down, it would help if you could try to give me a little more warning, when it's possible, and remember I do have a full-time job, even if it's mostly from home."

James sat silent, staring at the wall, one foot tapping.

Oh, dear. Well, let him stew a moment. Bree turned to Jessica. "And, honey, I don't mind having you stay with me right now—I'm never going to abandon you, either of you, when you have a real need. But it would help if you could let me know your schedule, when you'll be here for meals and when you won't, and maybe we can share the grocery shopping and meal prep sometimes. We can talk more later. We just need to find a rhythm that works for both of us."

"I get it." Jessica nodded, meeting her eyes. "I'm sorry if I've been insensitive. And I'm making progress with the credit counseling program, so hopefully I won't need to be here too much longer—maybe a couple of months."

So, her daughter was being the mature one tonight. Maybe all these trials and tribulations were finally bearing fruit.

"I'm sorry too." James's apology came slower. "I guess I had no idea. You always seemed so happy to have time with Luke."

"I am—I am. I love him. I love all of you—you know that. And much of this is my own fault. I'm just realizing it's okay to acknowledge that I have my limits and sometimes need help too, and we'll all be healthier if we recognize that."

"So..." James glanced at the entryway. "Shall we not ask you to do laundry anymore?"

Good, she hadn't had to bring that one up. "I didn't mind this time. I know you all have a ton on you right now adjusting to two little ones. But I wondered if I could chip in with you on a diaper service, if Abigail wants to keep using cloth."

James nodded. "We could talk about that."

"That's all I'm really asking, that we communicate more." Another lesson from Italy. Bree met both her children's eyes. "And if any of you really need me, don't you dare hesitate to call. I'll be there quicker than Spencer smelled that fire in the kitchen."

They all laughed, even Jessica, and the tension in Bree's stomach melted as she gathered her son and daughter into a group hug. *Thank you, Lord.*

❖   ❖   ❖

The weeks passed quickly. June, then into July, and before Pierre-René knew it the grand opening of The Gathering Place bore down only a week away, the final details assembling so fast he could hardly catch his breath. Not to mention his relationship with Bree was progressing nicely, so that whatever free time he did have he spent with her.

He lay awake long the night before their final health

inspection, running through not just a list but lists of lists in his mind as the wee hours counted away.

Under Pierre's supervision, Terrence had hired six more people and done a fine job. He still needed to find a couple more baristas—Jessica had been training those they had to prepare the various lattes, cappuccinos, and macchiatos, but Pierre was realizing, with baristas only being part-time, he needed more than he'd thought to cover all shifts. Jayla had been baking day after day, perfecting both Bree's recipes and her own into a bakery menu whose aroma made his mouth water each time he stepped through the coffee shop door. Yesterday she had finished training an assistant, a young vet named Chad.

Jason and Todd had spent last weekend helping Pierre complete all the finishing touches on the interior of the coffee shop and done a fabulous job. All the machinery was up and running, the walls painted—including Jessica's suggested border along the wainscoting. The slate-blue awning not only complemented the décor, but protected the two small tables set outside from the intermittent summer sunshine. Even the food license had finally come through, after weeks of frayed nerves over that.

Pierre turned onto his side. Now this meeting with the health inspector, to give them final clearance for opening. He'd heard horror stories of health inspections, but he and his staff had tried to cover every angle, keeping different types of food stored in color-coded containers and on separate levels, insisting all the employees wear gloves or use paper whenever they touched so much as a muffin, initiating a stringent cleaning routine for dishes, counters, utensils, everything. Surely they would be all right.

He resisted the urge to check the time again and focused on his breathing. In for four...hold...out for four. Despite his assurances to Bree, he hadn't been diligent about self-care lately and could feel it in every muscle and pound of his heart. No exercise except running forty directions at once with the coffee shop, too much fast food, not enough sleep. Once they were past the grand opening, he needed to get back on the ball. In for four...out for four. In...out.

Pierre woke sometime later to sunshine on his face. He jerked up in bed and shot a glance at the clock. Nearly 8:00 a.m.—how? His alarm had been set for six.

He launched out of bed, banging his shin on the corner of his dresser. The health inspector was due at The Gathering Place at nine. He'd barely make it, if traffic wasn't horrendous. Tension clamped his shoulders. He'd meant to leave by six thirty to avoid the worst morning rush and arrive at the coffee shop with plenty of time to spare.

Half an hour later, Pierre-René sat in the endless line of jammed cars on the 205 bridge, his blood pressure rising higher every minute. Was there an accident ahead, or just the usual traffic? Why did everyone have to leave for work at the same time anyway? Couldn't modern society have thought of some creative way to stagger rush hour? But no, they could make a tiny chip for a smartphone into a gateway to the universe and necessity for existence, but everyone still had to sit on the freeway like a herd of cattle.

He glared at the car radio clock again. No, no, no. He banged his palm on the steering wheel. There was no way he would make it in time.

Calling Terrence to see if he could cover for him grated Pierre's every nerve, but there was nothing else for it. Terrence lived much closer, with only surface streets to traverse. Pierre picked up his phone and clicked the speed dial, then set it to speaker.

"Hey, boss."

"Terrence. I'm extremely sorry, but I'm stuck in traffic on the bridge. I'm not going to make it by nine." He bit the inside of his cheek. "Any chance you could run over to meet with the health inspector? I don't want Jayla and Jessica to have to deal with that on their own."

"Ah." Terrence hesitated. "I would, boss, you know, of course. It's just my wife, she's not feeling too good."

"I see. Well, don't worry about it. I'll figure this out."

"You sure, boss?"

"Your wife and baby are more important. Hopefully there won't be any problems, and the ladies will manage. Thanks." He hung up and blew out a breath. The brake lights on the car before him dimmed, and hope leapt as Pierre eased forward—only to slam on the brakes once more. And utter words he'd promised himself to omit from his vocabulary.

Blast.

Since he wasn't moving anyway, Pierre grabbed his phone again and texted Jessica to warn her he'd be late. And the inspector—please, Lord. Let the health inspector be caught in a traffic jam too.

Forty minutes later, he practically screeched into a parking space down the block from the coffee shop—all he could find—and dashed down the sidewalk to the door.

He could hear strident tones before he even stepped inside.

Jayla met him at the door, apron and hairnet in place, wringing her hands. "I'm so sorry. I had no idea—everything in the kitchen was spotless, but I didn't know..."

"What happened?" Pierre hurried past her into the kitchen.

Jessica stood against the far kitchen wall, hugging her arms. Chad stood by the sink, trying to talk to a short, square-jawed woman with graying blond hair, a white coat, and an official name tag. She seemed to be ignoring the assistant baker, making notes on a clipboard so hard Pierre could hear the forceful strokes of her pen from the doorway.

Looking up to see Pierre, she aimed her pen in his direction. "Are you the owner of this place?"

"I am. Pierre-René Dubois." He held out his hand.

She ignored him. "And are you aware that you have a serious rodent problem at this location?"

Pierre froze. Time slid into slow motion. The exterminator. Had they never come back, to deal with that suspected mouse? Terrence had been following up on that, hadn't he? Or...was that supposed to have been Pierre?

"Serious?" He croaked the word. They hadn't seen any evidence of the mouse for weeks, surely it wasn't...

"I'd say so." The woman marched over to the storage room and flung open the door.

Pierre-René followed on numb legs.

The light had been left on inside the storage room. The health inspector strode to the back corner, where several boxes of disposable coffee cups and lids had been moved aside.

"There." She drew a small flashlight from her coat pocket and aimed it down at the corner. "Mouse droppings."

Pierre stared at the scattered black pellets. "We—thought we saw mouse evidence, once a couple of months ago. But I didn't—I hadn't seen anything for some time, I thought..." His tongue felt thick.

"And you took no measures to eliminate it?" Her eyes drilled into him.

"I set a trap, but nothing. I called an exterminator, and they didn't show..." He couldn't form words. He had dropped the ball, that's all there was to it. He remembered now—he had told Terrence he would follow up with the exterminator and schedule another time. And he had forgotten. How, how in the name of all that was holy, could he possibly have forgotten?

"We haven't seen any evidence for weeks." Jessica spoke

from the doorway. "Couldn't those be old droppings? The mouse is probably long gone by now."

"Not with the fresh droppings I also found on *top* of the boxes." The woman stepped back into the kitchen, making another slash with her pen. "I trust you know this is an immediate denial of your application to open."

No. Lord, no.

"Please. Ms.—?" Pierre stepped after her, desperation pushing words forth again.

"Mitchell," Jessica whispered as he passed her.

"Ms. Mitchell. Our grand opening is next week; all the advertisements have gone out. If we fix the problem, get rid of the mouse, can't we have another inspection and get approval?" He'd read about that.

"Sure you can. But I don't have any appointments available for at least another two weeks." She signed the form on her clipboard, ripped off the sheet, and handed it to him. "Contact us when you are certain—certain—you have eliminated the problem, and—we'll see. You'll just have to postpone your grand opening for now." She jabbed a finger at the paper. "You've got several other violations too. See that they all are dealt with before you request another appointment."

Pierre vaguely heard Jayla say something to the woman, but he couldn't comprehend anything but the paper in his hand. Denied. *Lord. How could this happen? We've come so far.*

The front door shut with a distant jangle. The bells Jessica had attached, at Pierre's request.

"Whew." Chad blew out a breath and shoved his hands in the deep pockets of his green apron. "Now what?"

"I thought the exterminator came and took care of the mouse weeks ago." Jessica cocked her head. "Can they really keep us from opening?"

"I'm afraid so." Jayla stepped back into the kitchen. She

must have seen the woman out. "The other violations were low risk level—someone forgot to replace the toilet paper in the bathroom, and there's something we have to fix about how the cloths for wiping the counters are stored. But those could have been fixed on the spot, though she would have still made note of them." She rubbed her elbow. "So what did happen with the exterminator? I thought Terrence told me you'd taken care of it."

"I—was supposed to." A fog crept over Pierre-René's brain. "They didn't show for the first appointment. I told Terrence I would follow up. With everything…I forgot." His voice seemed to come from a long way away.

Silence ticked away the seconds in the kitchen. Along with the growing smell of burned sugar.

"Drat it." Jayla sprang for the pot holders and opened the oven, snatching out a tray of cinnamon rolls, the tops singed dark. "I didn't even hear the timer."

"Too bad we didn't offer HRH one of those." Chad tried a chuckle. "Might have sweetened her disposition."

"Actually, I've read that offering a health inspector food or drink can be construed as bribery." Jessica's voice came flat. "So probably good we didn't."

"So." Chad raised his hands. "We get an exterminator. We get rid of the mouse, then we can open. Right, boss? We'll be okay."

"We've sent out those postcards all over the place, announcing the date of our grand opening," Jessica said. "But I'll talk to Michelle—maybe we can send out updated ones or something."

"And put out the new date on social media. Not saying why, of course."

"Yeah, I'll do that. Want me to call Terrence, Pierre, let him know?"

The voices swirled around him, the fog closing in.

Jayla laid a gentle hand on his arm. "Pierre? Are you okay?"

He shook her off and pushed himself across the kitchen, through the coffee shop of empty tables and chairs, out the front door.

❖   ❖   ❖

Pierre hardly knew how he got home, till he stood inside his front door, keys in hand. Had he locked the car in the condo garage? He couldn't remember. Didn't matter. He headed into his bedroom and dropped the keys on his dresser, then stood there staring dumbly at the photograph of him and Lynn, early in their marriage, her arms slung around his neck from behind, both of them laughing. Happy. At least on the surface.

He had failed her, failed to help his wife. Failed his kids, far too often. And now failed his employees, the vets counting on him for a hand up in this unkind world, everyone who had given so much to make this dream a reality.

Stupid, stupid fool.

His hands trembled. A fleeting thought crossed his mind of needing a drink, one he'd never given in to over the years, not after seeing what it did to Lynn. Only once, back in Italy before they were married, had he surrendered to the pull of the bottle, just to see if it would help. After—after what happened.

It hadn't.

The explosion of gunfire cut across his memory, and Pierre jerked, pressing his eyes shut against the images. But they flashed through his mind like a gruesome newsreel, relentless, taunting, as if knowing he lacked the willpower to suppress them any longer.

"God." He ground the heels of his hands into his eyes. "Oh, God."

A guttural sob wrenching his chest, Pierre crumpled to the bedroom floor.

❀   ❀   ❀

Bree sighed in satisfaction and hit SAVE on her Word document. She stretched her arms up, interlacing her fingers, then leaned her head side to side, easing the kinks from her neck.

She glanced at the clock. Almost 5:00 p.m.—wow. She'd been writing since late morning, nonstop except for runs to the bathroom and a scarfed-down energy bar from her desk drawer. But she had made progress, big progress, on the beginning of a first book for her new series. Her brain had finally broken open after the rewrite that nearly gave her heart palpitations, and while she'd been doing the breakfast dishes this morning, the ideas birthed in Italy suddenly unfolded in an epiphany that made her drop her cereal bowl in the drainer and dash for her computer. Before today she'd only had some notes and rough sketches for a new travel writer detective who solved mysteries in Europe...now the story premise, inciting incident, a strong start for the character arc, and the first chapter had unrolled before her fingers like a rich Italian carpet.

Thank you, thank you, Father. Not only a new series, but a new season for Bree Lindstrom. Of freedom, and trust, and widened boundaries—ironically because of setting some.

Her stomach rumbled. Goodness, she was hungry. Bree stretched her legs and headed into the kitchen. Grabbing a banana till she could figure out dinner, she picked up her phone to see if she'd missed any messages. Writing could make her dead to the world for a while.

She froze mid-bite of banana. Four missed calls from Jessica? And several texts too.

Her middle tightening, Bree dialed Jessica's number.

"Mom, where have you been? I was getting worried about you."

"I'm so sorry, honey, I was writing. What's going on? Are you okay?"

"I'm fine, but I'm worried about Pierre. I would have come home to find you, but I had a new barista to train at the coffee shop and then I had to run to my shift at Applebee's. I tried to call you on my breaks, just got off now."

"Pierre? What happened?"

"The health inspector came this morning, and she found mouse droppings. I guess Pierre forgot to follow up on that mouse someone suspected. I thought it was long gone—but anyway, she denied our application to open, and he...he just got really weird and left. Jayla and Chad and I are all worried about him." Jessica hesitated. "I know we're trying to not bother you with stuff so much, but I figured this was the kind of thing you'd want to know."

"Of course I do." Her adrenaline kicking in, Bree glanced at the clock again. "You say this happened this morning?"

"Yeah, around nine thirty."

A long time for Pierre to be alone. His recent revelations tugged urgency through Bree's veins. "I'll go over right now."

"Thanks, Mom. Love you."

"Love you too." Bree hung up. Oh, Pierre. *Lord, help me find him, and show me what to do.* She dialed his number while searching for her purse. No answer.

Praying all the way, Bree headed across the bridge toward Gresham. With rush-hour traffic, it was past six by the time she pulled into the condo parking lot, the summer air cooling toward evening.

She knocked on his door. No answer. She knocked again, then rang the bell. With still no response, she tried the door and found it unlocked. Dread tightened her gut. That wasn't like Pierre.

"Hello?" The rooms stood silent and dim. Bree shut the door behind her and peeked into the empty living room, the kitchen.

"Pierre?" She padded down the darkened hallway. The door to his bedroom stood ajar. Bree knocked lightly, then pushed it open and stepped inside.

Pierre lay on the bed in his business clothes, belt and shoes still on, curled in a fetal ball.

Chapter Twenty-Nine

Bree had never dealt with PTSD before. Mother instinct kicked in.

As the light outside his bedroom window darkened toward evening, Bree sat beside Pierre on the bed, her arm around his muscular shoulders as he sobbed.

Tears blurred her own vision. Yet she knew that this was right, she was where she should be, and Jesus was there with them, enveloping the room, stronger than the heartache that racked the strong man now crumpled in her arms.

At last Pierre-René sat up. He dragged his hand across his face and drew a long, shuddering breath.

"I'm sorry. I didn't—I never wanted you to see me like this."

"Oh, dear man." Bree laid her hand against his cheek. "Do you think I would want you to go through this alone?"

"Always thought it was better not to drag anyone else into my mess, after Lynn died." He blew his nose. "And then I met you. You chased that plan right out the window."

Bree ran her hand down his arm and squeezed his hand, lying beside her on the bedspread, open and vulnerable. "What happened?"

"The health inspector shut us down." He drew a ragged breath. "We can't open next week. I've failed everyone—

my employees, the vets, the community who's been looking forward to having this place—"

"No, I mean before. The accident you talked about, back at the air base in Italy. What happened there?"

Pierre sat silent a long time. Even in the dim light, she could see and feel his struggle. *Perhaps he isn't going to respond. Then what do I do?*

You wait. There was that voice again.

He leaned forward, dangling his hands between his knees. "During weapons training... I was teaching a younger officer, training him in how to train others, and the gun—I still don't know exactly what happened. I-I don't have any idea how it could have been misloaded, or faulty somehow. It... exploded—that's the only way I can describe it. Blasted a hole into his chest." A shudder shook Pierre's entire bed.

"Oh, my darling." Bree murmured as she smoothed her hand down his back. "But how can you think it was your fault? It was a horrible accident."

"But I should have checked the firearm again before we began. I knew that, it was protocol, but I was distracted—Lynn and I were engaged, and stuff was going on there, rough spots that should have warned me we weren't in for an easy ride—but regardless, I wasn't fully present. A supervising officer has to be fully present, at all times." He lifted his head, pressing his fingertips to his temples. "It's partly why I left the military. I didn't feel worthy of the responsibility, being in charge of others. And now, here I'm trying to do that again, and failing those who are counting on me."

Bree added steel to her voice. "You haven't failed, Pierre-René Dubois." She wanted to shake him, make sure he heard her. "You've had a little setback, that's all. So you have to change the date of the grand opening. Sure, that's a hassle, but it's far from the end of your dream."

Pierre bent his head and nodded, fingers massaging his

scalp. "You're right, I know. But my reacting like this, to a mere setback, proves again I'm not fit for this, leading other people, leading a company."

"No. It proves that you're human. Maybe you need to come to terms with that fact. I did."

Pierre lifted his head to look at her.

"I told you how, when we were in Venice, I couldn't get in the boat at first. How I froze. Then I missed our gondola tour, because I was just too terrified."

"Because of Roger."

"That was part of it. I hadn't gotten in a boat since he died, though I've always meant to, all these years. But it was more than that. It was being afraid itself that scared me." She paused and dropped her voice. "Shamed me, that I couldn't make myself do something I'd dearly wanted to do. I felt completely out of control, paralyzed by my own fear." She shook her head. "Never in my life. I'm not that person. Ever since Roger died, I've been the strong one, the mom, the one who makes everything work. Holds everything together." A subtle snort. "Can fix everything—or at least tries to." She heaved another sigh. "That's how I got in so deep with Jessica. You have no idea how hard it was to be on the other side of the world while she was struggling so, having the house literally catch on fire. But later on I began to realize maybe that's what the Lord wanted, to help me learn I'm not invincible. Not the one who has to fix everything. He is." A silence lengthened, ending with a shrug. "I'm human, and finally that's okay. That's why we need Him. And one another."

Pierre sat quiet a long moment, rubbing her fingers between his. "But you did end up on a gondola, right?"

"Nope. I missed out on that. Miguel, the man who helped me, was the captain of our motorboat the third day. I got to see the glassworks on Murano, and the lace making—it was all beyond-my-dreams beautiful. Thanks to Miguel, I got to see the two islands."

Silence fell for a time, but a good silence. The summer evening breeze wafted through the open window, soothing Bree's face and reminding her of the holy Presence with them.

"I don't know what the Lord wants me to do," Pierre said finally.

Bree leaned her head on his shoulder. "Then we'll ask Him. Together."

✿   ✿   ✿

With the dawn just peeping behind Mount Hood the next morning, Pierre-René took his coffee out onto the little balcony of his condo before the sun rose. Above the conifer trees that lined the property before the street, the sky pinked toward sunrise, dotted with tufts of rose and lavender clouds. Birds twittered a morning hymn of praise.

He wrapped both of his hands around his coffee mug. *Lord, thank you that your mercies are new every morning. Merci beaucoup.*

This new vulnerability felt as if a layer of armor had been stripped from him in the night. He wasn't comfortable with the feeling, not yet. Still, he sensed it a good thing, as when Aslan stripped the dragon skin from Eustace in C. S. Lewis's *Voyage of the Dawn Treader*. He hadn't thought of that story in years, though he'd often read it to his children when they were young.

Pierre sipped his coffee as the first fiery sliver of sun burst above the trees, gilding the edges of the clouds. He pulled his phone from his pocket. Still early, but Terrence was an early riser. He'd told Pierre anytime after six was fine to call—after all, a manager needed to be frequently available.

But this call wouldn't be about business, and that awareness set Pierre's heart thudding again. He didn't know all the steps God had for him to take now, but something needed to change. And the next step was right here.

. . . I know PTSD when I see it, man. If you ever want to talk, I'm here.

Pierre drew a deep breath and hit Terrence's number.

After a conversation that made him actually feel understood for the first time in years—and having left a message for the counselor whose number Terrence gave him—Pierre-René headed back to the coffee shop. He'd set up another exterminator appointment, a different company this time, but he wanted to see if he could find this mouse himself. Or at least where it was getting in.

His palms dampened as he approached the door of The Gathering Place, memories from yesterday threatening. Some of his employees would be inside, no doubt—what would they be thinking after seeing him check out like that yesterday? But he breathed deep and stepped through the door.

The whir of the coffee grinder and scent of lemon and sugar baking eased his angst. Jayla must be here. And Jessica stood behind the counter, training a young woman with a brown ponytail whom Pierre hadn't seen before. Must be Terrence's new hire, whom he'd mentioned this morning at the end of their phone conversation. Her and a man he'd hired as a janitor.

"Hey, Pierre." Jessica looked up with a smile. "This is Emily. Emily, Pierre-René Dubois, owner of The Gathering Place."

"Hi." Emily's ponytail bobbed as she beamed and nodded. "You've started a really great place, Mr. Dubois."

"Thank you. We're glad you're here, Emily." Pierre smiled at her, then looked to Jessica. "Jayla in the kitchen?"

Jessica nodded, and Pierre headed back. He reached the kitchen just as Jayla pulled a tray of muffins from the oven.

He stopped in the doorway and inhaled deeply. "Lemon poppy seed?"

"Lemon, cream cheese, poppy seed. New recipe." Jayla set the tray to cool and slipped off her oven mitts, then switched off the large mixer that was stirring something. "There, easier to hear now." She turned and cocked her head. "You okay?"

"I am." Pierre-René swallowed. "Sorry about yesterday."

"We were all worried about you."

"I appreciate that. I have some ... things, in my life, from my past, that I need to deal with. Yesterday just helped bring them to the surface." He paused and inhaled. "I'm a vet also, not sure if you knew that."

"I figured as much." Jayla nodded, then turned back to the mixer and removed the bowl from the base, giving it a final firm round with her spatula before stepping over to a waiting muffin tray. "Well, you let us know if you need anything, you hear? We're all here for you."

"Thank you." He fought the lump rising in his throat yet again. It seemed today his employees were taking care of him more than he was them. He cleared his throat. "Any sign of our mouse?"

"Not that I've seen. I checked all the doors and windows in here for cracks, and Jessica did the same in the front room." She raised her hands. "So far nothing."

"Well, I'm here to look some more." Pierre sighed. "Scour every corner of that storage room for one thing. That thing's got to be getting in somewhere. Did you know those little pests can squeeze through an opening the size of a dime?"

"Or just run in and out when a door is open. My grandma used to deal with mice."

"Great." Pierre reached in his pocket as his phone buzzed. "Excuse me. Thank you, Jayla, for everything."

She nodded and waved him off.

It was Bree. Pierre stepped into the restroom, trying to get away from the whir of machinery. "Hi." He felt strangely awkward after last night. Something had shifted between them again, he wasn't exactly sure what.

"Hey, you." Bree's voice sounded bright. "I'm bringing the family over to The Gathering Place for a bit, is that okay?"

"Sure. But why?"

"I was telling James and Abigail about all you've done there, and they want to see it. Plus we all want to help you look for that mouse."

"Well, that's just what I was going to do. Probably be boring for them."

"Truthfully, I think they just need an excuse to get out of the house with the little ones." Bree's voice lowered conspiratorially. "But extra pairs of eyes never hurt, do they?"

Pierre chuckled. "No, they don't."

Half an hour later, Bree arrived with James, Abigail carrying baby Cynthia Marie in a front pack, and Luke bouncing on his tiptoes with excitement. Paula came too.

"I haven't been here in far too long." Paula gave Pierre a hug. "My, it's looking wonderful! Jessica, didn't we do a fabulous job on those paint and curtain colors?"

Jessica grinned and dispensed hugs, then pressed a kiss to Cynthia Marie's almost-fuzzy head. "You need to let me babysit for you guys soon. You must need a night out, right?"

"Sure you're not just trying to drum up some more money?" James's grin took any sting out of his words.

Jessica punched his arm. "I'd pay you to let me spend time with my favorite kiddos." She tousled Luke's hair as he hugged his auntie's leg.

"By the way, Pierre"—Paula shook her head at him—"Bree tells me you've been fighting traffic every day, sometimes multiple times a day. I can't believe I didn't suggest it earlier, but why don't you move in with me awhile? At least till the business opens. I've got this whole house going to waste. It doesn't make sense."

Pierre stared at her. "Really?"

"Good grief, yes. Give yourself a break."

"Thank you." A weight lifted from his shoulders at the mere thought of losing that commute, even temporarily. "I might well do that. Been thinking about moving over here permanently, what with the business location. But for the time being—yes. I'd be grateful."

"Okay." Bree clasped her hands together. "Where shall we start looking for this mouse?"

"Well." Pierre-René glanced around, unsure how to best use this new crew. "Jessica and Jayla have already checked all the doors and windows. I want to clear out the storage room since that's where the droppings were discovered, so that's the biggest project. James, perhaps you and Bree could give me a hand in there? Then Paula and Abigail, if you wouldn't mind really examining the corners and walls and wainscoting in here. Any hole or crack, however small, is worth noting."

"Of course." Abigail smiled, soothing her sleeping baby with a mother's sway back and forth. "This sounds ridiculously fun. Have we been cooped up that long?"

"Yes." James's call came muffled from where he'd already headed to the storage room.

Amid the chuckles, Pierre-René went to join James with Bree behind him, his heart lifting. *Lord, thank you for this family*. Might they, one day, even become his family? The thought nestled somewhere deep within him.

Back in the storage room, he could hear laughter and chatter from the front room as Abigail and Paula searched, while Jessica and Emily continued to work on the coffees. Even if opening would be two weeks away instead of one— he prayed not more than that—they needed to be ready.

James helped him haul the big storage tubs and boxes out, stacking some to the side in the hallway, some in a corner of the kitchen. Bree insisted on donning gloves and cleaning up any mouse droppings, then scrubbing the area with old rags and disinfectant. Attacking the corner with vigor on hands and knees, gloved hands, and a bandanna over her short blond hair, she looked more alluring than ever.

"Hey"—grinning, James nudged him with his elbow— "eyes on your work."

His neck heating, Pierre refocused on helping James drag a heavy tub of coffee beans out into the hall. He straightened at a ding from his phone. "Let me see who this is." He stared at the text on his phone a moment, dumb.

"What is it?" James arched his lower back.

"Strange. The woman who did the health inspection yesterday, Daphne Mitchell. She says to check the pipes and drains, in case the mouse is getting in there." He certainly hadn't pegged her as the type to offer help, or even reach out by text at all, though he knew she had his number. Pierre texted back a thank-you and pocketed his phone.

"That's odd. Could be worth a check, though."

"I agree." Together they finished clearing the storage room, then inspected every inch. But the walls seemed tight, the cement floor solid.

Pierre shook his head. "I'll go check the kitchen pipes and drains now. That could definitely be a possibility, with the draw of food and water here."

But after an hour of climbing under sinks and getting in Jayla's way, he found no obvious gaps or leakage around the plumbing. The covers to the kitchen floor drains seemed too fine a grate for even a mouse to wriggle through. Pierre at last joined everyone in the front room.

The coffee grinder stood silent, Jessica and Emily having left for the day. Abigail sat in a booth, nursing the baby. Luke perched in one of the coffee shop high chairs between her and the edge of the counter, crumbling a lemon muffin.

"He got hungry, and Jayla graciously offered." Abigail ran her hand over her son's hair. "I hope you don't mind."

"Of course not. Let's just sweep up the crumbs after, especially till we find this little critter. Any success?" He sank onto a barstool next to Luke.

Paula lifted her hands and shook her head. "We found a couple of cracks, but nothing we think a mouse could get through."

"I'll have them patched anyway, just in case." Pierre rubbed the back of his neck. "Maybe it's just running in when the door is opened, like Jayla said. Don't know why I say 'it,' could be a whole family." His skin crawled at the thought. "I'll try setting a trap again and wait for the exterminator."

"Who would have thought one tiny mouse could cause so much trouble?" Abigail shook her head as she lifted Cynthia Marie to her shoulder for a burp.

"I see da mousie, Mommy." Luke poked at his muffin, then picked up a crumb and put it in his mouth.

"What?" She turned her head to stare at him.

"I see da mousie. Over dere." From his high chair, the little boy pointed behind the counter.

Pierre half rose from the stool. "You see the mouse? Where, Luke?"

"Dere. In da hole." Luke leaned so far to the side Pierre

lunged to grab his high chair lest it tip. Unconcerned, Luke stuffed another bite of muffin in his mouth.

Hardly daring to breathe, Pierre crept around the side of the counter to see where Luke had pointed.

The floor drain for the espresso machine, behind the counter. He'd forgotten about that one. Zoning laws required that the espresso drain hose run to a floor drain within a certain distance, so they'd had to install another in here.

But he saw no mouse.

"You sure, little man?" Pierre squatted a couple of yards from the drain, keeping his voice low. "You saw a mouse in the hole?"

"Uh-huh. Poke up head, den it hide."

Paula came to crouch beside Pierre. "Think it could be?"

"Maybe. Children can be far more observant than we."

The entire room seemed to hold its breath.

And then—he saw it. A tiny, quivering whiskered nose, then ears and beady eyes. The mouse poked its head out of one of the drain holes, just as Luke had said. It sniffed the air, ducked its head back. Then, all of a sudden, it popped its whole body through and skittered along under the edge of the counter.

Behind him, Paula screamed and fell backward. Scrambling to her feet, she scuttled across the floor to a chair and hopped up on it, squealing all the way.

Chaos, laughter. Everyone scrambling, trying to either head off the mouse or escape it. Luke yelled directions from his high chair. "Get it, Daddy. Get it!"

James grabbed a broom and tried to chase the mouse out the front door, held by Bree. The little creature dodged and scurried across the main floor, weaving under the tables, between the chair legs. Paula screeched whenever it came anywhere near her.

"What on earth?" Jayla appeared from the kitchen.

"The mouse." Holding up his hand, Pierre moved one step at a time toward the little critter, now huddled back in a corner behind the counter. No doubt it wanted to retreat to its safe hiding spot in the drain, but he couldn't let it. Not with them so close. Pierre grasped a basket from the counter, intended for packets of sugar. Approaching half bent, he crouched next to the drain, basket at the ready. He held still, holding his breath, only hearing the pound of his heart.

The mouse zipped from its hiding spot toward the drain.

Pierre popped the basket upside down over the creature and clamped it to the floor. "Got it." Exhilaration pumped through his veins. "Can someone bring me a box or something?"

Jayla appeared at his side with a small box and a piece of cardboard. Together they slid the cardboard under the basket, then deposited the whole thing into the box and quickly closed the lid.

"Whew." Pierre breathed again, then grimaced. "I'm afraid we'll have to get a new basket for the sugar." He passed the box off to James, who headed toward the back door.

"Well done." Jayla applauded. "Not even any casualties."

He chuckled. "Except maybe Paula." He scanned the room to find her being helped down from the chair by Bree. "I didn't know my sister-in-law was such an elephant when it comes to mice."

Paula waved one hand, the other held over her heart. "Give me spiders or snakes any day over mice or rats, little skittery things." She shuddered. "Guess I shouldn't have volunteered to come look for it, but I didn't want to miss out on the fun."

Fun. A chuckle started in Pierre's chest, then rumbled up into a laugh. He met Bree's gaze across the room, and her blue eyes lit and danced with his, her laughter rising like bells as the others joined in.

Fun was not what he had expected at the beginning of this day, nor last night. But a lot could change in twenty-four hours. At least when grace and God stepped in.

Pierre lifted his phone. "Excuse me, everyone. I need to make a call to our dear lady health inspector."

He'd intended to request a different health inspector altogether for the next visit. But after her text, and how she'd ended up being right about the drains...it was worth a shot.

What a day for miracles. Perhaps Daphne Mitchell might turn out to be another.

Chapter Thirty

Today was the day.

Bree stood on a chair in The Gathering Place, helping Michelle to finish tying blue and white balloons above the chalkboard menu, its lively handwritten selections specially chosen for the day. Emily ran the espresso machine behind the counter, while Jayla tucked a few more baked goods into the display case, then set out a basket of fresh cinnamon rolls, free today for customers to help themselves. Jessica and Pierre discussed something near the door, then Jessica hurried back behind the counter.

"Looks great, Mom, Michelle. You guys better get down, Pierre says it's almost time. The city council members will be here any minute."

Bree clambered down, welcoming Michelle's steadying hand, then helped stow the folding chairs away. She headed to Pierre, who stood adjusting his tie.

"You ready for this?" She touched his arm.

"I better be." He smiled at her, but she saw a flicker of trepidation in his eyes. Excitement underlay it, though, and that made her heart glad.

"There they are." He nodded to two gentlemen in business suits approaching the door. The council members would assist with the ribbon cutting. "I better greet them."

"Go." Bree gave his cheek a quick kiss, and Pierre headed to let the officials in, his charm and smile well in place.

She scanned the buzz of activity, inside and outside. Thanks only to a string of miracles were they actually having the grand opening on their originally planned date, and now all was happening so fast. Already local media lined up outside with cameras and microphones, along with an encouraging line of potential customers.

Inside, Jessica put final touches on the extra tables they had set up. Stacks of flyers and postcards, one table devoted to veterans' resources. Baskets of prizes for the raffle, whose proceeds would go to the local VA Center programs.

"Emily, you have the coupons to give out to customers for their next visit, right?" Jess called over her shoulder.

"Yep. And we're giving out both iced and hot coffee samples?"

"Right. Though iced will probably be most popular, in July. Make sure the ice machine is emptied so it will make more."

The bell on the door jangled, and Bree turned to see Pierre now greeting Terrence and a very pregnant auburn-haired woman. Must be Sarah, Terrence's wife, whom he had left to pick up a short while ago. Bree's eyes stung as she watched Pierre and Terrence embrace. Little had they known that Pierre's reaching out to this young vet would work the other way too. *Lord, you are so gentle and merciful with us all.*

Pierre said something to Terrence and the council members and glanced at the wood-framed clock on the wall. Bree followed his gaze—it was time.

She'd wanted to squeeze his hand once more, but Pierre was already heading to open the doors. So Bree slipped out the side entrance, whispering a prayer for her man, for this day.

Her heart swelled as she joined the crowd of customers

waiting outside, their anticipation a palpable hum. Look at what Pierre-René had done, with God's help.

"Exciting day, huh?" Todd, whom Bree had met when she and Pierre joined him and Jason for dinner a few weeks ago, elbowed through the crowd to stand beside her.

Bree smiled up at the tall young man. "It is indeed."

The crowd erupted in scattered cheers and applause as Pierre walked outside, followed by the city councilmen.

Jason stepped to his side and handed Pierre-René a microphone. Jason, a whiz with all kinds of technology and audio, had done all the sound system setup for today. Pierre took the mic with a brief squeeze of his son's shoulder.

"Welcome, everyone, to the grand opening of The Gathering Place." Pierre's smile turned into a genuine grin as he caught Bree's eye. "I am so grateful for the support of this community, our city council, my family and friends, and all our incredible employees for bringing us to this point." More cheers. "As some of you may know, this opening means not just another coffee shop for Vancouver, but a community effort to connect us all more with those who have sacrificed and served. As such, I have asked some of those on our staff who have served in the United States Armed Forces to assist in our ribbon-cutting ceremony."

The city council members stepped forward, holding a wide red ribbon between them. They stood on opposite sides of the open door, stretching it across.

Then, from within the shop, came Jayla with her husband, pushing himself along in his wheelchair, their little girl perched on his lap. Tears pricked Breeanna's eyes. Terrence came behind them, followed by Chad and Mark, the new janitor. The councilmen had to step farther forward to make room for them all.

Jessica passed forward a giant pair of scissors, then stepped back, beaming.

Jayla's husband helped his daughter wield the scissors to slice through the ribbon partway, then handed them to Terrence, who finished the job in one stroke. The red satin ends curled to the ground.

"As the owner of this business"—Pierre had to pause to clear his throat—"I declare The Gathering Place officially open."

More cheers, applause, whistles. The tears escaped to flow down Bree's cheeks now. A group of marine vets in the audience led a rousing "Oo-rah!" The employees hurried back to their stations, Jessica standing at the door to beckon the stream of eager customers inside. People grabbed Pierre's hand from all directions, congratulating him.

Bree wove her way forward toward him, through the crowd, reaching Pierre just as Terrence did. She paused to give them a moment.

His manager wrapped Pierre in a bear hug, slapping his back. "We did it, boss."

"We did. God did."

With a final thumbs-up, Terrence headed inside the coffee shop, and Pierre-René looked up to meet Bree's gaze. The look in his eyes caught her breath in her chest. *Lord, I think I love this man.*

"Mr. Dubois, can we get a statement, please?" A reporter and accompanying photographer from the local paper shoved a microphone into Pierre's face.

With an apologetic glance to Bree, he nodded and smiled, stepping in front of the business sign for a media-op.

Bree backed away. Duty called; they would have time later. Maybe she should see if Jessica needed any help.

But her daughter seemed to be running things beautifully, based on the flow of happy customers emerging from the shop, paper- or plastic-lidded cups in hand, munching baked goodies. The line still extended well beyond the coffee shop door, and quite a few folks milled outside, chatting or examining the literature on the outside table Michelle staffed. She waved at Bree with a grin.

Bree waved back. Such a community this was already, one only God could have built. Yet at the moment, she felt rather at loose ends. Unneeded, almost.

You don't always have to be busy, my child. She half chuckled at the heavenly whisper. True. Why was it so hard for her to just be and enjoy the day?

"Bree." Abigail hurried up to her, wailing baby in one arm and hanging on to a whimpering Luke's hand with the other. "I'm so sorry, Luke just had an accident. Could you possibly take Cynthia Marie a few minutes?" She grimaced. "I'm sorry to ask you, I know this is a special day..."

"Abby." Bree laid a hand on her daughter-in-law's arm with a smile. "Sometimes it's nice to be needed."

"Thank you." Abigail transferred the baby and, with a grateful smile, hurried toward the side entrance with Luke, murmuring mother reassurance along the way.

Bree cradled the small, warm weight of her grand-daughter against her chest, Cynthia Marie's cries quieting as she swayed back and forth. She glanced up at the sunlight filtering through the leaves of the trees just outside The Gathering Place. *Thanks, Father. You know sometimes I still need something to do.*

An hour later, the now-sleeping baby still on her shoulder, Bree stood chatting with a friend inside the coffee shop while Abigail got to actually sit and enjoy a frappe for once. Joy and energy hummed around her, people chatting and sipping coffee, Emily and the other baristas flying back and forth behind the counter, turning out iced lattes and mocha cappuccinos. A summer breeze blew in through the open door, setting the blue and white balloons to dancing.

Bree bid her friend goodbye and smoothed her hand

down her granddaughter's tiny, onesie-covered back. Nearby, James sat with a comforted and dry-clothed Luke at the kiddie table, where several small children scribbled on the coloring pages they'd received, child-size lidded cups of juice and cold chocolate milk nearby for refreshment.

Pierre and his team had thought of everything.

Lord, what a blessing this place will be to so many—no, already is. Thank you. I just wish I could tell Pierre-René how proud I am.

She glanced out the window again. Pierre was outside talking with Jayla's husband. Might there someday be a spot for him at The Gathering Place too? After warm handshakes a moment later, the younger man wheeled himself away, and a middle-aged woman approached Pierre instead. His attention certainly was in demand today, and rightly so.

"Ma'am, can we interest you in a coupon for your next visit to The Gathering Place?" Jessica appeared beside Bree, holding out a slip of paper and beaming. No wonder, since Ryan stood at her side.

"Don't mind if I do." With her free hand, Bree took the coupon and slid it into her purse. "How's it going, honey? Ryan, so good to see you."

"You too." Ryan grinned in that easy way she'd missed, then glanced at Jessica.

The look in his eyes…Bree's middle melted. These two seemed to be overcoming the challenges they'd faced. *Thank you, Lord.*

"It's going great—better than we even hoped." Jessica peered out the window. "Wait, why is Pierre talking to the health inspector again?"

"That's the health inspector?" Bree glanced at the window again.

"Yeah, that's Daphne Mitchell."

The woman whose change of heart had made this day

possible. "Well, they seem to be having a pleasant enough conversation."

Jessica shook her head. "Wonder what caused such a switch, that she moved our inspection up."

Ryan nudged her. "Didn't you want to show your mom something?"

"Oh, yeah." Jessica handed the stack of coupons to Ryan and pulled out her phone. "Mom, look."

Bree leaned toward the phone screen her daughter held out. *Confirmation of registration for classes...* She scanned the email, then looked at Jessica, her heart skipping. "Clark College? Jess, really?"

"Yep." Jessica smiled, a sheen in her eyes. "I'm registered for classes for this fall."

"Oh, honey." Tears stung Bree's eyes too. "I'm so proud of you. You were able to work it out financially?" It had been taking all her resolve the past few weeks not to offer to pay for her daughter's first semester.

"Michelle helped me figure out the financial aid options, and I'm making good progress on paying off my debts. So yeah, I think I'll be okay."

"What about the other thing?" Ryan nudged Jessica again.

"What other thing?" Bree asked.

Jessica's ears pinked. "Pierre offered me a job here full-time, being the assistant manager and training employees. That means I can quit working at Applebee's, so I'll only have one job to juggle with school."

"This makes me so happy." Bree hugged Jessica, eliciting a squeal of protest from little Cynthia squished between them. She stepped back and resumed jiggling. "Sorry, baby girl."

"Well, I better get back. I just saw the email come in on my phone so wanted to tell you." With a wave, Jessica hurried back to the counter, Ryan trailing her.

Lord, so many miracles to be thankful for today.

The crowd thinned as the afternoon waned. Bree passed Cynthia Marie back to her parents, and they headed home with Paula and two tired little ones. At last she made her way over to Pierre. He stood talking with Terrence near the urns of sample coffee, both sipping from small cups.

She stood back not to intrude, but Terrence waved her over.

"So what do you think, Mrs. L.?" He grinned at her.

"It's wonderful." Bree lifted her hands. "You guys have done an amazing job."

"Not without a lot of help from our women." Terrence shook his head. "Which reminds me, I should get mine home. You'll be okay here, boss?"

"We'll be fine. The others can finish up. Thank you, Terrence, for everything. See you in the morning."

"You bet." With a final dip of his head, Terrence went to collect his pregnant wife, who sat chatting at a corner table with Jayla and her little girl.

"Come on." Pierre snagged an extra cup of sample coffee, then, taking Bree's hand, tugged her toward a corner booth. "I've barely seen you. Sorry, I've been so tied up."

"Oh, yes, the owner should apologize for being busy during his grand opening." Bree raised an eyebrow at him as they both slid into the booth. "So, Jessica and I were curious—what were you talking to the health inspector lady about?"

"Oh, you saw that." Pierre-René chuckled. "Quite a story, actually. Turns out Mark, our new janitor, is her nephew's best friend—she's known him since he was a boy, seen some of his struggles since he served overseas. She had no idea he was working here, or even that this place was an outreach to vets, till she overheard him say something about not being able to start work as soon as he'd thought, because some health inspector just wouldn't cut them any slack." His eyes twinkled. "Wouldn't you know, last week some time opened up in her schedule."

"And here you are." Bree shook her head. "The Lord works in mysterious ways."

Pierre sipped his coffee, reflective. "She said she was touched by the ceremony, by how we want to make a difference, not just be another moneymaking coffee shop."

"The ceremony was beautiful, Pierre. Made me cry."

"You and me both." Pierre reached across the table and covered her hands with his, a look in his dark eyes that gave Bree the sensation of riding a quick elevator going down.

Her heart pounding, Bree swallowed. Whatever else she'd meant to say fled from her mind.

"I wanted to tell you." Pierre's thumb rubbed the back of her hand. "Yesterday I talked with the counselor Terrence referred me to. Sounds like the man is a believer, has a lot of experience helping vets. We've set up an appointment to meet next week."

"That sounds good." Bree gazed at their intertwined fingers, still having trouble thinking. "I'm proud of you."

"It may take some time before I make much progress with this thing. The PTSD. And some level of it will probably be with me forever. I don't want you to..." He hesitated.

"To what?"

"To feel tied down to this...relationship, with a hard-headed vet who happens to be French." His fingers tightened on hers.

"Pierre-René." She managed to pull one hand free and reached across the table to lay her palm against his cheek, tears springing to her eyes again. "I love you. Don't you know that by now?"

He looked into her eyes, his throat working. "And I love you, Breeanna Marie Lindstrom." Lifting his hand to the side of her head in turn, he leaned forward and covered her mouth with his kiss. "I love you," he murmured again against her lips.

Bree kissed him back, her heart full to overflowing. A Gathering Place this was indeed, for hearts, for lives, for broken people God was bringing together into a whole.

She could hardly wait to see what memories this place would hold next.

✦   ✦   ✦

One year later, beneath a rose-covered arch set up next to the counter, the wedding of Breeanna Marie Lindstrom and Pierre-René Dubois was held. A simple ceremony, with only their closest family and friends—including, of course, the staff of The Gathering Place. After pledging themselves to each other before God and man, they kissed and laughed and danced through the evening, stuffing themselves with French and Italian pastries instead of wedding cake, celebrating with toasts of champagne and, of course, coffee.

After they hugged their children good night and got into Pierre's streamer-decked black car, Bree leaned her head on her new husband's shoulder. "So, where to now, *amore mio*?"

Pierre-René kissed the top of her hair. "Wherever He takes us."

"Right." She smiled in the darkness as Pierre started the car. Surely the best was yet to come.

About the Author

Lauraine Snelling has been writing since 1980, with over ninety books published, both fiction and nonfiction, historical and contemporary, for adults and young readers. She received a Career Achievement Award for inspirational fiction from *RT Book Reviews*, and her books consistently appear on CBA bestseller lists. A hallmark of her style is writing about real issues within a compelling story. Lauraine and her husband, Wayne, have two grown sons, a daughter in heaven, and live in the Tehachapi Mountains in California with a basset hound named Annie, a tortoiseshell cat named Lapcat, and five chickens.